Where the
Wild Rose Blooms

Also by Lori Wick
in Large Print:

Promise Me Tomorrow
Whispers of Moonlight

Where the Wild Rose Blooms

LORI WICK

Thorndike Press • Thorndike, Maine

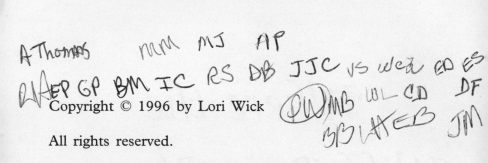

Published in 1998 by arrangement with
Harvest House Publishers.

Thorndike Large Print ® Christian Fiction Series.

The tree indicium is a trademark of Thorndike Press.

The text of this Large Print edition is unabridged.
Other aspects of the book may vary from the original edition.

Set in 16 pt. Plantin by Minnie B. Raven.

Printed in the United States on permanent paper.

Library of Congress Cataloging in Publication Data

Wick, Lori.
    Where the wild rose blooms / Lori Wick.
        p.   cm.
    ISBN 0-7862-1525-9 (lg. print : hc : alk. paper)
    1. Large type books.   2. Frontier and pioneer life —
Rocky Mountains Region — Fiction.   3. Man–woman
relationships — Rocky Mountains Region — Fiction.
I. Title.
    [PS3573.I237W485   1998]
    813'.54—dc21   98-23162

To Diane Barsness,
an old and *new friend.*
How far we've come because of
God's grace.
I thank you, precious friend,
for your love and caring.
I trust that the future will bring
only continued growth and closeness.
I dedicate this book to you with my love.

ACKNOWLEDGMENTS

So much of my writing is done alone. My office is in the center of our home, but even though someone else is in the house, I am alone at the computer. I am the only one who knows where I want to go with the story and what I hope to project. However, there are many people who fill the rest of my world. On this page I would like to acknowledge just a few of them.

To my son, Tim. Thank you for the poem. It was my favorite during your fifth-grade year. Thank you for having a tender heart, warm smile, and marvelous sense of humor. I love the sound of your laugh.

To my friend and secretary, Mary Vesperman. I can't imagine a more wonderful team. Thank you, Mary, for every jot and tittle, but most especially for being you.

To Harold and Norma Kolstad. Thank you for telling me your story. It was my strongest inspiration.

And finally to my husband, Bob. As imaginative as I am, I could not have dreamed of the joy I would know in our relationship. Even if my feelings were somehow cut in half, I would still be head-over-heels in love with you.

27 December 1872

Dear Morgan,

If this letter finds you, God has certainly heard my prayers. This year marks the third Christmas without my Clara, and even though this season is the most lonely, the rest of the year is not much better. The store here is profitable, enough for three families, but success is lonely when not shared.

I would very much enjoy seeing you and Adaline; in fact, I would like to present you with a business proposition. I have moved into the rooms above the store. I still have my home, but it's too large and full of Clara. I do not know how business stands for you in Boston, so much changed with the war, but if you've a longing for change, a position and home await you here. I feel the years that separate us now more than ever, and I can't continue on here — not on my own, feeling every one of my 63 years.

Many of the mine owners live here, so there is a school and a church, and as I stated before, business is good.

Winter lasts for months, but spring is worth the wait. I do not want to paint a false picture. I work hard and the hours are long, but if you've fathered a bunch of strapping sons, the load will be light.

Enough of the sales talk. You now know where I stand. I send this with hopes that I will hear from you soon, even if you decline to join me. I do ask myself, however, how brothers could have become so separated. I hope you come, but even a letter from the only family I have left would be more than welcome.

Sincerely,

Mitchell Fontaine

Georgetown
Colorado Territory

Dear Mitchell,

We received your letter with great pleasure and are at this time making plans to join you. Look for Addy, the boys, and me sometime in July. We look forward to the change and business opportunity.

Until then,

Morgan Fontaine

Boston, Mass.
17 March 1873

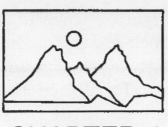

CHAPTER 1

Cut right out of the side of a mountain, Georgetown was filled with narrow streets and friendly businesses. The town of more than 3000 residents sat in a deep valley. Rocky-faced mountains, with just a sprinkling of pines, rose on three sides. The high elevation caused snow to remain on the tallest peaks even in midsummer. Amid the beauty, silver miners built shacks and moved equipment in to plumb the earth. Mine tailings made their own hills and valleys, looming dark and mysterious in the landscape.

Streets lined with houses ran north and south, east and west. Their colors ranged from white to more somber grays, with the occasional pink or bright-blue facade. Clear Creek, flowing fast and clear as its name, ran through the middle of town. Children of all ages loved to cross or stand on the wooden bridge that spanned it, its sides supported with heavy wood beams.

Clayton Taggart, a town local, waved to a few of the creek-gazers as he stopped his wagon in front of the general store and climbed down. He rubbed the small of his back and then looped the horses' reins over the hitching post. He'd been in the saddle for days, and the seat of the buckboard had not felt comfortable. However, his mother had a long list of supplies she needed from town. Milly, Clayton's younger sister, was ill, or his mother would have come herself.

Clayton walked across the street to the barber shop, thinking, as he often did, that there must be an easier way to make a living. Land and mine surveyors were in demand, but they couldn't live, like the mine owners, in town. A dream, one he'd had for years, flashed into his mind, but he forced the thought away. It was going to take more time, and he was going to have to be patient.

"Well now, Clay," the barber greeted the 18-year-old warmly once he was inside the shop.

"Hello, Hap. Have you time for a cut?"

"The chair's all yours."

The regular crowd had gathered in the mismatched wooden chairs along one wall, some smoking and some reading the weekly news. They mumbled greetings as Clayton dropped his hat onto the hook by the door and took a seat in the huge barber chair. The striped drape billowed in the air as it swung around his frame and settled below his throat.

"Yer pa still out?" Hap wanted to know.

"Yeah. He'll be back in a few days."

"Musta been nice and cool in those hills," Charlie Parks offered. He held a section of the paper in front of his nose, and Clayton only smiled. Georgetown itself was over 8500 feet in elevation, making the temperatures quite cool year round. However, it was true that the mine where Clayton had been working had been even cooler.

"It's still a lot of hard work," Clayton commented softly, but no one seemed to hear.

Hap snipped along for a time, working in silence, before Clayton asked, "So what's new in town?" If someone didn't talk to him, he was going to fall asleep.

"Well, now." Hap seemed pleased. "Young Doc Edwardson broke his leg."

"How'd he manage that?"

Hal gave a wheezy laugh before answering. "Him and the missus had a fight, and he went slamming out the back door after dark. Fell down all four steps and busted his leg good. Had to call his own pa to set the thing."

Clayton was amused but sympathetic.

13

"Billy Roper and June Hawley have decided to get married, kinda suddenlike. Some say she's in the family way."

Clayton's eyes in the mirror became very stern, and Hap cleared his throat and changed the subject.

"Mitch Fontaine's brother and his family have moved into town."

Something in Hap's voice caused Clayton to study him closely, but the older man's look gave nothing away.

"Yes, indeed," he continued. "Name's Morgan. Got a right pretty wife too."

"Where're they living?" Clayton's curiosity got the best of him.

"In Mitch's old place. Hey, you have been gone awhile, haven't you, Clay?" Hap suddenly interjected.

"Six weeks." Clayton's deep voice was mild.

"I wonder that your mother didn't tell you."

"I just got in last night, Hap, and Milly's sick."

"Is she now? That's a shame. Gonna miss the first day of school next week?"

"She's hoping not."

"Mitch's havin' a sale." Charlie Parks' voice once again drifted out from behind the paper.

"A sale?" Clayton asked skeptically.

"Yep," Hap took up the ball. "First ever. Morgan told Charlie here they're going to be moving some new stock in, so they've put old items on sale."

Clayton almost shook his head but remembered Hap's scissors just in time.

"All kinds of changes goin' on over there. You planning to stop, Clay?"

"Yeah. Ma sent a list."

There was a certain amount of rustling from the chairs against the wall, but Clayton took little notice. Hap was finished with his haircut and fussing about his neck and ears with a small brush. Clayton flipped a coin to the older man and went for his hat.

"Be sure and have the boys help you out when you get there," Charlie interjected one last time, the paper still in place. To Clayton's confusion, Hap and the other men howled with laughter.

"Yes, sir, Clay," Hap nearly shouted. "Meet the whole family and be *sure* those boys help you with your load." Rumbles of laughter still sounded from the chairs, but all Clayton did was shake his head.

"Thanks, Hap."

The old man never heard him. Clayton exited to calls of advice and more laughter. He stepped off the boardwalk and into the

15

dirt street and headed to the general store, wondering over Mitch Fontaine's brother. Clayton didn't think Georgetown had room for any more characters.

"Tag!" A voice rang out just as he reached the other side, and Clayton turned to wave at a friend. The other man was headed into the bank, so Clayton continued on his way. He stepped into Fontaine's and, while the bell was still ringing in his ear, noticed the change. Not only were things rearranged, they looked cleaner and tidier, like in the days before Clara had fallen ill.

The store sported two front doors, one for hardware and the other for dry goods and groceries. Clayton's list was for dry goods, but the smell of leather that beckoned from the adjoining door tempted him to check out the saddles and riding gear. Clayton's thoughts were interrupted when Mitch greeted him.

"Well, Clay," he said easily.

Clayton looked up to see the older man approaching. With him was a man who could only be his brother. He was younger, but the family resemblance was there.

"Hello, Mitch." Clayton greeted him with a longtime familiarity.

"Good to see you, Clay. Meet my

16

brother, Morgan," Mitch added with great enthusiasm.

"Hello, sir," the younger man said respectfully.

"Clay, was it?" Morgan asked.

"Yes. Clay Taggart."

"Good to meet you, Clay. I'm Morgan Fontaine, and this," he waited until a woman approached from down one of the aisles, "is my wife, Adaline."

Clayton removed his hat. Hap may have exaggerated about the other things, but his estimation of a "right pretty wife" was more than true: Adaline Fontaine was a beauty.

She had come to stand with Morgan, and he performed the introductions. "Addy, this is Clay Taggart."

"Hello, Mr. Taggart." Her voice was rich and cultured.

"Hello, ma'am."

"What can we do for you today?" she asked.

Clayton reached toward his breast pocket, and a moment later they started on the list he withdrew. Everything from sugar to sewing needles was piled on and around the counter. Mitch and Morgan did most of the work, and Clayton fell into conversation with Mrs. Fontaine. He learned they had

17

just moved from Boston, and she learned that his was the only home past their own.

"Your mother must be Elaine."

"Yes."

"Please tell her how thankful we were for the baked goods she left at the house, and also apologize that I've not had time to come to see her. I do plan on it."

"I'll tell her, but there's no rush to come. My sister is ill and it might be best if you wait."

"I'm sorry to hear that. Is there anything we can do?"

"Actually, she's on the road to recovery, but thank you for asking. I'm sure my mother would welcome a visit. Maybe sometime next week."

"I'll plan on that, Mr. Taggart."

"Please call me Clay."

"In that case, I'm Addy. I've noticed that people in town use first names, and to tell you the truth, I'm more comfortable with that."

The two exchanged a companionable smile, and Morgan joined them.

"I think that's everything, Mr. Taggart."

"Please call me Clay."

"Clay it is. I'll start these out, shall I?" He lifted a sack. "Where are the boys?" Morgan suddenly asked Addy.

"In the storeroom," she told him simply.

"Ed! Jack!" Morgan raised his voice to a shout. "Come out here."

Clayton had just thrown a sack of oats onto one muscular shoulder when they appeared.

"Boys," their father continued. "Help Mr. Taggart out with his things."

Clayton couldn't move. The *boys* were two of the most gorgeous females he'd ever laid eyes on. One was cute and the other was drop-dead beautiful. They weren't very tall but already showed signs of lovely womanhood. They both had clean, starched-white aprons covering their dresses, which only worked to accentuate their dark blue eyes and mahogany-colored hair. Clayton knew he was gawking but couldn't seem to help himself. He took in the amused gaze of one of the young women and still stared, but when his eyes swung to her beautiful sister, he saw only haughty disdain. Suddenly, Clayton's amusement matched that of the first girl.

"Come on," Morgan urged, and both girls lifted parcels and started toward the door. Clayton came behind them, his eyes on the girls' hair, which they both wore long and shiny down their backs.

"Here you go," Morgan spoke. "We'll

19

bring the rest out for you, Clay. We'll only be a moment."

Clayton was only too glad to stand and wait; it gave him a chance to get over his shock. Morgan Fontaine made one trip and said goodbye, as he had other customers to wait on, but the girls made two more trips. On the final load the lovelier of the girls tripped on a high board and almost fell on her face. That Clayton found this amusing was more than obvious.

She caught his laughing eyes, and he watched in fascination as her chin went into the air. She tossed her hair back with just the movement of her head, and her eyes flashed dark blue fire.

"A gentleman would never laugh," she told him in a contemptuous tone.

Clayton's smile only deepened. "Well, then, we both know where I stand."

Anger covered her exquisite features before she turned away and returned to the building in a huff. Watching until she disappeared, Clayton's eyes swung to the remaining sister. They grinned at one another.

"She doesn't like you," she said cheekily, and Clayton's shoulders shook with silent laughter.

"She made that quite clear." Clayton's

voice was deep. "Are you two really named Ed and Jack?"

"Edwina and Jacqueline. Eddie and Jackie to everyone but Father, who always wanted boys."

"But he got girls," Clayton clarified unnecessarily.

"Yes." Her dimples were still in place. "Five of them."

"*Five?*"

"Yes."

They both laughed now, and when Clayton sobered he said, "Are you Jackie or Eddie?"

"I'm Eddie. Jackie is the one who doesn't like you."

Clayton only laughed again. "I wonder if I'll be able to do anything about that."

Eddie cocked her head to one side. "I think you probably could, but something tells me you won't."

Clayton shook his head. It was disconcerting to be read so easily. He could probably sweet-talk circles around the lovely Miss Fontaine, but Eddie was right, he wouldn't.

"Well, Mr. Taggart, I'd best get back to work."

"Please call me Clay, or Tag, like my friends do."

The adorable head cocked again. "Well, now, since I hope we'll be friends, I'll call you Tag."

Clayton smiled at her, but a moment later his eyes went back to the door.

"Would I be out of line to ask how old you ladies are?"

"Yes," Eddie told him good-naturedly, "but I'll tell you anyway. I just turned 18, and Jackie's 15."

"And the rest of you?"

"You are nosey," Eddie teased. "Danny is 13, Lexa is 12, and Sammy is 10."

"Lexa?"

"Alexandra," Eddie supplied. "Father calls her Alex."

Clayton nodded, his smile back in place. "Well, Eddie, it's been a pleasure. I hope to see you again."

"Don't tell lies, Tag," she coined his nickname immediately. "You hope to see *Jackie* again."

Clayton didn't reply to this but threw her a huge grin. A moment later he'd climbed onto the buckboard and started the team toward home.

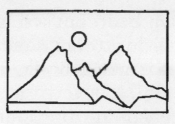

CHAPTER 2

"Is that you, Clay?" his mother called from the bedroom as he walked in the door.

"Yes, I'm back."

A moment later Elaine Taggart came into the kitchen of the small house.

"I think I got everything on your list."

"Thank you, dear," she said as she crossed the room to take one of the sacks from his arms and place it on the table.

"How's Milly?"

"You can ask her yourself. She's not had a fever today, but she's bored with her own company."

Clayton started toward the stairs that led to two bedrooms, Milly's and his parents'.

"No, Clay, she's in the front room. Settle in, and I'll bring you both some lunch."

Clayton walked quietly into the living room. His sister was curled on the sofa, covered with a light blanket. Her eyes were closed, and Clayton assumed she was asleep. His own bedroom was a small room right off the living room, and he stepped quietly inside to get a book. Returning to the living room, he took a comfortable chair. He opened the book and had read only the first page when he glanced up to find his sister's eyes on him.

"You got a haircut," she said unnecessarily.

Clayton's hand went to the back of his neck. Since he'd arrived late last night and left that morning before she was out of her room, she hadn't seen how much he'd needed one.

"Did you see Dad when you were out?"

"Yes. He's just up at Silver Plume, and I would think he'd be home by the end of the week. Probably sooner if he'd known you were sick."

Milly smiled at the thought. She loved her father dearly and missed him so much when he was away. The way she was feeling at the moment, she knew she would cry if she kept on thinking about him, so with a small note of desperation in her voice she asked, "Who did you see in town?"

"The regulars were at the barber shop," Clayton began and then obliged her with a detailed account of all he'd seen and done. He finished with his talk with Eddie while

24

in front of the general store and Milly spoke up.

"I met Eddie Fontaine one day when Mom asked me to take them some muffins. I think the youngest girl was there too."

"About ten years old?"

"Yeah."

"That would be Sammy. Eddie told me there are five, all told."

"And all with boys' names."

"Well, the nicknames their father has given them may be masculine, but *they're* definitely feminine."

"What's Jackie like? Isn't she the one my age?"

Clayton's brows drew together. He did not usually speak ill of people, but Jackie was hard to describe. "She's your age, all right, but I would say that you're going to have a hard time liking her very much."

"What exactly does that mean?"

Clayton dropped his eyes. He should never have put ideas into her head.

"I'm sorry, Milly. That was wrong of me. You might get along fine, but I sense that the move here wasn't the easiest for her. Georgetown's not Boston, and I don't know how much of a sense of humor she has."

"Is this your way of saying she's a snob?"

Clayton grimaced slightly; his sister was

no fool, but he'd seen something in Jackie's eyes that was difficult to describe. Finally he replied, "I think she's more scared than she is a snob, but it's not going to come across that way."

Milly nodded. Though she didn't have a fever or headache today, she was still tired, and the conversation was wearing her out. It was a relief to have her mother come in with large mugs of soup and thick pieces of bread. Both Elaine and Clayton stayed with Milly while they ate, but she was soon in need of a nap. Mother and brother left her alone. Elaine had baking to do, and Clayton had some letters to open and answer.

"Okay, Dan," her father panted. "Lift that end now."

Thirteen-year-old Danny tried to do as she was instructed. She was able to lift the box, but it was just too heavy to move once she had it in the air.

"It's too heavy."

Morgan frowned at her, but the young teen took it in stride.

"Where's Ed?"

"Reading a letter from Robert."

The frown turned into a dark scowl.

"That's quite a face," Addy commented softly as she approached. A reluctant smile tugged at Morgan's mouth. He could grow angry, and often did with nearly everyone in the world. However, just the sight of his precious wife was enough to calm him. She had given him all girls when he had specifically asked for boys, but he'd even forgiven her that. She now smiled into his eyes and put a gentle hand on his chest as she passed. Morgan took a quick glance around the store before he landed a quick swat to her backside. She turned indignantly.

"Morgan Fontaine! We're in the store!"

"No one's here, Addy," he replied reasonably.

"You call Danny 'no one'?"

"You didn't see anything, did you, Dan?"

"Not a thing," she told them with eyes wide to match her smile.

Addy shook her head in mock despair and heard Morgan tell Danny to go for Eddy.

"She's reading a letter from Robert," Addy informed him in a voice that caused Danny to stay still. Her mother had a way with her father.

The words still caused Morgan to scowl, but he said, "Then where is Jack?"

"Oh, she's home, trying to figure out what to wear for the first day of school," Danny informed him calmly.

"The first day of school is next week," he grunted in mild exasperation. "Run home and tell her to come down here, Dan. Alex too, if you see her."

Danny had only just walked from home and didn't want to go all the way back, but she did as she was told.

"Thank you." Addy's voice came softly to her husband's ears.

"For what?"

"For not making Eddy come."

Morgan frowned. "I don't like this correspondence with men."

"Not men, *man*. Just Robert Langley."

"I still don't like it."

"Oh, my darling," Addy's voice was still soft, "I wish you would accept the inevitable."

"Meaning?"

"Morgan, she's in love with the man. My sister said it happened the moment they set eyes on each other."

"Lacey can't possibly know such a thing, Addy."

Addy looked at him for a few moments. He returned her look. "I'm going to ask Eddie about the letter tonight, and I want you to watch her reaction," she said.

"I don't know what that will prove."

The bell rang, signaling a customer entering the store, and Addy had time only to whisper, "Just watch."

"Jackie," her younger sister called as soon as she entered the front door of the deep, narrow, two-story house.

"Upstairs," came a faint reply.

"Father wants you at the store."

Danny was still standing right inside the front door, watching as Jackie appeared at the top of the stairs wearing only her underclothes.

"But I just got home," she protested. "Where's Eddie?"

"Reading a letter from Robert."

Jackie was as easy to anger as her father, and had it been anyone else, she would have given vent to her temper. But Eddie had the same effect on Jackie that Addy had on her father, so Jackie turned back to her room to dress. Twenty minutes later she was at the store, her hair not even brushed. Still she was in trouble with her father for taking far too long.

"You're much too worried about the way you look," he scolded her, and Jackie, the only one of his five children to ever do so, answered back in equal anger.

"School begins next week, and I've nothing to wear!"

"You have a closetful of clothes and then some."

"I hate all of them! I need something new!"

"I can barely get a moment's work out of you, but you want new clothes."

The 15-year-old's mouth swung open. She had done nothing *but* work since she arrived in Georgetown, and the expression on her face reminded her father of that fact.

"Okay, Jack," he conceded, "we'll discuss your clothing tonight, but right now I want some work done."

"All right," Jackie acquiesced, but made it plain that she wasn't happy about it.

Ten minutes later Eddie made an appearance as well, and much was accomplished before the store closed for the day. Addy invited Mitch to supper that night, but he declined with a gracious smile. He was tired, he admitted to Addy, and looking forward to the quiet of his spacious rooms above the store.

The Morgan Fontaine family made their way home. Addy was still amazed at how perfectly the large house fit them. The downstairs had a lovely parlor, a formal dining room that lacked only table and chairs, a large, spacious kitchen with a walk-in pantry, and a small bedroom off the back. Four bedrooms surrounded the huge landing upstairs, and there was even a room with a water closet and large freestanding bathtub. Addy praised God every day for His provision and could well understand why Mitch didn't want to rattle around by himself in the large structure.

Hands were washed and aprons put in place, and after a half hour's work in the kitchen where there were numerous chairs and a large table, they sat down to their evening meal. Morgan spoke for a time as they all began to eat, thanking his family for their hard work, but also urging them to work harder still.

Adaline remained quiet during his talk, but when Morgan appeared to be through, she broke in with a quiet question to Eddie.

"Danny mentioned that you received a letter from Robert today."

Suddenly shy, Eddie only nodded and dropped her gaze to the edge of the blue-and-white china plate.

"How is he?" her mother persisted.

Eddie's entire demeanor changed. She tucked her lower lip under her teeth, and her eyes shone with happiness.

"He's fine," she breathed.

Addy exchanged a swift look with her husband, who was frowning, before gently pressing her daughter.

"What did he write about?"

"Well." Eddie's face was still alight with love. "He says that he envies us the cool of the mountains. Boulder has been very hot. He also said business at the bank is excellent, but he's getting tired of his small, downtown apartment." She hesitated and then added quietly, "He's looking for property and hopes to build a house someday."

"That would be exciting," Addy said smoothly before Eddie's sisters joined in the conversation. They asked Eddie many things she didn't know, but her shrug was so adorable that everyone but her father ended up laughing. He had stopped frowning but didn't comment or join in the fun. His wife could see that he was determined to talk to Eddie directly after the meal, but Addy caught him while the girls did the cleanup. With her hand gently holding his, she pulled him down the front hallway and into the living room. She lit a lamp and spoke, her eyes looking seriously into his.

"You don't like me to be right, so I'll not ask you to admit it, but I must say this, Morgan. You're certain in your mind that this wouldn't be happening if we'd had boys, but I can't agree with you. They would still grow up, fall in love, and move away. Some might stay, but certainly not all. We must accept this.

"Robert is a wonderful man, and Eddie has never disobeyed us. This is not some whim. If you forbid her this, it will break her heart. She'll obey you because of the love between you, but you'll crush her sweet heart until she's positive she's going to die."

"But we don't even know this man!" Morgan broke in in a desperate whisper.

"So let's invite him for a visit and get to know him. Let's encourage Eddie and not beat her down." Tears filled Addy's eyes. "My father never approved of you, but I ran away because you stole my heart. Before he died, my father realized he was all wrong about you. Eddie would never choose to rebel as I did, but you could be all wrong about Robert too."

Morgan's sigh was huge. He pulled Addy into his arms and just held her. He could never handle her tears. His sweet wife would never know it, but part of the reason that everything turned to success in Morgan's hand was because Addy's father had said it would never happen. Morgan Fontaine easily grew restless. They had lived in many places and he'd had his hand in many a business, but all had been successful, mainly because he'd been challenged.

He looked down now to where Addy's head lay on his chest. She tipped her head back to see him, and he pressed a kiss to her brow.

"I don't care what you say, Adaline, boys are easier." He was doing his level best to sound stern.

"Be that as it may, Morgan, we have girls."

Morgan only shook his head and kissed her again. It sounded like Lexa and Sammy were arguing over something, so he gently released his wife and moved to the kitchen. Morgan threatened to find additional chores to keep them busy until bedtime if the girls could not get along, and things quieted swiftly. Addy had come in slowly behind him, still praying that Morgan would accept what was to come. Her heart was greatly lifted when she heard him speak to Eddie.

"Does Robert ever talk about visiting Georgetown, Ed?"

"He did once," she told her father, "but I wasn't sure it would be all right, so I didn't reply to it."

"But you'd like him to come."

Eddie's anxious eyes flew to her father. She looked at him with such longing that she suddenly looked much younger than her 18 years. Her mouth opened, but no words

34

came out. She finally just nodded.

"Well then." Morgan's voice had become soft. "I guess you'd better ask him."

Eddie threw her arms around her father's neck and squeezed him with all her might. He laughed and hugged her in return.

"Well, if you thought it was hard to get work out of Eddie before," Lexa now commented, "it'll be dang-near impossible now."

"You shut your mouth, Lexa Fontaine," Jackie told her in no uncertain terms.

"That's a very good idea," Addy broke in with a firm but much calmer tone. "And if you use that kind of language again, Lexa, I'll find a bar of soap with your name on it."

"Yes, Mother." Lexa was suitably cowed by her mother, but when she turned away, Jackie received a dirty look. It did nothing to intimidate the older girl, however, and her lovely chin only rose in challenge until Lexa's gaze dropped.

That night in bed, the incident with Lexa put out of her mind, Jackie had more questions for Eddie. The girls shared a very feminine room as well as a large, soft bed, and as usual, ended the evening with talk about the day.

"Do you love Robert, Eddie?"

"Yes," the older girl said softly. "I think I loved him right away but then thought it must be a crush. Then after we started to write each other, I knew it was real."

"Do you get excited about living in a house that he built for the two of you?"

Eddie only laughed. Her mind hadn't gone that far.

"I'm never going to fall in love," Jackie declared as she got comfortable on the pillow. "I think men are a pain."

"You might change your mind, Jackie," Eddie said gently.

"Never! I'm still amazed that you spoke to that Clay Taggart today. I just hate him."

Eddie smiled as she rolled to turn down the lantern, but didn't speak. However, she was still thinking, *You might change your mind, Jackie.*

CHAPTER 3

Clayton dropped Milly off at the school-house on the first day of September and told her to have fun. Their father was still not home; he'd been expected on the week-end so that *he* could take his daughter to school. Milly had been disappointed but smiled at Clay anyway and then walked toward the group of other students waiting for the school bell to ring.

They had a new teacher this year, a Miss Bradley. None of the students had met her, but rumors were already circulating that she was strict. Milly knew some apprehension over this, but it was forgotten as she looked over to see the Fontaine sisters approaching. There were four of them, all with thick ma-hogany-colored hair and eyes in various shades of blue. Milly tried to remember their names. The oldest, the one she had met at the house, was not among them. She'd also met a younger sister and now spotted her, but still could not recall their names.

She was telling the Lord that she would make a good effort to get to know them today when she spotted her longtime friend, Padriac O'Brien. Milly would have gone to him, but his attention was riveted on something. It took a moment for her to see that it was not a something, but a someone — the oldest Fontaine girl. Indeed, nearly every eye in the group was on her. Milly's mind grappled with her name and finally came up with Jackie.

At the same time a spark of jealousy rose in Milly's chest over Paddy's interest. There was no commitment between the two of them, but they had been very close for many years. Seeing him now as smitten as all the other boys caused a deep pain in her heart. She was saved from dwelling on this too deeply when the bell rang. The children went forward as one, but the Fontaine girls hung back.

"I wish we had met more kids this summer," Sammy commented softly as she brought up the rear.

"I feel sick," Lexa added, and Danny put a hand on her arm.

Jackie didn't feel much better, but she wouldn't have admitted it under threat of death. She had been very aware of the eyes on her earlier, and where she usually enjoyed the attention, today she felt unsure about the style of her pale blue dress and wished she could have been invisible. It would have helped tremendously to have Eddie along — kind, confident Eddie — but she had finished her schooling in the spring while still in Boston.

"Take your seats, please," the teacher's voice rang out. "Older students in the rear, younger near the front."

Jackie sat in the last seat in the row nearest the north wall and hoped she wouldn't be moved. Every boy she'd ever sat in front of pulled her hair, and she didn't think she could take one more year of that.

"I am Miss Bradley," the tall, thin woman spoke from the front of the room. She smiled, but her eyes were serious. "I've written my name on the board so you can see how it is spelled, and now I wish to know your names. We will start with this row," she said, indicating the row nearest the south wall. "When I point to you, you will stand, state your full name and age, and then be reseated. Does everyone understand?"

There was a chorus of "Yes, Miss Bradley," and then they began. Sammy was near the front but not in the first row, and as it was, Lexa was the first of the Fontaine girls to give her name.

"Your full name is Lexa?" Miss Bradley questioned her with a frown.

"No, ma'am," Lexa nearly whispered.

"What is it?"

"Alexandra, ma'am."

"Then Alexandra it shall be. I do not use nicknames," she now told everyone. "We will proceed, and you will give your full name."

Again they were off. Red faces peppered the room as students with names like Bartholomew, Millicent, Danielle, Padriac, Matilda, Susannah, and Jacqueline were announced.

For Jackie it was the start of a morning that dragged. She was already hungry for lunch and tired of the looks the boy beside her was sending her way. How she envied Eddie. As much as Jackie hated stocking and dusting shelves, she wished she were at the store right now.

"Well, hello, Elaine."

"Hi, Mitch. How are you?"

"Can't complain, can't complain. Yourself?"

"I'm fine, but I miss Kevin."

"When do you expect him?"

"Two days ago."

Mitch chuckled. "Say, Elaine, have you met my family?"

"I'm sorry to say I haven't."

"Addy," Mitch called to the rear, "are you back there?"

A moment later she appeared. Elaine smiled as Mrs. Fontaine came forward, a picture of grace and beauty.

"Addy, this is Elaine Taggart," Mitch began.

"Of course," Addy said as her hand came out. "Please forgive my lack of response to your gift, Mrs. Taggart. We're still trying to find things."

Elaine laughed. "Call me Elaine, and think nothing of it. Moving can bring such upheaval. My Milly has been sick, or I'd have been to see you much sooner."

"We met your son, and he told us about Milly. Is she feeling better?" Addy asked.

"Yes, she's at school today. Clayton told me he enjoyed speaking to you."

"He's delightful," Addy told her sincerely. "Eddie had a nice talk with him too."

"Your husband?" Elaine questioned and received a chuckle.

"No," Addy's eyes sparkled. "My oldest daughter."

At that moment Morgan and Eddie made an appearance, and both met Elaine. Morgan questioned Elaine about Kevin's return, and because they were her closest neighbors, he told her to come if she needed anything, day or night. By the time Elaine left, they had made plans to get together soon. She hoped Kevin would be home by then. She was missing him more than ever and asking God to bring him home soon.

"What's eating you?" Paddy O'Brien asked easily as he lowered himself to the grass beside Milly.

Milly looked at him for a moment and debated what to say. He'd been gawking at Jackie Fontaine for most of the lunch hour, and Milly, in an effort to protect herself, had moved away so she didn't have to watch. In a flash, she decided on honesty.

"I realize Jackie Fontaine is pretty, but I'd rather not sit and watch all of you stare at her."

Sixteen, but mature for his age, Paddy looked thoughtful. Instead of teasing her, he regarded her statement seriously.

"Yeah," Paddy answered, his eyes on the walls of Clear Creek Canyon. "I guess we were all pretty obvious. It's like that with anyone new. It'll wear off soon enough. Were you jealous?" His gaze swung to her.

Milly met his eyes squarely. "A little, but

more than that I'm confused."

"Over what?"

"Over why boys are attracted to a pretty face no matter what the girl is like. I mean, look at Susie. She's the nicest girl in school, but she's not pretty so no one gives her a second look."

Again Paddy stared at her. Personally, he thought *Milly* was the nicest girl in school and pretty to go with it, but he saw her point. He was not able to tell her, however, since Danny and Sammy wandered by just then. Sammy gave them a shy hello, and when both Paddy and Milly greeted them in a friendly fashion, they stopped.

"I can't remember your names," Paddy told them honestly.

"I'm Danny, and this is Sammy."

"I'm Paddy O'Brien, and this is Milly Taggart."

"Would you like to sit down?" Milly asked.

The sisters exchanged a look and then sank down under the tree.

"You're new in town, aren't you?" This came from Paddy.

"Yes. We used to live in Massachusetts. Boston, actually."

"What was it like?"

"Oh, nice," Danny commented. "We've

lived many places, so in some ways, Boston was just another town."

"Where all have you lived?" Paddy, who could not remember ever being out of Georgetown, was intrigued.

"New York, Vermont, and Pennsylvania," Sammy informed him.

"I've lived in South Carolina, as well," Danny added.

"I have a friend that I write to in South Carolina!" Milly exclaimed, and the two of them had an excited exchange until the bell rang. Sammy ended up walking back to the schoolhouse with Paddy, and because he was the youngest in his own family, they found quite a bit to talk about.

"My brothers have all moved away."

"I think my sister Eddie will. She's in love with a man who lives in Boulder."

"It's a good thing they don't all leave at once. It can be pretty lonely when that happens."

Sammy nodded as they went up the steps. Her light blue eyes sought out those of the handsome, dark-haired Irish boy and gave him a sweet smile when he gently tugged on her braid.

The letter began *Dear Robert,* and Eddie concentrated with all her might to make every letter and space perfect. She wrote about Georgetown and the things that had been keeping her busy but hesitated over anything too personal. She had been tempted to write Robert since she had received his letter the previous week, but she wanted very much to take time to think and pray. Asking a man to come and visit you was in a way an invitation for something very personal. Eddie wanted that something personal very much, but she was hesitant to be the initiator. She had proceeded with caution and more prayer and decided that now was the time to plunge in.

> *My father has been uncertain of our corresponding because he and my mother have never met you. I do not want to presume upon your interest or go the other way and make you feel as though your letters are not welcome, but my father asked me if you'd ever expressed a desire to visit Georgetown.*

Eddie frowned at what she had written. "I sound like a little girl."

"Says who?"

Eddie jumped at the sound of her mother's voice.

"I thought I was home alone."

"I just got here. You must have been so intent you didn't hear me."

Eddie sighed.

"What is it, dear?"

"I'm writing to Robert."

Addy's brows rose. "Why did I think you would have done that long ago?"

"I wanted to, Mother, but when you ask a man to come and see you, well, I just didn't want to —" Not knowing how to go on, she stopped.

"I think I understand," Addy told her softly. "Are you a little uncertain of his feelings for you?"

"Yes."

"He sounds quite smitten to me."

Tears filled Eddie's eyes. "Oh, Mother. He's so wonderful, and I just can't think what he sees in me."

Addy's arms went around her oldest child. A lovelier, sweeter Christian girl she had never known, but Eddie always believed herself homely next to her beautiful sister, Jackie. Indeed, Jackie was lovely, but Eddie didn't realize how lovely she herself was. Addy pulled a scented lace handkerchief from her pocket and tenderly wiped her daughter's face. She cupped her daughter's soft cheeks in her smooth hands and spoke earnestly into her deep blue eyes.

46

"Robert Langley was blessed by God the day he walked into your Aunt Lacey's home in Boulder and saw you sitting there. I've talked to my sister, and she said he was enchanted before he could take his next breath. He wouldn't have felt that way about a little girl. She said he couldn't keep his eyes off you. And what did you tell me he said?"

"That he'd been waiting for me for a very long time."

Addy smiled. "Finish your letter, dear, and run downtown to post it."

"Thank you, Mother."

Addy was on her way from the room when Eddie spoke again.

"Why are you home?"

"Because your father wants me to meet the girls every day, and school lets out in less than an hour."

Eddie hadn't realized the time. She finished the letter, saying just what she'd wanted, and then grabbed her bonnet and rushed for the door. She wasn't overly tall, but her stride was swift, and in less time than she would have expected, she was at the post office and pushing her coin and letter across the counter. The postmaster smiled warmly at the lovely young woman, and Eddie beamed at him before turning to go. She was on her way through the door when a voice stopped her.

"Good afternoon, Miss Fontaine."

Having recognized that voice, Eddie turned with a ready smile.

"And to you, Mr. Taggart."

"What are you up to this warm afternoon?"

"I was mailing a letter. How about yourself?"

"I was doing the same."

"Someone special?" Eddie asked with a cheeky grin.

"Business," Clayton told her dryly. "How about you?"

Eddie bit her lip, her eyes sparkling. Clayton would have been blind not to recognize the look.

"What's his name?"

"Robert," she breathed. "Robert Langley."

"Where does he live?"

"Boulder."

"I see. And does he tell you that he's been looking for you for the whole of his life?"

"Oh, Tag," Eddie breathed. "How did you know?"

Clayton's smile was tender. She was a girl in love, all right. He thanked God that he hadn't lost his head the first time they'd met.

"God was smiling on Robert Langley the day he found you, Eddie Fontaine."

"That's what my mother says."

"And she's right." Clayton suddenly flipped his watch out of his pocket. "I've got to run. I told Milly I'd give her a lift home. Would you like a ride?"

"No. I have to get to the store."

"Good day to you then, Miss Fontaine."

Eddie threw him a beaming smile and swung away. Clayton placed his hat back on his head, climbed aboard the wagon, and swung the team toward the schoolhouse on the hill.

CHAPTER 4

II

Milly and Danny left the schoolhouse still talking. They had hardly noticed each other before lunch, but once they had returned to class both realized that they sat just two seats away from each other. When Miss Bradley told the class they could pair up for a reading exercise, Danny immediately looked to Milly who slid over on her bench so the younger girl could join her. Jackie had ended up sitting with Susie, and both girls looked miserable.

But now the day was over, and many of the students hit the door running. Miss Bradley had been strict but fair, and in her fairness she had warned them that she was an unyielding disciplinarian. She did not believe God had created stupid children, which meant if they were not learning, then they were not trying, and that meant the strap if you were a boy or the ruler if you were a girl. Punishment would be meted out at the front of the room, but that would

50

be the end of it. No staying after class or writing sentences for the better part of the day. Miss Bradley had no doubt that a session with the strap or ruler would be more than enough impetus to learn your lesson or alter your behavior.

"Here's Clay," Milly said as the girls gained the warm afternoon sun. "He told me he'd come for me. Hey, Clay," Milly called as she approached, "can we give Danny and her sisters a ride home?"

"Sure," the young man responded readily enough. "Hop in."

Danny, Lexa, and Sammy scrambled aboard with Milly, but Jackie, who had just come upon the scene, stopped short. Clayton's amused gaze swept over her affronted features.

"Are you going to join us, Miss Fontaine?"

That chin went into the air.

"Come on, Jackie," Sammy urged her. "Get in."

"No, thank you," she said with a regal air. "I'd rather walk." With that she turned, her skirts swirling around her, and started home.

Clayton grinned and raised the reins to slap the team, but Paddy hailed him from the schoolhouse steps and he stopped. The

51

younger man had a question and a message from his father that he'd forgotten to tell Milly. The two talked together for a few minutes. The girls took no notice but spoke of the day and made plans for the week.

By the time Clayton moved his team down the road, Jackie was far ahead of them. He slowed the team ever so slightly as they came abreast of her, and Clayton smiled to himself when he felt the wagon bounce slightly. The unapproachable Jackie Fontaine had climbed aboard. Clayton pulled up in front of the Fontaine home less than ten minutes later, and the three younger girls scrambled out with calls of thanks and goodbye. Jackie remained silent. Clayton deliberately turned his handsome blond head and watched her. Jackie caught his look and tossed her chestnut curls.

"Not going to thank me?" he murmured softly and watched as she flounced into the house. She shut the front door a little too hard and said to the entryway at large, "I hate that Clayton Taggart. I tell you, I do."

No one in her family commented, and Jackie stormed up the stairs telling herself that when her sisters saw what a colossal conceit he had, they would feel the same way.

In the meantime, Milly had come up beside her brother on the wagon seat, and as they pulled away, she commented, "I don't think she spoke to anyone all day."

"Jackie?"

"Yes."

"Maybe she was afraid."

Milly shook her head. "I don't think so. She thinks she's better than the rest of us."

"Her sisters aren't like that."

Milly thought about that. The Fontaine sisters were all so much alike in looks, but like night and day in temperament. Sammy and Danny were both warm and friendly, but not quite as lovely as Lexa and Jackie. *They* were the beauties of the family, their eyes rimmed by dark lashes and framed with perfect brows — a perfect foil for the burnished mahogany hair that was the hallmark of the family. Their attitudes, however, were much more guarded, making them seem standoffish and conceited.

"No, they're not all like that," Milly finally agreed. "Which is something of a miracle, since they're all pretty."

They fell silent, busy with their own thoughts, and the ride was quiet for the last hundred yards home — quiet, that is, until they spotted their father's horse. Kevin Taggart had finally come home.

★ ★ ★

Milly was in bed, and Clayton and his father sat together at the kitchen table. They had talked about the mine he'd been surveying and now they discussed the next jobs.

"I've got a letter out to McBride about his newest mine, but Paddy O'Brien told me today that his father is laid up with a leg injury. I didn't have time to go see him, but that means the Moonbeam #3 is going to be open for a surveyor."

"The Moonbeam is set in horrible terrain," Kevin commented.

"That's probably why Cormac O'Brien is laid up."

"At least it's close," Kevin put in. "I'm weary of the trail."

"Tell me about it," Clayton said softly, and his father laid a gentle hand on his shoulder.

"Still have that dream?"

"I sure do. I think that's why I'm so eager to pick Milly up from school. Every once in a while her dress will smell like chalk and all the other classroom smells combined. I can just see myself there, at the front of the class, chalk in hand."

Elaine had poured them all cups of coffee in heavy, dark mugs and had taken a place at the table. She looked across and smiled at her son.

"God will show you the way, Clay. You believe that, don't you?"

"I do, Mom, but I must admit that at times I chafe at God's timing. I want this now, while I'm still young."

"You are getting old," his father said, and it was clear where Clayton gained his sense of humor. "We'll find a way, Clayton." He turned serious just that fast. "Trust and keep on here. We'll find a way."

Clayton nodded, and Kevin's gaze swung to his wife. His eyes caressed her face and dark blonde hair before he reached for her hand. Clayton slipped away from the kitchen with a very soft good-night to his parents, but they barely noticed.

"Welcome home," Elaine said lovingly.

"Thank you." He continued to study her. "Tired?"

"Not a bit," she told him.

Kevin's gray eyes warmed perceptibly, and as their fingers locked they leaned simultaneously, their lips meeting, warm and familiar. It was lovely to be home.

The week moved on with a strong pattern. Kevin took Milly to school, but Clayton picked her up. Each day the Fontaine sisters rode with him. Jackie never thanked him or even spoke to him, but he could get a rise out of her with just one look. And that was the confusing part. If she hated him, why did she look at him? If she had simply ignored him and gone her way, she'd have never seen the amused glance that set her blood to boiling. Clayton mentally shook his head in wonder because she did it every time. He had started to say "You're welcome" even though she hadn't uttered a word, and instead of snubbing him, she looked into his eyes every time. One time Clayton even winked at her and then watched her turn red with fury, her eyes flashing ominous fire before she flounced away to the house.

In the midst of this was Milly. Milly loved her brother, and she loved her new friend Danny, but Jackie was more than she could handle. Jackie didn't speak to the kids at school or show a drop of the kindness offered to her by various classmates, and in Milly's opinion she just wasn't worth bothering with. Milly was not comfortable with her own attitude, but she didn't know what to do. One day she even discussed it with Danny, who simply said, "I'm sorry it's so strained between the two of you, Milly, but anything I would say would only sound like

I'm making excuses for Jackie."

"Does she get along with anyone?"

"Oh, yes, but she doesn't like school and doesn't make friends easily."

"I couldn't stand not to have friends."

"But she does have friends," Danny told her gently. "She has her sisters, especially Eddie. They're very close, and Jackie loves Eddie more than anyone."

Milly looked at the younger girl with new respect. If she had a sister that Clayton loved more, Milly knew she would be absolutely crushed, but Danny was accepting and even seemed glad for Jackie. Danny had gone on to say that her father and Lexa could be just as prickly, and that sometimes a person could be aware of a problem but not be able to do anything about it except pray.

Had Danny only known what was taking place at the store, she would have been amazed at how closely her words echoed those of her mother. Addy was talking with Mitch while Morgan was busy with the books.

"I can talk to Eddie and Danny — even Sammy — but not Jackie or Lexa. They're just as prickly as Morgan."

"Has he shown any signs of interest, Addy?"

Addy smiled gently at her brother-in-law. "That's just it, Mitch. He thinks he is a believer. He thinks he's very interested. He goes to church, he believes in God, he cares for his family, so of course he's going to heaven."

"But, Addy, what does he do with verses that say without God's plan we are lost?"

"He would say he has God's plan, and that he does believe in Jesus Christ."

The two fell silent for a moment. It had come as a great surprise to both of them to discover that they both had come to a saving knowledge of Christ, but it had been a tremendous letdown for Mitch when he realized his brother had never made that step.

"I keep praying, Mitch, but I also must thank God. I know Morgan loves me, and when I think of how it could be, I praise God for His grace and provision."

"I'm not sure what you mean."

"Only that he is a wonderful father and husband. He adores the girls, and even though he can be very dictatorial, he always acts in our best interest. So you see, I have much for which to give thanks."

Mitch nodded and also expressed his own heartfelt thanks. His brother had married a wonderful woman who honored him and was making a strong attempt to raise her

58

girls to understand God's greatest gift. A sudden pang stabbed through Mitch's heart as he thought of his own Clara. Mitch himself had not realized his need for Christ until after her death. He had no idea where she was spending eternity, and all he could do was rest in God's sovereignty.

Boulder, Colorado

Robert Langley rocked his chair back onto two legs and smiled at the letter in his hand. Eddie wanted him to come for a visit. She had not come right out and said so, but it was there. Robert's eyes closed as he pictured her in his mind, and again he smiled. He had told her that he'd been looking for her for a very long time, and this was quite true. She was everything he could possibly hope for in a wife. She shared his faith in Christ, she was gentle, kindhearted, and lovely. He had spent only three hours with her, but it felt like they had always known each other. And when they parted, he touched her hand oh-so-briefly, but even now his heart thundered in his chest at the thought of holding her in his arms. How soon could he leave . . .

A knock sounded on his office door, and

Robert was forced back to the world of banking.

"Come in," he called and stood up with a smile when his friend, Travis Buchanan, came in.

"Travis," the men shook hands, "what brings you into town?"

"Just a little business. We're starting a cattle drive soon and I needed a newspaper."

"Well, since you're here, I'll buy you lunch at the hotel."

"With an offer like that, I wonder why I don't come into town more often."

Robert reached for his suit jacket, and the men made their way through the bank and out onto the street. The contrast in their mode of dress was fascinating, and they caught many eyes, but some of this probably could have been attributed to their height. Robert Langley was no midget at 6'2", but Travis was the main attraction at 6'4". He was a rancher by trade, and with his dark jeans, plaid shirt, broad shoulders, and worn cowboy boots, he appeared even larger. Robert was also a large man, but his dress was very much that of the banker, with black serge pants and jacket, snow-white shirt, and a dark tie at his throat. Both men were well known in town, so seating in the dining room at the hotel was immediate and comfortable.

"What day do you expect the cattle to go?" Robert asked. They had placed their orders and been served large mugs of strong, black coffee.

"It looks like two weeks from Thursday, but I'll need to be back in town the day before." A sudden smile split Travis' face, and he said, "Shall I buy lunch that day?"

Robert smiled as well, his expression rather wistful. "As a matter of fact, I don't think I'll be around."

"Business?" Travis felt free to ask.

"No," Robert told him with quiet contentment. "I'm going to Georgetown."

Again Travis smiled. "Tell Eddie that I look forward to meeting her."

Robert only nodded, but he looked pleased. A moment later the waitress arrived with their food.

It did not go unnoticed by Jackie that Clayton Taggart sat directly behind her in church the next Sunday. It was not planned, but suddenly there he was. Her father liked to be very punctual when attending church — he told her one time that it impressed God — so they were often early and in a pew far to the front. Jackie would have preferred to sit a little farther back, but she was not given this option.

Now today she wished she could think of some reason to leave. The Fontaine girls were expected to take care of their needs before church began, so that excuse would never work, but Jackie thought if she could look sick enough . . .

Her thoughts were cut off by a sudden itch on the bottom of her foot. Jackie wiggled her foot out of one shoe in order to scratch it with the toe of the other, but she never put the shoe back on because her mind was distracted by a woman moving toward the front to sing.

Jackie steeled herself for an awful screech and clamor and was not disappointed. "All About God's Love" was a song her mother liked to hum while she worked, but this woman was spoiling it. And the woman's hat looked like a windblown bird's nest! Jackie rolled her eyes in disgust but looked over to catch her father's stern gaze. His serious eyes were enough to make her alter her expression and sit up straight. At the same time, she remembered her shoe. With her stocking-clad foot she felt around on the floor but couldn't locate it. She began to move a little more, searching as far as she could reach, but Eddie suddenly leaned close.

"Father said if you know what's good for you, you'll sit still."

Again Jackie did as she was directed, but her mind was not on the sermon that was just beginning. Indeed, the next half hour was torturous. Where in the world had her shoe gone?

"I would like to close with this verse," Jackie was relieved to hear Pastor Munroe finally say. "Joshua 1:8 says, 'This book of the law shall not depart out of thy mouth, but thou shalt meditate therein day and night, that thou mayest observe to do according to all that is written therein; for then thou shalt make thy way prosperous, and then thou shalt have good success.'

"I read this, dear friends, because I want you to understand that Sundays are not enough. You must be reading and studying your Bibles all through the week, and my prayer for you this day and always is that you will understand this truth and act upon it. Let us pray."

Jackie had never been so glad to hear the end of a sermon in her life. Her toes were sore from all the bumping around, and she still had not found her shoe. She was nearly bent double now, searching the area but finding nothing. She was bounced into by two of her sisters who moved past her to leave, but the shoe was nowhere to be found. The church was emptying fast when Jackie finally stood and turned around.

Seated on the pew behind her, the shoe dangling from one finger, was Clayton.

"Lose something?" he asked solicitously.

Incensed, Jackie leaned to snatch it away. All Clayton did was grin.

"You are insufferable," she told him between clenched teeth, her shoe finally in place. Clayton only stood, his movement lazy, and tried to look hurt by her words.

"I take it you won't be heartsick when I leave town this next week."

"Not in the least," the young beauty told him with flashing eyes. "I hope you never return."

Again Clayton was not offended. He gave Jackie a lazy smile and nod before moving on his way, his hat held loosely in one hand. Jackie was angry that he would go out ahead of a lady, but she was through talking to him. Indeed, she believed the man was impossible and vowed at that moment never to speak to him again. However, she watched as he walked all the way to the double church doors, put his hat firmly in place, and stepped out into the morning sunshine.

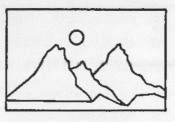

CHAPTER 5

"Now, girls," Adaline gave instructions the next morning, "everyone is to come home right after school. We are invited to the Taggarts' for dinner."

"What did you say?" Jackie questioned her mother. She hadn't been attending her words.

"You should have been listening," was all Addy would say. "Now, whether or not Eddie and I are here, I want your chores done and no bickering."

The girls all agreed respectfully and finished their breakfasts, but as Jackie, who had finally understood, was leaving the table, she mumbled under her breath, "At least Clayton won't be there."

"Why do you say that, dear?" her mother, whose hearing was keen, wished to know.

"He told me he was leaving town."

"He is. So is Mr. Taggart, but not until Tuesday. That's why we were asked over tonight." Addy turned away then, missing her daughter's face. To look at her, one would have thought she was carrying the weight of the world on her shoulders. Indeed, something told Jackie it was going to be a very long day.

"A telegram?" Eddie questioned the kind man. "For me?"

"Well, if your name is Edwina Fontaine, then it's yours."

"Thank you," she said faintly and then turned to find her parents' and uncle's eyes on her.

"I received a telegram," she explained unnecessarily and then stood there.

"Are you going to read it?" her mother asked gently.

"Oh!" Eddie started. "Yes." She unfolded the thin piece of paper and read the few short lines.

EDWINA STOP AM LEAVING BOULDER BY STAGE STOP SHOULD BE WITH YOU FRIDAY STOP ROBERT LANGLEY

"He's coming," she now whispered, her eyes flying to meet her mother's. "I never actually asked him; I just sort of hinted, but he's coming. Next Friday he'll be here. Oh,

Mother, he's actually coming to George-town!"

Something clenched around Morgan's heart as he watched his wife move forward and hug his oldest daughter, his precious Ed. *She's really going to leave.* His heart faced the fact for the first time. *She's really going to be married and go away.* For an instant the pain of it threatened to rob him of breath, but he was swift to recover. Suddenly he knew it was good and right and also realized that he'd come to this conclusion none too soon. Eddie was now turning to him, the need for approval lingering in her eyes.

"You still feel it's all right, don't you, Father?"

Morgan held out his arms, and Eddie welcomed his embrace, hugging him in return. He then held her at arm's length.

"It will take a very special man to be good enough for my Ed, but I am looking forward to meeting your Robert."

Eddie, who couldn't have asked for more, beamed at him. Her heart felt like it was going to float from her chest. *Your Robert* had been her father's words. Eddie felt his acceptance in those words, and her heart knew a soothing rest.

Jackie held her body poker straight as she

walked into the Taggart home that night, but there was no need. It had seemed to her she would be walking into the enemy camp, but nothing could have been further from the truth. Mr. and Mrs. Taggart were kind to a fault, and neither Clayton nor Milly gave her any undue attention.

With the seven Fontaines joining them, the families were forced to sit at two different tables. The adults, along with Clayton and Eddie, were at a makeshift table set up in the middle of the living room; Elaine had decorated it with a white cloth and flowers. Milly and the rest of the Fontaine girls were around the kitchen table. There were no flowers, but the pale blue tablecloth was clean and pressed. The food was wonderful, and it wasn't long before Jackie felt herself relaxing. Indeed, Sammy was telling a riotous story about something that had happened in the store, and she had her eating companions in stitches. Jackie nearly forgot all her previous fears.

"This certainly sounds like a lot of fun," Kevin Taggart commented when he came through at one point.

"Oh, Dad!" Milly gasped. "You should hear this story."

Sammy repeated it for her host's benefit, and during the telling of it, Clayton appeared. He laughed as hard as his father, but for Jackie the tenseness had returned. She watched Clayton's eyes rest on her for a moment and dropped her own. With his warm, brown eyes and sun-blond hair, all set off by a dark tan shirt and brown pants, she had to admit that he was handsome, but she still disliked him.

"I think we'll wait on dessert," Elaine said as she came to the kitchen. "Milly, will you please help me with the dishes?"

"I'll help too," Danny offered.

"All right," Elaine accepted with a smile. "Clay, why don't you take Sammy to the barn and show her the kittens."

"You should go too, Jackie," Addy said as she came from the living room with her hands full of dishes. "Jackie is our animal lover," she added to her hostess.

"Come on, Sammy," Clayton invited the youngest girl. "Let's head to the barn."

"Aren't we going to take Jackie?"

Clayton's eyes showed his amusement as they swung to the older girl. "I'm sure she won't be interested."

Jackie's chin lifted to the challenge. "As a matter of fact, I would love to see the kittens."

A smile split Clayton's face. He never dreamed she would accompany them, but he didn't comment. A moment later he stepped aside so that Sammy could lead the way. She threw a smile his way as she passed, but Jackie, who also walked in front of him, refused to look in his direction.

"Clay's a terrible tease," Elaine commented when they were gone.

"That might not be all bad," Addy told her softly. "Jackie takes herself much too seriously."

"I love the smell of barns," Sammy told Clayton enthusiastically. The blue eyes that were so like her mother's smiled up at him.

"So do I," he agreed. "I think it must be the hay and horses."

The sky was growing dark, so the spacious barn was dim with the fading light. Clayton moved to a post below the hayloft and took down the lantern. The light flared in the shadowy barn as he led the way to a nearby stall. He need not have bothered. The sound of kittens crying could be heard from several feet away and would have led them with ease.

"Hey," Clayton spoke as he knelt in the straw, "where's Princess?"

"Oh," Sammy breathed, and Jackie, who had remained very quiet, bit her lip, her eyes alight with pleasure.

"Aren't they adorable, Jackie?"

"Oh, they are," the older girl agreed. Clayton thought he'd never heard her voice so sweet.

"Look, Jackie! A gray stripe. Your favorite." Sammy gently lifted the kitten and placed it in her hands. Jackie let out a breathless laugh, unaware of the way Clayton's eyes studied her.

"She's so soft."

"This one is too," Sammy exclaimed as she cuddled a tiny red kitten close to her cheek.

The two remaining kittens found Clayton's lap, and he lazily stroked their tiny heads while watching the wonder of his guests. He'd never known so much physical beauty in one family. Morgan was a handsome man, and Addy was downright beautiful. The girls were all lovely as well, but he wasn't completely convinced that all was as it should be. Things seemed to be in place with Mrs. Fontaine, Eddie, Danny, and even Sammy, but the others were a mystery to him. His thoughts were interrupted when a large calico cat sauntered into the stall and meowed loudly to her children.

"Here's Princess," Clayton commented. The girls' kittens were no longer content

71

in their arms, and the two from Clayton's lap were swiftly making their way toward supper. A minute later all four were eagerly lined up along their mother's side, and purrs of contentment rumbled throughout the stall. The three watched for a few minutes, and then Sammy jumped up to explore the rest of the barn. Jackie rose as well, and Clayton followed slowly.

"How many horses, Tag?" Sammy asked.

"Just three."

Sammy skipped on ahead, and Clayton caught up with Jackie. She veered off to look in one of the stalls, and Clayton, acting instinctively, took her arm.

"Watch that pitchfork, Jackie. I must have forgotten to put it away."

Jackie jerked her arm from his touch and stepped away. Clayton was bending to put the fork against the wall when Jackie spoke in the voice he was accustomed to hearing.

"I'm surprised you didn't look forward to seeing my foot stabbed."

Clayton's head whipped around, but his face was in the shadows so Jackie couldn't see his shocked expression. He felt as though someone had thrown cold water over him; indeed, he nearly gasped. It was startlingly clear to him at that moment that his teasing had gone too far. He never dreamed she was taking him seriously. At last, his voice came softly, soberly, from the shadows.

"Contrary to what you obviously believe, Jackie, I'm not a monster." With that, Clayton turned to join Sammy. They talked about the horses and then visited the kittens again before Clayton hung the lantern back in place and blew it out. He did so without thought until he heard a small gasp and a voice of panic.

"Sammy? Where are you, Sammy?"

"I'm right here. The door's this way."

"What's the matter?" Clayton asked but was ignored.

"I can't see!" Jackie finally cried, and Clayton, hearing that she was on the verge of panic, moved back to the lantern. It flared into life a moment later, and Clayton found Jackie gripping Sammy's small arm frantically.

"It's okay now, Jackie. The light's on." Sammy's soft voice floated through the barn, but it took a moment for Jackie to relax her hold. When the older girl found Clayton's eyes on her, her chin went into the air. Her look dared him to laugh, but she need not have worried. Clayton was not cold or aloof to Jackie, nor did he dare show any pity, but where she was concerned, all teasing was gone.

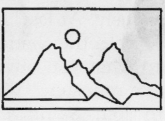

CHAPTER 6

Early the next morning Kevin and Clayton
said goodbye to Elaine and Milly and rode
out together. Though they were not going
to the same mine, they were headed in the
same direction for several miles. They left
town in silence, but it wasn't long before
they started to share. Clayton spoke of the
way Jackie had responded in the barn, and
his father was sympathetic.

"She really thought I would enjoy seeing
her hurt, Dad. I can't tell you how much
that bothered me."

"She seems rather sensitive," Kevin commented. "She hides behind a lovely face
and a nonchalant manner, but I sense that
she could be hurt quite easily."

"I wouldn't have agreed with you before
last night, but I think you must be right. Do
you suppose people have used her?"

"What do you mean?"

"I mean, gotten to know her just because
she's pretty and then hurt her in some way?"

"It's hard to say."

"It's strange," Clayton went on. "She acts so spoiled, but I don't think Morgan spoils any of his girls."

Kevin had to think on this for a moment. Finally he replied, "I know what you're saying, Clay, but Morgan does something worse — he's led Jackie to believe that she should look out for herself and no one else. I know Morgan is a good family man, and I can see that he cares, but his main concern seems to be himself."

Clayton nodded. His father had put his finger on the very thing that had eluded him. Morgan gave the appearance of being a righteous man, but Clayton could see that something was missing. He prayed for Morgan Fontaine right then, asking God to show him the way of true righteousness found in Christ alone.

"How long will you be out?" Kevin suddenly asked.

"I really should be gone for about a month, but I'll be coming back next weekend to meet a friend of Eddie's."

"A man friend?"

Clayton smiled. "Yes. Someone she's quite taken with."

Kevin frowned.

"What did I say?"

"Nothing, except watching the two of you over dinner last night, I thought maybe . . ."

Clayton was already shaking his head. "Eddie is just a friend, and besides, she was in love with Robert Langley before we even met."

"Well, he's a blessed man. She's a very special young lady."

"That she is."

"Of course, maybe you were thinking she would make a nice sister-in-law."

The younger man didn't feign ignorance. "Jackie is still very young."

"But young ladies grow up."

"Be that as it may, I've got a teaching career to pursue."

"Oh, speaking of which," Kevin now reached into his breast pocket, "I've a letter here from your grandmother."

"How is she doing?"

"Well."

"Does she speak of Denver?"

"Yes. She says it's hot, but she still managed to gather the information I needed about a certain training college."

Clayton brought his horse to a standstill and stared at his father, who had stopped as well. The older man shifted lazily in his saddle, pushed his hat back on his head, and grinned at his son.

"Do you mean it?" Clayton finally managed.

"Certainly. It's too late for this fall, but a year from now. . . . Are you willing to wait?"

"I'll wait," Clayton told him without a moment's thought, his voice almost breathless. "The time doesn't matter; just knowing it's really going to happen is all I need."

Kevin heeled his mount forward, a smile still splitting his beard. Clayton moved with him, a hundred questions swarming in his head. When had his father written about his desire to teach? When had the letter arrived from Denver? And why had he waited until now to tell him? How much did it cost? Was his grandmother helping? Maybe he could live with her.

It was all such a blur in his mind that Clayton couldn't voice a single word. A glance at his father told him he was still feeling very pleased with himself. Clayton let his eyes slide shut for just an instant.

I'm going to school, Lord. I'm going to teach. I prayed, and I waited on You. Thank You, Lord. Thank You with all my heart.

Eddie climbed up onto the double bed beside Jackie, but she did not touch the lantern. Jackie had already closed her eyes, but

77

a moment later she realized something was wrong. She opened her eyes to find Eddie sitting and staring at her.

"Aren't you going to turn out the light? I'm tired."

"He's probably going to fall in love with you."

"Who?" the younger girl frowned in confusion.

"Robert."

"Why would he do that?"

"Because all the men who meet you fall in love with you."

It did seem that way, so Jackie didn't deny it, but she did try to reason with her older sister.

"Eddie, Robert already loves you."

"That's because he's never met you."

Jackie now pushed herself up against the headboard. "Do you really think he's coming all this way just to lose interest?"

Eddie dropped her eyes. She was always the sure one, but tonight she wanted to panic. Robert was coming the day after tomorrow, and she was ready to snap under the pressure.

"Eddie?"

The older girl looked up.

"Do you think I would try to take your boyfriend?"

"No, Jackie!" Eddie was horrified. "I didn't mean that at all. It's just that we met for such a short time, and I'm afraid he's forgotten what I really look like. And I can't help but ask myself if you'd been there that day if he'd have fallen in love with me in the first place."

Jackie leaned forward in a rare show of affection and hugged her older sister. She spoke with her arms holding her tight.

"Robert Langley loves the woman who writes the letters you've shared. He might have been attracted that day at Aunt Lacey's, but his real love for you has come through your letters."

Jackie wasn't sure where the words had come from, but Eddie looked relieved. She admitted, "At first it felt like he would never get here, but the time has flown. I just don't know if I'm ready."

"You're ready. I know you are."

They fell silent for a time until something compelled Jackie to ask, "Eddie, what are you really afraid of?"

Eddie sighed deeply. "I think I'm afraid that he'll ask me to marry him, and I'll know it's right. Then I'll be torn between two worlds."

Jackie didn't need her to elaborate. She had thought of this same thing many times herself. Where would they all end up? Her father and Uncle Mitch had been separated for years and by many miles. The war had torn families apart from coast to coast. Where would they all be in ten years' time? Jackie reached for Eddie again and they clung together. Neither one wanted to cry, but suddenly separation felt imminent.

At that moment the door opened with a low groan. Addy came in without rebuke and joined them on the bed.

"It's getting late." Her voice was hushed.

"We were just talking," Eddie told her.

Addy nodded. She reached and brushed a wayward curl from Jackie's cheek and then tenderly stroked Eddie's.

"He'll be here before you know it, and then you'll know your heart. He'll either be everything you remember and more, or your heart will be cold."

"What if his heart is cold toward me?" Eddie couldn't keep the tremor from her voice.

Addy smiled. "If that was the case, then he wouldn't be taking a southbound stage to see you."

Both girls suddenly smiled at their mother. When Addy stood they lay down, dark heads finding comfortable places on the pillows, and their mother tucking them in like they were young. Addy moved to Jackie's side first, pulling the covers high and then bending to kiss her. She received a surprisingly tender hug for her efforts before moving to Eddie's side. They kissed and embraced as well, before Addy turned the lantern down and moved to the door. Her soft "Good-night, my darlings" floated over them like a warm caress.

Once in the hall, the door closed behind her, Addy trembled from head to foot.

He's going to come and claim her heart, Father, and I don't know if I can stand the separation. He's going to take my Eddie, and even though I see the love in her eyes whenever Robert's name is mentioned, I'm not ready to let her go.

Morgan had fallen asleep in his chair downstairs, but Addy didn't go back down. She moved further along the upstairs hallway and into their room to ready for bed. Her movements were laden. She was tired, and that always produced exaggerated emotions. She knew that sleep was her best option right now. As her own head lay on the soft pillow, and the light quilt settled around her, Addy said another prayer.

Help me to remember how far You've brought us, Lord. Help me to remember to trust as I've done before. You love Eddie more than I do. Help me give her to You. Robert too. And bless Morgan, Lord. As always, help him see that this time on earth is like a speck in light of eternity.

"One minute I feel like I just wrote that letter, and the next it feels like an eternity has passed."

Addy smiled but didn't comment. It was no good telling Eddie to sit down, for she would only pace on.

"Is it unkind of me to be glad that the girls won't be home for several hours?"

"No, dear." Addy's voice was calm as she went on with her quilting. "Your father and I certainly don't want you children with us 24 hours a day."

Eddie suddenly sat down so close to her mother that she was nearly stabbed with the needle.

"Mother, were you terribly afraid of *that* part of marriage?"

Addy looked into her eyes. "A little. But I love it when your father takes me in his arms. And if you and Robert love each other, you're going to love *that* too."

Eddie's smile was dreamy. "He took my hand before he left Aunt Lacey's."

"And what if he wants to do more than hold your hand this time?"

"Well," Eddie's brow furrowed in thought. "If he's asked me to be his wife, and I've agreed, then it's all right."

"How much is all right?"

"Oh." Eddie finally understood her mother's full line of thought. "What do you think?"

"I think it's all right if he holds your hand."

"All right," Eddie agreed. "What about kissing?"

"Well, it's like you said, it depends on whether or not he's declared his intentions."

Eddie nodded, clearly ready to talk. "Okay, let's say he's asked and I've accepted. What then?"

Addy's eyes came off her sewing again. Suddenly her daughter sounded very young, but what other time would she have asked about this? Morgan had never even allowed the girls to date.

"I think that if you plan to be husband and wife, then you can hold hands and hug and kiss, but I must warn you, Eddie, it's very easy to go too far. Until you become husband and wife before God, you must show restraint. Robert will certainly desire you, and I assume he will be respectful as well, but you must be fair with his feelings. The time to stop is long before you sense

83

things are spiraling out of control."

Eddie nodded, her eyes intent on her mother.

"The place to find out about the intimate side of marriage is in your bedroom on your wedding night, not in some buggy parked in the shadows of the woods. God will honor you both if you will obey Him in this area of your lives."

There was a note of fierceness in her mother's voice that Eddie had never heard before, and it caused her to ask a question she would normally never have broached.

"Did you do it the right way, Mother . . . with Father?"

"No, Eddie, I didn't," her mother told her with a sigh. "I saved myself for your father, but not for our wedding night, and I will regret that for all of my life."

Eddie saw in that brief sentence how hard it had been for her. The younger woman leaned close and kissed her mother's cheek. Just as she drew back, a knock sounded at the door. Eddie's eyes flew to her mother.

"It could be Father."

Addy smiled. "Your father wouldn't have knocked."

Eddie's eyes were huge as she rose slowly and walked from the living room. Her hand was slick with perspiration as she opened the door. There he was, taller than she remembered and so handsome in a dark suit and white shirt that it took her breath away.

"Hello, Eddie." His voice was mellow and kind.

"Hello, Robert. Won't you come in?" Eddie stepped back and let him enter. His bag bumped the wall as he moved in, and Eddie hoped he would be comfortable in the room they had prepared for his arrival. She expected him to at least glance around and see what he could of the house, but he turned and his eyes came immediately back to her. The warmth she saw in them made her blush.

"When I left your aunt's home in New York, I took your hand. You blushed then." Robert's voice was warm with remembrance. "My head was on nothing but business and then there you were. I've never been so glad that I got the wrong address. I never did make that appointment, but I didn't care."

Eddie's blush only deepened. She gave a self-conscious laugh, and her hands gripped the fabric of her dress. "I can't seem to help myself."

"Don't apologize."

Not wanting to seem so young and naive, Eddie shrugged a little and cast about in her mind for something to say. "How was your trip?" came out in a sudden rush.

"Fine, now."

"What does that mean?"

"Only that I wasn't certain what I would find, but I need not have worried. You're everything I remembered and more."

Eddie's breath caught in her throat. Those had been her mother's very words.

"Would you like to come in and meet my mother?"

"Very much."

Eddie gestured with her hand, and Robert placed his small black bag in the entryway and preceded her through the door into the living room. Eddie looked at his dark suit and noticed how his broad back filled the jacket. Her heart raced as she thought of his words to her.

If I doubted my feelings for you, Robert Langley, I doubt them no more. I am a woman in love.

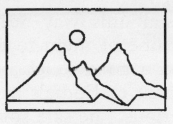

CHAPTER 7

Eddie watched as Robert laughed at a comment from Lexa and mentally shook her head. How could she have thought he was coming all this way only to fall in love with Jackie? He'd been laughing and teasing *all* of her sisters since they'd come home from school, but the eyes that turned tender with love were for her alone.

"All right, girls," Addy admonished, sticking her head in the door. "Come help me with dinner."

Robert rose as the four younger Fontaine girls stood, but Eddie kept her seat.

"What about Eddie?" Sammy wished to know as she exited, but Addy told her youngest only that Eddie had the evening off. Robert sat back down when their footsteps died away, his eyes immediately finding Eddie's.

"Your sisters are fun."

"They like you too," she told him and then looked away. "I actually thought you might come all this way and decide you might prefer one of them to me."

Robert had a good laugh over this until he saw the pain in Eddie's eyes.

"You're serious," he said softly. Eddie felt a fool. "Eddie," Robert leaned forward and went on gently, "I did a horrible job of expressing myself if you believed that."

"I'm sorry, Robert."

"No, Eddie. I'm not trying to wring some sort of apology out of you, I'm trying to tell you how I feel." He stopped then and looked out the window, his mind racing. Moving from where he stood across the room, he settled on the sofa within a few feet of Eddie, who faced him on her favorite chair.

"Let me put it this way," he whispered caressingly. "If your feelings for me are even a fraction of what mine are for you, then you're head-over-heels in love with me."

"Oh, Robert," Eddie breathed, her heart in her eyes. "I only dreamed, but I never hoped to know this soon. I've loved you for months."

Robert's eyes closed for an instant, and then he reached for her hand. Eddie never imagined that it would happen so quickly. She had wondered what she would do if he left and she still didn't know his intentions.

Eddie realized that her hand was being crushed, but she didn't care. Robert loved her and she loved him. Eddie asked the Lord right then to help her be the wife He would have her to be. Robert hadn't asked yet, but somehow she knew he would. With that she had a sudden thought.

"What is it?" Robert asked when she sat up very straight, taking her hand from his grasp.

"My father. You haven't met my father."

"Are you worried that he won't approve?"

"Maybe a little. He can be rather strict, and sometimes quite unpredictable."

With those words they both heard voices, one distinctly feminine and the other a man's. Eddie and Robert exchanged a look. Eddie's face was worried, but Robert was quite at ease. He gave her a tender wink as the voices neared. A moment later Morgan Fontaine entered the room.

"I hope you won't think me presumptuous to ask your wife to join our conversation, Mr. Fontaine, but I feel this involves both of you." It was hours after supper, and the three of them were seated in the living room.

Morgan nodded equably to Robert's remark. It had never occurred to him that his daughter's guest would ask for her hand in marriage this soon. Assuming Robert had some sort of business deal to discuss, he called Addy and then sat back comfortably. Indeed, Morgan hoped it was just that. Over dinner he'd become very impressed with this young man and felt it would be a benefit to both of them if they could work together in some capacity.

"I would like to marry Edwina."

Morgan was brought abruptly back to earth. He wanted to shout with outrage but worked at keeping his expression neutral. No easy feat this, with the way Addy was smiling from a brocade chair between them.

"Does Eddie know how you feel?" she asked, pleasure highlighting her voice.

"Yes, she does. I know it seems rather sudden, but she admitted to me today that she feared I would come and be interested in one of her sisters. It didn't seem that there could be a better time to tell her what's in my heart. I know I'm over ten years older than her 18 years, but Eddie tells me that doesn't worry her. I believe I could take very good care of her."

"But you only just arrived." Morgan finally found his voice.

Addy looked at her husband with compassion but wondered if he'd heard a thing Robert said.

"They've corresponded for many months now, Morgan," she reminded him.

Morgan looked at her as though seeing her for the first time. His gaze then became quite fierce.

"How does Eddie feel about this?" He asked his wife, but his eyes swung to Robert. "Can you tell me that?"

Robert remained silent. He hadn't known what to expect. Eddie had given him the impression that it had been her father's idea that he come, but now Mr. Fontaine seemed so offended. Before Robert could utter a word, Addy came to his aid.

"I'm sure Eddie is still awake," Addy said. "Would you like me to get her, Morgan?"

"Yes." He sounded relieved, as if Eddie would settle this misunderstanding once and for all. Addy rose, leaving an awkward silence in her wake. Robert was a guest and felt he should not try to make conversation. Besides, Morgan was looking very put out, so they just sat. A good ten minutes of this torture passed before Addy was back, bringing Eddie with her.

"Please sit down, Ed," her father instructed.

Eddie was careful to not look at Robert or sit anywhere near him. Morgan took this as a good sign and jumped right in.

"Robert has asked for your hand in marriage. Did you know he planned to do this?"

"Well, I wasn't sure, but I thought he might."

"And how do you feel about this?"

"I hoped you could come to some sort of agreement."

Her words were almost more than Morgan could bear. It was all happening too swiftly.

"You'd like me to say yes." Morgan speared Eddie with his eyes, and all she could do was nod. "And if I don't?" he added.

Eddie bit her lip, and a look of misery covered her features. She looked at the hands clenched in her lap for a moment and then back at her father. Her voice was just above a whisper when she replied, "Then I would tell him no."

Morgan couldn't think. How had things gotten so completely out of his control?

"You may return to your room, Ed."

Eddie did so without looking at anyone. Robert stood when she rose, and before he could be reseated, Morgan came to his feet.

"I'm going to need time to think about

this. I'll talk to you tomorrow, Robert. Come, Addy."

Adaline dutifully rose and bid her guest good-night before she swiftly preceded Morgan from the room. The hallway was dark with the lantern behind her in Morgan's hand, but Addy didn't slow her flight. She nearly ran to the room they shared and waited only until the door closed before she turned on her spouse.

"How could you do such a thing?" She spat the words in fury, huge tears filling her eyes. Morgan's hard expression softened when he saw them, but Addy was far from through.

"Why did you think he'd come here, Morgan — to buy land? How could you look into your daughter's face and put her through that? She loves and trusts you, but you've asked her to pick between the two of you. And to leave them hanging! Neither one of them will get a moment's sleep this night. Now, isn't that a grand way to begin Robert's visit?" With that she turned her back on him, a sob breaking in her throat.

Morgan didn't think Addy had ever spoken to him in such a way. Then Eddie's face came to mind, and he knew his wife had gone easy on him. He'd known very well why Robert was coming to Georgetown. Why was he fighting this when all he wanted was Eddie's happiness?

Addy was still crying softly when Morgan placed the lantern on the bedside table and lit another. Leaving one of the lights for his distraught wife, he moved back down the hall to Eddie and Jackie's room. The bed showed just one sleeping figure, and Morgan raised the light to find Eddie. She was in a chair by the window, and even though she'd scrubbed at her face with the sleeve of her gown, the evidence of tears was very clear.

Morgan stood for a long moment and looked down at her. While he did so, another drop slipped down her cheek. Morgan reached out to cup her face with one hand, and his voice was rough.

"Marry your Robert, Ed, with my blessing."

"Oh, Father, do you mean it?"

"Yes. I'm sorry I didn't tell you earlier."

Eddie would have risen, but Morgan put a hand on her shoulder. "Get ready for bed now and go to sleep. I'll see you tomorrow." With that he was gone. He took the stairs on silent feet and moved through the kitchen to the door of the small room they had prepared for their guest. He knocked and waited.

Only seconds passed before Robert came to the door. His jacket and tie were missing, but he was still dressed. The two men looked at one another for several heartbeats. Robert was much taller, but his look held respect.

"She's never had jewels or finery," Morgan began, "but she's had love. I would want no less for her."

"Love I can give her, sir, with all my heart."

"Then do so, Mr. Langley. I ask only that she be allowed to turn 18 and a half before the wedding."

Robert nodded, his mind moving. "That would be the end of February, wouldn't it?"

"Yes. Are you willing to wait until spring?"

"More than willing, Mr. Fontaine. Anything you ask in order to make Eddie my wife."

Morgan nodded, and his hand came forward. The men shook, and Robert smiled.

"Sleep well, Robert," Morgan added softly before turning away.

Robert's smile widened. "I shall, Mr. Fontaine. I shall indeed."

It was not with a light tread that Morgan took the stairs. He knew he'd done the right thing, but his heart was heavy. Boulder. His daughter would be moving away to Boulder in six months' time. Morgan stopped in his path. Or would she? Why did Robert have to live in Boulder? He and Eddie could settle here.

It was with a much lighter step that Morgan covered the remaining distance to his bedroom. First he had to thank Addy for helping him to see how harsh he'd been, but then he had some planning to do. It would take no small amount of talk to bring Langley around. It crossed his mind to make the marriage conditional on the move, but he knew that would not be fair to Ed. He wasn't daunted, however; he was quite a salesman and knew his strengths. He was certain he could make Robert see that he and Eddie needed to live in Georgetown.

"Did he change his mind?" Eddie asked Robert anxiously when he came in the door, but he only took her hand and led her into the living room.

That morning Morgan had gone off to work early, but he'd left word with Addy that he wished to see Robert at his earliest possible convenience. All the girls were expected to work in the store on Saturday mornings, so when they left Robert had gone with them. Eddie had remained home. She

96

wanted to do some baking, and she and her mother were already making wedding plans.

"No," Robert spoke when they were seated on the davenport. "He did not change his mind, but he wants me to move to Georgetown."

Eddie sat back in surprise. "He what?"

"He wanted to know if I'd ever considered setting up a bank here, or going into some other business in town."

"Did you tell him you'd think about it?"

Robert shook his head. "That wouldn't have been fair, Eddie. Moving to Boulder was not some whim on my part. I think the town has great potential, and that's where I want to live. I assumed you'd be fine with the idea, but we've never discussed it."

"I am fine with the idea, Robert. I mean, I'll miss my family, but I never dreamed you'd want to live here." She paused. "Was he terribly upset?"

Robert smiled. "Oh, no. He's still certain he can talk me around."

Eddie sighed. "It's not going to be a very nice visit for you, is it?"

"On the contrary," Robert replied while looking into her eyes. "I'm sure it's going to be a wonderful time."

And without a moment's warning, he leaned forward and kissed her. Eddie's eyes became very soft and warm, and Robert gently shook his head.

"You don't know how tempting you are, Eddie."

"Isn't that good?"

"It will be when you're my wife, but right now it's a lot of work."

Eddie's look became very serious, and she gently placed her hand on Robert's coat sleeve.

"I won't do anything to make it harder for us, Robert."

"That I can believe, but I think that Boulder will be the best place for me in the coming months. Have you and your mother decided when I can come back and make you my wife?"

"I think so. The snow can be pretty heavy in February and March, but we're going to try for March 14. How does that sound?"

Robert pulled a small book from his breast pocket, and Eddie saw that it was a tiny calendar.

"Twenty-four weeks from today," he finally commented quietly. "Nearly six months."

Eddie couldn't tell what he really thought. "It doesn't have to be that day, if you'd prefer another."

"No, I think this is fine. Would you rather

I come ahead of the wedding and then leave right after we're married, or come the day before and plan to stay longer afterward?"

Eddie didn't have to think very long. "I'm afraid something will keep you from getting here for the fourteenth, so I'd rather you come early."

"What would keep me from coming?"

"The snow."

Robert heard the fear in her voice and put his hand over hers. She was his Eddie. Their letters were always so full. They had spent less than 48 hours in each other's presence, but he knew this girl. She had told him all about herself, and he likewise, on the pages of their letters. They'd shared every dream and prayer on those pages, and it was no surprise to Robert that he was already in love.

It was an added blessing that her hair was thick and shiny and that her blue eyes were huge and rimmed with long, dark lashes, but the girl he loved, he loved from the pages of her letters.

"I thought I heard you come in, Robert," Addy spoke now as she joined them. She sat on the davenport, taking Eddie's other side, and put a loving hand on her daughter's arm.

"Did you discuss the wedding date?"

"Yes. Robert thinks it's fine. Mother, did you know what Father was going to talk to Robert about this morning?"

Addy sighed. "He mentioned it last night. I didn't encourage him, but he seemed to think it was a great idea. Has it ruined your stay, Robert?"

"No, Mrs. Fontaine, but I did have to tell him no. I want Eddie to come home as often as she likes, and I hope you'll visit us in Boulder, but I really do believe that's where the Lord wants us."

"Maybe someday we'll have a home and you can even stay with us," Eddie told her mother and then turned to smile at Robert. He was looking rather surprised.

"I think someday might be sooner than you think" was all he said.

"What do you mean?"

Robert hesitated and Addy stood.

"I think it's time I left you alone."

Robert swiftly came to his feet. "No, no, Mrs. Fontaine, please don't go; I just can't believe I forgot. Excuse me a moment, ladies."

He slipped from the room, and mother and daughter exchanged looks. They didn't have time to talk about it, however, because Robert was right back, a roll of paper in his hand.

"I brought house plans with me. There's a man in Boulder ready to go to work, but I didn't want him to start until I'd checked with you, Eddie."

"Oh, Robert!" Eddie exclaimed when the plans were opened. "It's wonderful."

All three heads bent over the pages as Robert's hand walked them through the downstairs. The entryway was large and ornate. Oak stairs, leading to the second story, rose just 20 feet from the wide front door. Immediately to the left of the entryway was a formal living room. The dining room was off that, and the entire back of the house was pantry and kitchen. A hallway could be taken from the kitchen to arrive at Robert's study or back to the main staircase. You could also reach the top floor from a narrow set of stairs that rose from the kitchen. The second story was beautifully laid out as well and sported four bedrooms. Robert's and Eddie's rooms were across the front of the house, with tall windows looking to the east, and the other rooms looked like they would be airy and spacious as well. Robert had designed the house himself, and Eddie was thrilled.

"What do you think?" Robert wanted to know.

"I think it's wonderful."

"It's not too late to change something. Do you have any suggestions?"

Eddie thought a moment, and both Robert and her mother were sure she would say no. She surprised them.

"It might be too costly, but would it be possible to put in another fireplace? Right here in the entryway?"

"A fireplace in the entryway?" Robert's tone spoke of his doubt.

"Well," Eddie became rather self-conscious. "It's probably too expensive, but that area is so large and what better place to warm up than when you've just come in from the cold."

Robert looked at Eddie and then back at the plans. Put like that, he could see that it was a marvelous idea. He turned back to look at her, his eyes intent now on her face. Addy decided it was time for her to leave.

"We don't have to, Robert," Eddie spoke when they were alone. "I won't be upset if you don't like it."

"I'm not building this house for me, Eddie. Before I met you I wasn't even interested in a home. Are you certain that's all you want changed?"

Eddie nodded, and Robert took her hand.

"You'll have your extra fireplace, Eddie. Count on that."

Eddie linked her fingers with Robert's and thought about his words. Yes, she was certain she could count on having the other fireplace, but suddenly it occurred to her that it was *Robert* who could be counted on. A sudden peace stole over her. God had sent her a wonderful man.

Eddie's thoughts were still dwelling on the wonder of it all when Robert put an arm around her and pulled her close.

CHAPTER 8

"Is that Clayton Taggart's voice?" Jackie whispered furiously as she darted into the kitchen.

"Yes" was Eddie's casual reply. "He came to meet Robert." She was making some refreshments for her guests and continued to do so calmly.

"But I thought he was out of town!"

"He was, but he made a special trip home because I told him Robert would be here."

Jackie dropped into a chair as though the world had come to an end. Seeing her face, Eddie wiped her hands and sat down across from her sister.

"Jackie, will you please tell me why you have such a problem with Tag?"

Jackie sighed. "I just don't like him."

"You sound like a five-year-old."

Jackie's face flushed with rage, but Eddie put a hand in the air.

"You don't have to buddy up to him, Jackie, but this outrage every time he's near or offers you a ride from school is wrong." Eddie placed strong emphasis on the last word, but the younger girl calmed upon hearing her sister's kind voice.

"Have you prayed about this, Jackie?"

"No," she admitted.

"Then do so," Eddie urged her. "Take some time right now. Robert and Tag are just getting to know each other. He'll probably be here for the better part of the afternoon and tomorrow after church as well. You could join us if you'd come to grips with your feelings."

Jackie nodded, and Eddie knew she had said enough. She loaded a serving tray with the good china plates and cups, and then added napkins, knives and spoons, cream, sugar, butter, a full pot of tea, and some freshly baked scones. Her Aunt Lacey always served tea and scones, and Eddie had a taste for them often. She hoped Robert would enjoy them too. She glanced at the table as she left, but Jackie hadn't moved or spoken. Indeed, Jackie was not even aware of her sister's departure.

I don't have to have a reason to hate him, she told herself. *I just do and that's that!* She then remembered her sister's admonition to pray. Jackie sighed in the stillness of the room.

She knew her attitude was wrong. Her mother was kind to everyone, but her father only bothered with people he liked. She knew her father was wrong to be so hard at times, but what could you do if you just didn't like someone?

Suddenly Clayton's eyes came to mind, and the way they looked the night her family had gone to the Taggarts' for dinner. At the beginning of the evening they'd been laughing, teasing eyes, but then after the incident in the barn, his eyes had been serious. He still looked at her in a way that told her he thought she was pretty, but the teasing glint and some of the friendliness was gone.

"It's just as well," Jackie stood and spoke to herself, her decision made. "I don't want to have anything to do with him anyhow."

Clayton walked back up the road to his house feeling very pleased that he'd made the effort to come home. Robert Langley was as fine a fellow as Clayton had met in a long time. There had been no awkwardness between them, no time of testing; they'd hit it off in the first five minutes. And it had done nothing but good for Clayton's heart to see the way Robert looked at Eddie. She was so lovely and sweet, and God had truly blessed her with a man who would obviously cherish all the love in her heart.

Milly and Elaine were waiting with dinner on the table when Clayton got home, and he was enthusiastic in his telling of Robert and Eddie. Milly thought it was the most romantic thing she ever heard, but Elaine had another thought.

"Maybe the Lord will lead you to teach school in Boulder someday, and you can see more of Robert Langley."

Clayton hadn't thought of it, but he smiled his appreciation at his mother. They bowed their heads to pray for the meal, but Clayton was a bit distracted. Why had the thought of teaching in Boulder made him wonder where Jackie would be living by then? He nearly shook his head. He hadn't seen her all day, and thinking of her in that way now seemed odd to him. A moment later he dismissed it; he was probably still just pondering the way she'd responded that night in the barn. Well, he'd done everything he could to make things right. It was up to her if she wanted to have anything to do with him.

"I can't believe you have to leave tomorrow."

Eddie and Robert were walking hand-in-hand along Clear Creek, the sun was sinking in the sky, and the sound of the rushing water caused Eddie to raise her voice slightly. Robert heard her quite clearly, but as hard as it was for him to leave, he didn't comment. Right now he just wanted to be near the woman he loved, holding her hand and not thinking about a six-month separation.

"Do you think the time will go by swiftly?" Eddie asked.

"That all depends."

"On what?"

"On the time of day. When I'm at the bank, at my desk or even overseeing a teller's window, the hours will fly by, but in the evening when I'll wonder what you're doing and if you had a good day, the time will drag." Robert stopped then and pulled Eddie close with one hand. With his free hand he traced the line of her brows and then drew his fingers down her cheek until he had taken gentle hold of her chin.

"I love you, Eddie, and I don't want you to forget that for one second."

"I won't. You won't forget my love, will you?"

"Not for an instant. And when I come again, we'll be husband and wife."

With that he caught her in both arms and kissed her. There were houses along the creek, but the trunk and branches of a large tree sheltered their tender kiss of love and anxiousness, and when they broke apart to walk back to the house, Eddie's thoughts went again to the forthcoming wedding.

"Are you certain your family won't come?"

"Quite certain. When I return to Boulder I'll write and let them know how things worked out, but it's such a long way from Pennsylvania, and my mother is not in the best of health. She'll want us to visit as soon as we're able. I know they're looking forward to meeting you, so we'll go soon after we're married."

"What if I'm expecting right away?"

"I hope you will be, and if that's the case, we'll wait and the three of us will go."

"What if it's twins?" Eddie asked, and Robert laughed because he knew she was being outrageous.

"In that case," he was outrageous in return, "we'll leave one of the babies with a neighbor so it will still just be the three of us."

Now Eddie laughed as well. As they neared the house, they heard Jackie's voice in the yard. She appeared to be waiting for them, and indeed she was, hands on her waist.

"I know you want him all to yourself, Eddie, but this is Robert's last night, and we want to visit with him too."

"All right," Eddie's hands went in the air as though in surrender. "I just had to get him away for a little while so you could do my job with dinner."

Jackie smiled hugely. "Well, it worked. Mother roped me in as soon as I came through the kitchen."

Eddie liked that a lot, but Robert turned on some mock sympathy. He put an arm around Jackie and walked her toward the house. His voice was full of fun when he asked, "She's very cruel to you, isn't she, Jackie?"

"Who? Mother or Eddie?"

"Both."

"Yes," Jackie told him emphatically and just barely held her laugher. "They all are. I'm under such persecution."

Robert laughed. Sammy darted from the house right then and took Robert's free hand. Eddie held back just a few steps so she could watch him walk with her sisters.

I never thought about how he would feel about my sisters, Lord, but this is so special. He brings out the best in all of us. I don't know how I'll stand it when he leaves in the morning.

With that Eddie slowly made her way inside, determining to throw off any hint of sadness. This was Robert's last night, and she needed to make the best of it. After all, she had only a week of memories to carry her for the next six months.

"Now," Addy spoke with determination. "I decided to get you a Christmas gift from the catalog, Eddie. It won't arrive before Christmas, and I'm going to have it mailed directly to Robert because it's for your new home." Addy set a Montgomery Ward catalog in her daughter's lap. "You choose which mantel clock you want."

"A mantel clock? Oh, Mother, are you certain?"

"Indeed I am. With the changes happening in the economy, I'm sure things are going to be tight in the days to come, but your father and I discussed it last night and he said you're to have the one you want. It can go over the fireplace in your bedroom, the one in the living room, or that wonderful fireplace you wanted in the entryway."

Eddie gave the older woman a hug before they bent their heads over the pages.

"Which one do you suppose Robert would like?"

"I don't know, Eddie," she said thoughtfully. "You could pick out a few you like —

111

you know, circle them and then tear the pages out and send them to Robert. He could mark the ones he likes and send them back. I know it's supposed to be a Christmas gift, but you won't be married for three more months, and that's more than enough time to pick out what you like."

"All right," Eddie agreed, and again both turned to the pages before them.

"That's pretty," Addy said as she pointed to one of the clocks.

"Oh, Mother, that's a Seth Thomas, and it's almost $7!"

"Your father said you were to have the one you wanted, Eddie."

Eddie chewed her lip. "I really should mark more than one."

"Not if you only like one."

"I like this one too, but it's $8."

"Mark them both," Addy said decisively and stood. "I have a dozen things to do before the girls come home from school, so you go ahead and take care of it, Eddie. I'm sure Robert will be pleased either way."

Addy left the kitchen then, but Eddie just sat. It was hard to imagine how their home would look and even harder to see the clock on a fireplace that existed only in her mind, but it wasn't at all hard to see that she and Robert were going to be very happy.

"Now, Jacqueline," Miss Bradley spoke clearly. "It's your turn to recite the original 13 colonies in the order they were admitted to the union, and also their capitals. Please come forward and face the class."

Jackie did so without fuss or nerves. She had worked long and hard with this memorization, and she knew them all by heart. However, Jackie didn't count on the way she would feel when every eye in the class was trained on her. It wasn't the admiring looks she received from some of the boys; it was the looks of dislike that many of the girls gave her. In order to get started, Jackie dropped her eyes to the floor in front of her.

"The capital of Delaware is Dover. The capital of Pennsylvania is Harrisburg. The capital of New Jersey is —"

"Look at the class, please," Miss Bradley interrupted from the rear.

Jackie raised her eyes and swallowed hard. "The capital of New Jersey is Trenton. The capital of Georgia is . . ." Here she faltered. She tried to keep her eyes glued to her teacher, but they kept darting about the room. Jackie felt her face turn red, and Miss Bradley suggested kindly that she begin again.

Jackie thanked her with a smile and started out all right, but faltered again at Georgia. She knew all of these, but her mind had suddenly gone blank. She wanted to tell the teacher, but she couldn't find those words, either. Her heart sank when after several strained minutes Miss Bradley rose and moved to her desk.

"Come here, Jacqueline." Her voice was stern. Jackie turned, thankful at least that her back was to the class, and stood before her teacher.

"I am very disappointed. You have had weeks to learn these." Her voice wasn't angry, but Jackie knew it would do no good to try to explain.

"Hold out your hand."

Jackie did as she was told, and her entire body convulsed as the ruler came down across her knuckles five times. She thought her hand would break with each blow.

"Return to your seat."

Jackie did so, her eyes blinded by tears. She didn't look at anyone or lay her head on her desk and sob as she longed to do, but sat looking straight ahead at the portrait of George Washington, blinking rapidly to dispel the moisture. Miss Bradley began to say something to the class but then faltered. Jackie would have been surprised to know that her own sister had caused the stumble. Lexa was looking at Miss Bradley with something akin to hatred.

"Mitch," Morgan called into the back room. "Have we received that order from Denver?"

"Not yet. I expect the snow has something to do with the holdup."

Morgan came into the room now, and Mitch turned to look at him. The light from the window shone full in his face for several seconds, and Mitch was alarmed by how tired and old he looked.

"You know, Morgan, I didn't ask you to join me in Georgetown so you could work yourself into an early grave."

"Why," Morgan asked with a grin, "am I looking half dead?"

"What time did you come in this morning?"

Morgan shrugged. "I couldn't sleep."

His avoidance of the answer told Mitch that the noise he'd heard around 4:00 A.M. was Morgan arriving for work. The older man slowly shook his head.

"We have different strengths, Morgan, and I'm thankful for that. You're more aggressive than I am, but we're not going to starve if you take a little time off. You've been down here every day since you arrived in July. I live right upstairs, but I've never had the desire to be here as often as you do. I really think you need to slow down, spend some more time at home. Eddie will be leaving in three months. Take as much time with her as you can."

"That's just it, Mitch."

"What is?"

"Eddie's leaving. It's shown me that I won't have my children here forever. I need to be sure I'm established now, while I'm still young enough to do the work. They won't be around forever, so I've got to see to Addy and myself on my own."

Mitch's heart ached. *If only you were seeing to eternity the way you see to this life on earth, Morgan. My heart would find rest knowing you're going to be with me up there.*

"Do you ever think about the folks?" Morgan asked out of the blue.

"Yes. I think about them a lot."

"So do I. They nearly worked themselves to death in their old age. That's why I'm working now."

Both men were silent for a moment.

"At least they're at rest now."

"Are they, Morgan?"

"What do you mean?" The younger man frowned at Mitch.

"I'm just saying I'm not sure."

"Well, of course they're at rest," Morgan said a bit testily. "They were good people. They deserve to be in heaven."

"Is that really what you believe, Morgan? That good people go to heaven?"

"Well, of course. Don't you?"

"No."

The single word hung between them for several uncomfortable seconds, and then the bell sounded at the door that led to the hardware.

"I'll get it." Morgan spoke quietly, but when he turned away his face did not hold his usual enthusiasm for any and all customers.

CHAPTER 9

The entire wagon was quiet on the way home that afternoon, and Clayton couldn't help but notice. Sammy was beside him on the seat, and she looked so sad that Clayton was tempted to put an arm around her. He planned to ask Milly about it as soon as they were home, but the snow was deep in places and the ride was taking longer than usual. He realized he should have brought the large sleigh.

"Everything okay, Milly?" he questioned as soon as he'd pulled into the barn.

"Sure," she answered easily enough, but her voice held no conviction.

"It seemed like everyone was pretty quiet today."

"Well," she shrugged, "we're probably all just tired of school and ready for some time off for Christmas."

Clayton stared at her, but Milly didn't notice. What she just described should have made them all restless and happy, not depressed. But Milly was already moving toward the path their father had shoveled out so they could reach the house. Clayton settled the two roan horses and wagon and then followed her. They found their father at the kitchen table filling out a survey report and working on some letters, but he put it all aside when they came in and joined his wife and children for hot coffee and fresh muffins.

Barefooted, Lexa stood in the hallway outside of Eddie and Jackie's room, a small jar clenched in her hand. It was late, time she was in bed, but welcome or not she had to see Jackie. She took a deep breath and knocked.

"Come in," Eddie called from within.

Lexa pushed the door open just enough to slip inside and then shut it behind her. Like Lexa, both of the older girls were in long flannel nightgowns, but the light was on and only Eddie was under the covers. Lexa made herself go to the other side of the bed, right up to Jackie, and speak.

"Uncle Mitch gave me this ointment a long time ago when I cut myself. I thought you might like to use it."

Jackie stared down into her sister's hesitant eyes and took the jar from her outstretched hand.

"Thanks, Lexa."

"You're welcome," she said and then just stood there. Jackie spoke next, her voice fierce, but not toward Lexa.

"I knew those states and capitals, Lexa. I knew every one."

"I know you did. I heard you say them to Mother."

Quiet descended until Eddie said softly, "I know it's Saturday tomorrow, but you'd best get to bed, Lexa."

"All right. Good-night, Jackie. 'Night, Eddie."

The older girls wished her a good night as well, and when Lexa slipped back out of the room, Eddie pushed herself up against the headboard. When Jackie climbed into bed still holding the ointment, Eddie immediately reached for her hand.

"Oh, Jackie," she whispered when she saw the marks, tears filling her eyes.

"Don't cry, Eddie!" Jackie's voice was sharp, but Eddie ignored her. Seeing those tears, Jackie's fell as well.

With tender movements Eddie took the small jar and removed the lid. She carefully smoothed the white cream over Jackie's swollen hand, moving painstakingly and sniffing back her tears. When she was done, her voice sounded as fierce as Jackie's had.

"Tag would never do this."

"Tag? What are you talking about?"

"Clayton Taggart. I don't think he'll hit anyone when he's a teacher."

Jackie shifted in order to get a better view of Eddie's face.

"Clay is going to be a teacher?"

"That's his dream."

"How do you know that?"

"Jackie," Eddie's voice held a note of rebuke. "I talk to the man. We visit every time he comes to the store, and whenever he's home he stops here to see Mother and me."

Jackie was frowning at her sister as though she didn't have the right to Clayton's company. Without speaking she took the jar from Eddie, replaced the cap, and set it on her nightstand. She settled her head on the pillow, her back to the sister who had just shown her such kindness.

"You're going to be 16 in a few weeks, Jackie. Don't you think it's time you gave up this childishness?"

"What about Clay?"

"What about Clay?" Eddie asked back. "Honestly Jackie, you have no grounds. He couldn't be kinder to us if he tried. He doesn't even tease you anymore."

Jackie was well aware of that fact but tried again to divert Eddie's belief.

"Well, anyway, Clay's too young to be teaching school. I, for one, would never respect him."

"Clay is no child, Jackie. He was 19 in October, and by the time he finishes his training he'll be even older than that. Like I said, you have no grounds for disliking him outside of your stubborn pride, and in my opinion that's no grounds at all."

With that Eddie blew the light out. The tender way the older girl had ministered to Jackie's hand seemed to be forgotten. Both girls fell asleep without sharing another word.

"What are you doing?" Milly called down to her brother from her place in the hayloft. He'd just moved the ladder away and stranded her above him.

"Moving the ladder."

"I can see that. Why?"

Clayton tipped his head back and stared at her. "You can come down when you've told me what's bothering you."

"Oh, Tag."

"Don't 'oh, Tag,' me. Now what's going on that's ruining your weekend, Milly? Even Dad and Mom have noticed."

He heard Milly's sigh from his place on the barn floor. A few more seconds went by and she said, "Let me down from here and I'll tell you."

Clayton did so, and after they had both taken seats on the bench by the stalls, Milly explained what had happened in the school-house the day before. It wasn't long before she was crying. Clayton put an arm around her.

"I feel just awful, Tag. Anyone can forget, and it's so hard to stand up there and have everyone looking at you. I know Miss Bradley must have hurt her. Her whole body jumped, and Miss Bradley didn't just do it once either. She must have hit her five or six times."

She turned her face into her brother's coatfront and cried. In so doing, she missed the clenching of Clayton's jaw. He could hardly stand the thought of anyone being hit on the back of the hand, but with Jackie, somehow it was worse. He was certain her pride had taken a beating, but that wasn't what bothered him. He had looked at her hands many times. For a girl who often helped in the general store, her hands were remarkably smooth and soft-looking with no jagged nails or calluses. He could well imagine what a few whacks with the ruler must have done.

The most frustrating part of this was realizing his position; he had no place in this situation. It was not his job to go to the teacher, nor could he even talk to Jackie and try to bring her comfort. Indeed, he was quite certain what her response would be if he tried.

"I think the worst part —" Milly had calmed enough to go on and voice Clayton's own thoughts — "is that I'm not close to Jackie, so I can't even tell her how sorry I am."

"No," Clayton agreed quietly. "She wouldn't welcome that."

"I could see that Danny was upset too. Lexa and Sammy probably were also, but they had their backs to me."

"We'll just pray for her, Milly. It doesn't have to be one of us to help her. We'll just pray that Danny or Eddie or maybe her mother will talk to her and make her feel better."

Milly sniffed and Clayton produced a handkerchief. She thanked him and sat up straight to repair her face. The subject of Jackie was dropped, but she was still heavy on both of their minds.

The Saturday before Christmas brought heavy snows to the mountains in Colorado, but many made it out for church the next

124

day. Christmas was on Thursday of that week, and excitement was high. The Fontaines planned to have Mitch and the Taggarts join them for Christmas dinner. Addy and the girls would be doing the bulk of the meal, and Elaine was to bring the dessert and rolls with fresh butter. Eddie was planning a splendid tea for the afternoon, and Danny and Milly already had their heads together about their own activities for the day.

At the moment, however, they were all bundled to their ears and getting ready to go home after the sermon. Pastor Munroe had ended his message with a tender prayer for blessings on his congregation in the week to come. He had asked God to remind them that His Son was to be celebrated all year long. Eddie had gone up to thank him for the reminder.

"And how are the wedding plans coming, Edwina?"

"Just fine." She smiled. "Less than three months now."

Pastor Munroe chuckled. "I may seem old to you, but I well remember the day when I counted the hours until my wedding." Mrs. Munroe had come to his side, and he sent her a warm smile.

"Robert wrote and told me he'd been in

touch with you and that you'd like to meet with us when he arrives."

"Yes, I would. I met him of course last fall, Edwina, but I think it might be a good idea to see you both again."

"Weather permitting, he and a friend plan to leave Boulder in time to arrive here on March 6."

"Well, fine. Why don't you come by and see me as soon as it works into your schedule?"

"Thank you, Pastor Munroe. I hope you both have a wonderful Christmas."

"You do the same," Ora Munroe told her kindly, and Eddie smiled her thanks.

Eddie turned to find her family gone. Indeed, Morgan was headed back inside to locate her. He hustled her into Mitch's waiting wagon and took them all home. Eddie helped with Sunday dinner as usual, but she was slightly preoccupied. As soon as she could get away, she took her stationery to her room and lay on the bed to write Robert a long letter.

Christmas is Thursday, and I hope and pray with all my heart that it will be the last one we spend apart. How I love the snow and the way it turns the mountains white, but my true longing

126

is to be snuggled together in our own home, watching it together. Even if the house cannot be complete, just to be with you will be enough.

I spoke to Pastor and Mrs. Munroe today, and they were very kind as we talked about the wedding. I'm looking forward to meeting Travis Buchanan since you've written so much about him. It's a shame Jackie's too young for marriage; he sounds wonderful.

And speaking of Jackie, I don't know what Christmas day will be like with her strong aversion to Tag. Honestly, Robert, I don't know what her problem is, unless it's as you say, "She protests too much." It's nearly inconceivable that under all that antagonism she could be fighting stronger feelings for him, but you might be right. I do wonder what she would say if he got hurt or she was never able to see him again. Well, I guess time will tell, and a little growing up wouldn't hurt, either. I keep praying about it.

Uncle Mitch says he has a surprise for us. He won't tell me what it is, but he's going to give it to both of us when you arrive. Do you remember the day you counted the weeks to our wedding?

Well, we're down to less than 12 weeks now. Eleven weeks and six days to be exact.

Eddie had to stop writing so she could roll onto her back, hug her pillow, and just smile at the ceiling. She was going to be married. She was going to be Mrs. Robert Langley. A huge sigh escaped her. It was wonderful, but the busy week was suddenly catching up with her; Eddie felt a certain lethargy creep over her. She might have fallen asleep if someone hadn't knocked on the door. A moment later Sammy came in.

"Eddie, are you busy?"

"Not real busy. I'm writing a letter."

"To Robert?"

"Yes."

"When you're done, will you play a game with me?"

"Certainly. I'll come down in a few minutes."

Sammy smiled her thanks and started to leave, but then she stuck her head back in. "Tell him hello for me, Eddie."

"I'll do it, Sammy," she told her with a huge smile. "I'll do it right now."

"Well, that was the meal to end all meals," Robert told his host as he rocked onto the back legs of his chair.

"Lavena is a real find, I assure you, Robert," he said of his crotchety but faithful housekeeper. "If your Eddie needs any help with the house or cooking, just pop out here to the ranch for a few tips."

Robert chuckled, thinking of the scones and tea Eddie had prepared. He shook his head at Travis. "I think my Eddie will do just fine, but thanks for the offer."

"Speaking of Eddie," Travis continued, "what were her plans for the day?"

"She's with her family, including Uncle Mitch, and I think Clay Taggart and his family had been invited to join them."

"You've mentioned Clay several times," Travis commented.

"Yes. I was very impressed. He lives in Georgetown, and he's even a mine surveyor, but he's not caught up in that world of trying to get-rich-quick. Eddie tells me that his dream is to teach school."

"Well, we can certainly do with some well-qualified men and women for that profession," Travis said fervently. "If the rumors in town can be trusted, Boulder's new schoolteacher is not what they hoped she would be."

"Yes, I'd heard that as well. It's a large class, and I don't think she's assertive enough."

Lavena chose that moment to scurry into the room. She was the tiniest woman Travis had ever known.

"That was a feast, Lavena," Robert told her.

She managed to look pleased without smiling. "Did you save room for pie?" she demanded.

"Not at the moment," he admitted, hands in the air.

Lavena speared Travis with her eyes. "You see that he stays around long enough to enjoy some of my pie, Travis Buchanan." With that she was gone.

The two men shared a smile.

"Lavena has spoken," Travis said with a false shudder.

Robert only laughed.

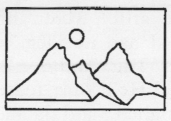

CHAPTER 10

"Now, who is this?" Clayton asked, pointing to the daguerreotype in the album. He turned his head to study Sammy's adorable profile as she answered.

"That's Mother's sister, Lacey. She lives in New York." Sammy turned to him and added, "It was at Aunt Lacey's house that Eddie met Robert."

Clayton's smiling eyes went to the glowing bride-to-be. "I haven't heard this story," Clayton told her. "I assumed you'd met Robert after you moved."

"No," Eddie said softly and would have elaborated, but Sammy jumped back in.

"Oh, no. She went to Aunt Lacey's before we went to New York, and while they were having tea, a man knocked on the door; it was Robert. He had the wrong house, but when he saw Eddie, he stayed for three hours!"

"Well, now." Clayton's expression was warm and teasing as he rose from the kitchen table and poured himself some more coffee. "I had no idea."

"Oh, stop it, Tag. And don't tell him any more, Sammy. He'll only tease me."

Clayton laughed, and Jackie chose that moment to come moodily into the kitchen. Christmas dinner had been over for an hour, and Lexa had gone off with Danny and Milly to one of the rooms upstairs. All the adults were in the living room. Since Eddie, Sammy, and Clayton had taken the kitchen, she felt she had no place to go.

"We were just going to play a game," Sammy told the sulking teen. "Want to join us, Jackie?"

"What are you going to play?" Her voice told of her disinterest.

"Across the Continent."

Jackie studied the toe of her shoe and then glanced at Clayton. His expression toward her was as it had been all day, completely noncommittal, and as much as she hated to be in the same room with him, she hated her boredom more.

"All right," she said after a moment. "I'll play."

Sammy had wanted to show the rest of the family photos to Clayton, but she thought Jackie would leave if she took the time. *Across the Continent* was always more

132

fun with four players, and even better with six or eight. She quickly put the photo album aside and waited while Eddie took the game from the cupboard.

"I've never played this before," Clayton admitted as they all took seats.

"I'll help you," Sammy offered, but Eddie did the honors.

"Your main objective is to travel across the continent and back. You see," Eddie spoke as the board was displayed, "It's like a map of the United States showing the large cities and the railway lines. You have a ticket and must pay travel expenses with the play money."

Always good with numbers, Jackie had taken over as banker and was now giving everyone their allotted finances. Lining up his play currency as he'd watched the girls do, Clayton waited for someone to explain the first move. Rummaging in the box, Jackie muttered something about the game pieces being gone, and Sammy jumped up.

"Oh! I think they're in my room. I'll run up and get them."

Jackie thought nothing of this until her father called to Eddie from the living room and a moment later she found herself alone with Clayton. Her eyes darted to him, but he was studying the board. Jackie relaxed until Clayton said out of the blue, "Does your hand hurt, Jackie?"

Jackie's eyes flew to his, but he was looking at the faint bruises on the back of her hand. Jackie swiftly buried her hand in her lap, and then Clayton sought out her eyes. She looked defiant as usual.

"I'm not going to tease you, Jackie," he said quietly. "You don't need to worry about that."

Silence hung between them for just an instant.

"Why did you stop teasing me, Clayton?" The question was out before she could stop it.

"It had gone too far."

"What do you mean?" Jackie's brow was furrowed; she honestly didn't understand.

"I mean, if someone actually thinks that I want to see them hurt, then my teasing has gone too far."

Jackie suddenly remembered the scene with the pitchfork in Taggarts' barn. She felt the first inkling of softening toward Clayton Taggart; he really had been concerned about her. Unfortunately, he was about to unwittingly destroy this tiny seed before it could grow even a millimeter.

"I realized," Clayton continued, "that either I was being too harsh, or you just couldn't handle that type of jesting."

Clayton watched Jackie's eyes flash with dark-blue fire and knew he'd stepped on her pride.

"I can take anything you dish out, Clayton Taggart!" she hissed. "Just don't you forget that."

Sammy came back into the room just then, and Eddie was close behind her, so Clayton was not able to reply to Jackie's venomous outburst. The game was played, and Jackie won hands down, but Clayton gave it little thought. However, he nearly mourned at how close he'd come to seeing her soften, only to have her turn on him again.

January 2, 1874, was Jackie's sixteenth birthday. It was a Friday, and she went to school wearing new ribbons in her hair and new mittens, but she wasn't feeling as ecstatic as she normally would have. The depression that had hit in the East in September '73 had now spread toward the West. Her mother had managed to make Christmas feel normal, but just days after December 25, her parents had warned everyone that things would be different. Since Jackie's birthday was the first in the year, she was the first to feel the changes.

There would still be a cake and a special meal, but the new dress she usually received, the book or game, and the special box of candy were going to have to wait for another time. Added to this was the upcoming wedding. One day while Eddie had been out of the house, Addy had sat down with the girls and told them her desire to make Eddie and Robert's wedding everything it could be. It meant cutting back in many areas, and although Jackie was the first to agree wholeheartedly to help in this, she had not anticipated the way she would feel when she had so few gifts to open on the morning of her birthday.

Though she was careful not to let on to anyone, it did not put her in the finest of moods. Her father's attitude was no help. He enjoyed birthdays but saw no reason to let them interrupt the workday. Friday the second was Jackie's day to work in the store, and Morgan expected her to be on time. After school she came through the doors in a towering rage but was careful not to let her father suspect.

"Sweep out the back room, Jack," were his first words, and when Jackie was finished, the room had never looked so good. She took out every ounce of resentment on that floor and had the dust flying so high she had to open a window.

Uncle Mitch came by at one point and gave her a birthday hug, but she was still out of sorts. The mood only worsened when her father told her she'd have to mind the front. Mitch had business at the bank, and Morgan planned to work in the office. Hoping with all her heart that no one would come in, Jackie obeyed and slowly walked toward the front. The bell rang just moments after she arrived behind the counter, and her heart sank when she saw it was Clayton.

He walked easily until he spotted the girl behind the counter whose eyes were hostile enough to make his step falter. Clayton had not had time to give the girls a ride home today, so he hadn't seen that Jackie would have walked downtown and not accepted his offer anyway. Knowing that nothing he could say or do was going to help the relationship, Clayton almost turned and went back out. However, he was out of time. His mother's birthday was in two days, and he had to leave the following morning.

"May I help you?" The question was asked with complete indifference. Clayton shook his head.

"I'll just look around."

"Suit yourself."

Clayton turned away with a small shake of his head. Maybe it was time for a confrontation. They both shared the same faith in Christ, but Jackie was nothing short of hateful when it came to him. He knew that all believers struggled with certain sins, but this seemed out of control.

Clayton pulled the watch from his pocket. He really didn't have time this afternoon, but when he returned to town, he would put things out in the open. Right now, however, he had to think of his mother and what would please her. He didn't have a lot to spend, but Milly had mentioned his mother's interest in a collar pin to go at the neckline of her lace blouse.

Clayton didn't move directly to the jewelry counter as he longed to do, but wandered around a bit, hoping that Mitch or Morgan would appear. He stepped to the large doorway that led to hardware, but that side of the store was empty. He knew he was going to have to get down to business.

With a soft sigh he turned back and stepped to the jewelry counter, which was separate from the others and sat in the middle of the store. He looked down through the glass and began to peruse the goods. He spotted the pin Milly had described almost immediately, but Jackie showed no signs of

138

coming to help him. He considered going home, giving Milly the money, and asking her to return the next day, but the snow was very deep these days and he didn't want her struggling with the sleigh. At last he heard Jackie's footsteps and steeled himself for the worst. She did not disappoint him.

"Did you want to see something? Because if you don't, I have things to do."

In that instant, Clayton had had enough. Anger leapt onto his back so swiftly that it nearly took his breath away. What had he done to deserve this? How could she hate him this much? These were just two of the questions that exploded in his brain, and his feelings must have shown on his face because Jackie looked rather startled.

"I am a paying customer in hard times, Jackie," Clayton bit out, doing nothing to disguise his outrage. "Now are you in the business of selling goods or not?"

Jackie blinked several times before saying in a much subdued tone, "I'd be glad to sell you something. Was there something special you wanted to see?"

"That pin, please." His voice had calmed, but he was still tense.

Jackie unlocked the cabinet and brought out a black velvet square covered with pins. She placed it gently on the counter and

139

watched as Clayton picked up a gold pin. Both ends were rounded and there were roses etched in the center. It was lovely. There was another one, nearly identical to the first except that it had a tiny diamond set in the center.

Clayton would have dearly loved to buy the one with the diamond but it was $2.50. The one without the stone was only $.78. Clayton lifted both in his hands and studied them, unaware of the fact that while he concentrated, Jackie was moving into a fine fury over the way he'd just put her in her place. Indeed, it was Jackie's impatient sigh that brought Clayton's head up and reminded him of the time.

"I'll take this one." He gestured toward the pin in his right hand, trying hard to ignore her returned ire.

"Fine," Jackie said shortly and reached to nearly tear the other pin from his left hand. Even in her anger, she noticed the way Clayton jumped slightly.

Both sets of eyes, one huge and the other intense, dropped to his hand and watched as a drop of blood welled to the surface. Clayton calmly placed the pin he had chosen on the counter and reached for his handkerchief. He wrapped his finger and then looked at Jackie. He blinked with surprise to see tears standing in her wide eyes.

"I'm sorry, Clay," she whispered.

"It's all right, Jackie," he told her, the sight of her tears touching his heart. "I'll take this one."

For a moment Jackie looked at him as though completely unaware of what he might be talking about, but then she looked down and saw the pin before him. With trembling hands she replaced the other pins, locked the cabinet, picked up Clayton's choice, and moved to the cash register. Her hands were still shaking when she took his money and made change from the drawer.

"Is it a gift?" The question was nearly whispered.

"Yes," Clayton told her simply and then watched as she placed it in a small box and painstakingly wrapped it in crisp, yellow paper. When it was ready, she held it out to him, her eyes still troubled.

"Thank you, Jackie."

"You're welcome, Clay."

Clayton stood for just a moment. Replacing his hat, he put the small parcel in his coat pocket but didn't walk away. He looked back at Jackie, his eyes serious.

"I'm headed out in the morning, but when I get back I think we should talk. I don't know what's brought on this hatred, but it's not right."

Jackie's heart clenched. Treating Clayton like she hated him had become almost a habit. Why had she acted this way?

Now, still speaking very low, she said, "I don't hate you, Clayton — not really. And I am sorry about your hand."

Clayton nodded his acceptance. "I'll see you later, Jackie."

"Goodbye, Clayton. Have a good trip."

"Thank you."

With that he turned away and moved out the door. Jackie stood still long after the sound of the bell faded away. A noise in the back finally made her move. She reached for the feather duster and turned to work on the shelves behind her. Tears slid down her face. This was turning out to be the worst birthday of her life.

The older woman closed the bedroom door firmly and gestured to the bed. She waited until her daughter took a seat on the edge and then moved to sit beside her.

"You've been quiet for a week now, Jackie. What's going on?" The question came from Addy, and it wasn't the first. However, this time she was not going to be put off. When Jackie was not in the mood to talk she was like her father. She told people to leave her alone and expected to be obeyed. This time Addy was not going to go away until she had some answers.

"Was it your birthday? Was it a terrible letdown for you?"

"It was," Jackie admitted, her eyes averted, "but not from anything you did. I had a bad day, but it was all my fault."

"Can you tell me about it?"

"I don't really want to."

"I would accept that, Jackie, but you've not been the same since. What is going on?" Addy's voice was just firm enough to tell her daughter that she wanted answers. Jackie gave a very light sketch of what had happened in the store.

"I nearly cried when I saw that blood," she said, looking at Addy. "Oh, Mother, I've treated him so badly, and now I just want to forget it. I don't know what I'll do if he wants to talk."

"So you still hate him?"

Jackie shook her head. "I don't think I ever did, but I don't want to talk it over with him either. I think I'd die of embarrassment if I had to explain. And Mother," Jackie wailed, "I just don't feel that comfortable around him! If we talk he'll think I want to talk and joke with him like Eddie."

"Would that be so bad?"

The question totally disarmed Jackie. She stared at her mother in complete bewilderment.

"Jackie," Addy went on gently, "I can't help but notice that you don't make friends easily. If Clayton is offering friendship to you, why can't you accept it?"

"What if he wants more than friendship?" The question came out in a tortured whisper, and Addy knew they had finally come to the crux of the matter.

"Oh, honey, acting like you hate a man is not going to make your feelings for him go away."

"But what if he finds out that I kind of like him, and he's *not* interested that way? I'd never be able to look at him again."

Addy reached for Jackie, gently putting her arms around her lovely daughter. She didn't know if Jackie had ever faced her feelings as she was now doing. Addy chose her words carefully.

"You are so afraid of being hurt that you never take risks. Love is a risky thing, Jackie, but we can't live without it. If you stay somewhere in the middle, you're never going to find out."

Jackie sniffed, and Addy just held her. The younger woman's head was against her mother's chest, and she spoke softly from that position.

"Eddie is so selfless, Mother. She puts others ahead of herself all the time, just like you do. I feel like I have to take care of myself. So many people have taken an instant dislike to me over the years that I found it was easier not to have anything to do with them. That way they couldn't hurt me."

Addy hugged her almost fiercely. "You're growing up, honey, and you're finding out that it doesn't work that way. Yes, we might be hurt, but we have to trust God and be willing to love and give of ourselves."

"Do you know how it all started?" Jackie pulled slightly away and looked at her mother. "Clayton stared at me the first time we met in the store last summer. I pretended that I didn't like it, but I did, and when we walked out with his purchases, I tripped." Tears filled her lovely eyes. "I felt like such a fool, but he laughed and only made it worse. It wasn't a cruel laugh — I think Eddie might have laughed too — but I decided then and there to hate him forever. But if I hate him, why do I want to look at him all the time? And why do I really care what he thinks of me?"

Addy smoothed Jackie's hair from her face and tenderly stroked her cheek.

"You still have some thinking to do, honey, but you'll find your answers. God does not want you lost and hurting. Trust Him for this. I'm not trying to push you and Clayton together. In fact, he doesn't even plan to stay in Georgetown that long."

"You mean his schooling?"

"That's right, but I do think he could be a good friend to you whether he lives here or not. I've seen how kind and tender he is with all your sisters, and I guess I trust him to be kind with you as well."

Jackie nodded.

"We'll just keep praying," Addy said softly, hugging her daughter once again.

CHAPTER 11

My Darling Eddie,

Today I write from our bedroom. I sit before the window, looking at the snow and wishing as you have in the past that we could be here together. I know as I write this that you are picturing my apartment above the bank. This time you are wrong. I now sit with paper on my knee in our new home, having just moved in yesterday.

I fear we will hear nothing but echoes for the first year, until we can afford some more furniture and rugs, but I'd rather shop with you and at a time when it will not cause a financial burden. The only thing I truly fear is loneliness for you. As of this writing we have only one neighbor. They are an older couple, very dear, but you are used to being surrounded by loving family, and I do not wish you to pine overly for them.

At that point Eddie had to stop reading. She was too overwhelmed to go on. The house was finished! She was not going to be married for six weeks, but her home was waiting for her. She smiled when she thought about the lack of neighbors. Didn't Robert understand that she was coming there for him? Eddie understood that she might be a bit naive about the future, but she was going to be married to the man she loved, and a lack of neighbors seemed of very little importance at the moment. She had to read on.

Our home sits on the road that leads to Travis' ranch, so I expect we'll see quite a bit of him. Maybe he will take a wife from one of the women at church and you will have a special friend in her. In any event, I know you'll meet some women of like interest, and I shall always have a buggy at your disposal. You might feel a little shut-in during the winter, but our snow does not remain on the ground as long as it does in Georgetown. Maybe God will bless us with children our first year, and I will never have need to worry for your loneliness again.

I count the days until we can be together and look forward to my return trip to see your family. You have all been in my prayers. How are things with Jackie and Clayton? I have praised God many times that her heart has become kinder.

Please tell Sammy that I received her letter and will be writing her soon. She told me about some cookies she was baking. I hope she'll make some more after I arrive. Thank your mother for setting things up with your Uncle Mitch so that Travis and I will not have to stay at the hotel. I will book a room for our wedding night, but the apartment above the store is much more practical for the week before the wedding.

A verse from Philippians says, "I thank my God upon every remembrance of you." My heart could feel no less. I love you, Eddie.

Yours always,
Robert

Eddie's eyes slid shut, and a huge sigh escaped her lips. He was so wonderful, and if he thanked God for her, Eddie nearly *shouted* her praise to God for him. She would have liked to lay on her bed and pray

149

for the next hour, but Jackie came in. Eddie wasn't angry over the interruption, but she decided right then to write Robert after she'd asked Jackie his question.

"Hi," Eddie said, sitting up. "What's up?"

"The sky" was Jackie's reply before she grinned. Eddie laughed and wondered at the change in her in the last few weeks. She wasn't anywhere near as moody as she had been, and her attitude was softening toward everyone in the house.

"Robert asked about you in his letter," Eddie told her.

"He did?" Jackie seemed very surprised.

"Yes. I talk to him about everyone, and he wanted to know how you were feeling about Clayton these days."

Jackie looked away for a minute. "I had a long talk with Mother about it, but I don't know."

"What do you mean?"

"Well, I was going to be kinder to him; I mean, I wasn't going to hold his hand or anything . . ." Jackie's face was comical. "Mother made me see that he didn't deserve to be treated the way I've been treating him."

"So what is it that you don't know now?"

Jackie shrugged. "He hasn't been around. I think I've only seen him twice in the last month. The first time he was all the way across the church, and the other time he walked by the store but didn't come in."

Eddie nodded. "This really isn't a very good time of year for socializing."

Jackie's gaze turned to the window. "I think the snow is going to be here forever."

They were quiet for a time before Eddie spoke.

"What changed your mind about Tag, Jackie? What was it Mother said?"

"She didn't really say anything." Jackie now looked at Eddie, her voice quiet. "I waited on Clayton at the store one day, and I was so irritated that I grabbed a collar pin from his hand and poked him in the finger. He bled, Eddie." Jackie's voice was tortured. "I've never been so ashamed in all my life. He didn't get angry or anything. He just wrapped it in his handkerchief and went on his way."

Eddie thought that sounded like something Clayton would do, but Jackie wouldn't have known that about him. It was very exciting to Eddie that her younger sister might be giving the man a chance. Not that she was hearing wedding bells or anything quite so dramatic, but Eddie saw Clayton for the fine man that he was, and she knew that Jackie was going to be lonely when she moved away to Boulder.

"The time will come for you to talk," Eddie predicted. "Probably at church or maybe at the store. You'll see."

Jackie nodded, and her gaze went back out the window. It was hard not to know, but at the moment she was amazingly calm inside. The meeting probably would be when she didn't expect it, but maybe that was best. A spark of fear and then anger lit in Jackie's soul. Fear threatened to choke her — fear of his rejecting her, laughing in her face, or treating her like a child. The only way Jackie knew to fight that kind of fear was to get angry at it and everyone around her, but she didn't want to do that again. With one small hand clenched in the folds of her skirt, she managed to tamp the feeling down. It took a few minutes, but at last she was calm.

There's no point in getting all shook up, Jackie, she said to herself. *It's impossible to know when or where, so you might as well relax.* But Jackie found that this was easier said than done, and as the end of January gave way to early February, which gave way to the middle of the month, Jackie wrestled almost daily with her feelings.

"We have a special guest this week," Miss Bradley announced on Monday morning.

"Mr. Clayton Taggart is going to be observing us all this week." She looked at Clayton. "I'm proud to tell you, Mr. Taggert, that this class is full of the brightest students I've ever taught. They do not always apply themselves," she added almost dryly, "but their potential is tremendous."

"Now," the teacher's voice turned more serious as she again faced the class. "Many of you may know our guest on a first-name basis, but this week he is Mr. Taggart. Is that understood?"

"Yes, Miss Bradley," chorused the occupants of the room.

"Now, to start off, Mr. Taggart is simply going to observe, but beginning this afternoon I will be choosing students from each form to sit in the back with Mr. Taggart and explain a subject to him. You will speak clearly if you are spoken to while still at your desk and answer all questions to the best of your ability. Let us begin."

Jackie had never had such a hard time with concentration. She was as aware of Clayton's presence as anyone could be. Questions plagued her, tortured her even. Would he try to humiliate her or get back at her for the way she'd treated him? If only she'd had a chance to talk to him before.

Jackie was completely unaware of the way

153

her thoughts showed on her face. She felt as vulnerable as if she'd been asked to sit in school in her underclothing. Her tormented thoughts eased a little when she saw Clayton put a hand on Paddy's shoulder, and more so when she saw him smooth Lexa's hair, but she was still in a panic. In fact, she was so troubled that unknown to her, her eyes pleaded with Clayton when he came by. He hadn't planned to stop, but her eyes were so miserable that he paused.

"How's it going?" he asked, his voice low and completely normal. Jackie trembled with relief.

"It's fine," she told him softly and was rewarded by his kind smile before he passed on to the next row.

The day got better from that point, and Jackie even managed to thank Clayton for the ride home. His eyes were warm but not teasing as he acknowledged her words, and Jackie went into the house feeling like she'd been given the day.

"I ate lunch with Paddy today," Milly told her brother. They had gone into the barn, but cold as it was Milly seemed in no hurry to rush inside. She stood holding her books in front of her, her hat and mittens still in place.

"I saw you." Clayton stared at her over the back of the horse.

"He said something about Jackie."

"Oh?"

"Yes. He wondered if the two of you might be seeing each other. He said she watched you the whole morning."

Clayton nodded. He'd been more than aware of her gaze.

"I don't think she hates you anymore, Tag," Milly continued. "I don't think she hates anyone anymore."

Clayton came out from the stall, patting the roan-colored rump as he passed. He stopped before Milly.

"Maybe she's growing up a little."

"Maybe. She still doesn't have many friends, though," Milly said sadly.

"It takes time for a person to live down a bad reputation. Sometimes it never goes away."

"But you've never been angry back or hated her, have you, Tag?"

"Well, not for long. Where Jackie and I are concerned, I brought some of her feelings on myself. I pushed in and teased her, and hurt her in the process. I know better now."

Milly suddenly had to hug her brother. "You're going to make a wonderful teacher,

Tag. I know that with all my heart."

Clayton gladly hugged her in return. Nothing else she could have said would have warmed his heart more.

"Jacqueline, you will go to the back now with Mr. Taggart. Please explain the Upper Form mathematics. Go over what we've been learning and be certain to take your book."

"Yes, Miss Bradley." Jackie's voice was subdued, but she obeyed. Her legs shook just a little as she rose and turned to the back. Jackie sat in the last seat so she didn't have far to go to the table and two chairs that had been set up at the back. Clayton was waiting for her, ready to hold her chair. Jackie thanked him in a soft voice and waited until he sat opposite her. She thought they would get right down to business, but Clayton surprised her.

"Why do you suppose Miss Bradley chose you to tell me about this?"

"Oh." Jackie faltered for a moment and made her hands lie still on the table. "Well, I think maybe because I'm good in this subject."

"Is it your favorite?"

Jackie looked into his eyes and then down, feeling very self-conscious.

"No, but I like it all right."

"What is your favorite?"

"World history."

Clayton smiled.

"Mine too."

Jackie bit her lip, but her smile stretched through. She forced herself to ask, "Did you want to hear about math now?"

"Sure," Clayton answered easily, and Jackie felt herself relaxing. She knew, however, that Clayton would have been just as content to sit and talk with her about something other than math. She opened the book, and Clayton leaned forward intently.

Jackie was very good at explaining things, and everything was familiar to Clayton, who was also good in math. He couldn't have said exactly when she lost him, but at some point the young man stopped listening to math and started listening more to the young woman.

The sound of Jackie's voice and the way her slim-fingered hands moved captivated him. The deep blue of her eyes was nearly hypnotic, and Clayton wondered when his feelings for her had moved from concern to something deeper. He was still concerned for her and cared more than he could tell her, but there was another feeling sinking deeply into his heart.

The funny part was that Clayton didn't know why. Jackie was not sweet and gentle like Eddie, or sensitive and kind like Danny, but she was Jackie — just Jackie. She was a girl in whom Clayton had seen serious faults, but he still cared. And although she tried her hardest not to disclose herself, he also saw a vulnerability in her that tore his heart nearly in two. Maybe she was like the students he hoped to teach one day. He simply ached to "take her on" and help her to be all she could be.

Clayton now forced his mind back to the book Jackie was holding. He was going to have to go slowly here, and well he knew it. His emotions could easily take him out of control. He knew this because as much as he wanted to teach students of all shapes and sizes, he didn't have the desire to kiss any of them the way he did Jackie Fontaine.

"Did that make sense?"

"Yes." Clayton swiftly gathered his thoughts. "Yes, it did. Now will you be through with this book before the year ends?"

"I don't think so. We have some more difficult steps coming up." Jackie swiftly turned to the back of the book. "See? Right here. Miss Bradley says we'll be taking extra time on these."

Clayton studied the pages. Very involved fractions. This too was familiar. He then thanked Jackie and asked her if she would want a ride home.

"I'm not going home today," she told him. "It's my day to work at the store, but thank you."

"I can swing you by," Clayton offered and watched Jackie's cheeks flush.

"You don't have to," she told him and closed the book.

"Well, it's up to you. I won't do anything you don't want me to do."

There was something in his tone and the way he said the words that made Jackie think he was talking about far more than a ride in the wagon. She stood swiftly and pushed her chair in. Clayton rose also.

"I'd appreciate a ride," she nearly whispered, her eyes not readable. "Thank you, Clayton." With that she slipped away to her seat, and Clayton was left to wonder just what he had said.

CHAPTER 12

The following Saturday morning Jackie was sitting quietly in a kitchen chair while Eddie trimmed her bangs. She kept her eyes closed but had a tendency to wrinkle her brow, and Eddie kept telling her to hold still. Indeed, Eddie really scolded her when Clayton's voice was heard coming through the house. He was talking as he walked, and it was clear that he had come in the front door and was heading their way.

"Just put them on the table, Clay," Addy instructed as she entered, the young man behind her. "I'll run upstairs and get those things for your mother."

"Well, now," Clayton spoke when his hostess had left, his smile huge. "Can I be next?"

"No," Eddie told him without hesitation. "Jackie is the third one since 6:30 this morning, and I'm at my limit."

"My loss," Clayton announced and sat down to watch. "I think you're missing

160

some on this side."

Eddie smiled, her eyes still on her work, but Jackie couldn't see that.

"Oh, no!" Clayton exclaimed. "Look at that big mistake. And right in the front too!"

Jackie wiggled a little, a smile on her face as well, and Eddie told her to hold still again.

"Watch it, Eddie. Don't make it any worse," Clayton continued to tease as Sammy came to see the commotion.

"Hi, Tag. What are you doing?"

Clayton opened his mouth to answer, but Jackie suddenly said, "Making a pest of himself."

Clayton's mouth remained open, but this time with incredulity. Both Eddie and Sammy were laughing, but he was sputtering like a boiling teakettle.

"A pest! She called me a pest!"

Jackie took a peek at him, her eyes brimming with laughter.

"Hold still, Jackie."

"Are you nearly finished?"

"Yes."

"She called me a pest," Jackie heard Clayton say again. "Well, that's the last time I help you get a haircut, Jackie Fontaine!"

Jackie only smiled, glad that she could

keep her eyes closed.

"All right, Clay," Addy said as she returned, "these are for your mother. Tell her I'll get the baskets back to her right after the wedding."

"Will do," Clayton told her. "Is there anything else, Addy?"

"Are you headed into town or home?"

"To town."

"Can you run the girls to the store? They're already late."

"Sure."

"Great." Addy thanked him with that one word and went to the stairs to call Lexa and Danny. They tumbled down a moment later, glad to be getting a ride, but Jackie, who was now finished at the table, hung back. She had enjoyed teasing with Clayton when she couldn't see him, but now she felt foolish. The others had gone to bundle into warm things, so Jackie found herself alone with Clayton.

"Did you want a ride?" he asked.

"No," she said without looking at him. "I have to clean up, so I'll just walk."

"The snow's pretty deep; I'd be glad to wait."

Jackie finally looked at him.

"Whatever you want," he added.

Jackie looked at him for a moment more.

162

"I'll hurry," she said, feeling oddly breathless and dashing for the stairs.

Clayton stood quite still, his heart beating like a trip-hammer in his chest. Had he really seen something there, or had he just wanted to see something? Only time would tell.

A week and a half later Clayton was in the general store with a special gift in mind. Mitch was on hand to help him, but the older man seemed strangely preoccupied.

"Maybe I should get Jackie from the back," Mitch finally suggested.

"Oh, is she here? Why don't you? Tell her the pest is here."

Mitch smiled and moved away. A few minutes later Jackie emerged from the back, trying very hard not to smile herself. She knew her face was flushed, but Clayton looked and sounded very normal.

"Hello, Jackie."

"Hello, Clay. Uncle Mitch said you needed some help."

"Yes. I'm looking for something for Robert and Eddie. My mother bought them a gift from the whole family, but I'd like to get a little something myself."

"Oh, that's a nice idea. Let's see." Jackie turned slowly and tried to think, her mind

163

dealing with the facts. It was still unbelievable that Clayton was offering kindness to her. And she was finding that when he was close, concentration was difficult. She felt as though she'd been rescued when she thought to look in the household goods.

"Actually, you have many choices," she said as she moved toward that counter. "If you want something practical, these cut-glass salt and pepper shakers are five cents each; if you're after a little more decorative item, this vase is 38 cents."

Clayton studied all of them. "I wish I'd thought to ask Eddie."

Jackie shook her head. "It wouldn't have done any good. I don't know what all women are like who plan to be married in ten days' time, but Eddie's feet are not even on the ground."

Clayton chuckled. "She told me Robert comes Friday."

"Yes, and she's praying every day that the snow will begin to melt a little. She said she doesn't care if he and Travis get snowed *in*, she just doesn't want them snowed *out*."

Clayton was smiling, but as he watched Jackie his look was very intent. It rather unnerved her. Beginning to feel flustered, Jackie grabbed the closest thing and held it in the air.

"Potato masher." She waved the metal object in the air. "You could give her that."

Clayton laughed. "Oh, I don't know. I was thinking maybe a combination rat-and-mouse trap."

Jackie really laughed at that, but then turned serious. "I do know something she and Robert would enjoy." Jackie reached beneath the counter and brought out a small box. "These are from England, so they're not as large as American ones. They're teaspoons, and Eddie loves to make tea. She would probably use them all the time. The only problem is the cost. I can't break up the set, and they're twelve cents each." She sounded apologetic.

"How many are there?"

"Eight. Would you like to see them?"

Ninety-six cents. Clayton's brain was calculating fast. If he looked at them and liked what he saw, he'd have a hard time saying no, but a dollar was a lot of money out of his pocket right now.

"I'll look at them," he said after a moment, and just as he suspected, they were beautiful. He was putting aside literally every penny for his schooling in the fall, but Eddie and Robert were very special to him.

"I'll take them," he said at last, and Jackie offered to wrap the box.

Well satisfied with his purchase, Clayton left the store just a few minutes later, his mind still on Jackie. She had definitely changed toward him, but he could tell she wanted to keep things lighthearted. She called him a pest when he thanked her for the help and had swiftly turned away to busy herself with the shelves behind the counter. Clayton wondered if he would ever really know where he stood with that girl.

Old Doc Edwardson stared across the room at his patient, knowing it had to be the other man's decision but not agreeing with it.

"What if it were Morgan? Wouldn't you want to know, Mitch?"

"Yes, but then my daughter's not getting married in a few days. I won't do anything to spoil that joy."

The old doctor nodded. He could hardly argue with that.

"Well, take it easy. Maybe that old ticker of yours will give us more time than we think."

"I'm already taking it easy," Mitch told him calmly. "Have been ever since Morgan and Addy came."

The doctor pursed his lips, his eyes

thoughtful. "I wish I could do something for you."

"Thanks, Ed, but I'm not worried. I've something better waiting on the other side."

Doc Edwardson smiled. He too believed in life after death for those who understood and believed in the work done on the cross.

"I can give you something for the pain. Are you interested?"

"How bad is it going to get?"

"It might get very bad, or you might just drop down dead," came the doctor's blunt reply.

Mitch thought a moment. "I'll take the bottle, Ed. I don't want anyone to know until after the wedding, and I was pretty uncomfortable last night."

Doc Edwardson rose and filled a small bottle from his sideboard dispensary. He handed it to Mitch and then waited while the other man stood. They shook hands, and Mitch took his leave. He walked out into the cold, glad that the snow was starting again. It was early in the day, and had the weather been better, more folks would have been out and he might have been questioned. Eddie's wedding was a week from Saturday. Mitch wasn't ready to talk about his need to see the doctor until sometime after that day, if ever.

★ ★ ★

Eddie's heart thundered in her chest as the knock sounded at the door. She put a shaky hand to the lace at her throat. It might not be Robert and Travis, but Eddie was certain that it must be. She walked with unsteady steps to the front door, and her heart melted within her as she saw him standing there.

"Hello, Eddie." His soft, deep voice came to her ears, and Eddie couldn't help herself. She threw her arms around his neck and hugged him with all her might.

"I didn't think you'd ever get here," she whispered close to his ear as he bent to hold her.

"It felt like years, but not now. Now I can hold you and take you home with me."

Eddie moved slightly away from him so she could see his face. He was smiling at her.

"We're heating the out-of-doors."

"Oh! Right! Come in and get warm."

Not until Robert was inside did Eddie notice he was alone.

"Where's Travis?"

"We stopped at the store to leave our gear at Uncle Mitch's. Travis said he'd come home with your father this evening. He had some idea that I might want to see you alone."

Eddie smiled. "And did you?"

"Yes."

Eddie bit her lip. "Mother's in the living room. Would you like to come in and see her?"

"Not yet," Robert told her, and the smile fell from Eddie's face. Robert was taking her in his arms again and kissing her in a way that made her forget she had a mother. When Eddie came up for air, she could only stand and look into Robert's eyes. She had prayed that he would arrive safely, and God had seen to the task.

"I'm so glad you're here."

"As am I. How are you?"

"Fine. Ready to be your wife."

"No last minute plans to chase after?"

"No. Everything is ready, so we can enjoy my family this week. We have only to see Pastor Munroe at some point and work at keeping my nerves at bay."

Robert smiled and kissed her again.

"Eddie," her mother now called from the next room. "Bring Robert in so I can say hello."

"All right, Mother," she answered and turned to her fiancé.

"Lead the way," he offered, and Eddie thought he was such a gentleman. She'd have laughed if she'd known he did it for himself; Eddie was as delightful from the back as she was from the front.

"Welcome, Robert." Addy stood and offered her cheek as they came into the room. Robert gave her a warm hug as well, and they sat down to reacquaint themselves. Addy told of how she received a letter from Robert's family and had already answered in return. Robert seemed very pleased. There was so much to share. They talked for nearly an hour before Addy rose to get them some refreshment.

"I'm looking forward to meeting Travis," Eddie told him. "I hope Father comes soon after the girls get home."

"I don't know if I'll be ready by then," Robert commented, but he was smiling.

Eddie cocked her head to one side. "Now, what did that mean, Mr. Langley?"

"Only that you feared I would fall for one of your sisters, and now I think I just might lose you to Travis."

Eddie laughed and Robert joined her.

"Well," she said primly, still smiling at the man she loved. "*That* is not going to happen."

"Are you sure?" He was still teasing.

"Yes. Aren't you?"

"You haven't seen him, Eddie."

"Good-looking?" Eddie's brows rose with

feigned interest, but this time Robert didn't answer. He smiled at her, however, and picked up her hand. Eddie knew it had all been in fun; nothing could change her feelings for Robert, but she did wonder what the other man looked like.

CHAPTER 13

Lexa and Sammy could do nothing but stare at Travis Buchanan that evening, and Danny blushed to the roots of her hair every time he glanced in her direction. Eddie had never seen her sisters behave this way. She had exchanged more than one amused glance with Robert as well as Travis.

When Travis first arrived with their father, he, Robert, Morgan, Jackie, and Eddie all ended up visiting in the living room. The younger girls were helping with dinner, but they thought of innumerable reasons to come and ask something of Eddie or Jackie. At one point, Eddie mentally shook her head.

A rancher by trade, Travis looked the part in his dark jeans and cowboy boots. His wavy, dark brown hair was a little long on his neck, but his eyes were light blue and clear as a child's. His teeth were startlingly white against his rugged features, and he was taller than Robert by two inches. His manner toward the family was courteous and gentle, and Eddie could tell that the girls felt very special when he spoke to them. Travis *was* very handsome, but the way her sisters were acting, she'd have thought they had never seen a man before.

Eddie was relieved when it was time for them to go off to bed. Even Jackie, who had been the only one not staring, was sent on her way, and the adults were finally alone. Eddie was on the verge of apologizing, but Morgan hadn't noticed a thing and began to question Travis about the cattle business.

"How many head do you have?"

"About 1500. It fluctuates."

"And to whom do you sell?"

"Whoever is buying. We drive cattle into the Denver stockyards and as far as Cheyenne."

Morgan leaned forward intently. "How many men do you have working for you?"

"That varies with the season. I need more hands during roundup and less in the winter months."

"Do you have trouble with thieves?"

Addy cleared her throat, and Morgan turned to her and smiled sheepishly. "Am I monopolizing the conversation, dear?"

Addy smiled in return. "Something like that. Sammy asked if you would come up and kiss her good-night."

"All right. If you'll excuse me," Morgan said to the room at large and exited silently.

"I wonder if the girls will ever get to sleep tonight," Addy commented. "It must be the wedding. I've never seen them this distracted."

Eddie tried to stop herself, but at that moment she looked at Robert and they both burst out laughing.

"What did we miss?" Travis asked as his confused gaze met Addy's.

"I don't know," replied the equally confused hostess.

"Mother," Eddie nearly gasped. "They weren't distracted; they were beheaded. And it's not the wedding; it's Travis. I've never seen Danny blush so many times in my whole life."

Addy finally caught on. Her amused gaze went to Travis, who now understood as well. "Should I be worried that you're going to elope with one of my daughters, Mr. Buchanan?"

Travis chuckled. "As lovely as they are, Mrs. Fontaine, I'm not in the market for a wife."

They all laughed before Addy changed the subject and asked Robert if they were settled in at Mitch's.

"Yes, we are. It's very hospitable of him."
Robert hesitated. "He seemed tired, however."

"Yes," Addy agreed. "I don't think he feels well. The winter is dragging on, and I think the wedding is on his mind. I might suggest he go see Doc Edwardson after next weekend."

"He mentioned that he had something special for Eddie and me."

"Oh, yes," Eddie said, remembering that Uncle Mitch had said something to her before.

"He asked if we would come by sometime early next week and stay for dinner, just the two of us."

"Oh," Addy said, and Eddie turned to her and smiled.

"Do you know what it is?"

"Yes," Addy smiled in return. "You're going to be very pleased."

Eddie was still smiling over this when Morgan joined them once again. They talked much too late. The following day was a workday, but a week was such a short time, and they all felt anxious for every moment.

Robert and Travis finally made their way to the back door of the store, through the shadowy interior, and up the stairs to

Mitch's rooms. His apartment had a door at the top of the stairs, but the main part of the living area was down a hallway, where the apartment split into several smaller rooms, all on one side. One room was a kitchen and dining area, and one was Mitch's sitting room. The rest were bedrooms. Some of the rooms connected, and others stood alone. The original builder and owner had probably intended to rent the rooms out, but Mitch kept them for himself.

Now the two guests moved as silently as possible in order not to disturb their host. Once in their room, which sported two small beds, they found he had left a lantern burning.

"Well, what did you think?" Robert whispered as both men sat on their own beds to undress.

"I think you're marrying the kindest woman God put on the earth."

Robert smiled, his chest filling on a huge sigh of contentment. "She's wonderful. That big house has been just plain lonely without her."

"It isn't long now."

"No."

The men were silent as they continued to ready for bed. Robert was under the covers first and said, "It's too bad Jackie's not a little bit older."

"It wouldn't matter, Robert; she would still seem too young. Even Eddie seems young."

Robert raised up on one elbow and stared across the room.

"I don't know what you mean, Travis. You're younger than I am by three years."

"It's not a measurement in years, Robert. Eddie is very mature, and she's going to make you a wonderful wife." Travis fell silent then, and Robert gave him a moment. "I haven't shared a lot with you, Robert, but my life before Christ was pretty worldly. I did a lot of wandering. I look into the eyes of those sweet girls, and I know they haven't seen anything of what this sinful world has to offer."

This Robert could understand. A man wanted a wife who would understand him, and even have an understanding of what he was thinking before he said it. Eddie had done that on countless occasions in her letters; she could read between the lines and guess Robert's thoughts before he voiced them. Travis was not saying he wanted a worldly wife, just one who would understand where he'd been.

"I'm glad you told me, Travis."

"Yeah, me too. Good-night, Robert."

"Good-night, Travis."

"Now," Mitch's eyes sparkled, his color looking better than it had all week, as he locked the front doors of the store and turned to his niece and Robert. "I've made some dinner, but first I want to give you your gift."

Eddie smiled in anticipation. Mitch's mood was infectious.

"My gift to you is to pick out anything you'd like."

Eddie gasped. "Oh, Uncle Mitch, how sweet." She turned to Robert. "How shall we ever decide?"

Robert looked surprised as well and shrugged helplessly. "I don't know."

"Well, there must be many things you need, settling into a new home and starting a life together," Mitch said with vigor as he began to move about the store. "You're sure to need this satchel, Eddie. And here, Robert, is your shaving brush in good shape? This hairbrush is a good one; I've carried this brand for years. And these gloves, Eddie. Even if yours are in good shape now, you could lose one on the trip to Boulder."

It took Eddie and Robert a moment to realize he meant anything and *everything* they needed. Eddie was shaking her head, but Mitch spoke with the firmest voice she'd ever heard from him.

"I want to do this, Edwina. You're my niece, and I have a store full of goods that you won't be able to shop for in the future. I will do this."

Both Robert's and Eddie's protests stopped in their mouths. They nodded and let Mitch move about the entire store, selecting things for their home or their own personal needs. Eddie was feeling overwhelmed but managed to mention the shipping cost.

"There's no need to worry about that," Mitch told them. "I've two trunks in the back that belonged to your Aunt Clara. We'll load those up, and they'll go with you."

Eddie's sigh was heartfelt, and she hugged Mitch tenderly.

"You'll have to come and see us, Uncle Mitch, to see how we've used all these things you've given us."

Mitch patted her back. "I'm getting a little old to be traveling about, honey."

Eddie only smiled. "Well, we'll be back often, and we can write and tell you everything in between."

Mitch only smiled.

"I'd better run to check on this dinner you have started," Eddie offered, moving toward the stairs with graceful strides. Mitch watched her go, but then looked back to see Robert studying him intently. The younger man thought about Eddie's words but saw the truth in Mitch's eyes. The older man was very aware that he'd been found out. It took a moment, but his voice finally came low and solemn to Robert's ears.

"I don't want anything to spoil this Saturday for her. Do you understand that, Robert?"

"Yes, sir, I do."

Mitch's hand came out, and they shook. Robert thanked him, but it was an effort to push the words around the tightness in his throat.

"Uncle Mitch, Robert, I've put supper on."

"We'll be right up," the older man called. With one more glance at each other, they started toward the stairs.

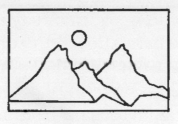

CHAPTER 14

Eddie and Robert's wedding day broke crisp and clear, the sun shining off the snow and nearly blinding the Fontaine family as they headed to the church. Eddie's face was pale with excitement. Seeing it, Jackie reached to squeeze her hand. The older girl didn't notice. Lexa directed a question to her oldest sister, and her response, or rather lack thereof, was the same. Jackie looked to Lexa and shrugged.

"I hope I get married someday," Sammy said with a wistful sigh.

"Are you also hoping that Travis Buchanan will wait for you?" her mother asked from the front seat.

Surprisingly, Sammy didn't blush. "He's so handsome" was her only comment, and Addy watched as a smile widened Morgan's mouth.

"You must think it's funny," Addy said softly for his ears.

"No." The smile was still in place. "I just

remember a young woman saying much the same thing when she didn't know that a certain young man was listening."

Addy smiled as well. "I knew you were there all along, Morgan Fontaine, and we both know I married you only because you were so homely I knew that no one else would have you."

All the girls, save the still-dreamy Eddie, wanted to know why their father was laughing, but he refused to tell. However, they could do their own figuring when Morgan brought the sleigh to a halt in front of the church and exuberantly kissed his wife.

An hour later Addy fussed with Eddie's dress and veil as Morgan, with Jackie at his side, looked on. Jackie's dress was a velvet in a deep burgundy color, but Eddie's was cream-colored satin, overlaid with lace across the entire bodice, up the high neckline, and down the long sleeves. When the mother-of-the-bride had finished her tucking and adjusting, she stood back and smiled at her lovely daughter.

"You're the most beautiful bride in the world, Eddie. Robert will be so pleased." Eddie smiled and the women embraced.

"I'd best get to my seat," Addy said to Morgan, and he saw her to the door.

"Come outside with me, Jackie," Addy called before she left. "That way you can tell Eddie and your father that it's time to start down."

"All right."

The door closed softly at that point, leaving Morgan and Eddie alone. Morgan turned to look at his daughter, his throat feeling oddly tight.

"Well," she said softly, "this is it."

"Yes," Morgan said inadequately, but then his head tipped to one side. "It's too bad that a man can't experience this before it actually involves him."

"What do you mean?"

Morgan sighed. "Your mother married me against her father's wishes. I haven't thought about what that day might have felt like for him until right now. You go with my blessing, but there's no way Robert can understand how I'm feeling until it's his turn to stand with his own daughter."

Eddie wanted to cry with the thought, but she forced herself to ask, "And how do you feel right now?"

"Proud," Morgan told her without hesitation. "Prouder than I've ever been in my life, but sad because you're leaving. I know we'll see each other, but it won't be the same ever again."

Eddie nodded. She'd had the same thoughts so many times.

"Change is not bad," she said softly, "but neither is it easy. I'll miss you more than I can say."

Morgan hugged her, and just ten minutes later Jackie announced that it was time. Eddie went very white upon hearing those words, but Morgan whispered words of encouragement, and it wasn't long before she was given over to Robert's waiting hand. Her heart calmed then, but the whole thing overwhelmed her just a little. Robert was pale himself, and Eddie knew he was feeling the same rush of emotion. The ceremony was over before she knew it, and family and friends were crowding around them to offer congratulations.

They stayed at the church for over an hour, talking and thanking people for coming, before Travis reminded them that they needed to get to the house. Morgan, Addy, Mitch, and the younger girls had all left, as had most of the guests, but Jackie, as maid of honor, was standing by to go with the bride, groom, and Travis, who had stood as best man.

"I think we had better get on our way," he suggested. "They're probably waiting for you."

Eddie didn't need to be asked twice. They had worked hard on the reception, and many people had offered to help. She wanted to be on hand to thank them all in person.

Travis bundled them all in the large sleigh, pulled by Mitch's team of matched black geldings. Jackie was in front with the best man and the newlyweds were in the back. They were no more settled in the seats when Robert grabbed Eddie and gave her a long, hard kiss.

"We're going to be entertaining everyone in town for the next several hours, so I thought I'd do that while I had the chance."

Eddie laughed in sheer delight and leaned to kiss him again.

"I think they're acting up back there," Jackie said loudly to Travis.

"I think you're right. I myself am blushing just at the thought."

They pulled into the Fontaine yard amid much laughter. Sure enough, it looked as if the whole town had already arrived. Eddie couldn't think how they would all fit in, but they managed. Food was served immediately, and folks stayed for hours. The cakes were delicious. With tears in her eyes, Eddie thanked her mother and Elaine Taggart for all their hard work. Both of the older

185

women looked utterly drained, but when most of the guests had gone on their way, family and close friends gathered in the Fontaine living room to watch Robert and Eddie unwrap their gifts. Uncle Mitch had asked to be excused, and Morgan had run him to the store, but Travis and the Taggart family were present.

Jackie and Clayton ended up on chairs close together. Other than smiling at Clayton a few times that day, they'd had no chance to talk. Clayton glanced at her lovely profile and wanted to tell her that she looked beautiful in her new dress, but there was something vulnerable about her right then and he refrained. It occurred to him very suddenly that this was the end of life as she had known it. Her closest sister, roommate, confidante, and friend was leaving. Clayton found himself praying for her heart as the gift-opening began.

"Oh, aren't they pretty," Eddie commented as she pulled out two embroidered pillow slips. "Look at the workmanship."

"Very nice," Robert agreed and worked on the next package.

"Who is this from?" Eddie wished to know.

"The card said 'The O'Brien Family.' "

"I think you met them, Robert. Paddy

O'Brien is a good friend of Milly and Danny."

"I think I did too."

"Oh, it's a bread tray!" Eddie exclaimed when Robert brought it forth. "Isn't it elegant?"

They loved the spoons from Clayton and had a wonderful time with all the gifts. Indeed, there was much laughter on several occasions. At one point Eddie opened a gift and held it aloft, her brow drawn down in puzzlement.

"What is it, Robert?"

"I was hoping you would tell me."

Both husband and wife looked to Addy and Elaine, who stared at the silver creation and then at one another. When everyone realized that neither one could identify it, the room erupted in laughter. The last burst of merriment came just a few minutes later when Eddie opened a box and inside was a baby's bib. She blushed to the roots of her hair and wouldn't hold it up. Robert took it and did the honors, a sweet smile on his face.

Eddie was still blushing amid the laughter when she said, "All right, who's responsible?"

No one would own up to it, but Eddie suddenly caught Jackie's eye. The younger girl could not hold her laughter.

"Jacqueline Faye!" Eddie scolded her, now laughing as well. "You rascal!"

"I saw it at the store and couldn't resist, Eddie. I'm sorry."

Eddie only shook her head, and after that, the party began to break up. Addy announced that she was going to fix something to eat and everyone was welcome to stay. Elaine, Milly, and Danny went with her, and Robert took that moment to lean close to his bride.

"Are you hungry?" he asked.

"Not a bit, but I am starting to feel tired."

"I think we'll say our goodbyes and head to the hotel. If you decide you want to eat, I'll have the hotel fix us something."

Eddie nodded, and Robert went to tell the others. Thankfully, only Addy and Morgan came to the door with them.

"We'll be over to join you for lunch tomorrow after church," Robert informed them. "Eddie's tired, and I think we need to sleep in."

"All right, Robert," Morgan agreed with him. "I'm not sure we'll even make it out ourselves, but we'll look for you around noon."

Addy hugged them both, and Travis came through the front door to tell them

188

that the sleigh was ready. Just minutes later they were on their way.

The hotel staff was very accommodating, and one of the men came out to stable the horse for the night. Robert had seen to the baggage that afternoon, so without fuss they walked up the oak staircase to the second floor of the hotel. Room 6 was spacious, with two double beds and a private bath. Several lanterns were lit, and Eddie preceded Robert into the room. Robert closed the door and leaned against it. He stared at Eddie where she had stopped at the corner of the bed.

For a time they didn't speak, but then Eddie, feeling self-conscious, began to move around the room. She went to the windows and glanced down at the alley below, but it was too dark to see outside. She inspected the chandelier, peeked into the closet and bathroom, and then moved to sit on the edge of the far bed. Robert pushed off from the door and moved to sit on the bed opposite her. He stared at her for several more seconds before he shared the thoughts of his heart.

"Every day I confidently run a large bank in a booming town with a certain measure of ease, but here, now, with you, I feel completely unsure."

189

"Unsure about me, or about this night?"

"This night. I'm 29 years old, Eddie, but you're the only woman I've kissed who wasn't my mother, aunt, or cousin. I've saved myself and I'm not sorry, but this is the first time in a long time that I haven't known exactly what to do."

Eddie shrugged as an adorable grin covered her mouth. She wasn't very sure herself, but the hard worker was coming to the fore.

"Well." Her voice was bracing. "It can't be too complicated." She shifted a little, and the mattress bounced beneath her. "I mean, we love each other, and I think we start with a kiss, and we both enjoy that." Again she shrugged and smiled.

Suddenly Robert wanted to laugh with hysterical joy. She was unlike anyone he'd ever known. He stood just long enough to take her hand in his and bring her over next to him to sit on the bed. They settled in, side-by-side, and just talked. Robert relaxed and Eddie leaned against him, her adoring eyes on his face as they shared their thoughts from the day. There was no pomp or ceremony when they began to kiss and hold each other, just warmth and caring.

"I love it when you kiss me," Eddie told him, blue eyes twinkling into gray. "For a moment there I thought you were going to suggest we each take a bed."

Robert chuckled low in his throat and kissed her again. He should have known that God would honor his desire to stand righteously before Him on his wedding night. After all, God had given him Eddie, and at the moment Robert could find nothing over which to be more thankful.

The time after Sunday dinner the next day was a little busier than Eddie had hoped for, but there was much to be packed before she, Robert, and Travis left the next morning. The trunks were readied, the newlyweds spent some time with Uncle Mitch, and they also went to see Clayton. Eddie wanted to cry when they parted, but Clayton reminded her that he would be living in Denver in the fall, and just maybe there was a chance he could get to Boulder later in the year.

This did comfort Eddie some, but her throat was still tight. As she left, all she could do was pray that she would make it through this separation from her family and friends. She also asked God to help Clayton and Jackie grow closer. Jackie needed someone, and so did Clayton. It seemed so ideal to the young bride that her sister and friend should form a friendship.

That evening Robert and Eddie spent a wonderful few hours with Eddie's whole family. Travis was with them as well, and it was a night full of memories to be cherished. Travis went back to Mitch's for that last night, and Jackie took the small room off the kitchen so Robert and Eddie could take the bedroom she'd shared with Jackie all these months. When they were settled in the room, all the changes in Eddie's life overwhelmed her. Wondering how she was going to leave them all, Robert held her as she cried.

"What if one of them dies before I can see them again?" she sobbed.

"You know where they're going," Robert comforted her. "You'll see them in heaven someday."

"Not my father," Eddie whispered fearfully. "I've never been sure about him."

"But he must be placed in God's care as well, Eddie. It's the only way you'll have peace."

Eddie continued to cry, and Robert prayed softly, his mouth close to her ear. Eddie calmed some and then kissed him with a kind of tender desperation. For a time their departure was forgotten.

In the morning only Morgan went with

them to the stage office. Eddie was trembling slightly, but God had touched her heart early that morning as she'd read the Word and prayed, and peace surrounded her. She was going to hurt over this departure, but this was what she had longed after and prayed for for months. She was Robert's wife, and it was right and good. Knowing that, she trusted God to take her on her way.

That afternoon Clayton picked the girls up from school and was not at all surprised to find them rather subdued. Milly had gained permission to stay and be with Danny for a time, and as it happened they all climbed out ahead of Jackie. She was just moving to step down when Clayton turned and spoke to her.

"Are you all right?"

Jackie sat back against the seat and looked at him. To his utter astonishment, he watched as tears filled her eyes. Clayton worked at not responding with the surprise he felt.

After a moment Jackie said, "I just can't believe she's gone. I gave her the bib as a joke, but she probably will have a baby, and I won't be there to be a part of it. There was talk that we might be together at

Christmas, but if Eddie's about to have a baby —" Jackie cut off and turned away. Clayton's voice came gently to her.

"Don't borrow trouble, Jackie. Eddie and Robert may not have children right away. It's impossible to know. And maybe your father will decide that all of you need to go and visit them this summer. So much can happen between now and then."

Sniffing, Jackie scrubbed at her face. Clayton watched her helplessly. Finally she turned back.

"Will you go and see them when you go to Denver this fall?"

"I don't know. I'd like to, but it all depends on my finances and studies."

Jackie nodded and glanced out over the snow-covered mountains and then down the canyon before looking back at him. He was still watching her. She hadn't wanted to talk about this on Saturday, and somehow he'd known that. Jackie thought he must like her some, but she was afraid to find out that she might be wrong.

"You had better get inside," Clayton said, breaking the silence, "or we're both going to freeze."

"Would you like to come in?" Jackie offered, feeling as though her heart had stopped.

"I'd love to," Clayton answered, his eyes drilling straight into Jackie's and causing what little breath she had left to lodge in her throat. "But I have some survey reports to chart before I leave town on Thursday."

Jackie told herself to make light of it. *Tell him you didn't mean it anyhow and that he's still a pest,* but the words would not come.

"I hope you'll ask me again," Clayton added, his eyes now smiling tenderly.

Jackie only nodded, her eyes still held by his.

"I will, Clayton. Thank you for the ride."

He watched as she climbed from the sleigh and then as she went toward the door. She turned and lifted a hand before she slipped inside, and Clayton managed to wave back in return. He was thankful that the horses knew the way home; he couldn't see anything but Jackie's huge blue eyes and the way they'd filled with tears.

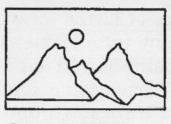

CHAPTER 15

The Fontaines found that spring did not come as swiftly to the Rocky Mountains as it did to New England. March passed into April and April headed toward May before there was any real sign of the snow leaving. They had a week of nearly hot weather, where the snow melted into rivers of water, but then they had a blizzard again the last week in May. Not until the first week in June did Georgetown begin to burst with new life, and when it got started there was no stopping it. Wildflowers bloomed in every direction, and the sight and sounds of local birds began to fill the air.

School was down to just four days when Miss Bradley gave the class an assignment. They were told to bring samples of the area's plant life to class for the following two days. They were divided into teams, and the goal was originality. Anything brought in that all the teams found counted for only a few points. Plants or flowers that just a few teams located were worth a little more. Foliage that no other team produced was worth nearly enough points to win the whole competition.

Paddy, Jackie, Milly, Danny, and Sammy had been assigned to a team, and they came from the schoolhouse with plans to start the hunt that very afternoon. To everyone's delight, Clayton was waiting for them. He'd not been home for well over a month, and the girls were not only excited to see him but ready to enlist his help.

"We need you, Tag," Sammy told him without any explanation. Clayton looked to Milly, who in her excitement, had left out many of the details.

"Aren't you supposed to do this on your own?" he finally questioned them.

"We will," Danny explained, "but our mothers are never going to let us go up on the ridge by ourselves. I mean, Paddy's with our team, but he might not be able to come. I know if you take us in the wagon, we can all go."

Clayton's eyes scanned the group. Sammy's face was filled with entreaty. Milly looked ready to argue if he said no, and Lexa was looking at some of the boys who rode horses to school and were now leaving. Jackie hadn't said anything during the conversation, but she was watching him with eager eyes.

"All right," Clayton said.

Shouts and cheers filled the air, and as the girls climbed in, Milly began to give orders like a drill sergeant.

"Okay, Tag. We'll drop the Fontaines at their houses so they can change. Then we'll rush to our house so I can change. Then we'll go pick them up. We know just the place we want to go, but we've got to be sneaky or we'll be seen."

"Why, pray tell, do we need to be sneaky?" Clayton's voice was dry with humor, but his sister was utterly serious.

"Clayton! This is a competition. If the others see where we go, we won't find anything unusual."

Clayton nodded, still not sure he understood. No one had bothered to explain the rules to him. He did as Milly asked, however, and it wasn't more than 30 minutes before they were back to get the Fontaine girls. Lexa was on another team and not all that interested in the hunt so she stayed home, but the rest had dressed in work clothes, and each had a basket. Addy came out to wave them off and warn them not to be overly late.

Not until they'd pulled away from the

house, though, did Danny lean close and say, "We're not going to the ridge."

"We're not?" Clayton asked, trying not to laugh at her conspiratorial tone.

"No. We only said that to throw the other kids off track. We want to go way down the creek to the meadow."

"All right," Clayton whispered back and Danny beamed at him.

"You're a good sport, Tag."

"Thank you, Danny. So are you."

The plan would have been ideal if several other groups hadn't thought of it. Clayton heard the girls sigh. He knew they were feeling let down. Surprisingly, Jackie, who usually said little in his presence, was the one to make everyone feel better.

"There are thousands of varieties out here, you know. We can go along the creek bed and probably still come up with something new. All of our houses are surrounded by plant life. We can always go home and try there."

"Yeah," Sammy said. "Let's start here and then try at home."

With that they piled from the wagon and walked through the grasses that would be knee-high by late summer. Although she was very aware of Clayton's presence, Jackie did nothing to show it. However, he was suddenly beside her, the others now racing on toward the banks of the creek.

"How are you?" Clayton asked politely.

"I'm fine. How was your trip?"

"Profitable. The land was extensive, far more than the owner thought, and we found an extra rock outcropping, ideal for mining. Which," Clayton added with delight, "brought in extra finances for everyone's pocket, including mine."

"So your schooling is all set?"

"Just about. I'll have to put in some time this summer, but it won't be outrageous."

"Where will you live?" Jackie suddenly asked.

"With my grandmother, as long as it works out."

"What could go wrong?"

They were at the creek now, and Clayton stopped by the water, a small tree at his back, his face reflective. "Nothing *wrong* exactly, but I'm not sure how far it is to the school, and my grandmother may have certain house rules that won't work for me. I'm not anticipating trouble, but I am trying to keep my mind open."

Jackie nodded. She wanted to say more, to be witty and amusing — anything to keep him talking — but no words would come. Feeling suddenly very shy with him, she knelt and began to pull flowers from the ground. Clayton took his cue from her and moved off a little way to do the same. While he was working over the grasses, it came to him very suddenly and without regret that Jackie was not the woman for him. At times his heart had dreamed of her taking an interest in him and even growing old enough to know her true feelings, but now he could see it was not going to work.

Clayton thought about Eddie and once again realized how he missed her. Although not in love with her, he did know she was the type of woman he was looking for. Maybe in a few years Jackie would be like that, but by then he would be away from Georgetown for most of the year. Depending on the available teaching positions, he might never live in Georgetown again. As he fingered a tiny bloom, Clayton felt an incredible peace steal over his heart. At one time he would have mourned not having something deeper with Jackie, but now it was all right.

He chanced a look in her direction and found her back to him. Clayton rocked back on his heels and just stared at the back of her. It was amazing, but now he felt utterly detached. Jackie could even fall in love and marry someone else right now, and Clayton would say nothing more than congratulations. He still cared, but then he cared for all of the Fontaine girls.

Clayton now looked over to see how the others were doing and rose to join them. He hadn't taken two steps when Jackie cried out.

"It's in my collar! What is it? I'm going to get stung!" She was frantic in a matter of moments, and Clayton rushed to her side.

"What is it?"

"I don't know," she howled. "I'm afraid to touch it."

Clayton saw what looked like a flutter of wings at her throat, and risking the sting, he reached up and plucked at the insect's legs.

"A grasshopper," Clayton said with relief and tossed it to the side. "Are you okay?"

"What's the matter?" Danny shouted from way along the creek line. Jackie turned in alarm. Milly and her sister had stopped to stare at her. She'd been screaming like she was on fire. Her face now reddened with embarrassment, and she turned swiftly away.

"It's nothing," Clayton, seeing her embarrassment, called to the others. He turned to Jackie. "Are you all right?"

She wouldn't look at him. "Yes, Clayton." She sounded angry. "I'm fine. Just leave me alone."

Clayton hesitated for only a moment. Turning to join the other girls, he realized he'd come to his new resolve just in time. He saw then that he'd been walking around Jackie as if on eggshells. Well, no more kid gloves. He was a kind, fair man, but he wasn't doing her any favors by putting her on a pedestal. From now on he was going to treat her like he did everyone else.

"I just don't understand," Milly admitted to her parents when Clayton was out one week. "First he tries to be kind to her, and she hates him. Then she's kind back, but now Clayton acts like he doesn't care one way or the other. He's back to teasing her. Jackie laughs more than she ever has and watches him whenever she doesn't think anyone notices, but Clayton's not making any effort to get closer to her."

Elaine sighed gently and made herself leave the dishes. Kevin was already at the table with Milly, so she joined them.

"May I tell you something, Milly?"

"Sure, Mom."

Elaine sat quietly for a moment and then began. "I think your father would agree with me if I told you that I'm not a very complicated person. I lived in the same house from the time I was born until I married your father. I had a father, mother, and brother who all loved me. I had my share of crushes on members of the male population, but nothing like what I felt when I met your father. I had some adjustments when he wanted to move from Denver to Georgetown, but our life here has been wonderful. I have you and your brother, and I have God's Word and your father. Your father and I have remained faithful to each other, and God has repeatedly blessed us. It hasn't always been easy, but God has taken care of us and we've kept our eyes on Him.

"I grew up next door to a girl whose name was Nadina. Some of the boys from church were attracted to Nadina, but she was always interested in the wild boys at school. We were fairly close, but she never wanted to talk about Christ or the things of the Bible. I realized later that my parents struggled with how close we were, but they prayed for me daily, and with God to strengthen me I was spared much heartache.

"Nadina and I haven't had any contact for years, but my mother used to keep me informed. Nadina never married but had babies with several different men. She eventually left them all, her children included, and went to California. The last I heard, she'd committed suicide."

Milly bit her lip, but she was still listening.

"Now, what's my point?" Elaine continued. "I'll tell you. We are all responsible for our choices, but sometimes life is complicated. Sometimes we cause the complication and sometimes others make it that way. I don't know why it was so different for Nadina and me, except to say that I was a simple girl."

"You understand that your mother is not talking about intelligence, don't you, Milly?" Kevin cut in. "She talking about how simple life can be if we obey God; not easy, but simple."

Milly nodded and Elaine went on. "I would say that Jackie is not a simple girl. Eddie is. Here they are, sisters, raised in the same home and yet completely different. Eddie trusted God for the man she loved, and she is able to give of herself. For reasons that no one seems to understand, Jackie guards herself carefully. If she were a poker player, I'd say she keeps her cards very close to her chest. She doesn't let herself out, nor does she let anyone in.

"When you can't give of yourself, Milly, your world is very small. Addy Fontaine came to town, and I befriended her. I took a risk. For all I know, she could have hurt and used me in a terrible way, but she didn't. Jackie is not willing to give of herself. She's pretty, so Clayton was probably attracted to her, but I think he's found that she's not the girl for him. Remember how you felt when Pastor Munroe's nephew was here?"

Milly was blushing, but she nodded.

"You wouldn't go out the door unless every hair was in place. We were late for church all summer because you took so much time in front of the mirror fretting over your appearance. Do you worry like that when Paddy's around?"

"No," Milly admitted with a smile.

"Do you understand what your mother is saying, Milly?" her father wished to know.

"I think so. Clayton can relax now because Jackie's just a friend."

"Right."

"How do you know all of this, Mom?"

"Clay has talked to your father off and on. His heart is so big and caring, but he wants a woman who will care as much as he does and not keep him at arm's length.

206

Changes come with age, but by 16 you can usually tell what a person is going to be like. Outgoing, independent, shy, talkative, bold, levelheaded . . ." Elaine shrugged. "It usually comes to the surface by the time you're Jackie's age. I think Clay is seeing this and feels that a relationship would not be what's best for both of them. Besides, he's leaving at the end of the summer. It will make it all the harder to leave if his heart is committed here in Georgetown."

Milly nodded. It made so much sense. Her young heart had prayed many times about this, and now she understood.

Had she only known it, she would have continued her prayers for someone down the road who was struggling as well — someone much closer to Jackie than herself.

"I wish I understood, Danny," Addy said softly, trying not to cry. "I told Jackie that she couldn't be afraid of the risk, and now Clayton treats her like anyone else. For a while there I thought there might be something special. I think she's going to feel betrayed."

Danny looked with compassion at her mother, but said, "She's having a better time with him these days, Mother. I mean, she's laughed more in the last few weeks

207

than I've seen her laugh in a long time."

Addy nodded. "She's missed Eddie more than any of us do."

"And in all fairness, Mother," Danny now spoke beyond her years, "Jackie is very prickly if she gets embarrassed. She's also arrogant and sometimes behaves like a child when she doesn't get her way. It's a wonder Clay even *wants* to befriend her."

Addy burst into tears, and Danny felt terrible. She went to her mother and sat close.

"I'm sorry, Mother; I shouldn't have said that."

Addy took several minutes to compose herself. Danny sat quietly, feeling utterly wretched.

"I'm sorry, Mother," she repeated.

"It's not your fault, Danny. You spoke the truth, but a mother never thinks it's going to happen to her child. A mother never thinks *her* child is going to be the unlovable one. Years ago I knew a girl who was so inquisitive that no one wanted anything to do with her. She listened in on conversations, read our diaries if she had the chance, and then went home and told her mother everything. She was so intrusive that we just shunned her." Addy sighed. "And now my own daughter is so hard to get close to that people won't even give her a chance."

Danny didn't know what to say, but a little bit of anger was kindling inside of her toward Clayton Taggart. She knew it wasn't his fault exactly, but Danny didn't want Jackie to be hurt.

"Have I upset you, Danny?" Her mother had been watching her face closely.

"I feel angry with Tag," she admitted.

Addy turned her daughter's face toward her and spoke gently, reminding herself that Danny was rather young to be burdened with this. "As you reminded me, honey, Jackie is having a good time with Clay right now. That means Jackie's hurt is probably bigger in my mind than in real life."

Danny nodded.

"You won't say anything?"

"No."

"Good girl. We'll just keep praying, Danny. We'll pray until we get this right."

CHAPTER 16

"Why do you want to teach school, Clay?" Jackie asked.

"Yeah, Tag," Sammy added. "I can't wait to be done with school, and you want to be there every day, all day!"

Clayton smiled at her incredulous tone but admitted, "It's just a dream I have." His voice turned wistful. "I love kids, and I love the thought of seeing them discover new things. I think to teach a child is to touch his life and help him to go out into the world more prepared."

Jackie stopped and stared. Sammy halted on the hot, dusty street as well. The three of them were a block off the main street of town. June had already turned to July, and Clayton, whose shirt was damp with perspiration, had to squint into the sun as he looked at both of them.

"What did I say?" he finally asked.

Jackie shrugged. "I've just never heard anyone talk about their work like that. For the first time I see how much this means to you."

"Then you haven't been very observant, Miss Fontaine," he teased her, "because I've been going on about this for months."

Jackie playfully put her chin in the air and walked on. Clayton tugged on her hair as she passed, and Sammy only smiled. They both heard Jackie sigh.

"We'd better get back, Sammy. Father will think we've left town."

"What will you do now, Tag?" Sammy asked him.

"Oh, I might get a haircut or just go to the livery and wait for Milton to finish the repairs on the wagon."

"I think you should come back to the store so we can put you to work," Jackie told him.

"Now who's being a pest?" Clayton asked and watched her laugh.

When they'd arrived back at the main street, Clayton said, "I'll see you two later." He turned and waved. The girls did the same and moved on toward the store. When they arrived at the store, just a few doors down, Jackie hesitated before going inside. She stood at the hardware door and watched Clayton go up the street, the sun turning his hair a shiny gold color. He moved past the barber shop and into the livery. Sammy observed her sister's actions, tilting her head to one side much like Eddie used to do.

"Are you going to marry Clay, Jackie?"

Jackie immediately dropped her eyes but did not grow angry. "He doesn't like me in that way, Sammy," was all she would say.

The younger girl didn't push the point. Jackie was relieved, but in her heart she was talking to Eddie as if she were present.

I did it, Eddie. I made friends with Clayton Taggart. And just like you said, he's wonderful to the people he cares for. Thanks, Eddie.

Sammy had moved into the store, and Jackie now followed more slowly, still thinking it was wonderful to have Clayton as a friend. And somehow, at that very moment, Jackie knew they would be friends forever. The fact that he was getting ready to leave in just a little over a month was not to be considered; Jackie had become very proficient at pushing it from her mind. She did so now as she went for the broom and began to work on the front walk.

The calendar read July 9, 1874, almost a year to the day that the Fontaines had arrived in town. Addy gave strict instructions to the girls about the day's activities before leaving for the store. Morgan had been suffering with a raging summer cold, and although he was feeling better, Addy actually convinced him to sleep in. Lexa would accompany her mother to the store, while the other girls were to work quietly and not bicker or disturb him.

Addy and Lexa let themselves in the back door and found that all was quiet. Addy wasn't certain but thought this might have been unusual. It seemed to her that Mitch was always up and around in the morning but tended to go to his apartment long before the store closed. Addy shrugged and got busy. Morgan enjoyed staying late and also coming in early. Mitch had surely begun to bank on that, and it gave him the freedom to lie-in once in a while.

However, as the first hour of work progressed, Addy became uncomfortable. She didn't wish to disturb the older man, but something was not quite right. When there were no customers in the store, she moved to the stairs.

"Lexa," Addy called to her, "I'm going to run up to your uncle's for a moment. Be certain to stay out front."

"All right, Mother," came the obedient reply as Lexa came from the rear and worked on a tall display of canned goods.

Morgan came in the back door just seconds after Addy left, and Lexa calmly told him where her mother had gone. Morgan nodded, still feeling a little out of sorts. He had come, telling himself that he must not overly burden Addy and the store couldn't run itself.

"Mitch?" Addy called softly as she knocked for the second time. There was still no answer. She bit her lip in indecision. She had never invaded his privacy before and only hoped as she turned the handle that he would understand her concern.

"Mitch?" she tried again, stepping into the hallway of his apartment. Things were dark and rather dreary for a summer day with all of the window coverings still drawn, but Addy knew where Mitch's bedroom was and moved quietly past the sitting room to that doorway. The door stood wide open. She peered into the rather shadowy interior and tried one more time.

"Mitch, are you all right?"

A low sound came from the direction of the bed, and Addy swiftly moved to the window. She drew back the heavy curtains on one window and then on the other before rushing to the bed.

"Mitch!" Addy's voice was low and urgent. "What is it, Mitch?"

The old man rasped. "It was bad last night, Addy . . . so bad."

"I'll get help, Mitch. Just hold on." Addy turned and fled the room. She dashed down the stairs, nearly falling in her haste and shouting to Lexa.

"Go for the doctor, Lexa! Hurry!" She was turning to dash back up to Mitch when she spotted a thunderstruck Morgan.

"Oh, Morgan, please come with me. Mitch is in a bad way."

She turned and ran once again to her brother-in-law's side. He hadn't moved in the bed at all. Addy grabbed a chair and positioned it close to his side. She bumped the edge of the mattress, and the old man's eyes suddenly opened.

"I'm sorry, Mitch." Addy was barely holding her tears. "I didn't mean to disturb you." Morgan had arrived as well and stood in the doorway, unnoticed by the two people within.

"It's all right, Addy. I need to rouse myself and talk to you."

"No, Mitch," she protested. "Just rest."

His head moved on the pillow. "I have things to say. The medicine is no longer helping. It won't be long now."

Addy spotted the small vial on the room's

lone nightstand and realized that this was no passing illness. She recalled how poorly he looked just before and after the wedding, but he had seemed fine later. She was going to tell him to see the doctor, but suddenly there hadn't seemed to be a need.

"Addy?"

"I'm listening, Mitch." Addy could say nothing else.

"Make sure he knows."

"Morgan?"

"Yes. There's more to this life than work and money. I took too long to find out, but it's true. Make sure he sees where his real treasure must be stored."

"I will." Tears poured down Addy's face. She reached to take Mitch's hand. His grip was surprisingly strong, and Addy wanted to sob.

"Tell the girls I love them," he managed. Before Addy could assure him, old Doc Edwardson came through the door.

He moved silently to the bed and picked up Mitch's wrist. The dying man struggled to open his eyes and look at him.

"You've been a horrible patient," the doctor scolded him gently. "You were supposed to come back and see me."

"Didn't need to. I still had medicine."

The doctor only grunted in reply.

Suddenly Mitch grabbed his hand. "Make sure Addy knows that I love her, Ed, and the girls too."

Doc Edwardson squeezed his patient's hand. "They know, Mitch. You've shown them a thousand times."

Mitch seemed to remember suddenly that Addy was there and turned to her. "It's meant so much to have you here, Addy. I can't say —"

Addy was sobbing now, feeling like her heart was going to burst, but still managed to reply, "I'm not ready for you to go, Mitch."

"I know, Addy. That's why you've got to make Morgan see."

The doctor, moving his head to look at the man still framed in the doorway, brought Addy's head around as well.

"Oh, Morgan," she said softly. "You're here. He's here, Mitch," Addy said, turning back to him. "You can tell him."

Feeling like a man in a nightmare, Morgan came forward awkwardly. He knew his brother hadn't been doing well and that he'd been tired lately, but death had never occurred to him. It just couldn't be. The doctor moved aside for him, and he forced himself to sit on the edge of the bed. Mitch immediately reached for his hand, and

Morgan grasped his firmly.

"I couldn't ruin the wedding," Mitch got out. "God brought you here so I could tell you the way, but you haven't listened. Addy understands, Morgan. Don't let your pride send you to hell. Ask her. Ask her today."

His breath left him with those words, and Addy heard a soft disturbance at the door. Her four daughters stood looking in, their eyes wide with fear and tears. Addy motioned them to the foot of the bed.

"The girls are here, Mitch," Addy told him gently.

"Good," he gasped. "Tell them, Addy. Tell them how much their Uncle Mitch loved them. Eddie and Robert too."

His eyes fluttered, and Addy's panicked gaze flew to Doc Edwardson, but he was taking Mitch's pulse.

"He's still with us," the physician spoke gently, "but it won't be long."

A shudder ran over Addy's frame. She wanted to cry, but she also wanted to be aware of everything. If she let herself go, she might miss someone needing her. She asked God for wisdom right then. This was so clearly His timing, and Addy, even in her grief, desperately wanted to be used to see to His work. A moment passed before she could find her voice, but a few seconds later she began to recite.

"The Lord is my shepherd; I shall not want. He maketh me to lie down in green pastures; he leadeth me beside the still waters. He restoreth my soul." All four girls joined her, their voices soft in the hushed room. "He leadeth me in the paths of righteousness for his name's sake. Yea, though I walk through the valley of the shadow of death, I will fear no evil; for thou art with me; thy rod and thy staff they comfort me. Thou preparest a table before me in the presence of mine enemies; thou anointest my head with oil; my cup runneth over. Surely goodness and mercy shall follow me all the days of my life; and I will dwell in the house of the Lord forever."

"Amen," Doc Edwardson spoke solemnly, and the girls moved around the bed to be near their mother. They would have gone to their father, but he looked carved from stone.

They all watched as Uncle Mitch moved slightly on the bed. He didn't thrash. His arm raised in seeming agitation, his breath came in a gasp, but his eyes remained closed. His hand then went to his chest, clutching at his nightshirt. Tears filled Addy's eyes once again as she thought he might be in pain. A second later he lay completely still.

Doc Edwardson moved to the bed one more time. He held Mitch's wrist for a long time and then gently laid the limp hand on the old man's chest. Then he stepped back and stood against one wall.

Addy was openly sobbing now, and so were the girls. Only the old doctor heard Morgan's hoarse voice when he said, "Goodbye, Mitch."

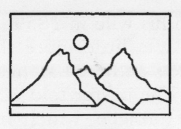

CHAPTER 17

It seemed that every resident of Georgetown turned out for the funeral of Mitchell Fontaine. Pastor Munroe held the service at the graveside, and it was to God's glory that he was able to point out the basis for the differences in Mitch's behavior in the last few years. His voice was kind as he spoke, but his words carried great weight.

"I could stand here and tell you that Mitch was a good man, and it would be true. I might also tell you that because he was good, we know he is in heaven, but there I must draw the line. Mitchell Fontaine is not in heaven because of anything he did. Mitch is in heaven because of his belief in Jesus Christ and His saving work on the cross. You may not want to hear or accept this — Mitch almost didn't — but he understood his need before it was too late."

Pastor Munroe talked a little bit about Mitch's life in Georgetown. He'd come to the area with his wife in 1859. At that time Georgetown was little more than a settlement of miners gathered along Clear Creek to prospect. The pastor told of some of the civic-minded projects Mitch had been involved with, and with his eyes on the crowd, some of whom were the wealthiest mine owners in town, he ended with yet another word about Mitch's decision, urging anyone in need to come to him.

"There will be some of you who think I only want more money for the church, but nothing could be further from the truth. Our church building does have some minor needs, but nothing compares to the need for all of you to know Christ."

Long after the crowd had pressed close to share their regrets and then moved on their way, the Fontaines stood by the grave. Sammy was inconsolable for many minutes.

"I need to see Eddie," she kept repeating. "She's going to be so upset, and she's so far away. I have to see Eddie." She sobbed uncontrollably against Danny's side. Not even her father, lifting her in his arms, could abate the storm.

"She has Robert." Addy came close to her husband's shoulder in an attempt to console her youngest daughter. "He'll take care of her."

"I know, Mother," Sammy replied, the tears still falling, "but she's so far away, and I know she'll be just crushed when she hears."

And indeed Sammy was correct. Eddie was very upset to hear of her uncle's passing. Robert delivered the telegram himself and held her while she sobbed. However, Eddie's greatest tears were for her father.

"I don't know what he'll do now, Robert," she cried. "He's lived with Mother for so long, and nothing has ever touched him. Now, Uncle Mitch, the man who could have helped, is gone."

"We can't stop trusting, Eddie. God will find a way. He always does."

Eddie continued to cry in her husband's arms, but she prayed as well. She prayed with all of her heart that her father would be touched. If she could only have seen through the walls of her parents' bedroom the next night, she'd have prayed for her mother as well.

Mitch had been buried for little more than 48 hours when Morgan responded to the things his brother had said. His response was not volcanic, but it was unsettling to Addy. They were getting ready for bed, and Addy could feel his tension from across the room.

"That's a fine way to end things with my brother." The statement came from out of nowhere. Addy turned, her blouse clutched in her hands.

"What do you mean?"

"I mean," Morgan replied as he nearly tore his necktie off, "it's just fine to learn when Mitch is on his deathbed that he thinks I deserve to go to hell."

Addy forced herself to hang the blouse in the closet. "That isn't what he said, Morgan."

"Oh, really." Morgan's sarcasm was biting. "Just exactly what did he mean? He seemed to think that you would have all the answers, so why don't you tell me just exactly what my brother meant."

"I don't think you're in any mood to hear it."

"*Don't* patronize me!" The words were like a lash, but Addy remained outwardly calm as she turned to him.

"My grief is as great as yours, Morgan. Please don't take this out on me."

Addy turned away and unbuttoned her skirt. Morgan watched her. He wanted answers, but he was so angry that he could have put his fist through a wall. He was still just standing and staring, the tie dangling from his fingers, when Addy began to brush out her hair. Only the normalcy of her routine kept her from bursting into tears. She was nearly done with her hair when Morgan forced himself to speak calmly.

"What did Mitch mean when he said my pride would send me to hell?"

Addy turned away from the mirror.

"I believe he was speaking to the fact that you think all good, hardworking people go to heaven."

"What's wrong with that?"

"It's not true, Morgan; that's what's wrong with it."

"How can you say that?"

"I don't say it." Addy kept her voice neutral. "The Bible says it."

"So you're telling me," Morgan returned, his voice was filling with rage all over again, "that all I've done, all I've worked for my whole life, isn't worth a thing?"

"Morgan, are you sure you want to talk about this?"

"*Yes!*"

Addy started and wished she hadn't asked. However, her own irritation was raised just enough to speak boldly. She knew this was not the right time — his grief was too fresh — but if Morgan wanted it, she would give it to him.

"Nothing we do outside of Christ is

225

worth a thing. Outside of Christ it's all useless." Addy's hand went into the air when Morgan opened his mouth. "And don't you dare ask me, Morgan, why I think you are outside of Christ. You know very well that something is missing in your life."

Morgan's eyes were fierce at this point, but Addy kept on. It was a temptation to rail at God for putting her in this position, but she thought she might have been too passive in the past. With a deep breath she continued.

"You go into church with your family well dressed and well behaved and line them up in a row and hope that God notices. You actually tell the girls that God is impressed if we're on time, yet you don't live like Christ matters. Your Bible looks like the day I gave it to you. The Bible says, in 2 Corinthians 5, 'If any man be in Christ he is a new creature; old things have passed away; behold all things are become new.' If that hasn't happened to you, Morgan, then Mitch is indeed right. You're going to hell."

Morgan's gaze could have drilled holes into Addy. He wanted to storm from the room, but his feet wouldn't move. How could she say this to him? He'd worked hard and been a fine provider. His eye didn't stray. What man wasn't tempted by the sight of a beautiful woman? But he had been faithful to Addy since the day he met her.

"Morgan," Addy's voice came softly to his ears. "It has to be God's way. All the girls came to Christ as little children because it's the easier way. We get older and our pride gets huge and then we try and tell God how we're going to come to Him. Only it won't work. He makes the call, and if we don't abide by it we're lost."

"So you think I'm a failure?"

Addy felt defeat wash over her. It was as if he didn't have a clue. She went to him and held his face in her hands.

"Morgan, you've been a wonderful husband and father, and you will go on being so, but something is missing. I think you can feel it, but you don't want to acknowledge it. All I'm asking is that you keep your mind open. You're so certain you have all the answers that you don't even listen. Pastor Munroe is not to be merely tolerated; he's there to teach us. The next time he speaks about heaven and how to get there, listen with your whole heart."

The room was shadowy, but he could see tears standing in Addy's eyes. He put his arms around her and felt her tremble, or was that his own body? Could he really be

227

wrong after all these years? And if he was, did good people really go to hell? Morgan's eyes shut in agony. He'd been so sure, and now his soul was in misery.

Better misery now, Morgan, than an eternity in hell. Where the thought came from Morgan couldn't say, but he was going to listen, this much was sure. He now tightened his arms around his wife, desperately needing to feel her close. He was scared. Like a child alone in a dark forest, he was terrified. It was a new sensation for him, and right now Addy seemed to be all that was real. He held onto her with a new desperation, not talking, just needing to have her close.

"You heard baby birds?" one little girl asked another.

"Yes. I know it's late, but they must have just hatched."

"I can't believe you were even in Henderson's field."

"Well, I was late getting home, so I had to cut across."

"Did your mother find out?"

"No."

The girls moved on, but their words echoed in Jackie's ears. Baby birds in Henderson's field. She knew where that was. And in July! Jackie glanced at the big clock on the wall. It was 1:15. She was done in the store today at 2:30. She had some chores to do at home, but she was certain she could work in a trip to see the birds' nest and still arrive home in plenty of time to do them. Henderson's property was off the beaten path, but it would be worth the walk.

Jackie suddenly looked down at her dress and scowled. What in the world had possessed her to wear something so dressy to work? The lavender fabric even had a row of snow-white lace a foot up from the hem! She continued to scowl at her own foolhardiness, but her frown soon faded to a look of wistfulness. She knew very well why she'd dressed up. She hadn't seen Clayton since right after Uncle Mitch's funeral and hoped beyond all hope that he would make an appearance today. So far it hadn't happened.

"Jack," her father's voice suddenly snatched her out of her dreams.

"Yes?"

"Take this in the back and put it on the shelf with the others." Morgan handed her a small satchel. "We have enough out front already. When you're through with that, sweep the front walk."

"All right."

"When are you done today?" His question stopped her before she could move six feet.

Jackie turned back, her heart beating with sudden fear.

"Two-thirty."

"All right," Morgan said as he turned away. Jackie's breath returned in a rush. She had thought he was going to say she needed to stay late. Her step was light as she moved to the back room and then to the front walk, the straw broom in her hand.

Two hours later, puffing from the warmth of her dress and the exertion, Jackie stopped below the tree in Henderson's field. There was only one, and she had to climb a fence to get to it, but she had arrived. She stood very still to calm her breathing, and then she heard them: Baby birds chirping and crying out to be fed. She stepped immediately underneath the overhanging branches and strained to see the nest. It was too high.

She knew they would be cute, and she had such a soft spot for baby animals. However, if she tore this dress, her mother would not be pleased.

"But if I don't see the nest," Jackie now spoke to the tree. "I've come all this way for nothing."

"Talking to yourself, Jackie?"

Jackie spun in surprise toward the voice and smiled as she spotted Clayton. He sat atop his horse, Miner, on the other side of the fence.

"Now what makes you think I'm alone," Jackie asked with a flirting glance. She started toward him. "There might be a handsome young man courting me from the tree."

He spoke when she'd stopped at the fence and looked up at him, her eyes sparkling with good humor.

"Now," Clayton drawled charmingly, "I wouldn't be calling you a liar, Miss Fontaine, but I think the only company you have out here is Henderson's bull."

"Is that right?" She sounded quite skeptical. "I think you might be doing the lying, Mr. Taggart. *I* haven't seen a bull."

Clayton's humor fell away. "He does have a bull, Jackie. I don't know if he's out right now, but Henderson does pen a bull in this field."

"Oh." Jackie turned serious, and looked in all directions behind her. She still didn't see anything, but the little girls' conversation from the store now made more sense.

"How'd you get in there?" Clayton suddenly asked, shifting in his saddle to scan the fence line. He spotted the gate across the way.

"Now that would be telling," Jackie said,

but she was looking away. She could feel her cheeks heating. Indeed, she had climbed over at a low spot in the fence but didn't care to admit this.

"Do you want some help getting out?"

"No, thank you." Jackie tried to sound nonchalant, but when she finally looked at him, she found he was eyeing her strangely. She watched as he pushed his hat back on his head.

"Everything okay?"

"Yeah." Jackie's eyes were huge, and she could feel her face going red all over again.

Clayton felt hesitant to leave her but told himself he'd have to take her at her word. She was acting very embarrassed about something, but he couldn't imagine what. He wondered at that moment if she might indeed be meeting a young man. It would certainly account for her behavior, but within Henderson's fence? The guy must not be very romantic.

"You're sure you're okay?"

"I'm sure."

"I best be off then." Clayton adjusted his hat low over his forehead again. "I'll see you later, Jackie."

"Bye, Clay," Jackie said with a smile and then stood very still as he moved away. She sighed softly as the horse took his broad back out of view. She turned back to the tree, but suddenly the thought of seeing the birds wasn't all that enticing. If Clayton had stayed to see them with her, she would have enjoyed it, but telling him the reason she'd come this far out had seemed so childish.

Jackie stood below the tree and listened to the sound of chirping again. She reminded herself again that the tree would tear her dress if she tried to climb it, so with a rather slow, disappointed step, she started back the way she had come.

The tree was a little farther than the fence when she heard the hoofbeats, but she panicked at the sight of a bull charging her and turned to run like the wind back to the haven of its branches. She swung herself up into the limbs with an agility she didn't know she possessed and watched with horrified eyes as the bull ran a ways past the tree, snorting and stomping and looking for her.

Jackie was afraid to breathe. She moved only her head to see his every move, but the bull soon lost interest and wandered a short way off to graze. Jackie would have groaned if she hadn't been so afraid. How would she ever get home? Not even the sight of the birds, which she finally remembered to look at, could cheer her.

She tried to gauge just how fast she could run compared to the distance to the fence, but knew it was foolhardy in long skirts. She shifted around a bit in an effort to see the bull again, but a small branch gave way beneath her foot and for a second she was hurtling toward the ground. She stopped with a loud scream as she was driven pencil-like into a small square of branches. Her legs felt scraped, and she could feel that her skirts were twisted tightly around her knees, baring her stocking-clad legs from the calves down.

As soon as she landed she pressed her hand tightly over her mouth to keep from howling again. Her scream had alerted the bull, and he was back under the tree, looking in all directions. Jackie was sure if he looked up and spotted her he could stab her foot with his horn, so she didn't move a muscle — not even when a tear trickled down her face. She kept herself frozen until he once again moved on his way.

With that her mind began to move as well, and the thoughts were not happy. The image of being stranded here after dark, left alone in the blackness, was enough to make her tremble all over with fear. If she thought it would have helped she would have shouted with all of her voice for her father.

Indeed, she was on the verge of doing this when a tiny peep from the nest diverted her.

Jackie looked at them and knew they were getting hungry. The mother was naturally frightened away by her presence. *They can't even get their dinner until I'm out of here,* she thought miserably. What in the world am I going to do? A tear came, and then another, but no answers.

The wind blew through the tree just then, a cool wind, and Jackie shivered from more than just the cold. When the temperature dropped in Georgetown, nighttime was on its way. Jackie tried to move her legs, but she was jammed tight, and it hurt to shift even a little. Not bothering to subdue the noise this time, her tears came in a torrent of weeping. She was going to be stuck in the tree all night.

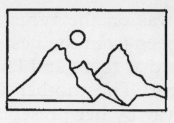

CHAPTER 18

"She wasn't at the store, Mother. Father said she left right at 2:30."

"Thank you, Lexa," Addy spoke from her place near the oven. Danny came into the room just then.

"Danny, have you seen Jackie?"

"No, not all afternoon."

Addy bit her lip for just an instant.

"Danny," she said, "run over to the Taggarts' and ask there, will you? Come right back and tell me whether she's been there or not."

"All right, Mother."

She left and Addy gave way to her concern, her face mirroring the anxiety within until she realized both Sammy and Lexa were watching her.

"Are you worried, Mother?"

"A little," she admitted, trying to smile. "It's nearly dark, and Jackie always does her chores."

The younger girls nodded and exchanged

a glance. Danny had exited a few minutes before, but every heart was with her as she walked down the road to the Taggart property.

"What's up?"

Clayton had just come in from outside to find Milly and his mother standing close by the front door. Elaine turned to him.

"Danny was just here looking for Jackie." She sounded preoccupied with her thoughts and didn't really notice the way Clayton tensed.

"She was finished at the store at 2:30," Milly added, "but no one's seen her since."

Even as she spoke, Clayton was reaching for the hat he'd just set down. "Go to the Fontaines, Milly. Tell them I saw her in Henderson's field this afternoon. If I'm not back here within a half hour, send help."

"Clayton," Elaine called before he could leave.

"Yes," he answered, stopping with his hand on the knob.

She looked frightened but managed, "Are you thinking she's been hurt? I mean, Henderson's bull is —"

"I don't know, Mom," he cut her off gently. "I'll be back just as soon as I find out."

Elaine had little choice but to let him go, but the direction of her thoughts caused her to tremble. Milly went out the front door at the same time to take word to the Fontaines. Elaine, a dishtowel still in her hand, sank down at the kitchen table to pray.

Jackie had been trying to pray for hours, but her mind was going numb. The light was already so dim that the mountains that rimmed the valley were beginning to lose shape. Evening was falling and her panic caused her to lose all reason. It even took a moment for her to hear the hoofbeats over the pounding of the blood in her ears. She twisted around frantically to see who was coming and nearly went to pieces when the rider came close but began to move away.

"Father?" she cried in a pitiful squeak. "Is that you, Father?"

"Jackie?"

It was Clayton's voice.

"Clay. Oh, Clay." Her voice was only a little louder.

"Where are you?"

"In the tree," she said before the tears came and took her voice away. She cried with relief but also pain. Her legs were in agony. *Her legs!* The words shouted in her head. This was not her father coming, but

Clayton, and her white-stockinged legs were exposed like a picture she'd seen one time of a dance-hall girl.

In the midst of all these tumultuous thoughts, she heard the horse draw near. Clayton must have come inside the fence. A moment later she looked down and saw him below her.

"Are you all right?" he asked.

"No, I'm not," she told him, sniffing. "It's getting dark, and I can't get free."

"Here." Clayton had moved until he was directly below her feet. "If I push your feet up, maybe you can grab the branch above you. Can you try?"

"Yes."

Clayton caught the sole of a shoe in each palm and pushed. The position was nearly impossible for leverage, but it gave Jackie just enough room to work. One foot lifted away from him to step on a strong branch and then the other followed. Clayton backed Miner off so he wasn't directly below her and then looked up to see her progress. She was standing easily now, but she was so far off the ground that he knew she shouldn't jump.

Clayton moved in yet again. "Here, Jackie, come down to this branch and then step down to me."

"Where's the bull?" Her voice wobbled.

"I can't see him right now." Clayton ducked his head to look around the field. "He must have wandered off. Go ahead and jump to me."

Jackie finally heard what he had said to her.

"You mean onto the horse?"

"Yes. I'll catch you."

"Oh, Clay . . ." Jackie's voice was trembling again.

"It's all right," he coaxed, and after several minutes' worth of soothing words she jumped. Clayton caught her just as he'd promised and settled her across the front of the saddle. She was trembling violently, and for a moment he kept his arms around her.

"Are you okay?"

"I just wanted to see the birds," she stuttered. "And then the bull came and my dress caught and they couldn't eat!" She was gripping his hand hard now. "They couldn't even eat while I was there, and they sounded so hungry."

It was too much for Jackie. She buried her face in her grubby hands and sobbed. Clayton knew it was time to get home. He heeled Miner forward to the gate and left the pasture. Jackie's shoulder was against his chest, and she was still crying into her hands. He didn't know what to say. Horrible images had flashed through his mind as he'd ridden to find her. He had been tortured with thoughts that she might have met some young man who tried to hurt her, and here she had only innocently come to see a bird's nest and ended up being chased by a bull.

"It's all right, Jackie," Clayton said when she began to calm. He looked up to see a rider coming toward them. "I think your father is coming."

Jackie's head snapped up. It was indeed Morgan.

"Please let me down, Clayton."

Clayton stopped immediately and helped Jackie to the ground. Her legs nearly buckled, and he leaned to keep hold of her hands, but a moment later he watched as she flew toward her father. The older man had come off his horse, and Clayton could hear her cries from dozens of yards away as Morgan held and comforted his daughter.

"It was getting dark," he heard her gasp as he drew near.

"I know, but I've got you now, Jack." Morgan looked up at Clayton. "She seems unhurt — just upset."

"Yes. The bull chased her, and then she couldn't get out of the tree."

Morgan nodded, but darkness was falling fast now, and Clayton could see him only dimly.

"I'll get home now," Clayton said, "before anyone worries any longer."

"Thank you, Clay," Morgan said simply. Because Jackie's legs still hurt, Morgan lifted her onto the horse. He led the animal home rather than sit with her, talking in calm tones as they moved. As soon as they arrived, Addy put Jackie to bed. She hovered over her for a long time and left a light burning in her room until she had fallen asleep. Addy still didn't know exactly what had happened, but at the moment it didn't matter. Some of the lace on Jackie's dress was torn, but she was home safe, and they could all start to breathe again.

"Hello." The word came quietly from Clayton as he came soft-footedly into the Fontaines' living room.

It was the afternoon of the next day. Jackie had heard her mother open the front door but hadn't heard the voices. She should have been working at the store this day, but her father had insisted she stay home.

"Hello, Clay," Jackie returned, putting her book aside.

"I came to see how you were doing." He sat in the chair across from her and thought she looked a little pale.

"I'm all right, but I managed to scare the life out of my father. He wants me to take it easy for a few days."

"That's not a bad idea," Clayton agreed, but Jackie only shrugged.

"What are you doing today?"

"Not much. My dad is due in any time, and when he comes back we'll be headed back out."

"You don't usually wait for him, do you?"

"No, but unless he needs me, I won't be going at all. I leave here in three weeks, and I want to spend as much time as possible at home."

"Three weeks?" Jackie questioned him quietly. "I thought you would be here until the end of August."

"No. I've decided to go earlier."

It was a good thing that Jackie's face was already pale, or Clayton might have questioned her more than he did. His simple words were enough to make her want to howl with dismay. He was going away. Not in six weeks, but in three. What in the world would she do?

"Are you sure you're all right?" Clayton asked.

243

"Yeah," Jackie lied, forcing a smile. "Thanks for coming to the rescue last night." She was pleased with her quick recovery. "I wasn't certain if I'd thanked you. It was so silly to be caught in that tree, and well, thanks, Clay."

"You're welcome," he told her warmly, relieved that her strained features were from thoughts about the night before. For a moment his mind dwelt on the whole incident. "Why does the darkness frighten you?"

Clayton watched her frown and look a bit irritated. He wished he had kept the question to himself. "Were you hurt?" he asked to fill the breech.

"Only some scratches on my legs." Jackie's face was expressionless, the irritation gone.

"I'm glad it was nothing worse."

The conversation was trailing off, and Jackie simply didn't have the stamina to keep things going. Usually all she had to do was ask Clayton about school and he would start talking fifteen to the dozen, but if she even thought about his schooling right now or how she'd felt the night before, she was going to burst into tears.

It wasn't a surprise that Clayton rose to leave just a few minutes later.

"I think I'd best get on my way, Jackie.

You still seem a little tired."

She managed to smile. "Yesterday was a long day."

"Well, take it easy. I'll see you later."

"Bye, Clay."

Jackie sat for a long time after he left. In fact, she was so quiet that Addy forgot she was even home. She wandered past the living room a little later and started in surprise.

"Jackie," she said with a hand on her heart. "You're so quiet that I forgot all about you." It was then she saw the tears in her daughter's eyes.

"What is it, honey?"

"He's leaving, Mother. In three weeks he's leaving. I thought it was six, but it's only three."

Addy came close now and sat on the arm of Jackie's chair. She couldn't find any words, but it didn't seem to matter. Jackie buried her face in her mother's lap and sobbed.

The next day began like any other for the Taggart family, except that Elaine was a little quieter than usual. Both of the children noticed but didn't comment. They missed their father as well, and talking about it wouldn't bring anything more than tears.

They both went about their daily chores with quiet efficiency.

Elaine was thankful for their lack of intrusion, because in truth she did not want to share what was on her heart. She had woken early, around 4:00 A.M., with an awful sense of pain. She wasn't actually hurting, but her breathing felt constricted and her body ached all over. She rose very quietly and checked on Clayton and Milly. When she found them both sleeping soundly, she returned to her bedroom to pray. She was well, and her children were unharmed, so it had to be something else.

Elaine had experienced this feeling once before — it was over five years ago now. Kevin had been late, and when he'd finally arrived home, she learned he'd been bitten by a rattlesnake. His leg was still swollen, and he was laid low for more than a week. Now the feeling was on her again. Elaine knelt by the bed she shared with her husband and let her head fall on his pillow.

I can feel something is amiss, Lord, she prayed in her heart. *I am not given to flights of fancy, but I know Kevin is hurt. He may even be with You right now. I trust You, Father. Give me the grace to make it through whatever You have for us. I would want him back, You know this, but You also know what's best. Help the children in this, Lord. Help them to keep trusting You no matter what.*

A tear slid down her face, a tear of pain for the man she loved. She hated the thought of his being alone and hurting, so she prayed that if he was injured, someone would find him soon.

I would like to see him one more time, Lord. I admit this freely to You, but again I ask You to help me to trust and believe. Touch Kevin now, Father. Help him to keep his eyes firmly fixed on You, no matter what the pain or circumstances.

When it was time for breakfast, Elaine rose stiffly from the floor to dress for the day, but she prayed often as the day progressed. In fact, she prayed constantly. It was just after lunch before she had any real idea as to why she felt so burdened.

Cormac O'Brien pulled into the yard with his longbed wagon. Kevin's horse was tied to the back, and Kevin lay in the wagon bed. There was no color in Elaine's face as she took in the sight of her husband's body, but seeing him didn't paralyze her. Cormac was talking, and she was listening to every word and already moving to do what had to be done.

"They brought him in in the back of a wagon."

"Is he dead?"

"I think he might be. Clayton was uptown, and Paddy came running into the bank to find him."

The sound of Clayton's name brought Jackie's head around. Fontaine's General Store was filled with almost as much gossip as the barber shop, and Jackie had already learned to block out most of it. However, Clayton's name was another matter.

"What happened?" Jackie broke a firm rule and intruded into the conversation.

"Kevin Taggart's been hurt, or maybe killed. They've sent for the doc."

"How?"

"I don't know, dear, but land surveyors live a dangerous life. He could have fallen or been attacked by a wild animal."

The older woman who was speaking finished her sentence, but Jackie didn't hear. She was already moving to find her father.

"Father, I have to go to the Taggarts'. Mr. Taggart has been hurt, and I have to see if they need me."

"Your mother was just here and told me, Jack. She'll go and see what needs to be done."

Morgan started to turn away, but Jackie grabbed his arm with bruising strength.

"Father," she spoke, her heart in her eyes. "I *have* to go."

Morgan looked down into her face and saw that it was true. She looked ready to come undone if he turned her down. And anyway, if she was that determined to go, she would be of no use in the store.

"All right, Jack."

The words were barely out of his mouth before Jackie ran for the door. Her father called something after her, but she never heard. Her mind was already at the Taggarts' wondering how she could be of the most help.

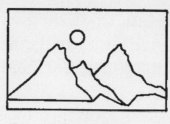

CHAPTER 19

Jackie knew better than to knock at the front door and disturb the goings-on within, but neither was she comfortable just walking inside Clayton's house. It was for this reason that she stood outside for quite some time and prayed.

"Please, God," she said softly. "Show me how I can help here. Show me what to do or say."

Doubts began to assail her. Reaching out to others was so new to Jackie that she didn't know where to start. Eddie and her mother always knew what to do, as did Danny, but Jackie was a complete novice. Jackie didn't know if she'd have made it inside at all, but Paddy's father chose that moment to come out.

"No need to knock, Jackie," he spoke kindly to her in his thick brogue. "Just go on in."

"Thank you, Mr. O'Brien." Jackie smiled with genuine relief and slipped inside.

The living room was empty, and surprisingly, so was the kitchen. Jackie could hear voices in the rooms upstairs, but she couldn't make herself go up those steps. She was casting her eyes around the room, still praying for help, when she spied the coffeepot. It was cold to the touch and not very full.

Jackie fought back tears of relief. *This* she could do. *This* she could handle. With simple movements and an efficiency born of years of practice, she made the coffee. From there she searched for food and began to cut vegetables for a soup. She had just started it in a big pot on the stove when she heard someone on the stairs. Milly came partway into the room and stopped in surprise when she saw her.

"Hello, Milly."

"Hi, Jackie." Her voice told of her wonder.

"I . . . um . . . just came to see if I could help. I took it upon myself to make some coffee and start some dinner. It's just soup, vegetable soup."

"Thank you."

"Would you like some coffee?"

Milly could only nod before she sank into a kitchen chair. Jackie poured her some coffee and sat across from her.

"Is your father going to be all right, Milly?"

"They don't know," she whispered. "His horse stumbled and rolled. It rolled right on top of him." Tears filled her eyes. "He can't feel his legs."

"Oh, Milly."

"He says he wishes he were in pain. He said it wouldn't be so scary that way." With that, Milly buried her face in her hands and sobbed. Jackie fought her own tears and pulled a handkerchief from the pocket of her skirt. She pressed it into Milly's hands. Milly worked at controlling herself, but it took a moment. After that they sat in silence with their coffee, a bit uncomfortable, but not as strained as usual.

Addy and Elaine came down the stairs a little later. The girls heard them talking as they came.

"He hasn't eaten for two days, but the doctor says to take it easy. No meat, and maybe a little bit of soup."

"I'll start that for you, Elaine," Addy offered.

"Jackie put soup on," Milly said, breaking into their conversation. Both women stopped and looked at Milly first and then Jackie. Jackie felt herself go red.

"It's not very fancy." Her hands moved nervously.

"Thank you, Jackie," Elaine told her sincerely.

Jackie looked over to see her mother smiling. It was a proud smile, and once again Jackie fought her tears. She hadn't felt this emotional since Eddie and Robert's departure or Uncle Mitch's death.

As soon as the Fontaine women were certain that everything was under control, they left. Addy explained to Jackie on the walk home that all they could do was wait. It was everyone's prayer that Kevin would regain some sensation in his legs, but right now, they waited.

Jackie fretted about how she could help, but almost of its own course, a pattern had been started. Jackie could be found at the Taggart home morning, noon, and evening. If she found dishes, she washed them. If coffee was needed, she made it, along with breakfast, lunch, or dinner. And when she wasn't in the Taggart kitchen baking or cleaning, she was home in her own kitchen baking cookies or bread to take to them. If she arrived and there was nothing to be done, she left as quietly as she had come. The Taggart family rarely saw her, only evidence that she'd been there.

One evening, about ten days into this schedule, Jackie was still finishing up in the kitchen when Elaine and Clayton arrived on the scene. They'd both been upstairs, and

Jackie was a bit flustered in Clayton's presence. She was glad to be able to say she was on her way out the door.

"Please walk Jackie home, Clay," Elaine said after she'd thanked the young woman.

"Oh, no," Jackie protested softly. "I'll be fine."

But Clayton was already reaching for his hat, and Jackie did not want to make a scene. They walked silently out the front door. Jackie felt a little silly. It wasn't even dark yet.

"There really isn't a need, Clay. I know you want to be close to your family, and I can get home alone."

Clayton suddenly stopped on the road, and Jackie stopped beside him. He looked down at her. Jackie wished she could read his thoughts.

"I haven't thanked you," he said with surprise.

"For what?"

"For all your help at the house."

Embarrassed, Jackie shrugged and started to turn away. Clayton caught her arm. He held it for just a moment, and then let his hand drop. His eyes now lifted to the craggy, snow-topped mountains.

"I never dreamed of how it might feel to see my father laid up. I mean, he's always been the strong one." He looked back at Jackie. "My world has become that bedroom, Jackie. I sit in there most of the day, and when I go downstairs to my bedroom I think about being in there most of the night."

Jackie saw for the first time how tired he looked.

"He teaches me so much. He may never walk again, but he still has a smile on his face and praise for God when he speaks. Do you know what he said to me last night?"

Jackie was forced to shake her head, but her eyes encouraged him.

"He said, 'I may have lost the use of my legs, Clay, but my soul still has wings.'" Tears filled Clayton's eyes. "Why didn't we take the time before to really study God's Word, Jackie? I mean, we've always had Bible time before breakfast, but not like this, not with such depth and meaning." A tear spilled over. "Why did it take his getting hurt for me to see how important it is?"

Clayton's hand came to his face as he tried to quell the flood, but his tears would not be stopped. Jackie wanted to die with the pain of it. Her friend was hurting, and she couldn't do a thing. She reached for his hand but pulled back, afraid that her gesture would be taken wrong. A moment later, Clayton's tears subsided, but his breathing was still hoarse and deep.

He hadn't looked at Jackie, but now he did. To his amazement, he felt no shame. She stood looking at him, her expression tender and tears filling her own lovely eyes.

"You're a good friend, Jackie Fontaine."

"You are too, Clay. I just wish I could do more."

"You've been a great help."

Jackie nodded. "Please tell your father that I'm praying for him."

"I'll do that."

"Go on home now, Clay. I'll get myself home."

"All right."

Jackie turned and started away and didn't look back. However, she knew that Clayton stood on the road and watched until she reached her own yard.

Jackie wasn't the least bit hungry when she arrived so she begged off from dinner and went to her room. She took time to pray for Mr. Taggart, but her mind kept going back to what Clayton had said.

Her family never read the Bible together. In their family spending time with God's Word was up to each person, and the truth was, Jackie had never taken an interest in her Bible. Not like her mother and Eddie always did, and certainly not like Clayton and his father. For the first time in years she pulled it out and turned to a place in Jeremiah. There was a little marker at that spot, and she tried to remember why it was there. She read it to see if she could find a clue.

Starting in chapter 23, verse 19, she read softly aloud, "Behold, a whirlwind of the Lord is gone forth in fury, even a grievous whirlwind; it shall fall grievously upon the head of the wicked. The anger of the Lord shall not return, until he have executed, and till he have performed the thoughts of his heart; in the latter days ye shall consider it perfectly. I have not sent these prophets, yet they ran; I have not spoken to them, yet they prophesied. But if they had stood in my counsel, and had caused my people to hear my words, then they should have turned them from their evil way, and from the evil of their doings. Am I a God at hand, saith the Lord, and not a God afar off? Can any hide himself in secret places that I shall not see Him? saith the Lord. Do not I fill heaven and earth? saith the Lord."

Jackie did not understand much of what she read, but one thing had jumped out at her. Was God a far-off God, or was He near? Most times she would say He was very far off, but she closed her Bible and went to join her family before she could really gain an answer.

"I want you to go to school."

"No." For the first time in his life Clayton out-and-out defied his father.

"I'm not asking you, Clay. I'm telling you. Go to school."

"Absolutely not."

"It starts next week, Clay. I'm sure I won't be laid up here forever, and you've got to get there."

Clayton shook his head. His voice was gentle, but he held his jaw at a stubborn angle. "I'm going back to work tomorrow, and that's the end of it."

"We don't need the money," Kevin said, but he knew it was a half-truth.

Clayton looked clearly skeptical.

"We're good for a time, Clay. Please do as I ask you."

Clayton shook is head. "It's foolish to deplete your savings account when I'm capable of supporting this family."

"You're not touching your money for school, Clay." Kevin's voice went up a notch. "Do you hear me?"

"I'm not going to, but I am going out on the job with Cormac tomorrow, and that's final."

Kevin opened his mouth to say more, but Clayton turned away. He didn't look at his mother or father, but both heard him on the stairs and then closing the front door.

"Elaine." Kevin was reaching for her, panic on his face. "Make him go to Denver, Elaine." She saw the tears in his eyes. "He's waited for so long. Make him see. He's got to go. Please, Elaine."

Elaine sat down on the bed and leaned over to put her arms around him. She had never seen Kevin like this — so helpless and weak. It had been six weeks since he'd been put in this bed, and he hadn't moved from it. However, this was a blow that was harder to take than the accident itself. It had never occurred to Kevin that Clayton would change his mind about school. Elaine waited until she thought he might be a little calmer, but when she looked into his eyes, he still looked desperate. Tears came to Elaine's own eyes as she slowly shook her head.

"I can't tell him to go, Kevin, anymore than I could leave you myself."

"Oh, Elaine."

This was too much for him. Tears racked the body that was already becoming flaccid and weak, and Elaine held onto him with all her strength.

"He's dreamed for so long," Kevin cried, "and stayed to work long past the time he first knew he wanted to teach. I just can't stand the thought that he's staying for me."

Elaine smoothed the hair off his brow. They had washed his hair just that morning, and the effort had exhausted him.

Not many hours later, Clayton had come to say he was going back out to work.

"It's not forever, Kevin," Elaine soothed. "If God wants him at school, God will show us the way."

"But he could go —" Kevin began. Elaine cut him off. "No, Kevin, you're not thinking clearly. If he goes, then Milly and I must go to work, or we'll be forced to use up all the money in the savings account. What will we do after it's gone? It would be even harder to call Clayton home, I think, than for him not to go at all."

Her calm voice got through. She was right, of course, and he had to confess the panic and lack of trust. However, his mind was still praying, and a moment later he asked Elaine to write a letter for him.

"To whom?" she asked when she had sat close to Kevin, paper and ink at hand.

"My mother."

The married couple exchanged a long look.

"You want to know more about the position?"

Kevin nodded. "I would do anything for you and the kids."

"Even this, Kevin?"

"Yes. Even this."

With that, he began to dictate. Elaine took down every word in her smooth hand. However, her heart was beating fast. The contents of this letter could change their lives forever, but on second thought, Elaine realized that had already happened.

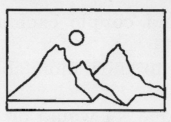

CHAPTER 20

Morgan walked away from the Taggart home, doing his best not to think. He knew it was cowardice, but right now he didn't think he could handle his own thoughts. How in the world did a man praise God after he'd been broken and laid down? Morgan could not even imagine, but that was exactly what he'd witnessed. Determined to apologize for not coming sooner, Morgan had gone to see Kevin to cheer up the bedridden man, but it hadn't gone anything like the way he planned.

"There was no warning," Kevin had told him. "One moment I was in the saddle, and the next instant we were falling. It must have been a deep hole. I'm surprised my horse didn't break a leg, but I was in too much pain to really analyze what was happening." At that point a peaceful smile had come over Kevin's face.

"Not that it really matters," he went on softly. "I'm alive, and we're praying every day for my recovery."

Such talk always made Morgan uncomfortable. Praying was the pastor's job. But Kevin wasn't through.

"But I'll tell you, Morgan," he said, the smile still in place, "if I never get out of this bed I'll still praise God because that would be His plan for me."

Morgan had sat thunderstruck, rescued only when Milly had offered him coffee. It tasted like bitter water in his mouth, but it gave him something to do with his hands and eyes. He drank every drop, and not long after he'd finished the cup, he'd taken his leave.

On his walk home, he moved very slowly. He hadn't thought about what he and Addy had talked about for weeks, but now it came to mind. He had listened to every word of Pastor Munroe's sermons, just as she'd urged him to do, but he still didn't like what he heard. Addy had told him not to harden his heart, and the words had been good. Morgan could see that hardening his heart was exactly what he was doing. He was doing it now. Walking away from Kevin Taggart, Morgan pushed all thoughts of God from his mind. He arrived home in a frightful mood, but no one in his family made comment.

★ ★ ★

Jackie held in the huge sigh that threatened to escape her and walked up the steps of the schoolhouse for the start of the new year. It was difficult to have shared a room with Eddie for all those years because it caused her to think of herself as older, when in fact she had two more years of school to go. Eddie was the lucky one. Her birthday had fallen right before the school year began, so when she turned 18 she was finished. Jackie wouldn't be 17 until January, which meant that even though she turned 18 in the middle of the following year, she would still need to attend. It was almost more than the 16-year-old could take.

At least the teacher was still Miss Bradley. Rumor in town had been that she was moving to Denver and would not be back, but she was there at the front of the room, looking much the same. Jackie had not enjoyed the punishment she'd received late in the last school year, but she had to admit that the woman was fair. Her praise was as noteworthy as her discipline.

Being in school also reminded her of Clayton and the loss of his dream. Jackie had cried buckets over this. Clayton had not. He had told her very calmly that this was the way it needed to be right now, and someday God would provide another way. Jackie had felt devastated for him nonetheless. She couldn't understand her own heart. First she was crushed that he was leaving at all, and now she was upset that he couldn't go. She'd finally gone to her mother and been surprised speechless by what she said.

"That's what true love is all about, Jackie. We put aside our feelings and wants to see to another's needs or happiness."

Jackie could not get the words out of her mind. True love. Is that what she felt for Clayton? Is that why she was so tongue-tied and felt so foolish around him? Her heart did the funniest things when he was near, and she was never hungry afterward. Was it love? Jackie could see that she had much to think about.

"I want you to be thinking about what you will write," Miss Bradley's voice cut across her thoughts. "And I will expect you to do your best. It can be any subject, but it must be thorough. The paper is due at the end of the month, September 30, three-and-a-half weeks from today. Yes, Padriac?"

"Can we work with a partner?"

"Not this time. I want you to do this on your own. Now, go get your math books and let's begin on page 6."

Jackie did sigh this time, but also reminded herself she had better start listening. She had a paper due on the last day of the month, and she wasn't even sure what was expected. She opened her math book to page 6 and told herself to get in line.

"A grizzly?" The little girl's eyes widened.

"Yep."

"How big was it?" Sammy asked.

"Big," Clayton told her and shook his head. "Ugly too, with a turned-up nose and a bunch of fur missing off his back."

"Maybe it was a she."

"Maybe," Clayton agreed and tweaked the end of her nose.

Jackie looked on. She wanted to be so light and carefree around Clayton, just like Sammy was, but she had decided that she *was* in love with him and now had even less to say than before.

Sammy and Clayton talked on about the bear some more, and then Clayton moved away. They were at a birthday party for old Mrs. Greeley. She was a regular customer at the store, and the whole Fontaine family had been invited. Elaine, Clayton, and Milly were there because Milly had taken piano lessons from Mrs. Greeley.

Jackie began to wander some herself. The

266

party was being held in the elderly lady's house and backyard, but Jackie moved to the front. She had decided to do her school report on wildflowers, and Mrs. Greeley's fenced-in front yard was full of them. Jackie moved among the different blooms, touching one here and smelling one there.

She wished she had paper along to take a few notes, but maybe she could come back and do that later. She was kneeling on the grass to look at an interesting species when she heard footsteps. Jackie looked up to see Paddy approaching, a grin on his face.

"Now, don't be telling me you're working on your report on a Sunday."

Jackie smiled in return; he was always so fun. "Well, Mrs. Greeley does have some perfect blooms, and since I was here . . ." The young woman shrugged.

Paddy sank down onto the grass. "I'll put mine off until the night before it's due and then write like mad 'til I'm done."

"Why, Paddy? Why not work a little at a time?"

"Because I've no interest in horses."

"Then why did you choose that subject?"

Paddy shrugged. "My mother has a book on horses, and it just seemed convenient."

Jackie shook her head. "You should have

chosen something you're interested in."

"My mother doesn't have any books on mines."

Jackie's mouth swung wide open. "Paddy! You don't need books. Your father's a surveyor, and you could get him to take you to a mine. Who needs books when you have all of that?"

Paddy stared at her as if he'd just seen a ghost. "Jackie, darlin', you're an angel." He breathed the words and stood. He felt so good that he even bent low and dropped a kiss onto her cheek. Jackie only laughed as he then shouted with glee and ran to find his father in the back. It would have been a wonderful scene if Jackie hadn't looked up and spotted Clayton coming her way. Had he seen the kiss? Would he think that she was interested in Paddy?

"What are you up to?" Clayton was beside her now, dropping onto the grass much the way Paddy had done.

"Oh, just looking at the wildflowers."

"Milly told me about your report."

"She did?"

"Sure. She said Miss Bradley looked quite impressed. Most of the class is doing an animal of some sort, and she thought the teacher must think wildflowers would be a nice change."

Jackie nodded but couldn't speak. Why was she so talkative with Paddy but utterly mute with Clayton?

"So tell me what all of these are." Clayton indicated the flowers around them.

"I'm certain you must know them all, Clayton."

"Well, tell me anyhow. It'll give you good practice."

"You're such a pest," she told him to cover her feelings, but she did as he asked. "This is Indian paintbrush, and this pink one is mountain hollyhock. Behind you is western coneflower and then blazing star."

"What about this one?" Clayton pointed to a flower colored in deep pink with numerous yellow stamens in the center. It was lovely to the eyes and had a small, delicate, light green leaf. Jackie reached for it and smiled.

"This is a wild rose. It's my favorite." She held it to her nose. "I love the fragrance." She let Clayton smell it, and he smiled as well.

With his eye on her face, he said, "Paddy's coming back. Would you like to be alone with him?"

Jackie's eyes flew to his. She blushed to a color that rivaled the Indian paintbrush. Clayton took that as a yes and rose. He

269

smiled at Paddy on his way by but said nothing else to Jackie. She was glad that she'd been a help to Paddy, and even that he'd come back to tell her that his father was going to help, but more than anything, she wanted to call Clayton back and tell him he had it all wrong.

Kevin's chest heaved from the exertion, but the sense of triumph he always felt was well worth it. This was the fifth time he'd sat in a chair, and the tingling he felt in his feet made him want to shout with joy. However, this was a solemn occasion. His wife knew what he was going to say, but Clayton and Milly had no idea. He took a deep breath and began.

"Your mother and I have been in touch with your grandmother in Denver. We've all done a lot of praying and thinking, and I've decided to take a job that she has offered me in the office at the mill."

Clayton and Milly stared at him and then at their mother.

"You mean move to Denver?" Milly whispered after a painful moment of silence.

"Yes," her father said gently.

"Why, Dad?" Clayton managed. "Why leave Georgetown? You and Mom love it here."

"Yes, we do, Clay, but your mother and I want you to get to school, and we can't wait too long or the snows are going to be upon us. It's the ninth of October, and I can't believe we're not snowed in already."

"You can't do this, Dad!" Clayton burst out, all calmness deserting him. "You love it here in the mountains, and I won't let you give it all up for me."

Kevin waited for this outburst to die down and then said, "I talked to young Doc Edwardson just this morning. He told me I would never sit in the saddle again. If I thought there was a chance, I'd stick it out, Clay, but I know in my heart he's right. I never thought I'd be happy behind a desk, but I'm so thrilled to be sitting in a chair right now that I'll take what I can get to support my family. And that is what I'm talking about, Clay," he added almost sternly. "It's my job to take care of this family, and any way I can do that, I will."

The room fell very silent now. Milly could hear the pounding of blood in her ears. Leave Georgetown? Leave Danny and Paddy? What would she do? She had no desire to live in Denver. *Why, God, why did this happen to Dad? Why must he suffer this way?* She began to cry. She told herself not to, but she couldn't hold back the tears. Elaine went to her.

"It's all right, Milly. I've cried too, and I know I'm going to cry again."

"So it's really all set?" she sobbed. "We're really going to go?"

"Yes, dear. We leave next week."

Milly cried against her mother's shoulder, feeling like her heart would break. Clayton didn't feel any better himself, but his father was saying something and he tried to attend.

"Clay, did you hear me?"

"No, I'm sorry, Dad, I didn't."

"You can go to school, son."

Clay nodded, but there was no joy in it.

"You don't understand," Kevin went on. "Your grandmother checked it out. You can start as soon as you arrive. Attendance was down this year, and they'll take anyone they can get. Or if you'd rather wait until the term break, you can start in January."

Clayton blinked at his father. That was good news, but not at the expense of this family.

"You're schooling is a factor, Clay, but it's not the only reason. Can you see that?"

"I'm trying, Dad, but it's just not working. I think the main reason you're doing this is because I went back to work."

"Exactly!" Kevin said triumphantly.

Clayton could only shake his head. "But you just said —"

"I just said the schooling is not the reason, but your supporting this family is."

Clayton only looked at him.

"Clay," Kevin said patiently. "If I had died, then I would expect you to stay here and take care of Milly and your mother, but I'm not dead. I'm not even an invalid. I can work. I can't do the work I've always done, but I can make a living, and that's what I'm going to do." He paused for a moment, a strange light coming into his eyes. "You know, Clay, I nearly forgot that your nineteenth birthday is three weeks away. You can do what you wish, but Milly, your mother, and I are moving to Denver. If you want to join us, you're more than welcome."

Clayton had to smile at this new tactic. He now understood. Kevin smiled in return.

"What day do we go?"

"Next Friday, the sixteenth."

"All right," Clay told him. He looked to Milly. She was still visibly shaken but holding on. Kevin asked everyone to pray with him, and they all bowed their heads.

"This is no mistake," he told his heavenly Father. "We're all going to hurt, Lord, but

You are here with us, and we know this is all a part of Your plan. Thank You for Your sovereignty and loving hand. Help us to trust you when we are tempted to fret. Surround us, especially Clay and Milly, with your grace. Make our peace greater than our pain, so that our lives may glorify You as never before."

God touched Clayton's and Milly's hearts in a special way during their father's prayer. They knew that they would hurt, but the move was for the best. Milly was able to hug and kiss her parents good-night with a genuine smile on her face.

Clayton, equally serene, went off to bed with plans running through his mind. They would have to work hard to be able to move in a week, but the snow would not allow them any more time. The temperatures were already dropping fast. Clayton was nearly asleep when he remembered Jackie. He would have to seek her out in the morning and tell her himself. Somehow he knew she would be hurt if she found out second-hand. He told himself he'd take care of it right after breakfast in the morning. She was heavy on his heart until he fell asleep.

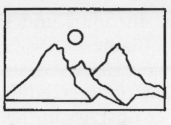

CHAPTER 21

Clayton was at the Fontaine home early the next day, but still he missed Jackie. Addy told him that she'd gone very early with her father to the store. He briefly explained why he needed to see her and was surprised when Addy ordered Danny to go with Clayton and take Jackie's place at the store.

"It won't take that long to tell her, Mrs. Fontaine," Clayton said when Danny went for her coat.

Addy stared at him. Why were men so stupid at times?

"Well," she said, "I think she might be sad, and Danny could help out until she feels like working."

Clayton shrugged and waited for Danny to come. He was completely unaware of the way Addy scribbled a quick note for Danny to put in her pocket and give to her father. She saw both Danny and Clayton out the front door and then bundled into her coat. The other girls would be leaving for the store in about an hour, and right now she had to talk to Elaine.

"Hello," Clayton greeted Jackie as soon as he found her upstairs in the kitchen. The cleaning of Uncle Mitch's apartments had been put off way too long, and now Morgan wanted it done. He'd taken Jackie with him early to see to it.

"Well, now." Jackie smiled at the sight of him. His face was red from the cold, and he was so handsome in his heavy leather coat that her heart ached. "You're certainly out early today to pester people."

Clayton smiled in return and did some admiring of his own. Jackie's face was flushed and just a little dusty, and he thought she looked like an adorable street urchin.

"Yes, I am. I've come to tell you something."

"Good news?"

"Yes."

"What is it?"

"I'm going to Denver."

"Denver?" Her face held a puzzled expression for several seconds and then brightened. "Oh, Clayton, you're going to school! That's wonderful!" Jackie nearly hugged him but caught herself in time. She felt flustered by her own thoughts and shuffled the dust rag in her grasp from one hand to the other.

"Your dream, Clayton," she finally managed. "You get to realize your dream."

Clayton nodded. It was still not real to him, but he was very pleased at her genuine response.

"When do you go?" she asked suddenly.

"Next week."

Some of Jackie's elation left her. Next week. But of course, she realized, it would have to be soon, or the snow would hold him up. She opened her mouth to ask something else, but Clayton continued.

"There's more, Jackie. My father's been offered a job in Denver, so we're all going."

This time she took a moment to respond. "You're all going?" Jackie's voice was uncertain. Clayton liked to tease her, and she didn't want to be caught out.

"Yes. My grandmother still owns and operates a mill in Denver, and Dad will be taking an office job. It'll be hard to leave Georgetown — he loves it here — but we all feel a peace about this."

"Sure," Jackie said and wondered how normal her voice sounded. "I'm glad he's doing so much better. I'm sorry I haven't been able to come as often, but it's hard with school."

"Oh, Jackie, don't apologize," Clayton swiftly told her, his voice sincere. "You've done more than enough, and we'll always be grateful."

Jackie nodded. "Well, if there's anything else I can do, let me know."

"Thank you, Jackie. I'll let you get back to work now."

"Sure, Clay. I'll see you later."

He was gone in the next instant, taking the stairs in an easy stride. He probably hadn't needed to rush and tell her; after all, she took it very well. But he was glad he had. He suddenly shook his head. What had he expected? Screaming hysterics? It's not as if they were engaged to be married and the separation would upset their whole world.

Clayton was amused by his own worry and then realized he had to get home. There was plenty to do. He stopped for a moment to tell Morgan and Danny of their plans and then went swiftly on his way.

When he left, Danny turned to her father with tears in her eyes. Morgan looked at her with compassion. He'd asked his daughters many times to move from their friends, but never had Danny had a friend move from her. Addy was going to be equally upset about Elaine.

"Oh, no!" Danny suddenly exclaimed. "He's already told Jackie."

"Is that bad?"

"Oh, Father," Danny's voice was hurt. "She's in love with him."

Morgan's mouth opened in surprise, and then he asked himself why no one ever told him anything.

"You'd better go and check on her, Dan. Tell her that if she wants to go home, she can."

Danny went without another word and was surprised to find Jackie working. Her back was to the door as she knelt on the kitchen floor, scrubbing it with all her might.

"Jackie?" Danny called and came forward, but the arm motion didn't stop. Danny moved so she could see her sister's face. "Please stop, Jackie, and talk to me."

Jackie sat back on her heels and stared straight ahead. "What did you want to talk about?"

"Well, Father said that if you'd rather go home, you could do that."

Jackie shook her head, her eyes on the counter she had just scrubbed. "I think I'd rather work."

"Oh, Jackie." Danny started to say more, but the older girl shook her head.

"He doesn't have any idea, Danny. In fact, he's very excited about leaving. He gets to go to school now, and he's naturally pleased about that." Jackie finally looked at Danny. "I'm sorry that Milly's leaving. I know you'll miss her. Mother will miss Mrs. Taggart too."

"But what about you, Jackie?" Danny persisted.

The older girl shrugged. "I didn't think I would survive when Eddie left, but I did. I'll survive again." She went back to the floor. Danny wanted to burst into tears. She had never seen her sister give up so quickly.

I have to believe that she'll be all right, Danny said to herself as she returned downstairs. *She believes that she will be, and I must believe it too.*

But it was not to be. The news had come on Saturday, and by Wednesday Jackie was so drawn and pale that several customers asked Morgan if she was coming down with something. She and Danny had needed to keep busy, and so they worked at the store every day, but both were depressed.

Jackie almost invariably waited on Clayton when he came into the store, but on this occasion she was busy with two other customers. In fact, she didn't even see him. Danny went to the other side of the counter to see to his needs, but for a moment she could see only his profile as he stared at Jackie. Danny waited patiently until he turned.

"Did you need something, Tag?"

"Danny." His face and voice were serious. "Is Jackie ill?"

Danny frowned, and anger, anger she suddenly realized had been simmering in her since Saturday, came to the surface. She did nothing to hide this emotion.

"How thick can one man be, Clayton?"

Clayton was so surprised that he blinked.

"Have *I* done something, Danny?" His face was so vulnerable that Danny's ire broke and so did her heart.

"Oh, Clayton," she sighed. "You know better than anyone how hard it is for her to make friends. First Eddie goes and now you. How do you think she should be feeling?" Tears had come to Danny's eyes, and she dashed them away with an embarrassed move.

"But I thought she and Paddy —" Danny's mouth came open, and Clayton let the sentence hang.

"Paddy O'Brien?" Danny's voice came out in an incredulous squeak.

"Well, yes. I thought maybe they were —" The look of shock in Danny's eyes brought him to an uncomfortable halt.

Danny felt as if the wind had been knocked out of her. She looked down at her hands and then back at her customer, her voice suddenly tired. "What can I get for you, Clayton?"

"Lexa, dear," old Mrs. Greeley suddenly spoke in a loud voice from Clayton's side, "can you help me?"

"Go ahead," Clayton urged her in a low voice. "I'll look around."

"Lexa, can you help me?"

"Yes, Mrs. Greeley, and I'm Danny."

"Oh, thank you, dear." She was deaf as a post. "Now, Lexa, I need some thread. Blue. Not too dark and not too light."

Danny sighed but then thought it might be for the best. Maybe Jackie could help Clayton, and he would say something kind to her. But it didn't work out that way. Danny glanced up at one point to see her father attending to him. Clayton's gaze was still on Jackie, but she didn't notice. Mrs. Greeley was shouting again in order to hear her own voice, and when Danny looked one last time, Clayton was gone.

Addy watched Jackie pick at her food that evening and begged God for wisdom. Mother and daughter had prayed together every night over the Taggarts' departure, but Jackie acted like she was in mourning. In a way she was. Addy was much the same way when she was upset. She lost all interest in food or coffee. Addy was old enough to know she had to eat, but right now, Jackie simply didn't care. Addy worried she would come down sick before she felt up to eating again. She had tried to discuss it with Morgan, but his answer had been to order Jackie to eat and to punish her if she didn't. Addy wished she'd kept the concern to herself.

It was a surprise to everyone when Clayton came to the house that night. They were all aware of how hard the Taggarts were working to get ready to go, but Morgan had a rare moment of insight when he let Clayton in the front door.

"I'd like to talk to Jackie," Clay told him. "Is she around?"

"Sure, Clay. Go right into the living room. I'll send her in."

Morgan went back to the family still gathered in the kitchen.

"Clay is here to see you, Jack. He's in the living room."

"Oh," was the only reply he received, and for a moment he wondered if Danny had known what she was talking about. Sammy began to slip past him to see Clayton as well, but he caught the back of her dress.

"Not tonight, Sam. Let Jack go on her own."

Morgan was rewarded by Addy's loving smile of approval. That smile did things to his heart. Danny *had* known what she was talking about. Morgan decided then and there to ask Addy about it when they were alone; after that he would kiss her until they were both breathless.

"Hello, Clay," Jackie spoke as she came into the room. Clayton came to his feet.

"Hi, Jackie. I hope I didn't take you from anything." He tried not to look at how thin she had become, but it was impossible; her dress was beginning to hang on her frame.

"No." Jackie smiled, her voice sounding normal. "Just the dishes, and I won't miss those."

She sat on one of the chairs, and he sat across from her. To Jackie's surprise, an uncomfortable silence fell. If she hadn't known better, she would have said Clayton was nervous.

"Are you all packed?" Jackie rescued him.

"Almost. Tomorrow should be a pretty easy day, but then we have lots of goodbyes to make."

"I'll bet you do. Be sure and tell us all

goodbye tonight, and then you can scratch us off the list."

Clayton stared at her. Why had he never noticed how few demands she made on him? It wasn't that way at first. At first she had had all sorts of expectations, and he hadn't caught half of them, but in the past year she never made him feel bad about leaving or pressured him to do anything for her. He thought of her as another sister, but she was far less demanding than Milly, who was a wonderful sister in her own right.

"I'll write to you," he suddenly said, and watched a grimace of pain cross her face.

"Oh, Clay, don't say that," she said softly.

"Why not? It's true."

Jackie shook her head. "It never quite works that way."

"I don't know what you mean."

She sighed softly. Jackie usually had a hard time sharing her feelings for fear of rejection, but Clayton was leaving and suddenly she didn't care what he thought. She was going to be honest even if it hurt him a little.

"It's nothing intentional, Clay, but when a person goes away he sets up a new life for himself. Eddie hasn't written anywhere near what she'd promised, but I under-

285

stand. She has her life there in Boulder, and she's busy with that. I'm sure it's much more healthy than constantly trying to live in the past."

"I'm going to write to you," he stated emphatically, but Jackie didn't comment. Clayton let the silence hang between them for a moment. She wasn't even looking at him. How had he been so blind to her feelings and need for friendship?

"Jackie." He waited until she looked up and then asked plainly, "Will you write back to me if I write to you?"

Jackie let herself really look at him now, telling herself it might be the last time. She knew her heart would always melt at the sight of him, but she had to say what was on her mind.

"I honestly don't think you will, Clay, at least not over once or twice, but I'll answer every letter you send me."

Clay nodded. "It's a deal then."

Jackie actually managed a smile, but her heart knew the truth.

Clayton didn't say his goodbyes that night but came by briefly the next day with his mother and Milly. There were tears on nearly everyone's part, but Jackie was dry-eyed. Why this stuck out to Clayton more than anything else, he didn't know.

But even when the stage pulled out of Georgetown the next day, his father made as comfortable as possible for the long trip, the look in Jackie's eyes still haunted him.

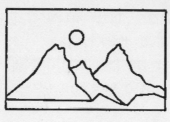

CHAPTER 22

The mails were in their usual winter holdup, but surprisingly enough, Jackie received three letters on the same day. One was from Eddie and two were from Clayton, who had been gone a month. She told herself not to get her hopes up. He was writing only because he said he would, but it would be no different than Eddie. The snow did slow things up, but this was Eddie's first letter to her in weeks.

Jackie opted to open the letter from her sister first. She was very cheered by the words inside, but felt sad when Eddie once again confided to Jackie that she wished to be pregnant.

"You hear of women who go childless, Jackie," she wrote, "but you never dream it will happen to you. I know Robert loves me as I am, and even laughs and hugs me if I mention my infertile state, but I so want us to have a child. I've never wrestled with anything as much as this. I have even been

288

angry at God. Please pray for me concerning my heart's attitude."

Jackie did pray for her, every night. She also prayed that someday they would see each other again, but it didn't seem likely to happen anytime soon. Jackie's mind swam in all directions for a while before she told herself to get on with what she was doing.

She picked up Clayton's letters, opened both of them just enough to see which one he'd written first, and then started in. She was in for a pleasant surprise.

"I thought we were going to be on that stage forever. *But,*" he had underlined that word, "we caught the train in Forks and was that an adventure! I've never moved so fast in my life. Poor Miner would have dropped dead from heart failure." Jackie laughed in delight at this description and thought of Miner, now housed in the stable behind the store. She avidly read on.

My grandmother's house is nothing like I expected. She has enough room to house the whole of Denver. I think I mentioned to you that I would stay with her only if it worked out. Well, believe me, Jackie, it has been fine. She's so loving and really delighted to have us here.

I haven't actually walked to the school, so I don't know exactly how far away the school is right now, but I'm going tomorrow. I'm a little nervous about checking in at the school, but Grandma says there's nothing to worry about.

My father starts work tomorrow too. My mother tried to get him to take it easy for a time, but he's raring to go.

It's certainly noisy here. I haven't slept as well because of it, but my mom says I'll adjust. Milly has cried every day for Danny and Paddy, but the sights and sounds of the big city have certainly helped to distract her.

Jackie had to stop reading. She was so amazed she couldn't go on. Why, it sounded just like him! At times it was difficult to picture Eddie and Robert, but Clayton's letters were just an extension of the man, and Jackie could see his face and hear his voice as she read. Relieved by this revelation, Jackie gave way to her exhaustion. She lay back on her bed and let the wonderfulness of it flow over her.

However, she sobered swiftly. It didn't mean he would keep writing. She finished the first letter and turned to the next one. It was just as much fun as the first and ended with a postscript. "Don't forget, Miss Fontaine, you said you would reply to every letter. You now owe me two."

Jackie scrambled off the bed, forgetting all about being cautious. She pulled out paper and immediately started to write. The things she could never say to Clayton's face now came easily. She swiftly told him that she missed him and all of his family and then went on to talk about events in Georgetown. She was careful to address only the things in the first letter with plans to answer the other one as well.

She started the second one by saying, "If you haven't received my first letter, don't read this or it will be all out of whack." She then put a little smiling face on the page and smiled herself. The second letter went on for three pages. Jackie would have written more, but her father stuck his head in the door and told her to get to bed. Addy came soon after to kiss her. Jackie scrambled up into the big bed, feeling five years old all over again.

"That's certainly a happy face," Addy commented, kissing her brow.

"He wrote, Mother. Clay wrote to me."

"Danny told me."

"Two letters, Mother, and they sound just like Clay."

Addy sat down now and just listened to the sound of her voice. Addy didn't know what she would do if Clayton didn't follow through. It would almost be easier never to hear from him again if he wasn't going to remain her friend, but that decision was out of her hands. Then Addy asked herself what she expected the man to do if he met a girl in Denver and fell in love. Right now she couldn't find an answer.

A moment later she kissed Jackie and told her good-night. She went to her own room, giving Jackie and Clayton over to God in prayer and taking them back again in worry not two minutes later. *Go to sleep, Addy,* she finally said to herself. *You can pray about this in the morning.*

Denver

Jackie's letter began with "Merry Christmas." Clayton smiled at the words and then laughed about her explanation.

"I assume my letters are taking as long to get to you as yours are to me, so I'm getting a jump on the stage. Who knows? I may even be 17 before you get this. I don't suppose a man of your advanced years (20, isn't it now?) can possibly remember these young,

292

carefree days, but I'll try to fill you in."

Jackie went on to tell him about an afternoon at school, followed by an evening of work at the store. He laughed until tears ran down his face. Everything that could go wrong, had, and then some. She asked him all about school and whether or not he'd had his first exam. She said she hoped he was making friends and wasn't lonely. Clayton finished her letter and then sat staring into space.

Had she really been so shy, or was another girl writing these letters? This was the fourth he'd received, and he couldn't believe what fun she was and how caring. School was such hard work that going to church and reading her letters were the only bright spots in his week. As had become the pattern, Clayton got ready to write back to her. He knew somehow that he would never hear from her unless he wrote first, and for some reason the idea of not getting a letter from her utterly depressed him. Christmas was still more than two weeks away, but if he mailed the letter tomorrow, he was certain that she would receive it in plenty of time.

In the sawmill where his father worked they had a machine that allowed them to call one another within the building. It was the most wondrous thing he had ever seen. His father could pick up the instrument at his desk and a bell would ring down in the warehouse. Someone could pick-up down there and talk to him. It would be wonderful to talk to Jackie through that instrument. It would have done his heart good to hear her laugh.

Clayton was about to put ink to paper when he heard his father's wheeled chair in the hall. A knock sounded a moment later.

"Come on in," Clayton called, turning from his desk to see his father come through the door.

"I saw your light. Studying late?"

"No, I'm just getting ready to write to Jackie."

"How is she?"

Clayton smiled. "Doing well, I think. A little tired of the snow but looking forward to Christmas."

"Your mother said that Eddie was in touch yesterday."

"Yes, she was. She and Robert are busy in a small church, and God is doing mighty things. She admitted she's so busy in Boulder that she feels likes she's losing touch with Georgetown and her family."

Kevin nodded. "Is that why you write Jackie regularly? Because you feel sorry for her?"

"It was at first," Clayton admitted, remembering how he'd told her he would. "But now I look forward to hearing from her. She's so different on paper than in real life."

"What do you mean?"

Clayton shrugged. "I don't know exactly, but I'd see her laughing with a group and then I'd come on the scene. She would act as though she was pleased to see me, but she wouldn't have two words to say. Her face would get red for no reason."

Kevin stared at his son. Could he really be so unsuspecting? Kevin thought about the way Jackie looked when she came up to his bedroom to say goodbye. She had not been upstairs one time before that day, but Elaine had told him of the way she'd come in and quietly helped around the house. They had never had much contact, and Kevin had still been thinking of her the way she was that first summer when she despised Clayton. He had struggled with his feelings toward her for that very reason, but the young woman who'd come to his room to tell him she was praying and to have a good trip was not the same girl.

"You have an odd look on your face," Clayton commented.

"Do I?"

"Yes. Are you going to tell me what it means?"

Kevin looked at him and made a decision. "You can't force feelings that are not there, Clay, but I want you to think long and hard about the way you just described Jackie to me."

Clayton's brow furrowed. Why would he ask him to do that?

"Just think about it, Clay. I'm glad you have tremendous respect for women, and that you have chosen to comport yourself in a way that pleases God, but you're being naive where Jackie is concerned."

Understanding came to Clayton like a bee sting. He literally started in his seat and stared, slack-jawed, at his father. He started to shake his head, but Kevin only smiled.

"I hope I haven't ruined things between the two of you, Clay, but I felt it was only fair to her that you should know."

"I can't believe it," he admitted softly. "I mean, it's not the way I would think anyone would act."

Kevin tilted his head to one side, his smile still in place. "I can't agree with you, Clay. I think that's exactly the way she would act. After all, you've never done anything to encourage her, so she couldn't exactly let her feelings show."

Clayton's hand came to his mouth and then rubbed over his jaw. He was still trying to take it in, but his father said a soft "good-night" and went out.

Oh, Jackie, how could I have missed that. I felt such a peace about not being in love with you that it never occurred to me that you might not share that feeling. The thinness of her wrists and the way her cheeks sank in just before he left Georgetown jumped starkly into Clayton's mind. The young man's eyes slid shut. Jackie was feeling more than friendship to have his leaving affect her like that.

He had been on the verge of picking up the pen to write to her about school, but now he only shook his head.

"Every letter is all about me," he told the quiet room. "Every letter is filled with Clayton's world." This was not exactly true, but Clayton was upset. "You are an incredibly selfish person, Clayton Taggart, and it's nothing short of self-centeredness that it has taken this long for you to see it."

Clayton did write Jackie a letter that night, but it was one with her in mind. He answered the questions she'd asked of him, but then sent back dozens of his own. He suddenly wanted to know so much. His heart ached that he'd been so insensitive.

He hadn't suddenly fallen in love with her because of his father's words, but he saw now that he could have been so much kinder and more caring of her needs. He mailed it the next day with a prayer that she would be encouraged. He was already in class before he realized that he hadn't remembered to say anything about her birthday.

"Happy birthday," Morgan said. Jackie's eyes widened. Her birthday had been over a week ago, but her father was holding a gift for her. "This came to the store."

"Oh!" Her eyes sparkled with pleasure. "Is it from Eddie?"

"Not unless she's moved to Denver."

Jackie became very still.

"Denver?"

"That's right," he said with a flourish, and set the box on the table beside her plate. Her sisters were all watching her.

"Aren't you going to open it?" Lexa wanted to know.

"Yes, but I don't want to hold up dinner."

"Well," her mother said practically, "let's pray and get started, and you can open it when you want to."

Jackie nodded and all heads bowed. It

was Sammy's turn to pray, but Jackie didn't hear a word. Her eyes were on the box. She put food on her plate without really seeing it. Morgan and Addy shared a smile when she took a huge helping of beets. Jackie hated beets.

"I want you to open it now, Jackie," Danny admitted suddenly. "The rest of us don't have birthdays for weeks to come and any gift, even someone else's, is fun."

Jackie looked at her and chuckled.

"You might as well, Jackie," her father put it. "You're sure not interested in eating."

She blushed a little at that and, using her knife, opened the box. There were all sorts of wrappings inside, and it took some work, but when the floor was finally littered with paper Jackie brought forth the most delicate crystal bell she'd ever seen.

"Ohhh." Her sisters gave a collective sigh as she held it up for inspection.

"Ring it, Jackie," Sammy urged her. When she did, the room filled with a delightful tinkling sound.

"I have to go and write to him right now," Jackie said in a dreamy voice. She began to move, but Morgan waved her back.

"After you eat," he told her in a voice that she knew better than to argue with.

Nodding, Jackie set the bell carefully by her plate and just looked at it. It was several more minutes before she picked up her fork.

"All right," she said to the sisters on either side of her. "Who's the joker? Who put all the beets on my plate?"

The whole family laughed at her expense.

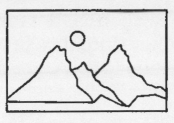

CHAPTER 23

Jackie had thought that winter would last forever, but the mud, sucking at her boots, gave lie to that myth. Spring was upon them, and the snow was melting fast and furiously. Flowers were already working their way out of the ground, and Jackie had only to close her eyes to envision how lovely they were going to be.

Her attitude at the moment could have used some of that same loveliness. The soggy ground was getting to her. She looked down at her skirt to see that she had spattered mud up the front of herself. She was going to have to go to work like this, and the thought made her want to explode with anger. She heard a wagon slogging its way along, but she didn't even look up. In her irritation she missed a step and fell down. By the time the wagon drew abreast of her, she was struggling up from her hands and knees and was literally black with mud.

She had just gained her footing when she

realized the wagon had stopped. Jackie looked up, straight into the eyes of her sister.

"Eddie," she whispered and then screamed, *"Eddie!"*

Eddie laughed and Robert joined her. Jackie nearly did a dance in her exasperation.

"You didn't tell anyone, and look at me — I can't even touch you!"

"Climb in the back, and we'll take you home," Eddie told her, a huge smile still in place. "We're going to surprise Mother."

"All right," Jackie agreed, "but just let me clean up quickly so I can see her face. Take the wagon around the back," she instructed Robert. "I'll let you in that way and she'll faint."

Eddie turned on the seat to talk to her filthy sister as Jackie climbed in. She turned a beaming face to her.

"You look wonderful, Eddie."

"You do too. I think."

They both laughed hilariously at this until Robert reminded them they were going to alert Addy if they didn't quiet down. They tried to be calm, but it was like being 10 and 12 all over again and both just wanted to giggle for the fun of it.

"How have you been?" Eddie asked in a soft voice.

Jackie gave her a mock frown. "You'd know that, Eddie Langley, if you wrote more often."

Eddie looked very contrite, but her eyes were still shining.

"Don't be too long," Eddie admonished Jackie when the team halted around back.

"I won't," Jackie promised, climbing down in an undignified fashion.

Robert had left the wagon as well, and leaning from his great height, dropped a kiss on her forehead. He managed to do this and not get anywhere near that mud. Jackie smiled up at him with loving eyes and darted into the back door.

"It's just me, Mother," she called from the kitchen.

"What's wrong?" Addy was dusting the front room and remained there.

"I fell in the mud. I'm going to change and head back out."

"All right. Be certain to leave your things in the kitchen."

Normally Jackie would have undressed without a thought, but with Robert in the backyard, she was careful to stay away from the window. She made quick work of her muddy face and hands and then dashed up the stairs for fresh clothing. She dressed in record time, and when she got back down,

Robert and Eddie were waiting right outside the kitchen door. She let them in silently, hugged them both, and then strolled nonchalantly to the living room to see her mother.

"All clean now, dear?" Addy only glanced at her.

"Yes, Mother. I'll get going pretty soon, but I wanted to ask you something."

"That's fine with me, dear, but your father will be looking for you." Addy's cloth attacked a small vase.

"Well, I'll hurry. Mother, do you think I could make my bedroom in the small room off the kitchen?"

"Whatever for?" Addy's face was still bent over her work.

"Well, I think it would be a nice change."

"I don't think so, Jackie." She set the vase down and positioned it on the shelf, her back to her daughter. "I mean it's so much smaller than your room, and I really don't think you'll be as comfortable."

"Well, couldn't I just try it for a week?"

"I don't know, dear." Addy shook her head, still not looking at Jackie as she reached for a tiny china doll. "I don't really see the point."

"But if she can't take that room, Mother," Eddie now stepped into the room,

304

"where will Robert and I sleep for the next week?"

"Eddie." Her mother breathed the word as she spun around. The doll and dust cloth landed on a chair as Addy swiftly navigated through furniture to get to her daughter. Eddie met her halfway across the room. By the time they touched, the tears were flowing unchecked. More than a year. Her precious Eddie had been Mrs. Robert Langley for more than a year. It was like a wonderful present from the Lord to be able to hold her again.

"Oh, Robert," Addy said, moving to hug her son-in-law. She then held him at arm's length and looked him over.

"You look wonderful, Robert. Married life must agree with you."

"Indeed, it does. If the girl is anything like my Eddie, I highly recommend it."

Husband and wife shared a smile, and Addy urged them into chairs.

"Have you been to the store? Have you seen Morgan?"

"Yes," Eddie answered. "He gave us the wagon and said he hoped Jackie would still be home."

Robert grinned. "She was the welcome party out on the road."

"Oh, no." Addy was swift to catch on.

"You fell in the mud in front of them."

Jackie shrugged, but she was not upset. Suddenly the mud didn't matter at all. Only last week she'd written Clayton and admitted that she was almost angry that Robert and Eddie had never come to visit, but now here they were, and she felt guilty for not trusting God for this.

"We saw Danny and Lexa with Father, but where's Sammy?" Eddie wished to know.

"She's in bed. She's had a touch of something for a week now, and all she wants to do is sleep. I should go and see if she wants to get up." Addy went out, and Jackie looked over to see Robert smiling at her.

"We got a letter from Tag last week."

"Did you?" Jackie smiled and tried not to blush at the sound of his name.

"Yes. He says that you correspond quite regularly."

Jackie did blush then, but only nodded in return. If the truth be told, they wrote to each other at least twice a week. It was still amazing to Jackie that they never ran out of things to say. And Clayton's letters had just gotten kinder and kinder with every passing month. He always admonished Jackie to take good care of herself. In turn, Jackie told him not to overdo on his studies, and that he wouldn't be fit to teach if he burned out during college. His plan right now was to take some summer courses as well, but Jackie wondered if he wasn't going overboard. He wanted to finish in two years, and he said this was the only way.

"I think we've lost her." Eddie's voice floated through the air.

"Yes," Robert agreed. "I think we lost her the moment I mentioned Clay's name."

Again Jackie lit up like a candle, and Eddie apologized.

"Forgive us, Jackie; we shouldn't tease."

"It's all right. I've always blushed easily when it comes to Clay."

"Does he know how you feel?" Robert asked the question so gently that Jackie wasn't offended.

"No, he doesn't, but that's all right. It's just fun to share letters with him."

Robert's head turned to his wife. "That's how I fell in love with Eddie."

"Oh, Robert, don't say that," Jackie begged him. "It hurts too much to raise my hopes."

Robert looked at her. "Why can't you hope for it?"

Jackie shrugged. "I just don't think it's going to be like that, and that's okay. I can live with it."

My, but she's done a lot of growing up, both Eddie and Robert were thinking. Nothing could ever dim her physical beauty, but she was now starting to be beautiful on the inside as well.

Robert didn't comment again, but he didn't think the idea of the two of them getting together was so hopeless. Tag hadn't actually come right out with it, but Robert had gained an impression from his letter that Jackie was pretty special.

"Hi, Eddie."

"Oh, Sammy." Eddie stood as soon as she saw her, her heart breaking a little. She was so thin and pale, and her hair was all over her head. Eddie went right to her. She hugged her, but Sammy needed to sit down. Eddie took the sofa so they could be close. Once Sammy was snuggled against her side, the little girl looked across the room at Robert.

"Hello, Sammy."

"Hi, Robert."

"I'm not sure you should be out of bed," he said gently.

"I had to," she answered in a tired voice.

"Why is that?"

"I have to ask you a question. How is Travis Buchanan?"

Robert smiled hugely. "Doing well. As

handsome as ever, I would say."

Sammy smiled and sighed and then laid her head against Eddie. Not a minute later, she was asleep. Everyone in the room was forced to hold in their laughter.

"Still not expecting?" Addy questioned Eddie gently when they were alone.

"No," Eddy sighed, but she was smiling. "I know it has to be in God's time, but I do wish for it."

"There's nothing wrong with that," Addy replied. "Even the Bible talks about the way children are a woman's pride and joy. I don't think we're in any way imperfect if we can't have children, but if we can, we should."

Eddie nodded. "I knew you would feel that way."

Both women were in Addy and Morgan's bedroom, and silence fell until Addy asked, "How does Robert feel about it, Eddie?"

"Oh, Mother, he's so wonderful. He keeps reminding me how long he waited to find me. He says that if we never have children, he'll still live the rest of his life in contentment with me at his side."

Addy smiled. "He's very special."

"Yes. I only hope that all my sisters find

men with half the love and tenderness Robert possesses."

"I think they will. After all, Sammy has claimed Travis Buchanan, but only when Danny's not looking."

They laughed, but then Eddie turned serious, her mind going to her sister.

"She's still head-over-heels, isn't she, Mother?"

Addy sighed. "Yes. I think I wrote to you about the way she looked when Clayton left last year."

Eddie nodded.

"She scared me to death, Eddie. She simply couldn't eat, and I didn't think she would ever get over it."

"What happened?"

"He wrote her a letter. In fact, he wrote two letters. She had made a deal with him that if he wrote, she would reply. So she wrote back, and lo and behold, letters from him just kept coming.

"She's been so excited at times that she's read a few to me. I don't know if this will go anywhere, Eddie, but he has far more care for her feelings than he did when he lived here. I know why he didn't get that close to her; I mean, Jackie was impossible, but now," Addy shrugged, "she's utterly smitten."

"I can see it in her face when his name is mentioned."

Someone knocked at the door, and a moment later Robert stuck his head in.

"I wondered where you'd wandered off to."

"Why, Robert." Eddie was surprised. "I thought you were having lunch with Father."

"I was, but he cut it short when I told him in no uncertain terms that we're not moving to Georgetown and setting up a branch office to my bank."

The women could only stare at him. Eddie looked crushed, but her mother looked furious. Robert didn't know what else to say and was a little sorry he'd interrupted them, so he quietly left.

"After all this time, Mother, he still doesn't accept this change."

"I know," Addy replied tiredly. "He usually discusses things with me, but this time he must have just been lying in wait."

The image so amused Eddie that she suddenly smiled. He was like that at times; he would rehearse his words and spring on someone, sure of what that person's answer was going to be. Right now it seemed quite laughable to her. Addy suddenly looked over and saw Eddie's smile.

"It's not funny, Eddie." The older woman was still frowning.

"I'm sorry, Mother, but it is. Father is just too outrageous for words. Not a word out of him when we arrive. He greets us like everything is fine and then he pounces on Robert as soon as our backs are turned." A giggle escaped her. "We might as well laugh as cry."

Addy shook her head. She was not angry, but neither was she amused. *Oh, Morgan,* her heart sighed. *What am I going to do with you?*

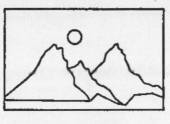

CHAPTER 24

Robert and Eddie left just over a week after they arrived. It had been a wonderful time, full of memories and fun. Some of the mud had dried up and although the temperatures were cool at night, the family had picnicked in the orchard on two occasions and gone for long afternoon walks. In the evenings they would pop corn and have hot cocoa and then visit until late at night. Even the younger girls had been given grace concerning the normal bedtime hour.

Nothing else was said about Morgan's proposal to Robert — not even Addy mentioned it — but it caused some strain for several days. Addy, Robert, and Eddie were all privy to the details and prayed fervently. By the end of the visit all was well. It was impossible to say when they would see the young married couple again, so everyone was extremely thankful for this good time together.

The day they left, Jackie and Morgan saw

them off and then went to the store. Jackie was feeling positively ecstatic about their visit and hummed as she worked, but Morgan, even though he'd been all smiles at the stage office, was rather short with her and even abrupt with one or two customers. Jackie noticed it but didn't have a chance to say anything until near noon.

"Would you like me to run over to the hotel and get us some dinner, Father?"

"No," he said shortly. "I'm not hungry."

Jackie stood silently by the desk. All morning he'd spent as much time in the office as possible.

"Maybe next time we'll get to visit them," she said softly. Morgan looked at her sharply. Not easily intimidated, Jackie stood facing him.

"What does that mean?" he snapped.

"Well, I know you miss them," she said kindly, "and I just thought it would cheer you to think about going to see them in Boulder. I know I would enjoy it."

"Is that so? Well, I for one have no interest in going to see where your sister has made a life for herself, one that does not involve anyone *but* herself." This was completely unfair, but Morgan only went angrily back to his work.

Jackie had always known that her father

was self-centered, especially compared to her very giving mother, but never was it so clear as right now. She knew her mother's father had never approved of the relationship between her father and her mother, but that hadn't stopped Morgan from taking her away and marrying her. He had other ideas now that it was *his* daughter. Not to mention the fact that he had given his blessing. It occurred to Jackie suddenly that her father did not like things he could not control and that she tended to be the same way.

Jackie could freely admit that she wished Eddie lived closer or wrote more often, but she could see that her sister was happy and blessed, and she wouldn't have wished anything else for her. And if their home was as large as it sounded, she had plenty to do.

Eddie had also told Jackie of the different people she and Robert ministered to. Her life sounded very fruitful and peaceful. How could their father want any less for his oldest daughter?

"Well," she said softly when Morgan continued to write, "I'm going across the street to get something to eat."

Morgan's head came up as she left, his brow drawn forward as he watched her leave. He knew he'd been unreasonably harsh, but he didn't feel like apologizing. Besides, why *couldn't* Robert set up here? Morgan knew just where and how it could happen. There was an empty store adjacent to his, and Georgetown needed another bank.

"Young and headstrong," Morgan muttered to himself. "I know what's best for him and Ed if he would only listen."

Once again the angry man went back to his accounts.

"The first of July —" Addy commented after lunch that afternoon. "It's hard to believe the month of June is already gone." Lexa was working at the store, and Danny and Sammy had gone on an outing with Paddy.

"I'll be back in school before I can count to ten," Jackie complained. Addy smiled understandingly but then turned to look at her daughter.

"What is it that you want to do so badly, Jackie, that you want to be finished with school?"

Jackie's hair swung to one side as she tipped her head in thought. "I don't know exactly. I like working at the store, but I guess I'd like to travel a bit."

How this dream would be financed was not mentioned, but Addy said, "Any place in particular?"

"Boulder," she said without hesitation. "I'd love to see Boulder and Eddie."

"Would Denver enter into the picture in any of those travel plans?" The question was kindly put.

Jackie hugged the dish she'd just dried against her chest and shook her head. "I don't think so, Mother. He's never even hinted at my visiting, and I simply couldn't go if I wasn't welcomed by Clayton himself."

Addy agreed softly but turned away before Jackie could see her face. Jackie's eyes were so wistful any time his name was mentioned that it almost broke her mother's heart to watch.

The kitchen was in good shape now, so she left her daughter to go work on the rooms upstairs. Jackie finished drying the dishes on her own and started some baking. It was dreadfully hot, but they were out of bread and Father's favorite cookies.

She had just put the bread dough together when she saw him. She had no idea how long he'd been standing there, but Clayton Taggart was in the doorway watching her. Jackie moved like a woman sleepwalking. She came around the table and stopped just two steps away from him. All the love she felt inside was written on her face before she could come to her senses.

Clayton watched her blush and said gently, "Hello, Jackie."

Eight months! She hadn't heard his deep voice for eight months! Jackie smiled suddenly.

"I can't believe you're here," she admitted and looked away from him, feeling rather flustered. How many times had she practiced what she would do and say if she ever saw him again. Now all of it flew from her head.

"Please," she nearly stammered. "Sit down. You must be tired."

"Thank you," Clayton said, taking a seat at the table. He couldn't stop looking at her. She was so different from the last time he'd seen her, and that Jackie was the only one he'd been able to visualize.

"Are you . . . um . . . I mean," she stumbled painfully, "would you care for some lemonade? I just made some."

"Sure, that sounds great."

Jackie nearly dropped her mother's good set of hollowware as she moved to the table, but she did finally manage to pour two lemonades. She started to sit down across the table from Clayton, but he pulled the chair out on the end and she sat beside him. It was her father's chair. Clayton was in the side chair where her mother always sat.

"How is your family?" Jackie blurted, and Clayton told her things she already knew.

"Oh, right. I guess you told me all about that in your last letter," she said with an embarrassed smile. After that she rattled on, making no sense at all until Clayton came to the rescue. He gently laid a hand over hers.

"Jackie," he spoke tenderly. "It's me, Clayton."

Jackie became utterly still. His touch was doing odd things to her heart. She told herself not to cry, and even managed to obey; however, she could no longer keep her thoughts to herself.

"Oh, Clay, I've missed you so much."

His hand came up then. He tenderly stroked her cheek with the backs of his fingers, and Jackie's heart melted.

"I was going to be so witty and charming when you came, and now I've been an idiot."

"I don't think you're an idiot." His hand was on hers again.

"How long can you stay, Clay?"

"I'm not certain," he admitted, keeping himself from adding, *It all depends on you.*

"Where are you staying?"

Clayton smiled. "I don't know. I was

rather hoping your father would let me crash at Uncle Mitch's."

"It's rented," Jackie told him. "Maybe I can ask Mother —" she stopped suddenly. "How did you get in here?"

"Your mother let me in."

"But I never heard the door."

"You were too busy making something in the bowl over there."

"Oh!" Jackie's hands flew in the air, and she dashed back to her bread dough. "I've got to punch this down, or we'll have a monstrosity."

"Would that be so bad?" He leaned back in his chair and just gazed at her.

"Well, I guess not. Especially if you like your bread the same size as the town hall."

Now *that* was something she would have said in one of her letters, and Clayton felt very heartened. He knew why he'd come, but he didn't dare tell her that his sole reason was to learn if the girl from the letters really existed.

"I read a story one time," Jackie now spoke conversationally, feeling suddenly at ease. "It was about a woman who had black hair. It would fall in her face. Naturally she would push it back, even while she baked. The people in the town did not believe any work should be done on Sunday. She wholeheartedly agreed with this, except that she showed up at church one morning with flour in her hair."

Clayton smiled. "What did the people do?"

"Oh, they were upset, but the pastor was new and he hadn't heard all the rules the town had imposed on itself. He took one look at her and fell in love, flour and all."

They both laughed at this, but it was short-lived. Clayton looked at Jackie's eyes, and Jackie stared back, her hands still buried in the bowl.

"I had to come, Jackie," he whispered. "Your letters are doing things to my heart, and I had to come."

"I'm glad you did. My mother asked me if I would ever go to see you. I told her I didn't think I'd be welcome."

"You'll have to tell her you were wrong. You'd be very welcome."

Jackie just looked at him. "I didn't remember how handsome you were, Clay. I'd forgotten the way the sun bleaches your hair and the way it falls on your forehead."

"You were about ten pounds lighter the last time I saw you."

Jackie looked down at the dough, her hands working again. "I was a little upset."

Clayton was next to her before she could

take another breath. Jackie turned and looked into his face. She loved the fact that he didn't tower over her. She knew Eddie loved Robert's height, but it was not for her. Clayton had only to lean in order to press his lips against her forehead. Jackie blushed at her own thoughts.

"You were more than a little upset, Jackie." Clayton ignored the color in her face and went on. "I'm sorry I was so insensitive."

"You were so pleased to be leaving, and I felt utterly crushed. It wasn't anything I could really share with you."

"I understand."

"And now," Jackie admitted painfully, "you're here to find the girl in the letters. Well, I don't know if you will, Clay. I mean, I just get all flustered when you're around, and I can't seem —"

She cut off when he placed two fingers over her mouth.

"I want you to listen to me. Will you do that?"

Jackie could only nod.

"Like I said, my heart is changing. For all I know, yours is too. I'm here to see if there's something between us, Jackie, not to hurt you or pressure you in any way." Clayton finally moved his hand. "I felt it was best to be right up-front."

Jackie nodded. "Thank you, Clay." She looked away to pick up the towel for her hands and then back at him. "I'll go and find Mother now and ask her if you can stay."

"All right, but I think maybe I'd better talk to her first."

Jackie looked at him for a moment but then understood. She found her mother in the living room and explained what she wanted.

"Of course he can stay with us, honey."

"Well," Jackie wasn't sure how to say it, "he wants to talk to you first."

Addy stared at her and then said, "Well, by all means, ask him to come in."

A moment later, when Clayton came alone to the living room, Addy was smiling. However, he looked so strained that she felt a prickling of fear. Had he told Jackie in plain terms that he was just here as a friend? Or had he come to ask of becoming engaged? When Addy had opened the door and seen him standing there, her heart had tripped with gladness. Was she right or wrong?

"Sit down, Clay. What can I do for you?"

"Thank you, Addy. I appreciate your hospitality, but I think I need to tell you that

I've come for a reason."

Addy leaned forward in her chair.

"I've come to see if the things I'm feeling for Jackie are real. I think you know that we've kept in touch while I've been in Denver, but I had to see her. If I still looked at her like a little sister, then I wouldn't hesitate to accept your offer, but I think you should know that my heart is changing."

"I see," Addy said simply.

"That isn't to say that I'd dishonor her in any way, no matter how my feelings have changed, but I thought you should know."

Addy's heart felt like a butterfly just released from its cocoon. "The fact that you've come to me, Clay, and laid your heart at my feet, tells me that Morgan and I have nothing to worry about."

Clay smiled. His own heart was feeling a good deal lighter all of a sudden.

"Thank you. I'll go and tell Jackie." Clayton rose to do this but never got to the door.

"Clay is here?"

The shout could be heard from the other room, and then Danny and Sammy were upon him. They both hugged him before Sammy dragged him to the sofa and began a line of a thousand questions. She seemed to have no concept of how far Denver was from Boulder and asked if he ever saw Robert and Eddie. It took some time to explain the geography to her, and while they were talking, Jackie joined them. Clayton didn't spend the whole time gazing at her, but he knew she was there. And for today, that was enough.

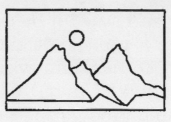

CHAPTER 25

"Jackie is working today?" Addy asked Morgan and then stared at him. He wouldn't look at her when he answered but bent over to fasten his shoes.

"Yes. I need her."

"I know, Morgan, but Clay is here and I —"

"*Yes,*" he bit out suddenly. "Clay is here. And the next thing you know we'll be watching our second daughter go away."

Addy sighed but kept quiet. Morgan had been in a terrible temper for weeks now, but things had grown noticeably worse when Addy confided in him the night before as to why Clayton was in Georgetown. And why was it, she asked herself, that Morgan never had a problem *before* the man showed up. He would encourage the girls, telling them to write, delivering the gifts that were sent, and even listening to them chatter on and act all dreamy when the beloved's name was mentioned. But when the man came on the scene, first Robert and now Clayton, Morgan was impossible to live with. Addy simply did not know what to think any more.

"Morgan, please let her have some time off," she tried again. "She works so hard and never complains. Please, Morgan."

But he was adamant. His mind made up, he left the bedroom and moved to the kitchen. However, he hadn't reckoned with his daughter. Danny and Jackie were in the kitchen. Danny had just agreed to work for her older sister, but her father said no. Both girls stared at him. He decided against breakfast and started toward the door. Clayton was not to be seen at the moment, but Jackie didn't want to risk a scene in front of him. She followed her father out of the house.

"Danny's going to work for me, Father."

"No, Jack." His tone told her not to argue, but she didn't heed it. "You come to the store as soon as you've eaten."

"Why?"

"Just do as I tell you, Jack." He was hitching the team now in a way that told his daughter he was finished.

"I'm going to spend the day with Clay," Jackie said firmly. "Probably tomorrow too."

Morgan's head rose slowly. "Are you defying me, Jack?"

"If that's what it takes," she stated with more calm than she felt.

Morgan's anger exploded. "How dare you!"

"How dare I what?" Jackie was just as angry now. "Danny is coming down to the store. Why do I have to be there?"

"I'll thank you to remember," Morgan bit out, "that you still sleep under *my* roof and eat *my* food, Jacqueline Fontaine."

"And I'll thank *you* to remember that I put in 50 hours a week in the store and 30 during the school year without a dime to show for it."

Some of the wind went out of Morgan's sails at that point, but Jackie went on quietly before he could speak.

"I didn't know you felt that way. Maybe I'll just not be a burden any longer. Maybe I'll just go to Denver with Clay when he returns." She turned to walk back to the house, but Morgan finally heard what he'd been saying.

"Jack."

She stopped but didn't turn around.

"Please come here."

Jackie went then, but her expression was defensive. She didn't want to draw too close, but when she was within arm's length, Morgan pulled her to him. He embraced her for a moment, and Jackie even hugged him in return.

"Go with Clay today. Have a good time."

His voice sounded oddly strained to her ears, but she still nodded.

"Thank you, Father."

Morgan went back to hitching the team, and Jackie went inside. Clayton was now in the kitchen and greeted her warmly, but Addy looked straight at her daughter. She asked to see Jackie upstairs, and the 17-year-old followed her mother from the room.

"You had words with your father?" Addy asked as soon as the bedroom door was closed.

"Yes. He's being completely unreasonable." Jackie was still a little angry. "He pushes you around, but he's not going to treat me that way."

"You will not speak to me in such a way, Jackie." Addy's voice told of her fury.

"It's true, Mother. You're his wife, so you have to take it. I don't."

"You're wrong," Addy said coldly. "You do have to take it, and if this is the way you're going to act when Clayton shows up, then maybe he should leave."

The anger left Jackie in a hurry. Her

mother was rarely upset with her, and she felt terrible. She spoke again, but her voice was subdued.

"He was wrong, Mother. What was I supposed to do?"

"You must respect him, Jackie."

"So you think I should have gone to the store?"

Addy suddenly felt tired beyond her years, and her face indicated as much. She turned away from Jackie and said, "I don't know, Jackie. I just don't know."

Silence dropped like a cloak onto the room. The clock could be heard chiming downstairs. Seven rings. So early in the day and already off on terrible footing.

"What did you and your father fight about?"

Jackie explained. "Then he made me feel as though I don't earn my keep. I never ask for money, Mother, you know that. So I told him that if he felt that way, maybe I should just go back to Denver with Clay."

Oh, Jackie, you must have crushed him with those words, her mother said to herself. Outloud she said, "What did he say?"

"He told me to go ahead and have my day. I think he was sorry, even though he didn't say it."

"So you did part on good terms?"

"Yes, but he still looked upset." Jackie shook her head. "Why, Mother? Why does he give us such a hard time?"

"It's very involved, Jackie, and I'm not sure I can explain." Something in Addy's voice bothered her daughter.

"Does it have to do with the fact that you and Eddie don't think Father's going to heaven?"

Addy could only stare at her.

"Oh, Mother, please don't be angry with Eddie, but she was upset before she and Robert got married. I asked her why, and she said that sometimes Father's lack of faith really upsets her. She told me she prayed for him every day. I didn't know what to say to her. It's not true, is it, Mother? Father will go to heaven, won't he? I mean, he's such a good man."

Oh, heavenly Father, Addy's heart begged as the breath left her body, *is she really so ignorant of the way of salvation? Did her confession as a child mean so little, or have I been remiss in my explanation?*

"Jackie," Addy finally spoke very slowly. "Do you really not understand about salvation by grace, not works?"

"Well, yes, I do, but I just can't believe that God would keep a good man like Father out of heaven. I used to get angry

331

with Uncle Mitch for talking that way too."

A knock sounded on the door just then, and Addy did not get a chance to reply. Lexa stuck her head in and spoke to Jackie.

"Clayton hasn't said anything, Jackie, but he keeps looking toward the stairs. I think you should come down."

"All right," Jackie answered and turned toward the door. She was almost out when she remembered her mother.

"I'm sorry, Mother. Was that all?"

The timing was wrong, and Addy knew it. She wanted to sit her daughter down and talk this out, but her heart would not be in it. The older woman eventually nodded her head and told Jackie to run along. She was in need of breakfast, but she had no appetite. Addy sank down onto the bed and prayed for a long time.

"Here's your favorite. A wild rose." Clayton held the flower beneath Jackie's nose. She breathed deeply before he slipped it into her hair. He then caught her hand when she tried to move it.

"Now, don't you touch it," he scolded. "I've got it just right."

She laughed. "It feels like it's sticking straight up in the air."

"Well, it is. What else is it supposed to do?"

Jackie took her hand back and reached for the flower. She placed it behind her ear, a vast improvement, and then posed.

"Well," Clayton admitted grudgingly. "I guess it looks a *little* better."

Jackie smiled at him and turned away from the warmth she saw in his eyes. She began to repack the picnic lunch they'd enjoyed. Clayton lay down on the pale yellow blanket, supported by one elbow.

"Why do you do that?" he asked nonchalantly as he fiddled with a blade of grass.

"Do what?"

"Why do you get busy with your hands every time I look at you?"

Jackie stopped all movement, but still didn't look up. What could she say to him? *I'm sorry, Clayton, but if I look at you and think I see love in your eyes when there's not, I'm going to be hurt beyond all repair.* The thought alone was enough to make her speechless with embarrassment.

"Can't answer," he coaxed softly, "or don't want to?"

"Oh, Clay, it's just that —" Jackie cut off and looked at him. He wasn't looking at her with warm interest now. Now he was just Clayton, and she felt a little better.

"I think I'm afraid for you to know how I really feel, and I'm afraid that if you look at me too long, I won't have a secret left."

Clayton smiled gently. "You do tend to carry your emotions in your eyes."

Jackie had to agree. Her family always knew what she was thinking.

"Did you by any chance have angry words with your father this morning?"

"Yes, I did."

"Did it concern me?"

Jackie nodded miserably. "Danny said she'd work for me, but he said I had to come in. We fought, but then he changed his mind."

"Is it me, specifically, Jackie, or any man?"

Jackie was so stunned by this question that for a moment she sat quietly.

"I never thought about it before, but it is all men. I mean, Robert is a wonderful man, but Father had a terrible time when he came. He kept it covered up most of the time, but we could tell. No, Clay, it's not you. It's Father. I think he sees all men as a threat to our family."

"Well, in some ways they are."

"I don't know what you mean."

Clayton chuckled and tossed the blade of grass he'd been holding. "Robert didn't come here to study the plant life; he came to propose to Eddie. Six months later, she was gone. And now I'm sure your mother must have told your father that I'm here to find out our feelings for each other. The man's not blind, Jackie; he can see the way I look at you."

"And how do you look at me?" The question escaped with no premeditation, but Jackie felt immediately better.

Clayton grew very serious. "It's like the letter you wrote me a long time ago about the wildflowers. For a while looking at them is enough, but then you want to touch. To really experience them, you need to hold them in your hands, smell them, and even rub them on your skin. I love looking at you, Jackie, but your father's a married man. He knows very well that I want to kiss you and hold you."

Jackie nearly panicked, but managed to speak.

"You've never talked about that in your letters."

"I didn't want to kiss your letters."

Jackie couldn't take her eyes from him. She wanted to; she wanted to busy her hands and mind a thousand miles from here, but she had to look into his eyes.

"I'm surprised you didn't start packing the lunch again." Clay had looked back at her, but now his eyes were smiling.

"I probably should, Clay, or I'm going to be the one to kiss you."

She so shocked him with that statement that his mouth came open. Jackie found this very amusing. Her laughter bounced over the meadow, and her grin was cheeky. The intense moment was broken, and right now it was for the best.

Addy waited until Morgan was finished with his customer and then approached. She wasn't fast enough, however. One of the older ladies in town snagged her, and she was tied up showing her bolt after bolt of fabric until the woman decided to go home and think it over. It seemed like hours before she could break away, but it must not have been. Morgan was leaning against the doorframe of the back room, just watching her. She hesitated in her step but kept on. When she neared, he dropped back into the room itself and over to the window. The act gave them privacy, and the window gave them light.

Looking down at her, Morgan stood in profile to the glass, his arms crossed over his chest. For a moment Addy felt like she was the one he'd fought with. She couldn't quite meet his eye.

"I was furious with Jackie when she told me she'd had words with you."

"I thought you would be angry with me," Morgan admitted quietly.

"I was, but not furious like with Jackie."

"She was right, you know. I was being unreasonable."

"And she was being disrespectful. I won't stand for that."

Morgan nodded but did not comment. It wasn't every man whose wife stood by his side even when he was behaving like a fool.

"I want to understand, Morgan, but I don't," she said suddenly. "Why could you take me thousands of miles away from my family, but not be willing to have anyone do that to your daughters?"

Morgan's gaze shifted out the window. The back of the building looked out over the mountains. It was beautiful beyond description. He honestly couldn't understand why anyone would want to live anywhere else, but he reminded himself that he hadn't seen the rest of Colorado's territory. It could be just as beautiful. In fact, if Eddie's letters could be trusted, it certainly was.

"I just take longer to adjust than you do, Addy. I'll get used to the idea of Jackie and Clay. Give me time."

"I'm glad to hear that, Morgan, but

337

you've been simmering with anger since Robert and Eddie left. Why can't you go see them? Go see how happy Eddie is in her home, and maybe you can lay it to rest."

"Go on my own?" he asked incredulously.

"Well, yes. I thought if I suggested we all go, you'd say we couldn't afford it. If you go alone, I'll be here to watch the store."

"I can always close the store," he mumbled. Addy's heart leapt. The hope must have shown in her eyes because Morgan reached for her.

"I'll think about it. All right?"

She nodded against his chest.

"Maybe this fall. All six of us."

Addy looked into his eyes. "Thank you."

"For what? I could still say no."

"I know, but your willingness to work on it makes it so much better."

He kissed her then, a long passionate kiss that dislodged hair pins and turned her face a bright pink. Coming into the back, Danny heard their low voices and moved back out front. Father always whistled the hours away when mother made a visit to the store. Danny decided her mother should come every day.

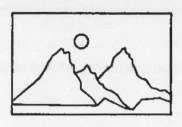

CHAPTER 26

Clayton leaned forward and gently pressed his lips to Jackie's brow. When he moved away, she looked into his eyes and admitted, "I've wanted you to do that for the longest time."

Clayton's eyes burned into hers, and a moment later, he lowered his head. Jackie back-pedaled as fast as she could go, a hand to his chest as she moved her head back.

"I don't think I meant to say that." Her voice was in a panic.

Clayton didn't push the point, but his eyes were eating up every inch of her face.

"Why can't I kiss you?" he finally managed.

"Because you can't know if you love me in five days' time."

"How much do you want to bet?"

She really wanted to run then, but he caught her and held her by the upper arms.

So much had happened in the last few days. Jackie had worked at the store some, but Clayton was with her even there. They'd talked of everything under the sun, and Clayton had finally come to realize that the only thing he could be feeling for this woman was love.

After the picnic the first day, they'd walked home talking all the way. With the passion of the moment behind them, they were able to discuss the possibility of kissing. Clayton told Jackie before they reached her house that he would not kiss her unless he was certain he loved her. Jackie had thanked him, knowing it was going to be hard, but very grateful for his honor in the situation.

And now they were outside after dinner. It was still quite light, but they could feel evening descending. They had walked around the side of the barn and stood talking. Clayton had surprised Jackie when he turned and kissed her brow, but she enjoyed it.

Now the hands that held her upper arms went around her back. Clayton pulled her into an undemanding embrace, and Jackie laid her head on his shoulder. How long had she dreamed of being held by him? But nothing could have prepared her for the real thing.

Clayton's shoulders were broad, and his

chest was hard. He didn't press his advantage in any way, but Jackie felt cherished and desired. It was a lovely time for the two of them, interrupted only by his next statement.

"I need to leave in a few days."

Jackie raised her head. "So soon?"

"Yes. I'll miss a little class time as it is."

"When will I see you again?"

Clayton sighed. "I won't be done with school until next spring, and I know your father would never agree to your coming and finding a place to live in Denver now."

"But you will come back?"

"Jackie," Clayton sounded stunned. "If you can doubt that, then I haven't told you how I really feel."

The sun was setting just behind Clayton's shoulder now, and he had a perfect view of her face. She looked utterly vulnerable at that moment and he asked God to help him be the husband she needed. He didn't think that now was the time to propose, but he could tell Jackie that he loved her.

"I love you, Jackie, and if you'll have me, I'll return in the spring and show you how much I mean it."

"Oh, Clayton, I've loved you forever."

She sounded young and ardent, and Clayton's heart felt very tender. He did kiss her then, but it was a gentle kiss, a kiss of promise for things to come.

"I've got to discuss this with your parents."

"Yes. I'll go with you."

But when the time came later that evening, Clayton was honest with Jackie and told her he'd rather she wait in the other room. She agreed, but it wasn't easy.

"I haven't asked Jackie to be my wife," Clayton told her parents, "but I have told her that I love her. We plan to continue our letters to each other, and when I do propose, it probably will be by mail. I'd like to come next year for a spring wedding, but it all depends on whether I get work.

"I haven't told you all of this in complete disregard of your wishes, but now that you know what I'd *like* to do, I'd like you to tell me if you think I'll suit. In other words, may I court your daughter, Jackie?"

"Yes, Clay, you may," Morgan answered immediately and surprised Addy into staring at him. "I've already given it great thought. It would please me beyond all reason to see you settle here, but whether or not you do, I know Jackie loves you, and I know you'll take care of her."

"Thank you, sir." Clayton was a bit choked up, but he managed the words. Not long afterward he joined Jackie in the kitchen.

"Well, I didn't ask for your hand in marriage, but I did tell them that I hoped it would come to that. The only thing I really requested was to court you."

"What did Father say?"

"Yes."

"Yes? Just like that?"

"He didn't even hesitate."

Jackie threw her arms around him for just an instant, and then they sat at the table, heads close and talking.

"Father's been more gentle in the last few days than I've seen him in a long time."

"Months ago now Eddie told me that she prayed for his salvation every day. I've prayed for him as well, Jackie. I wanted you to know that."

Jackie's face looked troubled. "It's funny you should mention it, Clay. Mother came to my room just two nights ago to kiss me good-night and questioned me for a long time. I must have said something to make her worry about my going to heaven."

"Did you clear things up?"

"I think so, at least *I* feel all right about it."

"Good. When *did* you come to Christ, Jackie? Were you a child?"

Jackie shrugged. "I've just always been, Clayton. For as long as I can remember."

Clayton had never heard it put that way before. He was thinking on the subject when Jackie started to talk about Robert and Eddie. The young couple visited for another half hour in the kitchen and then joined the rest of the family in the living room.

Clayton left three days later, but there was no grief on Jackie's part this time. He loved her, and if he was hired somewhere to teach, then in the spring they could be married. God had taken care of every other need, and Jackie knew He would bring them together. She also knew that nothing in the world could dim the happiness she felt right now. God had been so good, and she was walking on a cloud.

Clayton loves me, Eddie. I didn't think I would ever be able to say those words, but he does. It had taken Jackie a few weeks to come back to earth, but now she had to write and let her sister know that she was in love with a man who loved her in return.

I never completely understood the way you floated around after Robert had been here, but I do now. I'm 17 ¹/₂ and I'm in love. I can't believe it. It feels so good to write to you about this.

When Eddie received the letter, she could only shake her head. She read it to Robert, and they both laughed. Every paragraph was about Clayton or his time with Jackie. She had written about everything they'd done and talked about.

"And how long does it say they'll need to wait?"

"Next spring," Eddie told her husband.

He now shook his head as well. "It's going to be a long winter."

Jackie began school with much the same feeling as ever. Danny, Lexa, and Sammy were all glad to be back, but Jackie's heart was not in it. Her mother had had a talk with her about attitude, and although she was still struggling, she was working on it.

"I don't feel like a schoolgirl anymore, Mother. I'm contemplating marriage, and I just don't want to study math."

Addy stroked her hair. "I can see that it's going to be hard, dear; indeed, it's going to take a real step of maturity to deal with this."

Addy inadvertently challenged Jackie with those words. More than anything else, Jackie wanted Clayton to see her as a mature woman. She thought about the letter she'd already started, the one that did nothing but complain about returning to school. She decided then and there to tear it up and start another one.

It took a few weeks, but by the end of September she was doing well. Her father had cut her hours in the store, but she still worked all day Saturday and two afternoons during the week. She really did enjoy it, especially when she could rearrange the stock room.

"I can put this heavy stuff at the top," Morgan told her when she arrived one Tuesday after school, "but please work on these lower shelves."

"All right. Call me if you need me out front."

Morgan suddenly hugged her.

"What was that for?" Jackie was very pleased.

"I don't know. You're so cheerful and helpful these days. I think being in love suits you very well."

The young woman beamed at him and went to work. She was fast and efficient, and because her father didn't call her to the front at all, she was finished with the low shelves very swiftly. Morgan had said he would do the top shelves, but Jackie saw no need. She positioned the ladder and climbed up with the heavy tins of syrup and pails of river salmon. She was getting tired after two or three trips, but she had only two to go and stuck with it. Jackie had not faltered a single step in the last two hours, but suddenly, before she could put the tin in place, she was falling from more than six feet in the air, the tin coming down on top of her.

Morgan heard the crash from the front and walked swiftly away from the customer he was serving. Seeing Jackie unconscious on her back was nearly enough to make his heart stop. He ran to the front long enough to send the customer for the doctor and then back to his daughter's side. Bile rose in his throat as he saw that her nose and mouth were both bleeding. He couldn't stand the thought that she would be in pain, so he didn't try to wake her. He left her lying flat, praying for the doctor to arrive soon.

He wished he could have warned Addy before they arrived, but Jackie never awakened, not even when, accompanied by young Doc Edwardson, they took her home in the back of the wagon and carried her to her room.

An hour later, the screams that came from Jackie's room so terrified Sammy that Addy took her downstairs. Lexa and Danny stood huddled in the hallway while the doctor and their father remained inside.

"Try to keep her still," Doc Edwardson gasped as he grabbed for Jackie's flailing arms. Morgan would have been better at that position, but he'd grabbed her legs and still tried to reason with her from further down the bed.

"Jackie, it's all right," he called to her. "I'm right here."

"Help me!" she replied hysterically.

"Jackie," he tried again, but at that moment, she swung her own arm against her head and went completely still.

Both men froze, Morgan's pale face going even whiter. He looked at his daughter's still form, and then his eyes flew to the young doctor.

"What happened?" He demanded, his voice hushed.

"She's fainted," the doctor told him. Both men were panting.

Morgan's tortured eyes went back to Jackie and then to the doctor once again. "Please tell me it isn't so."

"I can't." The younger man rose slowly, his voice hushed as he gently put Jackie's arms at her side. "I saw this just recently, I'm sorry to say. There's not a thing that can be done." He looked at Morgan.

"I'll sit with her, Morgan. Go and see your family. They need to know, and you need each other right now."

"You're sure?" Morgan asked, tears filling his eyes, and the doctor knew to what he referred.

"I'm sorry, Morgan," he said resignedly. "I haven't seen much of this, but enough to know. The way she fell and then woke up — it can't be anything else."

Morgan stumbled to the door and then out into the hall. Danny's and Lexa's soft cries met his ears, and he went to them. He held them close for a moment.

"Where's your mother?"

"She took Sammy to the kitchen."

"Come on. I've got to see her."

It was a pitiful group that huddled close and descended the stairs. Addy came to her feet as soon as she saw them, her hand going instinctively to Sammy's shoulder.

"Oh, no, Morgan," Addy gasped when she saw his face. "She's not dead. Please don't tell me she's dead."

"No, she's not." He looked at Addy, but didn't really focus. "But she's blind, Addy. Completely blind. She'll never see again."

Dark spots danced before Addy's eyes. One minute she was standing and the next she was crumpled into a heap on the floor.

CHAPTER 27

"Mother! Mother!" the terrified voice called, and Addy rushed to her daughter's side.

"I'm here, Jackie. It's all right. I'm right here."

Jackie clung to her mother, trembling from head to foot. Jackie's fear of the dark had begun during childhood. Now she'd been plunged into a sea of blackness, and the slightest change set her off. Just now the wind had kicked up outside, and she'd heard a strange noise. It had been happening off and on for days. Addy's face was drawn with exhaustion, but Jackie couldn't see this.

"Here," Addy suggested, "the sun is shining right through this window. Move to the sofa now, and you'll be able to feel it."

"Help me," Jackie whimpered.

"I'm here. Take my hand."

They made the move with Jackie clutching at her mother's arm. Addy's skin was already bruised and scratched from Jackie's clasping hands, and she winced when Jackie hit a sore spot.

When Jackie was settled, Addy sank into a chair of her own and just stared into space. She wasn't certain how much longer she could do this. It was three weeks to the day since Jackie had fallen in the store, and although her headaches had abated, Jackie was terrified most of the time. The rest of the household had finally learned to sleep through her cries in the night, but Addy went to her every time. She never calmed down in less than two hours, and the days were not much better.

One afternoon just that week after a particularly difficult night, Addy fell into such a hard sleep in a living room chair that by the time she heard Jackie's cries the younger woman was inconsolable. Jackie had been almost impossible to live with since, terrified that she was being left alone in her blackness. Attempts to comfort her with Scripture, God's promises to never leave His children, fell on deaf ears. Jackie had nearly reverted to infancy.

Addy had thought it hard to have little ones under foot, but nothing could have prepared her for having a 17-year-old baby. She was dressing Jackie, giving her baths, and helping her eat. Addy didn't know how much more she could take.

From where she sat in the chair, she now rocked her head and looked at Jackie. The blind girl just sat there. Addy tried to understand but couldn't. Jackie didn't talk anymore or ask questions. Her world had shrunk until she was the only one who existed.

It's too soon, Addy told herself, but then an unfair thought came to mind. Jackie had always been more self-centered than any of the other children. Blind or not, Addy didn't believe she herself would be so unreasonable. A minute later guilt poured over her. She felt terrible for thinking this way. She was praying, trying to explain her weary heart to God, when she heard someone knock at the front door.

"What was that?" Jackie was instantly afraid.

"Just someone at the door." Addy rose to answer it.

"Are you leaving?" Jackie's hands were outstretched, and Addy rushed to her.

"I'm just going to answer the door," Addy answered. Jackie calmed a little at her touch. "Just sit tight; I'll be right back."

Jackie was shaking again, but Addy left her and rushed to the door. She was rather startled to see Mrs. Munroe standing on the small porch. Pastor had visited twice, but his wife, who was often busy with the town orphans, was the last person Addy expected. However, she was not unwelcome.

"I hope I won't be intruding, Addy, but I thought I could be of some help."

"Oh," Addy's manners returned to her in a rush. "Of course, Ora, please come in."

Ora Munroe was just two steps into the house when Jackie set up a hue and cry. Addy didn't explain, but turned and ran to her. Ora followed slowly. By the time she calmed Jackie down, the other woman was standing silently in the doorway.

"Come in, Ora," she bade gently, telling herself to forget the dust and grime that seemed to pervade the room, indeed, the whole house.

"Thank you."

"Mrs. Munroe is here, Jackie."

"Hello, Jackie," Ora greeted her softly.

"Hello." Jackie's voice was dull.

"How is your shoulder?"

Jackie didn't answer. Addy looked apologetic and spoke for her.

"It's fine really, just very bruised. Those tins of syrup are quite heavy. Doc Edwardson was rather surprised she hadn't broken any bones."

Ora nodded, and a momentary silence fell on the threesome. It didn't last, however, as Jackie suddenly lost her mother and began to call to her in terror. Addy was standing to go to her when Ora spotted a bruise and a scratch on her arm. She caught Addy's sleeve and shook her head.

"Answer her from here," she said quietly. For a moment, Addy only stared at her. "Sit back down, Addy, and answer her from your place in the chair."

"Mother! Mother!"

The cries escalated, but Addy made herself sit back down.

"I'm right here, Jackie; right in my chair."

"Mother." Again Jackie's hands were outstretched, unseeing eyes searching frantically.

Addy began to panic herself and turned to their guest, but Ora only shook her head.

"Jackie." The strange voice caught her attention. She'd forgotten anyone else was there. "Your mother is right here. She's going to answer you from her seat." Ora urged Addy with her head.

"I'm right here, Jackie. Can you hear me?"

"Yes, but I need to touch you." Jackie was crying now.

Ora shook her head vehemently.

"I'm right here." Addy's voice wobbled with her own tears, but she managed the words. "You can hear me."

Jackie's hands began to twist and flap. She was on the verge of hysteria.

"I have to touch you," she sobbed.

"No," Addy now said on her own. "I'm right here. Just listen to the sound of my voice."

"I can't."

"Yes, you can," Ora put in. "In fact, you can tell by the sound of her voice how your mother is feeling."

Jackie was shaking her head, but Ora went on, her soft voice compelling.

"Listen to your mother, Jackie, and tell me if she's angry."

Addy picked up her cue. "I'm right here, Jackie, right here in the room with you."

Jackie was still moving fretfully, but she was listening too.

"Is she angry, Jackie?"

"No, but I need to touch her."

"Does she sound like she's going to play a trick on you?"

"No." Jackie's movements were calming.

"No, she isn't, is she? If your mother tells you she's right in the room, then you know she's going to be here."

Jackie's breathing was returning to normal, and her hands now lay still in her lap.

"Go to her, Addy," Ora instructed, and when she did, Jackie clung to her in relief. Addy smoothed her hair and nestled Jackie against her. The exercise had been as draining for her as it was for Jackie. She finally looked to Ora.

"My mother was blind," the pastor's wife stated quietly. "I think I can be of help to you."

"If you run your right hand along the edge of the plate, Jackie, you will feel your cup."

Jackie's hand came to the table top. She bumped her knife and spoon but found the plate. It was a good thing it was empty, or she'd have put her hand right in the food.

"You must move slower, dear," Ora cautioned her. "Slow movements at all times, until you've found your way."

Jackie's left hand gripped the edge of the table, and Ora prepared herself for the outburst. They'd been working for two hours every morning for six weeks, and she knew all the signs. The progress had been very slow, but Ora was patient beyond all description.

"No one is going to clean up any messes you make today, Jackie. If you break another plate, you'll clean up the glass on your own."

At first Jackie was so shocked she couldn't speak, but a moment later she let out a howl.

"Mother! Mother!"

"Listen, Jackie." Ora's voice got through when Jackie was taking a breath. "She heard you upstairs. Listen to her footsteps on the stairs."

Jackie forgot her earlier irritation until she heard her teacher's next words.

"You can see, Jackie; you can see without your eyes."

"Don't say that to me!" she said through gritted teeth.

"But it's true," Ora insisted. "And as soon as you realize it, you're going to feel set free."

Jackie was still breathing heavily with irritation when her mother entered.

"Did you call me, Jackie?"

"Yes. I'm through for the day." She started to rise. "Take me upstairs."

"If you want to get upstairs," Ora cut in, "you'll have to go on your own."

"Mother!" she immediately cried. "Help me, Mother."

Ora didn't look at Addy or Jackie. She sat at the table and let them decide. In the past,

Addy had often helped when she shouldn't have. Ora had told her that in the long run it would make things worse, but too often Addy had not been able to withstand Jackie's tears.

"I think," Addy said softly, "that I'll let you go on your own today."

Jackie sat back down and began to cry. The women did not touch her or speak to her, and soon her tears became sobs. Morgan chose that moment to come in the door.

"What is it?" he asked immediately, not seeing anyone but Jackie.

"Oh, Father," she cried, taking immediate advantage. "I just want to go upstairs."

"I'll take you, honey," he offered and went right to her.

So taken was he with Jackie's fear that he didn't even notice his wife's face. Without further word to anyone, he took Jackie to her room.

Addy and Ora stared at each other before Addy admitted quietly, "Christmas is three-and-a-half-weeks away, and a week after that is Jackie's birthday. I wish they were already over."

"How can I clean it if I can't see it?" Jackie's voice was filled with anger, but Addy ignored it.

"It doesn't have to be perfect, but you can tell where the polish is. Just try."

"No. I don't want it all over me."

Addy worked to tamp down her own anger. If she told Jackie what she was really thinking, that she was a self-centered brat, it would crush her. However, she was not going to take no for an answer.

"I want you to do this," Addy said in an even tone. "I want you to at least try to polish this platter. If you don't, I won't read to you tonight at bedtime."

"You're treating me like a child," Jackie whimpered.

"Because you're acting like one," Addy snapped. She stopped herself just short of asking, *What would Clayton say?* But he was not mentioned anymore. His letters to Jackie were stacked unopened in her room, untouched and unanswered.

"I'll try," Jackie said quietly after a moment of uncomfortable silence. Addy thanked her and moved from the room.

I must stop this, Lord. I question You at every turn. I want answers as to how I'm going to carry on and how much longer I must struggle, but You have kept silent. I am becoming frustrated and distant with You, and I can't stand it.

Addy heard the sound of her own

thoughts and knew that she alone must deal with her anger and apathy. She took the first chair she could find and began to pray. Years ago she'd heard a preacher say, "The moment you don't feel like praying, get on your knees. And the moment you don't feel like reading your Bible, you'd better get that Book open."

The words came to her now, and Addy prayed. She didn't have the energy to go upstairs for her Bible, but she did pray. She confessed her anger and asked God for the strength to carry on. Jackie called to her a short time later, and she went to her, still praying. She talked to the Lord all the way to bedtime that night when she could finally escape to the quiet of her bedroom and write a letter to Eddie. She needed someone who would listen. Eddie seemed the ideal choice. Addy was tired enough to go to bed and sleep for 12 hours, but she fought the urge, sat down at her desk, and put ink to paper.

Morgan climbed the stairs to the bedroom late that same night. He was bone tired and told himself that he didn't really need to be at the store at 6:00. In fact, he had gotten so much done today, he didn't need to be there until right before opening at 8:00. Morgan was contemplating the loveliness of turning over in the morning and going back to sleep when he opened the door and found Addy slumped over the writing desk.

The lantern was burning, but she was sound asleep. He nearly shook her awake, but before he could do so, his eye caught some of the words of her letter to Eddie. Morgan carefully slid the paper from under her hand and moved beside her to catch the light.

Jackie looks like a scarecrow, and so do I. Never has weight control been so little a problem. Jackie actually polished a platter for me today but then threw a fit when I didn't get the polish off of her hands fast enough. I have prayed more today than I have in weeks, but never have I been so lonely. With Jackie not at the store to help him, Morgan is putting in double the hours, and knowing how much he worked before you can well imagine how little I see of him. When I came upstairs for the night, he wasn't even home yet. I don't know if the store needs him that badly or if he is running from this situation. I have been tempted to run myself.

I long for you, Eddie, as I have never done before. Please pray for me. Elaine in Denver seems a thousand miles away. I haven't even written to her. Every time I try to sit down and talk with Danny, Jackie screams for something. I know it's best to make her do things for herself, but most of the time I do not have the fortitude to deny her. She is still too dependent on me. I ask myself when enough is enough but gain no answers. I keep making excuses for her, telling myself that she needs more time, but they are hollow excuses even to my own ears.

I believe God is sovereign, and I believe He loves me, but I feel so frail. I ask Him to ease this load, but He has said no. I must carry on here, and for this I covet your prayers. I have an 18-year-old infant on my hands, an unsaved husband, and three other daughters who haven't had my attention since September 27 of last year. I haven't seen the inside of the church since that day, and even though I praise God for Ora Munroe, at times I think I will break under the strain of it all.

February is just around the corner, and I am asking God for something special. Maybe the snows won't be so harsh this late in the winter and spring will come early. This really would uplift my heart, especially if I could take Jackie outside or more folks would visit. Right now no one wants to be around her. At this point, I'd even enjoy working at the store instead of being with Jackie, but she will have no one but me or Morgan, and I've already told you where Morgan is most of the time. I ask again, Eddie, please pray for me.

Morgan set the letter down and saw that his hand was shaking. He put his hand on Addy's shoulders and cringed at the feel of her bones protruding under her flesh. How long since he'd last touched her?

"Come on, Addy," he spoke softly as he tried to lift her. She was like a boneless cat.

"I'm coming, Jackie," she mumbled incoherently.

"Come to bed, honey."

Morgan now lifted her and laid her on the bed. He removed her dress but left her in her shift. He divested her of shoes and stockings and then pulled the covers over her. She slept through it all. Morgan undressed himself and joined her, his head going down heavily on his own pillow. He didn't roll close to Addy, but lay very still. He had been so tired when he'd climbed the stairs, but now he felt wide awake. He saw the words on the letter again, and something terrible squeezed around his heart.

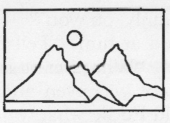

CHAPTER 28

Robert and Eddie received Addy's letter on February 17. Eddie was inconsolable for long minutes to follow. Indeed, Robert had been forced to read it to her, and he cried as well. They had certainly known about Jackie's blindness and been in touch often, but never had Addy unburdened as she'd done this time.

Robert waited until Eddie had calmed a little and then told her what was on his heart concerning Jackie's spiritual status. When he was finished she cried yet again, but Robert was patient, his own throat feeling rather tight.

"I have to do something, Robert," Eddie sobbed, her face still streaked with tears. "I can't play God, Robert, but there must be something. Please tell me what to do."

Robert smoothed her hair and used his own handkerchief on her face. "I have an idea, Eddie, but I don't know what you'll say. As with your mother, the burden would fall mainly on you."

Eddie looked at him. "Tell me, Robert," she whispered. "Whatever it is, tell me."

Robert's voice was even and well modulated as he told Eddie what was in his heart, but it was not easy. Eddie cried some more, but in the end she put her arms around him and held him tight. A plan — they had a plan — and that was better than aimlessly waiting. With that in mind she could wait for the spring.

"Write it, Lexa," Jackie ordered her miserable sister. "Write it now."

"Why, Jackie, why me?"

"Because your handwriting is the most like mine. Now, write what I tell you."

"But what about all of his letters? Don't you at least want to hear what he has to say?"

"Tell me, Lexa," Jackie said, her voice biting, low and furious. "Will you marry a blind man someday? Wouldn't it be exciting to marry a man who could never see you? You could guide him around like a stumbling child for the rest of your life. Now wouldn't that be fun?"

Lexa was openly sobbing now, but Jackie's heart hardened to the sound.

"Write, Lexa."

Still sniffing, Lexa adjusted the paper.

Jackie heard the rustle and began.

"Clay."

"Just 'Clay,' not 'Dear Clay'?"

"Clay!" Jackie spoke firmly. The younger girl tried to keep her hand from shaking. *Why,* she begged silently, *is this my Sunday to sit with Jackie?*

"Okay, what now?" she managed.

"I have met someone else," Jackie recited in a cold voice, "and fallen in love." She waited a moment, listening to the pen. "I never wish to see or hear from you again. Jackie."

"Oh, Jackie," Lexa began.

"Write it!"

Lexa was dying inside. She didn't know when she had been so upset. The whole house had been turned upside down last year, and they'd all walked around in a stupor until just a few weeks ago when their father got them all involved in Jackie's care. It wasn't that they hadn't tried before, but Jackie never wanted it. Now, in order to ease Addy's load, Father had them all on a schedule that included himself.

At first Jackie fought it, but the first time he'd stayed with Jackie himself and went so far as to take Addy from the house was a breakthrough. Jackie was out of control at the beginning, but now they'd developed a bit of a pattern. Today was Sunday. The rest of the family was at church, and Lexa had been put in charge. Not only was she to keep an eye on Jackie, she was to start lunch. Until this new schedule had begun, none of them had realized the stress their mother had been under.

"Don't forget to date it," Jackie added, breaking Lexa from her thoughts.

"I won't." Lexa was still so shaken she could hardly think.

"What is the date today?" Jackie demanded.

"March 12."

Jackie didn't speak, but bitterness coiled like a snake inside of her. Not even six months since her fall, but it felt like years. It felt like forever and always would. Blackness surrounded her, and that would never change. Clayton would go on. He would read the letter and hurt for a time, but then he'd find someone new, marry her, and live forever in happiness. He'd probably become a father. The thought so pained Jackie that she gasped.

"What is it?" Lexa asked.

"Nothing. Have you got it ready?"

"Yes."

"Dated?"

"Yes."

368

"Good. Now tomorrow, right after school, you take it and post it. No one is to know, do you hear me, Lexa? No one! And don't get any ideas in your head about writing to Clay."

"Don't you think he already knows, Jackie? Eddie or someone must have told him."

"No," Jackie said with confidence. "He doesn't know. I'm sure of it."

"How can you be?"

"Because he's still writing to me. If he knew I was blind, I'd never hear from him again. This way is best. He'll hate me, and that'll be the end of it."

Lexa couldn't find anything to say to this. She wanted nothing to do with this horrid scheme, but she felt trapped. For just an instant she wanted to strike her sister. She wanted to lash out, call her names, and rail at her for climbing that ladder, but when she looked up, Jackie wore such a look of utter hopelessness and despair that Lexa was crushed. She prayed as she'd been doing for the past five months. *What are we going to do, Lord? What are we going to do?*

Clayton's hands shook as he opened the letter. Even without seeing the contents, he knew Jackie's hand. She hadn't written in six months, and he'd about given up hope. He laughed at his own reaction to a simple letter, but still his hand shook.

"Clay," it began, and ended with "Jackie." Clayton read it over twice and then one more time. He stared at the words but couldn't take them in. He sat slowly on his chair. On his desk lay her last letter, dated in September. He'd read it so many times that it was torn and smudged. How could this happen? The letter from the fall was filled with happiness and love — love for him.

Oh, Jackie, his heart cried. *How could you do this to us? We love each other.* The flow of Clayton's heart stopped. *We did love each other. Now it's just me.* Clayton realized how true it was. Jackie might have fallen for someone else, but Clayton would never. The pain squeezing his heart was like a steel band. He looked down in front of him and spotted the letters he'd been writing. He was applying to three different positions he'd read about in the Denver newspaper. The one on top was addressed to the school board in Georgetown.

Clayton lay his hand on it and crumpled it into a ball. He might not hate Jackie or believe he could ever love again, but neither could he move there, teach school, and live near her and her new love. Again pain tore through him, and a sob broke from his throat. His mother, who came to tell him dinner was ready, found him crying at his desk. He told her the whole story but felt no relief. She cried with him but urged him to eat. He wasn't hungry. Right now he didn't think he'd ever be hungry again.

Robert and Eddie had prayed for an opening in the weather, and God gave them a time. They arrived in Georgetown on April 27. It was a surprise to all, but mostly to Addy. She never dreamed they'd come when there was still such a strong chance of snow, but she was thrilled to have them. As she stood in the kitchen with them, however, a strained look crossed her face.

"Father told us how bad she is," Eddie said quietly and before her mother could speak. "He's in the stable now, putting the horses in for the night."

"Your father's here?" Addy was amazed. "It's only 2:00, and no one else is with him today. The girls aren't even home from school yet."

"He closed the store for the day and brought us in the wagon," Robert put in. "We told him we can't stay long, and he said he didn't want to miss any time with us."

"Why are you here?" Addy was completely confused.

"To take Jackie back to Boulder with us," Robert stated.

Addy began to shake her head, but Eddie spoke up, "No, Mother. Don't try to get used to the idea right now. Just let it sink in."

"Eddie, you don't know what you're saying. You've never seen her like —" Robert stopped her with a hand to her arm.

"It's going to be all right," he said gently.

"What if she says no?" Addy asked just as Morgan was coming in the back door. "What if Jackie refuses to go?"

"She's not going to be given a choice," Morgan said kindly, but with a note of steel. "And neither are you, Addy. It doesn't have to be forever, but Robert and Eddie are right. It's time for this."

Addy nodded but had one more comment. "I won't tell you no, but I will say this — you haven't seen her or talked to her. It may not be me who changes my mind."

Robert and Eddie both looked at her. A moment later, the air was split by Jackie's piercing voice. The adults all exchanged looks, and then Eddie's chin went into the air. She was thinking, *Your big sister has come to town.* She sailed from the kitchen, a determined glint in her eye.

Jackie trembled from head to foot as she clung to Robert's arm, and her shakes were from far more than the cold. The journey to Boulder was ending, and she was so frightened that she could hardly breathe or move. How could they have done this? How could they have sent her away? She knew her home. She knew every inch of it. She had said this to her father, but he'd shocked her with his reply.

"You may know this house, Jack, but what's the point? You won't move an inch for fear of falling or bumping into something, and so you expect everyone to wait on you. Your mother shouldn't have to take it anymore, and I refuse to. You're going to go with Eddie and Robert, and you're going to do as you're told. We'll come to see how you're doing — maybe this summer or fall. But you are going."

She had screamed and cried, begged and pleaded, but it was no use. Four days later, on May 1, 1876, Jackie was packed up and taken to the stage office. Robert and Eddie were with her, but she was not comforted. She cried and trembled until Robert told her in no uncertain terms that the tears would stop. His voice was normal, kind even, but he made his feelings quite clear. Jackie told herself she didn't have to obey. After all, what could he do? But she didn't have the fortitude to cause a scene when the blackness around her seemed darker than ever. It might have helped if she'd realized that Eddie had been crying with pain for her, but so caught up was she in her own little world that she was not aware of this.

"Okay," Robert spoke from above her head. "Let's count."

"Count?" she asked breathlessly.

"That's right. These are the front steps to our home. You'll have to know how many there are, or you'll fall when you do them yourself."

Jackie would have denied him this, but he started forward, counting out loud at the same time. She had no choice but to follow.

"Ten, eleven, and twelve. There! We're at the top. Now five more steps forward and we'll be at the front door. Here we go.

Good. Now straight in front of you is the staircase. You're going to go up it. Count six steps and then the landing. I'll be right behind you."

Jackie was in a daze. The cold was receding, and a strange rug was beneath her feet. She grasped the wide banister and felt like she'd come into a huge cavern. She could smell a fire burning and even feel the warmth, but no light reached her eyes.

"Eddie!" Jackie cried so piteously that Robert had to hold his wife by the arm.

"I'm right here, Jackie," she managed through her tears. "You're doing just great."

"I'll fall," she whispered.

"No, you won't." Robert had let go of Eddie. "I'm right behind you. Are you counting?"

"No."

"Well, get at it. What did I tell you?"

"Six steps and then the landing."

"Excellent." Robert was very pleased because he wasn't certain she'd been listening. "And once on the landing you'll just circle it, keeping your left hand on the big ball, and then you'll have eight more steps to the top."

"All right. Is it hot in here?"

"Oh, here," Robert came forward. "Let

me have your coat."

"Will I ever get it back?"

"Of course," he laughed. "It'll be in the closet, which we'll save for another day."

"Another day?"

"Certainly. Today you're just going to learn your room, the stairs, and the dining room."

"Eddie?"

"Yes, Jackie, I'm right here behind Robert."

"Please don't let me fall in a hole."

"There are no drops at all, Jackie. Upstairs is all one level and so is downstairs. Just keep sliding your foot along. Not even the stairs will surprise you if you slide your foot along."

Jackie had no idea of the planning that had gone on in the last three months which allowed Eddie to say this. They had cleared their home of all but the necessities and counted every path and stairway in order to teach Jackie to move around on her own. In Eddie's and Robert's minds she was here to stay, and the sooner she learned her way around, the better.

Eddie had even gone so far as to remove all of her knickknacks and store them in boxes in the attic. When Jackie learned where each piece of furniture was, she would put them back. She knew that if Jackie broke something, she wouldn't want to take another step.

"You made it," Robert cried and Eddie followed more slowly.

"I'll fall backward," Jackie said, clutching at the railing. Robert put a hand on her back.

"I've got you. Now straight ahead is your room. Put your hand out and start moving."

"Oh, Robert, I don't think I can."

He could hear the exhaustion in her voice and knew that this had to be the last trial for the day.

"Just do this, Jackie, and I'll help you with the rest. Hand out, and slide your feet." He watched her carefully. "Now move your hand two inches to the left. Do you feel that? That's the doorway to your room."

Jackie felt her way all around, her hands smoothing the frame and wall and even walking a little bit inside. Robert came behind her and led her to the bed. She sat down hard when he backed her up to it and settled himself beside her. She promptly burst into tears, the first since they'd left Georgetown. Eddie sat on the other side of her and put her arms around her.

"Oh, Eddie, Eddie. How will I ever make it?"

"You did wonderfully, dear," she consoled her. "I'm so proud of you. In no time at all you'll be all over the house and yard."

"Why, Eddie? Why must I do this?"

"Because you need to take your life back, Jackie. You've become an invalid, and Mother is too close to you to change it. Robert and I are going to help you, but you're going to have to do the work. You're going to have to be willing to get bruised and spill things, because I won't allow you to sit around and neither will Robert. Trust me, Jackie, you will thank us someday."

Jackie didn't comment, and husband and wife exchanged a look over her head. They were both smiling and believed that it wouldn't be long before Jackie was smiling too. They would see to that. They would do everything in their power to help her reclaim some independence, if only she would make the effort. If they succeeded, they believed she would see far more in her world than she ever had with perfect vision.

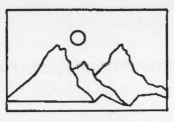

CHAPTER 29

"You did not tell me she was a beauty."

Eddie smiled at Lena, their housekeeper and cook. "She is pretty, isn't she?"

Lena put a hand over her heart. "Carl will faint."

Eddie laughed. Lena was always so dramatic, and her son, Carl, had an eye for a pretty face. Lena thought Robert was the salt of the earth and had begged to work for him even when he could barely afford her. Robert's bank had given Lena's husband, Raymond, a loan, and as far as she was concerned, Robert could do no wrong. His taking in of his blind sister-in-law only added to this adoration.

"I must take her food now."

"No, Lena," Eddie spoke, eyeing her sternly. "You will not wait on her or feel sorry for her. I was just up there. She had a great night's sleep, and she's coming down as soon as she brushes her hair."

"But she may have forgotten from yesterday. She may not know the way. This house is so big."

Eddie shook her head, and Lena relented. Robert had already left for the bank, and Eddie wanted to report to him at the end of the day that everything had gone well. If she started by babying Jackie, the day was going to be a disaster.

"Eddie?"

The young wife heard her name from the other room, and her heart leapt with joy. She moved to the bottom of the stairs and found Jackie standing uncertainly.

"Hi. You made it."

"Yes," she agreed, but she looked sad. "I can't remember how many steps it is to the dining room table."

"Nineteen," Eddie told her immediately.

"Eddie, how do you know that so fast?"

Eddie slipped her arm in Jackie's, not a comfortable position for the blind girl since she felt like she was in the lead. Eddie had done some reading and knew that the most comfortable position would be to have Jackie's arm in hers, with her walking half a step ahead of Jackie. But right now her mind wasn't on that.

"We did a lot of planning before you arrived," Eddie told her easily as they moved.

"Oh." Jackie's voice was still flat, and she

had no other questions.

They walked in silence until Jackie was at her chair.

"Have a seat, Jackie," Eddie began. "To your right is Lena. She works for Robert and me."

"Oh!" Jackie was startled. She'd heard movement but assumed it was her sister.

"Hello, Miss Jackie."

"Hello," Jackie answered, but her mind was moving. She had heard rustling upstairs after Eddie had left her and now knew that must have been Lena as well.

"Can you find everything there?" Eddie wished to know after Lena had put a plate before her. Jackie nodded. In truth, she wasn't too certain, but she was going to try.

"Where is my fork?" she finally had to ask.

"I think —" Eddie stayed in her place, but was helping her look. "Oh, yes. You pushed it under the plate."

"Oh, okay. I've got it now."

Eddie looked up to see Lena watching from the doorway, tears in the older woman's eyes. She swiftly averted her own so as not to join her.

"What's this?"

"Scrambled eggs, and to the other side are potatoes. Sausages are on the small plate to the left, and a cup of coffee is on your right."

Jackie started to eat, and for a time they were quiet. The new Boulder resident was the one to break the silence with a question that Eddie would have said was the furthest thing from her mind.

"Are you still as pretty as you were, Eddie?"

"Oh, my." Eddie's voice was exaggerated. "Much more so," she told her sister and was rewarded by the first small smile since they had arrived in Boulder.

It's going to be all right, Jackie. You'll see.

After Eddie had silently said these words, she asked God to enable her to do all she could with this sister of hers, and to have a heart that was glad for the privilege.

"Church?" Jackie's voice was horrified. "I can't go to church."

"I don't know why not," Eddie replied reasonably. "Lena has pressed your best dress, and I'll get you up in plenty of time. I'll even help with your hair."

"I couldn't stand it, Eddie. I know people will stare. I just couldn't stand it." Her voice was going higher and higher.

"Is there a problem?" Robert's voice came from the other side of the door.

Eddie made sure that Jackie's nightgown was in place and went to open it.

"She's panicked about going to church."

"I can't, Robert," she spoke as she heard his steps entering the room. "And you're not going to make me!" Her hands were clenched so tightly at her side that her nails were biting into her skin.

Robert came forward and without warning caught Jackie's jaw in his hand. It was not harsh, nor was his voice cruel, but he was master over her and she knew it.

"In this house we attend church on Sundays. What you get out of it is up to you, but we will be going, and you with us."

"Oh, Robert," she whispered fearfully, her hands now flapping in panic. "Please don't make me."

Robert moved his hand to her shoulder in a tender gesture. "Jackie, we're not here to humiliate you. Eddie will help you with your clothing and hair, and you'll look lovely. If people stare it will be because we have such an attractive sister who's come to live with us. Our church family will be delighted to meet you."

Jackie's breathing was still coming hard and fast.

"Jackie," Robert said, his voice still gentle. "The first time will be the hardest.

When the road dries a little more, you'll be going shopping with Eddie and doing everything she does. I believe with all my heart that you can enjoy a wonderful life." Jackie did not look convinced, but he finished with, "Get some sleep now; tomorrow will be a big day."

She never did agree, but Robert meant to have his way on this. He left Eddie to settle her in for the night — not something she usually did, but tonight Jackie needed it. They said nothing more on the subject, but when Eddie joined Robert in their bedroom, she shook her head.

"I'm not certain this is going to work."

Robert didn't comment but reached to unbutton the back of the dress Eddie was presenting to him. Both knew they would just have to wait and see.

Jackie could see the church but not touch it or be heard. Clayton was walking down the aisle. There was a beautiful blonde woman on his arm, and as Jackie stared, the woman and Clayton went to stand before the preacher. He said some words that Jackie couldn't make out and touched their heads, and then Jackie watched as they kissed. A bunch of little children ran out of nowhere, and Clayton gathered them all into his arms. His bride too. He looked so happy. Just as he left the church, he caught Jackie's eye and winked . . .

Jackie came awake in a rush, senses returning with a jolt. She sat up and was still panting when the clock began chiming downstairs. She counted. Only 4:00. Her chest was still heaving when she lay back down. It was a dream. Nothing but a dream.

"Oh, Clay," she said in the dark. "How will I go on? How will I live like this? If I thought you wouldn't stay out of pity, I might have written and explained, but I couldn't take that chance. If you pitied me, I would die, and I can't see your eyes to know the truth."

Her chest rose on a huge sigh as the pain of it all gripped her again. She put a hand to her ribs and could feel each one. She knew her breasts were smaller too, shrunken. She could circle one wrist with the fingers from the other hand and overlap them by what felt like inches. She knew she looked like a skeleton. It was surprising too, as she had always had a good figure and appetite. She might have run to fat if she hadn't been so busy all the time. But now, even though she spent most of her day sitting, she couldn't seem to gain any weight.

Well, not most of her day anymore. Eddie

had had her so busy in the last few days that she didn't know which end was up. And her mother. She missed her mother so badly that she ached inside. She wanted to hear her voice and feel her hands. A sob broke the stillness of the room.

How could you do this to me, God? What did I do to deserve this? Clay always talked of serving You, of us serving You together, but I don't think he really knows who You are. He doesn't know what You're capable of doing. I was happy. I was good. Why, God? Why me?

Jackie's tears were drying up instead of growing stronger, but her soul was drying up too. The only time she'd had a thought that wasn't for herself was when she'd asked Eddie how she looked. Her world had shrunken to the size of a robin's egg, and all thoughts were for Jackie, poor Jackie.

It took some time, but she did fall back to sleep. She woke with a feeling of dread, and for a time she attributed it to her dream in the wee hours. Then she remembered the day and Robert's hand on her jaw. They were going to force her to go to church.

"Oh, Jackie," Eddie's voice came to her ear. "Travis is here."

"Hello, Jackie." His voice, deep and kind, came from somewhere above her.

She remembered him, of course, but had forgotten how tall he was — even taller than Robert.

"Hello." Jackie greeted him quietly and continued to grip Eddie's arm. The older girl was certain to have a bruise.

She heard the two of them talk a moment but didn't really attend. Then Eddie was moving them forward.

"Here's our seat," Eddie was saying. Jackie put a hand out to guide herself along the pew. The wood was smooth, like the banister at Robert and Eddie's, and Jackie liked the feel of it. Someone moved beside her, and a moment later Robert spoke in a hushed tone.

"Well, people are staring, just like you thought." He watched her stiffen. "I think Carl, that's Lena's son, is never going to blink again."

Jackie moved her head as though she hadn't heard him right.

"And Tommy Walcott. He's only 16, but he looks like he won't hear a word of the sermon."

"Don't tease me, Robert," she finally managed, her voice just as low.

"Jackie." His voice was very serious. "The young men in this church are falling out of their seats looking at you."

"Then they don't know yet. They don't know I'm blind."

"On the contrary, they all know and have been praying for you for months."

"Good morning, everyone," a cheerful voice sounded from the front, and the conversation was cut off. Jackie, who was beginning to remember voices, tried to place this one and failed. Not that it would have mattered. Even after the singing was over and the sermon began, she heard very little. She was still trying to sort out Robert's words. It was inconceivable that anyone would find her even remotely attractive.

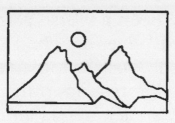

CHAPTER 30

"Hello, Jackie," the familiar voice called from the edge of the huge living room. Jackie turned to face the owner.

"Hello, Carl," she spoke softly, wondering if she would ever get over the wonder of it.

Carl had been to visit her every day for the last three weeks. He would wait until his mother was ready to go home in the late afternoon and then come on the pretense of seeing her home. Lena wasted no time in telling Jackie that her son had never seen the need to escort her home before, but Jackie could tell from Lena's voice that she was not at all upset.

"How are you today?"

"I'm fine," Jackie answered automatically as she always did. "How are you?"

"Fine." He said the words, and Jackie knew he was staring at her. She knew then, as she had before, that the attraction was purely physical.

This was not hard to figure out, as she

couldn't have been a worse companion. She said little and never laughed or smiled. It wasn't that she was trying not to, but she had so little interest in other people that nothing really struck her as amusing or worthy of her regard. In a way, she wanted to see Carl give up. She did not even know what he looked like because she had never asked. She had no intention of getting involved with anyone, and knowing that he was happy to just sit and stare at her did nothing for her heart.

"I am ready now, Carl." Lena called from the next room.

"All right." As usual he sounded regretful. "Have a nice evening, Jackie."

"Thank you, Carl. You do the same."

"Goodbye."

"Goodbye."

Here again was part of the routine. She would hear him walk across the floor, but he always paused. Jackie learned that if she turned her head away when his back was to her, he would take one final look at her and leave, but if she was still facing him, he took it as an invitation to talk to her again. Tonight she had her head turned, just as she'd done for the last two weeks. It was a relief to hear him move away and leave with his mother.

"Would it hurt you to talk to him a little, Jackie?" Eddie asked as she entered the room just a few minutes later.

"It might not hurt me, but it would him. I'm not going to encourage him."

"Why not?"

"To what end, Eddie?" Jackie sounded tired. "He's content to sit and stare at me, which means there's nothing deep about his attention."

Eddie couldn't argue with her there. Carl did like pretty girls, and Jackie was not a very fascinating companion these days. However, he was a sweet boy and had a strong love for Christ. Eddie knew it would do little good to tell Jackie that he was shy around her and afraid of saying the wrong thing. Eddie was certain that if he found the courage he could bring her sister out.

"How did you do on your mending?" Eddie had come to lean over her. "I swear Jackie," she said with a laugh in her voice. "I'm just going to give you the dark colors. You must have pricked your finger. There's blood all over your white blouse and the button too."

"I knew I'd stabbed myself, but I sucked on my finger for a while and thought it had stopped." She sighed deeply. "This is the blouse that goes with the navy skirt you gave me."

"How did you know which blouse it was?" Eddie said incredulously.

"It has a different feel to it, and see," she remarked, shifting the garment around. "The lace around the collar is very soft. The other one is scratchy."

"Well, I'll take it and work on it right now. If I can't get it out, Lena can. That woman's a wonder."

"Eddie," Jackie spoke when she began to move away. "You don't think Lena has encouraged Carl, do you?"

"I would say not, Jackie. She must know how you feel."

Eddie didn't elaborate, but it was very clear to anyone with eyes that Jackie was not in love. If she had been, the very mention of Carl's name would have brought color to her cheeks. Eddie walked away wondering what Clayton had said about the blindness. The older woman didn't have it in her heart to ask.

Jackie didn't comment to Eddie when she left either. Eddie had said that Lena knew how she felt. Jackie thought that nothing could be further from the truth. No one knew how she felt. How could she possibly let someone fall for her? It was like she had said to Lexa months ago now, how much fun would it be to lead a blind wife around for the rest of your life? "No thank you," was Jackie's reply to that. She didn't know how long Robert's and Eddie's patience would hold out, but at least she didn't feel humiliated in front of them.

In the midst of all these thoughts, Robert's voice could be heard. He must have just come home from work.

"Something smells good," Jackie heard him say just before he entered the room.

"Hi," he called as he moved toward her. "How was your day?" he asked, dropping a kiss on her cheek.

"The same as usual."

"Meaning?" Robert pressed her.

"Well, I sat here," Jackie recited in a dull voice. "I sewed a little. I sat some more. Carl came to stare at me. That's about the end of it."

Robert told himself to be patient, but it was not easy. His wife's sister had no interest in life at all. It was like her life had ended the same day her vision had. Was the blindness difficult? Yes. Was it upsetting? Undoubtedly. But it was *not* the end of the world. Did he wish it on himself? Absolutely not, but if it happened he would see the need to carry on and do so. The fact that Jackie had not done this; indeed, that she was willing to sit and let the world go by, infuriated Robert. He thought fast in order to keep his thoughts constructive. Growing angry with her was not going to do a bit of good.

"I want you to help Eddie with the dishes tonight, Jackie," he told her suddenly.

"The dishes?" she questioned, not having done them since she fell.

"Yes. I think it makes sense if you wash and Eddie and I dry. That way you can stand in one place and just hand things to us."

Jackie's mouth had gone very dry. That was her typical reaction every time Robert introduced her to something new. She didn't want to help in the house at all but knew better than to admit that. Robert would have given her a lecture. Indeed, Robert was watching her mutinous expression right now and felt pleased that she was restraining herself.

"Come on," he said conversationally. "Let's head to the table. I think dinner is almost on."

Robert stood and went ahead of her. Jackie fought down bitterness that she couldn't walk across the room so easily. She never talked unless someone was leading her, for it took all her concentration to remember where she was. Lately she was in the habit of asking God when it would all be over, but the answer was so painful that she would only push it from her mind.

Jackie collapsed into the buggy and put a hand to her head. Eddie knew she was completely spent but didn't comment. Jackie had been living in Boulder for a month now, and this was their first trip into town. The young woman had been terrified. They'd gone to the bank, to the general store, had lunch at the hotel with Robert, and even stopped at Pastor Henley's house. Taking everything in without complaint, Jackie had been very quiet the entire day, but Eddie felt her trembling each time she took her arm.

Now they were in the buggy and headed home, and Eddie knew that Jackie would fall asleep early tonight. She was sitting up, not laying back in fatigue, but one look at her face and Eddie knew she was just barely holding on.

Help her Lord. Give her strength. It won't be like this forever if only she'll keep trying and committing herself to You. I can't do it for her, Lord. Just show her the way.

"I don't want you to be such a stranger,"

Robert told Travis that very afternoon, but the younger man only shook his head.

"I can't do that to Jackie right now, Robert. I can see how hard it is for her, and my presence is only going to make things worse. I can tell that she thinks everyone is staring at her."

"Well, many of them do," Robert admitted, "but it's not in the pitying or negative way she imagines. She and Eddie came into town to shop today. We went to lunch. I could tell she was terrified, but Eddie plans to take her every week until she's more comfortable."

"She should enjoy that once she gets used to it."

"I hope so, but now we're off the subject. Why don't you come for dinner tonight?"

Travis began to shake his head, but Robert put a hand up, his voice at its most persuasive.

"It's already after 4:30, so there's no need for you to go all the way home, and you don't have to stay long after we've eaten, but I know Eddie would like to see you."

"All right, I'll come. When are you going to head home?"

"Around 5:00, but don't wait for me. Go on to the house and keep Jackie company.

She needs to get out of herself."

"All right."

The men stood. "By the way, how are things going at the ranch?"

"Well. Maybe I'll have a chance to tell you about it tonight."

"All right. I'll see you at the house."

"I can't remember what color your eyes are," Jackie admitted shyly.

"Blue. Light blue."

Jackie nodded, a little amazed that she'd been bold enough to ask, but Travis had a very calming effect on her. He'd also kept Carl away. When the younger man had seen him, he hadn't spoken to Jackie at all.

"Do you wear a hat, Travis?"

"Yes. A black cowboy hat."

"Felt?"

"Yes. Here," he lifted it off the seat beside him. "Feel it."

He pressed the hat into Jackie's hands, and she studied it through her fingertips. It was large and soft and smelled faintly of leather. Her fingers traced the braided hat band and told her why her nose had picked up the leather smell.

"What color is the band?"

"Black. Black on black. Not very exciting." His voice was kind.

"It's so soft."

"Here now." Travis rose and came to her. "Try it on. You live in Boulder now, and you have to look the part."

A small smile pulled at the corners of Jackie's mouth, and when he put the hat on her head, she asked, "How's that?"

"Fine," Travis told her, but a small spark of pain hit his chest. A seeing person would have moved it back. It nearly covered her eyes.

"Robert just came in," Eddie announced from the doorway. "Why don't you come in and sit down at the table."

"Okay. May I offer you my arm, Jackie?"

"Sure." She stood and waited for him to remove the hat. When the hat was back on the chair, he took her hand in his and drew it through his arm. Jackie was vaguely aware that his voice was now many inches over her head, and for some reason she shuddered. She worked to keep his image from her mind, but Clayton's face came so clearly to her. She had to bite her lip to keep from crying. Clayton was the right size. Clayton was perfect.

Forget it Jackie. Just put him from your mind. He wouldn't want you if he knew. So just stop.

It was a relief to sit down and have Eddie
tell her what was on her plate. It helped her
to remember who she was: a blind girl with
no chance of marriage. The sooner she accepted that, the better.

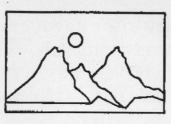

CHAPTER 31

Clayton looked out his living room window at the neat front yard and then to the schoolhouse beyond and felt a thrill run through him. His school. He was going to be Mr. Taggart. School was not scheduled to start until September, and this was only mid-July, but the board had had no problem with his arriving early and getting settled in. In fact, they were thrilled at his eagerness.

And he was eager. Never had he dreamed that the schoolhouse would be so new or the teacher's house so large. He'd been told that the first schoolteacher they'd hired had been a married man with six children. They'd built a house that would fit his needs. Clayton knew he would never fill these rooms with a wife and children, but he would still do everything in his power to make it a home. It was very exciting to him that his family could come and visit anytime they wanted, and he would have no problem putting them up indefinitely.

Clayton reached for the list in his front pocket. He'd written out the things he would need. He was going to have to be careful until his regular paychecks started. Although it would have been cheaper to remain at his grandmother's, once he'd graduated and been accepted as a teacher, he couldn't stand to stay in Denver. He let himself out the front door and moved around back to the stable behind the house.

Inside was the horse his parents had given him the funds to purchase. The man at the livery had been very helpful. He'd said her name was Sally, and Clayton had found her a gentle old mare. He saddled her and moved her to the front of the house to pull himself onto her back. From the saddle he took another long look at the schoolhouse. A moment later he turned and started Sally toward town, his heart thanking God for all that had come to pass.

"And don't let me forget the salt."

"But you have the list, Eddie," Jackie told her. "If it's on your list, how can you forget it?"

"Oh, right. Well, anyway, head to the buggy, Jackie. It's out front."

One, two, three, four, five, six, seven — the

count was immediately on in her mind. From the bottom of the stairs, to the front door, now across the porch. There was the first step. Eleven down, moving carefully. It was the same routine. Jackie told herself that someday she wouldn't have to count, but right now she would only add bruises if she tried it another way.

"Okay." Eddie sounded breathless as she climbed aboard.

"Eddie, what are you so upset about?"

"I'm not upset," came the genuine reply. "I just think I should have eaten a little more breakfast, and now I don't feel I have time."

"What's our hurry?"

Eddie came to a complete stop, the reins in her hand. "Well, come to think of it, there isn't one." She began to chuckle, but other than a slight smile, Jackie didn't join her. She wasn't angry, but nothing ever struck her as funny these days.

"Well, I'll eat a big lunch," Eddie said. "Shall we go to the hotel?"

"That's fine," Jackie replied apathetically. As usual Eddie prayed for strength.

She thanked God for how well Jackie was doing. She was getting along very well on her own, but her lack of interest was completely disheartening to her sister. The two women made the ride into town in near silence and started their errands at the bank. They were there longer than they expected to be, and because Eddie claimed she was starving, they ate next. The general store was the last stop.

Jackie was finally comfortable there. She now understood the lay of the things and took a slight interest. The bolts of fabric were all down one wall, but sewing notions were in the third aisle.

"Did you put lace on your list, Eddie?"

"Láce?"

"Yes. Didn't you say I'd torn some on my blouse and it would have to be replaced?"

"Oh, you're right. Let's go look."

It was after they'd stopped and Eddie had handed some lace to Jackie that she spotted him. Nothing could have prepared her for the sight of Clayton Taggart. Looking like a man in a dream, he was moving toward them. Jackie was intent on what she was feeling, and for the moment she required no assistance from her sister.

Eddie couldn't utter a word. She watched Clayton approach, his eyes fastened on Jackie. She also watched and knew that he was just finding out the truth. He had snapped out of his earlier trance and now wore a look of defiant protection. Eddie assumed it was for his own heart, but Jackie's movements changed his face yet again. Thankful that no one else was in the aisle, Eddie stood completely frozen as Clayton stepped up to within two feet of them. He stared at Jackie, and Jackie stared right through him.

"I think this one feels nice, Eddie. What does it look like?" The sounds of the store moved in and out of Jackie's mind, but nothing else.

"Eddie," she said uncertainly. "Did you leave me, Eddie?"

The slightly alarmed tone in her voice got through.

"No, no," Eddie assured her swiftly. "I'm right here. I don't know where my head is today."

"Eddie, is something wrong?" Her sister's voice frightened her.

"No, of course not. Now which one did you like?"

"This one."

"Oh, yes." Eddie was amazed at how normal she sounded with Clayton at her elbow. "This is very simple but elegant. It has large holes to the bottom, but at the top they're very tiny. Can you tell what I mean?"

"Yes. Is it very much?"

"I don't think so." In truth, she hadn't even looked. "Why don't we take some up to be measured. What would you say, a yard?"

"That should do it."

Eddie forced herself to concentrate on her sister and just get home. She moved Jackie on her way without ever looking at Clayton. They went to the front and paid for their purchases, Eddie needing three tries before the correct coins were offered and they could finally make their way toward the buggy. Eddie couldn't stand it anymore. She looked back at the front of the store to see that Clayton had come to the door to watch them. He looked utterly devastated. Eddie thought fast.

"Jackie, will you take the reins a moment? I need to run back for something."

"Oh, Eddie, what if the horse moves?"

"Here," she took the reins back. "I'll tie the lines back again, and he'll just sit here."

"All right. Will you be long?"

"No. Just sit tight."

She climbed down from the buggy with the help of a passing gentleman and moved back to where Clayton stood transfixed. He didn't look at her at first. His eyes were still glued to Jackie. When he did look at Eddie, his gaze was tortured.

"When, Eddie?" He could barely manage the words.

"Months ago. Last September."

There is no other man, Clayton now realized. *She stopped writing because of the blindness. There is no other man.* His mind raced on.

"Is it permanent?" he asked, his eyes drilling into Eddie's. She could only nod.

It was awful. Experiencing the news with Clayton was almost as bad as learning about it all over again for herself.

"I've got to speak to her."

Eddie shook her head.

"Tag," she said in a low voice, "please wait. Come to the house tonight. Come late when Jackie will be in bed. Robert and I will wait up for you."

He opened his mouth to protest, but Eddie shook her head.

"It won't work, Tag, not like this on the streets of town. She wouldn't be able to deal with the surprise, and I won't do that to her. Please come tonight," she pleaded, praying that Clayton would understand.

Clayton looked once again at the back of Jackie's head. The buggy was parked a little way up the street. He had to force his eyes away.

"What time?"

"After nine. Do you know where we live?"

"I'll find it."

With that Eddie turned and moved away. She forced herself to respond normally to her sister, but it was an effort. She was glad that Jackie wanted to sew that afternoon. Had she wanted anything more demanding, Eddie would not have survived.

Robert took one look at his wife's face and knew that her day had been rough. He also knew that she didn't want to talk about it in Jackie's presence. Her voice was just a little too cheerful as they ate and did the dishes, so as soon as Jackie went into the other room, Robert speared her with his eyes.

Eddie wouldn't look at him. She was not afraid, but she knew she was going to cry and that Jackie would hear her.

"Talk to me, Eddie," he said softly, his eyes on her profile.

"Later."

"No. If you're this upset, I need to know what's going on."

Eddie took a deep breath and shook her head.

Robert gently took her arm and moved her out the back door. It was private out on the rear porch, and Robert could still hear if Jackie called to them.

"If you don't tell me what's going on, I'll be forced to ask Jackie directly. What has she done?"

Eddie shook her head, and could no longer hold the tears. "Clayton Taggart is here," she whispered.

Robert looked thunderstruck. "You saw him?"

"And talked to him."

He let this sink in for a moment, and then asked, "What did Jackie say?"

More tears choked her voice for a moment. "She doesn't know. He wanted to talk to her, but I discouraged him. He's coming by later, after she's retired. In all this time she's never said a word about him. Why is he here, Robert?"

"Maybe he wanted to see her and tell her how sorry he was about the accident."

Again Eddie shook her head. "He didn't know. When he saw her he was so shocked he could barely function. Why is he here?"

Light dawned very swiftly. "You never wrote to him about the accident, did you?"

"No, and I think my family has lost all touch with his."

"The school."

"What?"

Robert took her hands in his. "I'll bet he's been hired on to teach school. I'm not involved, of course, but I know the board was looking for a new teacher."

"Oh, Robert, what does this all mean?"

He now took her in his arms. "I don't know exactly, but if he's graduated and is now able to teach, then he might be the answer to our prayers."

"Eddie," Jackie's voice preceded her as she moved slowly into the kitchen, something clutched in her hand. "Are you in the pantry, Eddie?"

"No," Robert answered and stood back so his wife could enter. "We were just on the back porch."

"Oh. Well, I can't get this knot out of my thread. Will you help me?"

"Sure," Robert offered, giving Eddie a chance to compose herself. "I'll have to remove the needle, I think."

Jackie stood silently and waited. She heard Eddie move then and spoke to her.

"Is that you, Eddie?"

"Yes."

"I think this is my last one. I don't know what I'm going to do tomorrow with nothing to sew or mend."

Robert's eyes met Eddie's for just an instant.

"We'll think of something," Eddie assured her.

The thread now adjusted and the needle back in place, Eddie offered Jackie her arm. It wasn't often that they led her around or waited on her, but Eddie felt a desperate need to touch her sister. She didn't know how she could act normally until Jackie went to bed and Clayton arrived, but Robert came to the rescue. He'd picked up a letter from Morgan when he left the bank. The women sat across the living room from him while he read.

Dear Robert, Ed, and Jack, business is booming and it seems that new strikes are found almost daily. As usual, we sell more mining supplies than food. One of the mine owners stopped his team of mules in front of the store recently and left a huge mess for me to clean, but as I said, business is good.

New houses are being built as well, and the latest is a bright yellow one almost next door to us. A young couple has moved into Uncle Mitch's apartment. They have a small baby, and your mother frets that the little guy will fall down the stairs. You were all raised around stairs; she's starting to sound like a grandmother.

We miss you, Jack, very much, but are thrilled you're getting out. I would enjoy seeing the general store there in Boulder. It never hurts to check out the competition. Miss Bradley has left us, but the new schoolteacher has already been installed. A man this time, and he has two boys and a girl who match the ages of Sam, Dan, and Alex. They've gotten to know each other some, and your mother has met his wife at church. His name escapes me right now, but I'll think of it later.

Your mother and Ora are making a quilt together, and she is there now because Ora has a large quilting frame. I'm supposed to be helping Sam with her math, but she fell asleep and I carried her to bed. Oh, I think I hear your mother coming in now. I'll close and let her write more to you later.

Love to each of you,
Father

Robert set the letter aside and smiled at his wife. Jackie did not comment, and not long after she took herself upstairs for the night.

★ ★ ★

Clayton had never experienced anything like this. His heart felt as if it had been torn in two. One half rejoiced that Jackie was not in love with someone else, but the other half could hardly bear the pain of what had happened to her. He wasn't angry; indeed, he thought he understood. If it had been him, would he have assumed that Jackie wanted a blind husband? The question took some real soul-searching.

His stomach growled as the house came into view. He hadn't wanted anything to eat after he talked to Eddie, and even now his stomach felt a mite queasy. Not with revulsion but with pain.

He was at the house now. Clayton tied Sally's lead to a bush and climbed the front-porch stairs to the door. Darkness was falling fast, but he could see his way. He knocked and waited. How could he get this close and not see her? Eddie said she would be in bed, but Clayton hoped she would be wrong. Eddie opened the door, and without words she stepped back and let him enter. A large fireplace sat against the right wall of the entryway and to the left was the double-doorway to the living room.

"I'll take your hat, Clay." Eddie spoke softly, bringing Clayton's eyes to hers just briefly. If he was here out of pity for her sister, she'd tell him to leave. Eddie herself didn't know where this fierce, protective attitude came from, but Clayton could see that his hostess was ill-at-ease.

"Robert is in the study. If you'll just —" Eddie stopped, and her head twisted around.

Slowly descending the stairs was Jackie. She was moving with deliberate care, her hand on the railing. Eddie shot a swift glance at Clayton, but he had eyes for Jackie alone. Eddie nearly panicked, thinking he would speak and ruin everything. They were both watching the blind girl when she missed the last step and fell into a heap.

Clayton moved so quickly to help her that Eddie had to step in front of him, arms outstretched. She spoke swiftly to cover the noise.

"Are you all right, Jackie?"

"Yes." She sounded more angry than hurt.

"Do you want some help?"

"No." Her answer was clipped.

A moment of silence passed, and Jackie turned her head slightly. "Are you alone, Eddie?"

"No." Again she tried to sound normal.

"Male or female?"

"Male."

"Are my legs covered?"

"Yes."

Jackie came to her feet then, feeling her way carefully. Eddie said, "I thought you were going to bed."

"I am, but I forgot my water glass."

"I'll get it for you."

Eddie moved off quickly, but not before she gave Clayton a look that told him he had better stay quiet. She was back very swiftly, an empty glass in her hand.

"Here you go."

"Thanks, Eddie."

"Good-night, Jackie."

"Good-night."

Once again they watched, only this time Jackie eventually moved from view. The look on Clayton's face broke Eddie's heart. With nothing but compassion she took his arm and led him to the study.

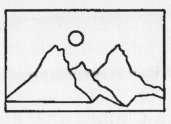

CHAPTER 32

Clayton was trembling so badly by the time he reached the spacious study that he could barely walk. Robert immediately offered him a chair.

He had thought it would help. He had thought if he could just see her he would feel better, but the sight of Jackie sitting in a heap was almost more than he could bear. If he'd been able to go to her, he might have been all right, but as it was, he felt as helpless as she must feel all the time.

Tears gathered in his eyes. He might have cried earlier in the day, but he'd been too shocked. Now he wanted to sob like a child, much the way he'd done when Jackie wrote and said she'd found someone new. At last he looked up to see his hosts watching him. Had only a few moments passed? They looked kind, and he felt free to speak.

"My mother commented to me several times that Addy had stopped writing her. It was the same for Danny's correspondence with Milly. I never once suspected that Jackie's letter might not be true."

"She wrote to you?" Eddie asked. "You knew?"

"No, I don't think she did write. She must have had someone else."

"But you did know about the blindness?" Robert asked.

Clayton shook his head. He knew he was making very little sense. "A letter came to me saying she'd met someone else and that she never wanted to hear from me or see me again."

Robert and Eddie both nodded. It was sad that Jackie hadn't told him the truth, but neither one of them was surprised. Eddie thought about how closely Lexa's handwriting resembled Jackie's. It was not hard to figure out.

"How long has it been?" Clayton now asked.

"The date was late September, so that would be almost ten months," Eddie responded.

"How did it happen?"

"She fell from a ladder in the back room of the store. She landed flat on her back. The doctor said it was the blow to the back of the head that did the damage."

"And she'll never see again?"

"Never," Robert told him quietly. They both watched as Clayton was overcome. He put his face in his hands and cried.

"Is she in pain now?" Clayton managed, tears still streaming down his face.

"No," Robert assured him. "They said she might have headaches beyond the first few weeks, and that would have been a good sign because it might mean that things were only damaged and not ruptured, but her lack of pain means that it's permanent."

Clayton nodded. He was feeling more in control now, and a thousand questions raced through his mind. Before he could utter one of them, however, Robert had some of his own.

"I'm sorry you had to find out this way, Clay, but may I ask what brings you to Boulder?"

Clayton used his handkerchief and took a deep breath. "I've been hired to teach here at the school."

Robert nodded. "Congratulations. I know it's what you've wanted for a long time."

"Yes." Clayton agreed with him but did not sound overjoyed.

"You're here rather early for school, Clay. Is there a reason for that?"

"I just wanted to get settled in." He sounded almost apologetic.

"So you're not actually working until this fall?"

"That's correct."

Robert shot a glance at his wife, but she was looking at Clayton. He knew he was taking a chance and prayed that she would not be upset.

"Jackie didn't retire until right before you came, Clay, so Eddie and I haven't even had a chance to talk about this, but I wonder if I could hire you for the summer and even into the school year."

Both other occupants of the room stared at him, and Robert tried to tell Eddie with his eyes to trust him.

"Hire me to do what?"

"Teach Jackie."

Eddie came to her feet, and Robert stood as well.

"It's all right, Eddie," he said gently.

"No, it's not, Robert," Eddie told him, completely forgetting Clayton's presence. "We can't do this to her. She was in love with him, and she won't be able to stand it. She'll be humiliated, having him here but not having his love anymore."

Clayton interrupted with a statement that completely snagged Eddie's attention. She stared at him in wonder, but saw the truth in his eyes.

She had to ask him, "What do you intend to do about it?"

"For starters," he replied, "I'll take up Robert's offer to teach your sister."

He turned back to Robert.

"When do you want me to start?"

"As soon as you can come."

Clayton's eyes searched the room but didn't really focus. "They don't teach you this at school," he nearly murmured to himself. "I mean, they assume all your students will have vision, but I think I can work this out. Can you give me a week?"

"Yes. In fact, just do what you can and get back to me. I see now that I shouldn't have surprised Eddie. In a week, you'll know if you can do it, and Eddie and I will either be in one accord on this or we'll forget the whole thing."

"All right."

"I hope you know that it's not you, Tag," Eddie said, finding her voice.

"I know, Eddie," he replied kindly.

"She's just been through so much and I know how upset she'll be if Robert suggests this."

"It won't be any party for me, either," he said quietly.

Eddie had to admit that she hadn't thought of his feelings.

"We'll all pray about this," Robert said, "and see if we can come to an agreement."

"What if Jackie says no," Clayton wanted to know.

Robert shook his head. "If Eddie and I decide this is the best for her, she won't be given a choice."

Clayton stared at him. "The Jackie I know wouldn't put up with that."

Robert shook his head a bit sadly. "She's not the same girl, Clay — that might be the first thing you should know. And I'm not promising this will be easy. More than likely she'll fight you every step of the way."

"But you would want me to maintain control, just like in a classroom."

"Yes."

"No." Husband and wife said the words in unison and then looked at each other.

"If he isn't firm enough with her, Eddie, she'll never respond."

"I can't see her crushed, Robert. No matter what, I can't see her crushed." Tears had come to her eyes, and Robert reached for her hand. He knew it upset her to have Clayton see them.

"I wouldn't do that, Eddie," Clayton said without heat. "I'm not that kind of teacher. I mean, there's going to be an adjustment time, that's a given, but I have no plans to humiliate any of my students, and that includes Jackie. However, I know very well what she's capable of and how intelligent she is, so my standard will be high."

Eddie suddenly felt more tired than she'd ever been in her life, and it must have shown on her face because Clayton made a move to leave. He bade Eddie goodbye, and Robert saw him to the door. Robert returned to put the lights out in the study and found Eddie sitting trancelike in a chair. He assumed she'd have gone up the back stairway to their room. She looked utterly drained.

"Eddie, if it's going to upset you this much, we'll drop the whole idea."

"I'm just so tired." She began to cry. "I can't even think straight right now."

Robert lifted her to her feet and then into his arms. He forgot about the lights and simply carried her up the stairs. Eddie cried the whole time he was getting her ready for bed and even after her head lay on the pillow.

"Just go to sleep."

"But you'll be gone in the morning, and I won't be able to talk to you."

"I'll make some time," he promised her, really worried at how this had upset her. "I'm sorry I didn't talk to you first," he told her, but she was already gone. Her breathing was a bit shuddery, but she was asleep. He told himself he would make things right in the morning.

But in the morning, Eddie was of an entirely different mind. She woke early and prayed for almost an hour. She then woke Robert and told him her heart.

"I think Tag should come."

"What changed your mind?"

"I wasn't really against it, Robert. I just couldn't put any more thought to it last night."

"But what of your fears? They might have some validity."

"No, they don't; I know that now. Clay would not hurt her, and if he wasn't firm with her, she'd have him waiting on her hand and foot. We've been asking God for weeks to show us a new direction, and I can't help but believe this is His answer." Eddie lay in the crook of her husband's arm. "When should I tell her?"

"I'll tell her," Robert said. "You can be there if you like. I'll probably wait until early next week, after I've talked to Clay."

"All right. Is there some reason?" Eddie rose to look into his face.

"To wait?"

"Yes."

"Only to make sure that Clay understands what she's going to be like, and to make sure he still wants the job."

"Maybe she'll surprise us," Eddie offered, but Robert looked skeptical. His face made Eddie doubt as well, and unfortunately, Robert was correct.

"I know I missed a year," Jackie argued for the fifth time, "but it can't be all *that* important. What does it matter now if I know my '12 times' table or the capital of Rhode Island?" There was a bitter tone to her voice that Robert chose to ignore.

"You need to gain more interest in the things around you, Jackie," he repeated. "This is one way to do it. I've even found you a teacher."

This gained Jackie's immediate attention. She sat very still, and a feeling of dread stole over her. She was not going to be able to talk her way out of this if he had already talked to a teacher.

"Who is it?" she asked in a resigned voice.

Robert glanced quickly at Eddie before saying, "Clayton Taggart."

Jackie rose from the settee as though on strings, the color draining from her face.

"You're lying. Clayton is in Denver."

"He has been hired to teach school here

in Boulder, and I just spoke with him yesterday. He's willing to come every day and tutor you until school begins. After September he'll probably come evenings and weekends."

"No." Jackie said the word softly and then with more strength. "*No,* I won't do it! You've had your way about everything. Well, you can forget this, Robert Langley. I *won't* be taught by Clay Taggart, and that's the end of it!"

Robert had known she was going to be upset, but he hadn't been prepared for this furious, red-in-the-face reaction. She was not just beside herself; she was hysterical with panic.

"I want to go home," she now began. "I want to go to Georgetown. *Eddie,*" she screamed. "Eddie, don't let him do this to me."

Robert was on her in a moment, putting his arms gently around her and talking in a calm voice, but Jackie would have none of it. She cried and pushed against him, even lashing out with her feet and screaming Eddie's name again and again.

Robert forced her back onto the settee, and when he had practically pinned her to the seat, his words got through.

"It's all right, Jackie; it's all right. I know

it's a shock, but it's going to be all right."

"Please don't make me, Robert," she whimpered when she could barely move an inch. Robert had to wall up his heart to make it. He knew this was best, but it was breaking his heart to see her so upset.

"It's going to be all right," he said with a catch in his voice. "You'll find out that he's still the same Clay, and his coming will give you something to look forward to. I know he's going to be a very good teacher."

Jackie turned her face into his coatfront and sobbed. "I can't stand the pity. I know he's just coming because he feels sorry for me. I can't stand it. I wrote and told him I was in love with someone else. Please don't make me face Clay."

"Shhh," he comforted. Looking over at his sobbing wife, he wished he could hold them both. He didn't regret this action for a moment, but he did hate to see his wife and sister-in-law in pain.

"Jackie." Eddie surprised Robert by speaking up. "I hate to see you this upset. Please don't cry."

The younger girl took a few great gulping breaths and worked hard to control herself.

"I just can't face him," she said so softly that they almost missed it. "He's going to know I lied, and after all we've been to each other, I just don't. . . ." The words trailed off, but she no longer cried. Her unseeing eyes stared sightlessly ahead of her as if she hadn't a friend in the world.

Robert broke the silence.

"I think you will find that Clay is every inch a professional. Whatever there was in the past is just that, the past."

He let this sink in for a time.

"I'm not saying it's going to be easy, Jackie," Robert continued in a very gentle tone, "but then you've had to learn in the last ten months that your life will never be easy again. Now, you can decide how you want it. You can work with Clay or fight him, but he will be here."

If Jackie had felt hopeless before, she now felt beyond despair. However, she did not feel helpless. For the first time since the accident, she told herself she was not going to ask for assistance or do anything that might make it look like she needed help. Clayton Taggart was not going to come and find some pitiful, waning creature in need of special care. She would do all he asked of her and more. She would work so hard that he wouldn't even need to stay the whole year.

Exactly how she was going to accomplish this she didn't know, but her mind was made up. She had told Clayton that she'd found someone new. It wasn't true, but it might as well have been: She was never going to let him know that she was still in love with him.

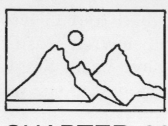

CHAPTER 33

Clayton's heart pounded as he lifted the crate up onto his kitchen table and pried open the lid. The box was from his mother, but he knew she couldn't have received his letter. Even before he'd remembered the books, he'd told Robert he would take the job. Other than rote memorization, he didn't have a clue as to how to teach Jackie, but he was not going to let this opportunity pass.

The lid was off now, and Clayton moved aside old newspapers and straw. Again he felt his breath quicken. She'd sent his books — all of them! It had to be the Lord.

He dug deeply into the box, his heart sinking a little. Then he saw them. Two volumes, one rather thick and one quite small and thin. He pulled the fat one out and dusted it off: *Braille: Methods and Management*. The other volume was a book of poetry written in Braille. They had been in his grandmother's library, and she had given them to him. He had never even looked at them. They'd been taking up space on his lower shelf for months, and he wasn't even certain if he still had them. He now turned to the first page of the manual, his hand shaking.

He read that a young French lad by the name of Louis Braille, who had gone blind at age three, developed a system in 1828 that was based on a six-dot configuration. Clayton had heard of this method — reading by following raised marks on paper — but he had never studied or given much thought to it. Now he read in amazement that there were 63 possible characters in the Braille system. With those dot arrangements a person could make the alphabet, punctuation marks, numbers, and some small words.

For the next three hours, Clayton didn't move. His neck grew stiff and the hand holding the book cramped, but he read on. He didn't know if he could learn enough in two days, but he was going to give it a try. If it didn't work, he would tell Jackie that they would be learning together. With the instruction book open under his left hand and the poetry book open in his right, Clayton tried to read with his fingers. It took another hour to learn even a few words, but he was getting it. He nearly shouted for joy when he turned to the back of the manual and found a long list of practice words.

Thank You, Lord. I know You've made this possible. Please help me to help her. You know that my heart has been involved in the past, but I don't ask this for myself. I ask for Jackie. Please help her to understand. Make me the teacher You would have me to be, patient and kind.

Clayton prayed for the next hour and then worked over the books some more. He did little else in the next 48 hours but sleep, study, and pray. When Thursday morning arrived, he knew he was as ready as he was going to be, and his heart thudded with a mixture of joy and apprehension, all the time telling himself to watch his expectations. He looked at the watch in his pocket constantly and nearly forgot to shave, but it was finally time to go.

Jackie pressed her damp palms deep into the folds of her dress and told herself she was not going to use the necessity again. Her stomach had been in knots ever since she'd awakened and realized that this was the day Clayton was scheduled to arrive.

How would it feel? How would it be to hear his voice but never see his wonderful face again? Jackie's heart thundered at the very thought. Her breathing came fast, and she nearly jumped from her skin when Eddie spoke to her from across the table.

"I'm sorry to startle you," she said, tears filling her eyes as they had been all morning. "Please try to eat something, Jackie."

"I'm just not hungry. I think if I eat, I'll be sick to my stomach."

Eddie sighed. It was remarkable how much weight Jackie could drop in a few days. For a while she had started to fill out a little, but now she was back to her cadaverous state. Eddie was feeling sick just thinking about what Jackie was going through.

"Just some toast," Eddie coaxed, but Jackie shook her head.

The young wife wondered if Robert would have held to his resolve if he could see Jackie now. It wasn't that Eddie disagreed with the schooling decision; it was just that she felt too emotionally involved to be the one to enforce this. Not that she expected Jackie to fight it; indeed, a frightening transformation had come over her sister since Robert had made his announcement. The younger girl looked hard now, implacable, and that was something Eddie was not accustomed to seeing. The vulnerable, frightened, and ofttimes apathetic Jackie was gone. This Jackie was defensive and angry. Eddie simply didn't know what to think.

"I think I'll wait in my room," Jackie suddenly said and rose.

"Are you sure? I thought you would want to be in the study before Clayton arrives."

"The study? We're going to be in there?"

"Yes. Robert thought it would give you the most privacy."

Jackie nearly fainted on the spot. She had assumed they would be in the living room. She didn't know the study like she did the other rooms in the house. She was sure to bump things if she tried to move around. There was only one answer.

"I will go to the study now, Eddie. Please give me some warning before he walks in the door."

"I will," Eddie promised, but stared after her in confusion. What was the problem with the study? Thankfully, Eddie realized the answer before Clayton arrived. She went to Jackie immediately and helped her find her way around. When the bell sounded at the front door, signaling Clayton's arrival, she left Jackie sitting at the inlaid mahogany writing table that Robert had set up for just that purpose.

Clayton's heart was a mixture of emotions as he stood and waited for the door of the Langley home to open. In some ways he was glad that Jackie wouldn't be able to read his face, but her blindness was still so shocking to him that he was having trouble taking it in. She appeared to be so accepting. First in the buggy, then when she waited for her glass of water, and then again at church, sitting silently through the whole morning, not even aware that he was in the room. Was she really so resigned? Clayton somehow doubted it. The door opened amidst the questioning of his mind.

"Hello, Tag," Eddie greeted him warmly, but the young man noticed a flush to her face.

"Are you all right?"

Eddie gave a small laugh. "Just a little tense. Jackie wants me to warn her before I let you in the study. In truth, I think she's scared out of her wits."

"Understandable." His voice was wonderfully kind. "I'm worse than a stranger. It's embarrassing because of our past, and at the same time she doesn't know me well enough anymore to really judge what I'll be like."

"Yes, I see what you mean. I'll go now

and give her a moment to get used to the idea that you've arrived."

Eddie found Jackie on the sofa. She sat up rather tensely and looked toward her sister.

"He's here, Jackie."

Jackie came to her feet. "Do I look all right?" Her voice was low, and her hands smoothed down the skirt of her light gray dress. It was a perfect foil for Robert's dark burgundy office. Jackie's question was the first sign of vulnerability Eddie had seen for days.

"You look beautiful," she told her truthfully. It was amazing that the blindness had done nothing to mar the loveliness of Jackie's eyes or face. Her mouth was no longer given to smiling, but she was still gorgeous. "I'll send him in."

By the time Clayton arrived, Jackie was back in control. Sitting had seemed so awkward, so she had remained on her feet and forced herself not to appear tense when she heard his footsteps at the door.

"Hello, Jackie."

"Clayton?" He sounded so different. Some of her confidence left her.

"Yes, it's me. Are you ready to begin?"

"Yes," she answered without thinking.

"Okay. Why don't you come to the desk

here." Clayton came forward to take her arm. "I have some books to show —"

"I can do it," she snapped at him. Clayton dropped her arm and swiftly stepped back.

"Of course," he said quietly. "I'm sorry. How would you like to handle this? Shall I assume you'll ask for help if you need it?"

"Yes," Jackie replied coldly, even as she told herself she would never ask him for anything.

Clayton waited until she was seated before he spoke, and in that moment he saw that she hadn't needed his help. She went directly to the table and sat down at the chair. Her actions reminded him of the calm way she'd come down the stairs the week before. It would have been nice if they could have engaged in some small talk, but Jackie's expression did not welcome it. Clayton felt he had no choice but to begin.

"I'm putting a book in front of you, Jackie. It's opened to the middle, and I'd just like you to touch the pages for a moment."

Clayton watched as she obeyed, and then studied her face as her brow furrowed in concentration.

"Have you ever heard of Braille, Jackie?"

"Braille?"

"Yes, it's a French name, and along with being a technique by which a blind person can read, it's also the name of the method's creator." Clayton nearly stumbled on the word "blind" but managed it. Other than a slight lift in Jackie's chin, she had no reaction. "As you can feel, it's a series of dots or small bumps, if you will. I'm going to teach you to read and write with this method."

Jackie's mouth went dry. She'd have told Robert or Eddie no and without discussion that she couldn't possibly learn such a thing, but not Clayton — never him.

"All right." Again the chin lifted.

"Here, let me have that book, and I'll give you another." Clayton slid the manual into her hands. "Now, we'll start with the alphabet. Right at the top you'll find A." He caused her to start when he took her hand and directed her finger. "Can you feel it?"

"Yes."

"What does it feel like?"

"Just one little bump."

"That's right. Read along to B and tell me what you feel."

Jackie's hand moved. "Two dots."

"That's right, but you've got to memorize their order. Are they on top of one another, or side by side?"

"On top."

"Good. Now go onto C and you'll understand why I asked."

Again Jackie's hand moved. "It's three
dots."

"No, you've moved too far to D. Go back
slightly."

"Oh." Jackie's voice actually sounded
pleased. "It's two dots side by side."

"Right. You're doing great. Now go back
to A and just go over A, B, and C one more
time. Say them outloud."

Jackie did as she was told. The letters
came slowly. "A, B, C."

"Excellent," Clayton praised her, carefully watching her fingers move.

The job done, her heart lifted for the first
time in months. Clayton's presence was forgotten. She could read these letters! It
seemed like a miracle to her. Clayton could
see the pleasure on her face and smiled but
didn't comment. His eyes softened as he
looked at her.

"Do I go on now?" she asked when he
grew very quiet. Her question snapped him
out of his thoughts.

"Yes. Go on to D, E, and F. They get a
little bit harder, but I know you'll get it."

And he was right. Jackie worked without
complaint for the next three hours. Clayton
was as excited as she was and never even

thought about lunch. They didn't stop until Eddie came to check on them.

"Lunch is ready," she said when there was a break.

"Oh." Clayton looked surprised and then glanced down at his watch. "I brought something from home."

"Well, you can take it home with you," Eddie told him kindly. "When you're here at noon, we'll just expect you for lunch."

"All right."

"Coming, Jackie?" Eddie wished to know.

"Yes." She stood but didn't move from around the table. Clayton looked undecided, but Eddie signaled to him with her hand, and he followed her out.

Jackie heard them leave and, with a rush, the morning's work caught up to her. She felt as though she could hardly move. The sofa was behind her to the right and if she could just sit down a moment, then she would go eat.

Clayton offered to look for her when she didn't arrive in the dining room right behind them. He made his way back to the study and started to turn away when he saw the empty desk chair. His eye caught sight of his sleeping student just before he left. He changed directions and moved back into the room. Jackie didn't rouse when his steps sounded on the floor or when he turned his desk chair around to face her. It was all done very quietly.

Eddie was just as quiet when she came to the door a few minutes later. She looked in and saw Clayton sitting with Jackie, his eyes resting on her face. She left them undisturbed. Lunch was easy enough to reheat, and even if it wasn't, she wouldn't have disturbed them for anything short of a fire.

When Jackie awoke, Clayton was gone. She couldn't remember why she was alone on the sofa, but when she softly called Eddie's name and then Clayton's, there was no answer.

Right then her stomach growled and lunch came to mind. Eddie had called them to come to lunch, and she'd been too tired to even eat. Jackie stood and made her way to the kitchen where Lena spotted her immediately.

"Oh, Miss Jackie, I'm so glad you came. Lena's heart is heavy when you do not eat. Come, I have your food."

It was two hours past the time when Jackie should have eaten, and the loving housekeeper was not going to stand on ceremony. She sat the girl down at the kitchen table and fed her until she was ready to pop.

CHAPTER 34

"Are you certain you don't want me to wake her, Tag?"

"Yes. I need all the time I can get to study this book, Eddie, and if Jackie's that tired, let her sleep."

"She's never napped before. It must be the mental effort of learning something so foreign." With that, Eddie went back to the quilt she was making for Robert's birthday. She actually preferred to quilt in the evening but wanted this to be a surprise. Her hands moved as lightly as her heart. Clayton had finally come to eat lunch, and they had talked.

"How did she do?"

"Excellently. I know she'll have it down in no time."

"She didn't fight you?"

"Not the way I think you're talking about."

"Meaning?"

"Meaning, that if I read her face correctly, Jackie has decided to show me that she doesn't need me for anything."

Eddie's eyes slid shut. Understanding dawned.

"I saw it in her," Eddie told him after a moment. "I mean, ever since Robert told her you were coming, she's been hardening her heart."

Clayton nodded. "It really makes sense, Eddie. She can't risk my rejection, so she's not going to let me close enough to hurt her."

"But what about you, Tag? What about your feelings?"

He'd been silent for long minutes. "Right now I'm here to teach Jackie, and that's all. If I don't watch my expectations, this is never going to work."

Eddie had done nothing more than nod and, once the meal was over, suggested they take coffee in the living room. Clayton had agreed, gone to the study for the manual, and been reading with very little interruption since.

Now, some 40 minutes later, movement at the door and Jackie's voice raised both their heads.

"Eddie?"

"Right here, Jackie. Did you want some lunch?"

"Lena just served me."

"Good."

"Is my lesson over for the day, Eddie?"

"Not if you're up to more."

"Clay is still here?"

"Yes. Would you like to continue?"

Jackie nodded, her look unreadable.

"All right. Head back to the study, and Clay will be right behind you."

Why neither one of them mentioned Clayton's presence in the room, no one knew, but the experience was good for the new teacher. Jackie was remarkably different with her sister. Her voice and expressions were more open and softer than when she was alone with him. Seeing her thus, Clayton determined to bring his student out. He didn't have to teach the children of Boulder for another five-and-a-half weeks. As Clayton joined Jackie in the study, he asked God to work a miracle between him and Jackie during that time.

"Oh, Robert, it went so well." Eddie's voice was breathless with excitement. They were already in bed for the night, cuddled together under a sheet and light blanket. The night was deliciously cool, and both could hear the familiar creaks as the house settled in the dark.

"She didn't really want to talk about it at dinner," Robert commented, pulling Eddie closer.

"No, but when I went in to say good-night she grabbed my hand. 'I did it,' she said. 'I read some words, Eddie.' You should have heard her voice."

"Did Clay say how it went?"

"We didn't talk before he left, but I could tell he was still ready to go on at lunch-time."

Robert pressed a kiss to her brow and then found her mouth. Eddie was ready to chatter on about the day for hours to come, but Robert wanted only to kiss and hold her. He loved Jackie, but having a live-in sister-in-law did have its drawbacks. They were able to say things with their eyes, something which would have been impossible with a sighted sister in the house, but it was still a challenge to find time for themselves.

Robert knew Eddie wanted to talk, but tonight he wanted her silence more.

"I take it you don't want to hear anymore?" Eddie questioned softly with a smile in her voice.

"Later," Robert murmured when his lips found her throat.

Eddie wouldn't have argued for the moon.

★ ★ ★

"Okay, let's have you stand and recite your '12 times' table."

Jackie slowly pushed herself to her feet. They'd been working together for more than two weeks, but for some reason she felt a little nervous this morning. Her hands fluttered for just a moment, but she managed to complete the assignment perfectly.

"Good. Now, we've been going over the early presidents. Can you name the first 15 for me?"

"I think so," she told him, but she stumbled to a painful halt after the eighth president, Martin Van Buren.

"Want to start again?"

"Yes." Her face was red now, and she was beginning to tremble, but she did start again. She got a little further this time but once again fell into an excruciating silence.

"Come on now." Clayton's voice was light and teasing, but in her humiliation, Jackie missed it. "You've got to stay with it, or I'll have to get out my ruler."

Clayton was not even looking at her or he'd have seen the sudden panic. Her hands went deep into the folds of her skirt and clutched together until they were nearly cramped.

"Is Eddie in here?" Her voice was high

and strange, causing Clayton to finally turn and look at her.

"No, she's not here right —"

"I need her," she gasped.

Clayton watched in amazement as her head whipped around in complete panic.

"Jackie, what's —"

"Eddie," her voice called like a frightened child. She began to edge her way to the wall, trying to keep her face to the man she couldn't see. "Eddie, I need you," she cried again, now having found the wall.

"Jackie, it's okay." Clayton came closer just as she ran into a bookshelf. He put his hand out and touched her arm but withdrew when she screamed in terror.

"Please don't, Clayton, please don't hit me. Eddie, Eddie, where are you, Eddie?"

Thankfully, Eddie wasn't far. She hit the door at a run, coming to Jackie's side and barely taking in the fact that Clayton was standing by in utter stupefaction.

"Jackie, Jackie, what is it?"

"Please, Eddie," she clung to the older girl. "Don't let him hit me."

Eddie told herself not to tell Jackie she was being ridiculous and, leading her to the sofa, tried to talk in a calm voice. Searching her mind for what went wrong, Eddie noticed that Clayton had taken a chair as far from Jackie as he could get. It was beyond him as to what had just happened, and he was afraid to approach until he knew.

"Now, Jackie." Eddie's voice was almost stern. "What happened? Clay would never hit you. What in the world is going on?"

The tears had stopped, but she was still trembling and holding onto Eddie's arm.

"I hated it when Miss Bradley hit me," Jackie said in a dull tone, "but it would be a hundred times worse if I couldn't see."

Before Eddie even had time to turn and look at him, Clayton was kneeling in front of Jackie. He took her hands gently into his own, his grasp warm and strong.

"Jackie." His voice was deep and soothing. "I'm sorry I teased you about the ruler. I don't even have a ruler with me, and I would never hit you. I'm sorry I was so insensitive."

The trembling slowly moved from her body, but Clayton still held on. Strangely enough Jackie made no objection, and now Eddie was talking in a comforting voice as well. It took a few minutes, but when Eddie asked if she could leave, Jackie agreed with the nod of her head. Clayton thought she would pull her hands away, but she didn't. He felt her thumb move over one of the knuckles on his right hand.

446

"Is this a scar, Clay?"

"Yeah," he managed to answer without revealing what her touch was doing to his heart.

"I don't remember it."

"It's been there. Barbed wire when I was about ten."

The caress continued for just a moment more. Then all at once, she took her hands back, her face becoming hard once again. A moment later she spoke.

"I'm ready to recite now," she announced, sounding like a queen addressing her court, "but I'd rather sit down."

Clayton moved away from her. He wasn't certain if he could keep the disappointment from his voice, but he tried. He hoped they were getting somewhere, but she'd pulled from his touch as if she'd been stung.

"It has occurred to me," Clayton began, "that maybe we should take a midmorning break. Now would be a good time, I think. Would you like me to get you some coffee or anything?"

"I thought you wanted me to recite."

"I do, right after the break."

"And if I'm ready now?" Her voice arched.

Silence fell over the room. Clayton was not about to pander to her tantrum.

"I'm going to go and have some coffee," Clayton told her evenly. "You can do as you like, but I'll expect you to recite for me when I return in 15 minutes."

"And if I refuse to be taught at all?"

Clayton shrugged, but Jackie couldn't see it. "You'll have to take that up with Eddie and Robert. They're the people who hired me."

Jackie was so furious that she couldn't move or speak. She heard Clayton leave the room, and so great was the rage within her that she thought she would explode. At the moment she hated him, or did she only hate the darkness that surrounded her? *No matter,* her mind told her. She planned to be back in control of herself by the time Clayton returned.

"I've decided we should work outside today."

"Outside?" The familiar feeling of cottonmouth over anything new came on Jackie.

"Yes. I've set out a blanket in the back. We'll still have shade from the house, and I think the change of scenery will do us good."

"I can't see how a change of scenery will do *me* any good," Jackie told Clayton, but still she rose to move for the door.

Clayton let her precede him. Something had happened a week ago after they'd had words over her recitation. She was no longer the biddable, if uppity, Jackie. She was now saying what was on her mind, and on a very regular basis. Her bitterness over her situation was plain to see. Up until that time, she'd been a cool, polite stranger. Now, she told Clayton in no uncertain terms that her life was awful and she hated it.

They made it down the back porch steps, and Clayton knew better than to take Jackie's arm or even offer.

"The blanket is just this way," he told her, hoping the sound of his voice would help direct her. Five steps later, she was down. Her foot had missed a low spot on the turf and she'd gone full onto her face.

The exertion on Clayton's part was unbearable. His hands clenched at his side, and his head went back in agony. His breathing came in rapid gasps as he stopped himself from going to her. She'd fallen one other time, in the house as they were walking to lunch, and without thought he'd reached for her. She had told him in scathing tones that he was never to touch her again. Now the effort to restrain himself as she spat grass from her mouth and struggled in a full skirt with nothing to hold onto was more painful to him than a lash from a whip.

"Over this way," he said when she had come to her knees. "You can almost reach it if you put your hand out."

The temptation to crawl onto the blanket was strong, but Jackie resisted it. She came awkwardly to her feet, nearly tripping on her hem this time, and moved very slowly to the blanket.

"There you go," Clayton said softly. "Have a seat." He wanted to reach out and pluck the grass from her hair and dress but knew better. He watched in silence as Jackie sank down onto the quilt, her composure swiftly returning.

"I'm trying to come up with some other books in Braille," Clayton began immediately to cover his own emotions. "But so far I've been unsuccessful. You'll have to read to me from the poetry book." He handed her the thin volume. "Please read me the poem on page 19."

Jackie turned the pages carefully and found the numbers with her finger. In order to use both hands, she set the book in her lap and began speaking, her voice clear and confident as she read over the lines.

As always, Clayton was amazed. Gone was the falling blind girl. Jackie had taken to

Braille like a duck to water, and it was obvi-ous in the way she read.

My Summer Day
by Timothy James

As I look over the horizon and see the setting sun, it reminds me of a fun summer day with my friends at the sea.

As the cool breeze blows in my face, I think of how as a child I would run along the beach where the sea breeze would hit me from the side and knock me down.

As the stars come out, and the moon shines bright I close my eyes and feel content. I feel the soft touch of a hand caress over my arm. I can tell who it is because of that smooth hand, and the soft voice telling me to come in.

"That was excellent," Clayton said softly. He had translated several poems the night before, but none of them had hit him the way this one did with Jackie reading it and using such expression. It seemed the only time she didn't play the part of the ice maiden was when she read aloud to Clayton.

In an effort to keep her on congenial

451

ground, Clayton asked her to read two more selections. She was still moving through the last one when Eddie came out. She sat on the blanket as well, and when Jackie finished, spoke in an excited tone.

"Oh, Jackie, that was wonderful!" But her sister only smiled cynically.

"Wasn't it, though? Just like a trained seal. Remember the one in New York, Eddie? Soon you'll be able to put me on display and maybe even charge admission. Then I can help pay for my school lessons."

Eddie told herself not to cry or even listen to the horrible, sarcastic tone, but in truth she was crushed. She came swiftly back to her feet, tears filling her eyes before she rushed to the house.

"Eddie," Clayton called to her, but she did not turn back.

A moment later Jackie found herself hauled to her feet. She was so shocked by the action that for a moment she didn't respond. Then Clayton's furious words found their mark.

"It would be just wonderful if you could actually think of someone besides yourself, Miss Fontaine."

"Let go of me," she hissed, but only found herself moved swiftly along the grass.

"I said, let go."

Clayton came to an abrupt halt.

"Just shut your mouth, Jackie. Shut it right now."

Again she was propelled forward several feet.

"The steps are directly in front of you," he told her tersely. "Find your own way inside."

The steps just inches from her feet, Jackie stood alone in the backyard long after she heard Clayton go up the stairs and into the house.

CHAPTER 35

Clayton found Eddie in the living room. He couldn't tell if she was still crying, but she stood at the huge north window, her back very straight and still.

"Are you all right?"

She didn't answer.

"Maybe I should go and get Robert. May I do that for you?"

"No," she said, shaking her head. "I have to handle my response. Jackie has to answer for her own. She knows the truth and rejects it, but that's not my fault. It's between her and God."

Eddie turned from the window. "I'm going to lie down for a while now, Tag. Please tell Jackie and Lena that I do not wish to be disturbed."

Clayton didn't speak as she left the room. There wasn't anything to say. He'd known. He'd been suspicious for weeks now but did not want to face Jackie's true spiritual state.

You're a fool, Clayton. You wanted it so

badly that you refused to see the truth.

Clayton sat down in a chair. At the moment he had no desire to seek out Jackie and continue their lesson. Clayton opened his heart to God. He prayed and tried to commit the future to Him. Worry was a strong temptation until Clayton remembered verses from Matthew 11 — verses that reminded him that the Lord's yoke, the Lord's burden, was light.

This heavy burden I feel is my own doing. If I'll just leave this with You, Lord, You'll be my strength. And strength was just what Clayton needed as Jackie came to the door.

"Eddie?"

"No." Clayton replied quietly. "She's gone upstairs to lie down. Please come in. I'd like to speak to you."

"Is it lecture time, Clayton?" The voice that was hesitant a moment earlier now turned hard.

"Yes. Get comfortable."

Jackie did as she was told.

"I've been hiding from the facts before me, Jackie," Clayton began quietly. "Even when I saw the truth, I didn't want to believe it."

This was nothing like what Jackie expected. For a moment she was confused. It showed on her face.

"It's been bothering me for weeks now as to why you're so angry and hateful to everyone and everything. I knew the truth, deep down, but I didn't want to face it. I shudder just a little at the thought that we were almost married."

"What do you mean?" She was angry now.

"I mean, the Bible is very clear. As a believer in Christ, my wife must be a believer too."

"What are you talking about?" She half rose from her seat on the sofa.

"I'm talking about my strong doubt concerning your salvation. If the fall had taken your life and not just your eyesight, I find it hard to believe that you would really be standing in the presence of God, Jackie. I'm sorry to be the one to tell you this, but you haven't the foggiest idea what true salvation means."

Jackie sat back now, her face a mask of shock.

"It bothered me so much when you said you'd just always been a Christian. I had never heard anyone say that before, and it concerned me. You've gone to church all your life and told yourself you're a good person, just like your father has, but you haven't a clue."

All color had drained from Jackie's face, and her chest rose and fell with her quickened breaths. Thoughts raced through her mind. *How can he say this to me? I am a good person. No one is perfect, but surely God wouldn't —*

For the first time Jackie couldn't finish the sentence. She'd certainly known, but for the first time she accepted the truth that God *would* deny her a heavenly home if she continued on as she'd been. Not because He wanted to, but because His holiness was so great, and as her mother always said, it's God's way or no way. So far she'd lived life all her way, and she had nothing but misery to show for it.

"I'll go now," Clayton was saying, but Jackie barely heard him. "Maybe you'd better have Robert get in touch if you want me to come back and teach."

Jackie couldn't say a word. She turned her head away from his footsteps on the floor and flinched as the huge front door shut. It sounded like a death knell in her ears.

The blackness that surrounded her — not the one that so terrified her when she first woke up and learned the truth about her eyesight, but the one that had been there all along — now crowded in again. She was going to hell, and somehow she knew that the day-to-day blackness she experienced would be nothing compared to the eternal darkness awaiting her.

Her mind raced as a new kind of terror embraced her. Her heart begged God not to let it be too late, but every verse she'd ever heard concerning eternity and salvation had slipped from her mind. John 3:16,17. What were they? And Ephesians 2:8. She was certain that there was another one, but how did they begin? She couldn't find a word.

Steps sounded in the hallway.

"Eddie?" she cried. "Clayton? Eddie? Is that you?"

"No, Miss Jackie, it's Lena." She came into the room and saw Jackie's tear-streaked face. "What did you need, dear?"

"Oh, Lena," she cried, on the verge of hysterics. "What is John 3:16? I can't remember. Please help me."

" 'For God so loved the world,' " she began calmly, and took Jackie's hand as she joined her on the settee.

" 'That he gave his only begotten Son,' " Jackie picked it up. " 'That whosoever believes in Him, should not perish, but have everlasting life.' "

"That's it, love."

"But Lena." Jackie's voice was still desperate. "What do I do? How can I believe?"

"It is not hard, Miss Jackie. Belief is to humble your heart and tell God what a lost sinner you are. Then you tell Him that you accept the salvation offered to you because of the cross. Some say to invite Jesus into your heart, but the words are not so important as the belief.

"Raymond and I believed at the same time, Miss Jackie, and all Raymond said was 'I have come to You, Lord Jesus, and lay my sin at Your feet. Please make me Yours forever.' And that was it."

"Oh, Lena," Jackie sobbed. "What if it doesn't work? I've been fighting for so long."

"No, no," her voice was tender and sure. "Nothing touches God's heart like true repentance, Miss Jackie. Confess and believe."

Jackie was trembling all over, but with excitement rather than fear.

"Would you like to do this now, Miss Jackie?" Lena asked with bold compassion. "Would you like me to help you pray?"

"Yes, Lena, please. I have so much to say to God. Do you think He'll really listen?"

"Oh yes, my dear. Just open your heart."

Jackie's breath came a little hard, but she began to pray.

"Lord God in heaven, I've always let my pride rule me. I didn't ever want to disagree with my father, and I was so certain he was good enough. Me too." She had to pause to catch her breath. "I've sinned against You, God. I've been headstrong and hated You for my blindness."

Jackie was overcome then, but Lena sat silently nearby. Realizing just how blind she had been was an earth-shattering experience for her. She had walked with perfect vision and a black heart.

"I can't go on alone anymore," she now whispered to the Lord. "Please take me as you did Raymond and Lena. Take all of me and let me into Your sight."

Arms came around her a moment before she smelled Eddie's perfume. The three women clung to each other and cried.

"He told me, Eddie. I could tell he was sad and upset, but Clayton told me he thought I was going to hell. It hurt so much, Eddie, but I had to know."

"I know, Jackie; I know. You've taken care of it now."

"You heard?"

"Yes. I didn't want to interrupt, but I was near the door."

"I tried to do it on my own, Eddie." Jackie grew very serious. "Just like Father, and for a while I thought I was succeeding. Clayton was so serious about it in his letters, and I wanted to be like him. I was kind and did things for others, but I was still empty inside. Most of the time I wouldn't allow myself to think about it."

Eddie smoothed the hair from her face and laughed softly. "You have grass all over your hair and dress."

"Oh. I fell outside before my lesson. Lena?" Jackie asked suddenly.

"Yes, dear?"

"Thank you," Jackie said simply.

Lena hugged her close and blubbered all over both of them. A few moments passed before Lena grew flustered by her own show of emotions. She jumped up and declared that the two sisters must be starving. She hurried off to fix lunch.

"Clay left," Jackie said softly.

"He must have wanted to give you some time."

"And take some for himself," Jackie added.

Eddie suddenly kissed Jackie's cheek. The younger girl put a hand on that spot.

"What was that for?"

"For thinking of Tag's feelings."

Jackie smiled just a little. "So much, Eddie. There's so much that's clear to me now. Can it really happen so swiftly?"

"Yes. It may not be like that all the time, but when it is, it's a lot of work."

"You knew, didn't you?"

"That you thought you were saved but weren't? Yes. I had a hard time facing the facts, but Robert was very firm with me, and I saw the truth. Don't forget that we shared a room, Jackie. We were about as close as two sisters could be. I was a fool not to see it long ago.

"Anyone can be afraid of the dark, but sometimes you would be terrified no matter how I tried to comfort you. When Robert spoke to me, it suddenly made perfect sense. I see now that the darkness outside was so frightening to you because there was no light inside."

"Oh, Eddie," Jackie said as the years came rushing back. "It's so true. I would lie beside you in bed and feel like I was suffocating, even when you would leave the lantern on for me. I was black on the inside, all right," the younger girl sighed. "I have so many things to apologize for. I have been horrid to you at times. Today I was just awful."

"That's behind us, Jackie. You'll be

tempted to beat yourself over the head with the past, but it does no good."

Jackie nodded, her face filling with peace. "I'm glad of one thing, Eddie."

"What's that?"

"That I didn't lose my sight because of some rebellion. Then I would feel that it's all my fault."

"It's wise of you to think that way, Jackie. You have much to be thankful for. If you had kept your vision, you might have wandered blindly for years."

"Yes. I'd already thought of that. Oh, Eddie, so much has happened in the last few minutes. I feel overwhelmed."

"Don't try to take it in all at once."

Lena came back to the room and told the women she had lunch ready. Their conversation never stemmed all the way through the meal and into the middle of the afternoon. They talked like they never had before. Jackie had dozens of questions, and Eddie tried to answer them all. Lena came and went as well, but she was already back in the kitchen working on dinner when Clayton's name was mentioned again.

"You're quiet all of a sudden," Eddie commented.

"I was thinking of Clay."

"What about Clay?"

"He said he was coming back only if Robert asked him. I'm sure he thought I would never want to see him again."

"Well, maybe a day or two off would be nice. You do want him to teach you?"

"Yes, but some time off would be welcome. Do you think he'll understand?"

"Certainly. I know Robert would be happy to talk to him."

"Who would I be happy to talk with?"

Eddie jumped up and ran into her husband's arms. He was home an hour early, and she barely accepted his kiss before she was talking 15 to the dozen and pulling him by the hand to Jackie's side. Robert cried when he heard her news and hugged her close.

"Oh, Jackie," was all he could say. His heart was so full. He asked questions of her, and when he learned the story, sought out Lena to hug her as well.

The three of them had a lovely dinner together before Robert told them he simply had to get some work done in his office. The women were left on their own, and Eddie could tell that Jackie had something on her mind. She waited and wasn't disappointed.

"May I ask you something, Eddie?"

"Certainly."

"Why do you suppose God did this?"

"You mean, allowed your blindness to happen?"

"Yes. I was only trying to help Father, and now I'll never see again. Why is it like that sometimes?"

"Can I read something to you, Jackie?"

"Yes." She listened as her sister rose, went across the room, and then reseated herself.

"This is a letter Mother wrote to me long before we brought you to Boulder. I'd like to share part of it with you."

"All right."

"Mother writes, 'The temptation to question is strong at a time like this. Why my daughter? Why my Jackie? But then I also have to ask myself, why *not* my daughter? I think of the blind man from John 9. The disciples asked Jesus, whose fault is it that's he's blind, his or his parents? Jesus told them it wasn't anyone's fault, but that the works of God would be manifested in this deed. I will do well to remember this. We live in a sinful world and painful, evil things happen. God allows them to show us our need for Him. I must be thankful for that sovereignty and not fight against it.

" 'I have found a verse, Exodus 4:11, that has been a comfort to me. "And the Lord said, unto him, Who hath made man's mouth? Or who maketh the dumb, or deaf, or the seeing or the blind? Have not I, the Lord?" This reminds me, Eddie, that He never lost control. Even as my precious girl fell and lost her sight forever, He was there. Will she ever again take enough interest in life to ask me about this? I don't know, but I have peace and I pray that someday she will live as she never has before.' "

"Oh, Eddie." Jackie had tears in her eyes. "She answered my question, and I'd never even asked it. I might have never known."

Eddie hugged her for a long time before they fell quiet. Then, for the first time since Eddie could remember, Jackie asked her to read from the Bible.

She was more than happy to comply, and Jackie listened, her head tilted to hear every word until she realized she was getting a crick in her neck. She told Eddie that they could stop when she heard the older girl yawn, but Eddie insisted they keep on. However, she suddenly stopped a few verses later.

"Eddie?" Jackie called softly, moving her hand along the davenport. She felt her sister's skirt and knew she was there.

"Eddie. Are you all right?"

Jackie turned when she heard footsteps.

"She's asleep, Jackie," Robert told her.

"Oh. Okay."

"Would you like me to read to you?"

"Don't you want to go to bed?"

"Not yet."

Robert settled in next to his wife and arranged her against him. She woke, but he pushed her head back onto his shoulder. He began to read, and she fell back to sleep almost instantly. Taking up where Eddie had left off, he got right into the chapter she was sharing from Genesis. It took several minutes for him to see that he'd lost Jackie as well.

"No, I don't want you to," Eddie told her husband, circling the table in his study, keeping it between them. "I will see the doctor."

"But I know all about these things," he said with a twinkle in his eye.

Eddie shook her head and tried not to smile. "I want to hear it from him. I don't think I trust you."

Robert barely held his laughter.

"All I'm going to do," he said as he came around the table after her again, "is span your waist with my hands. Then I'll know."

Eddie laughed but did not let him catch her. She countered, "And the next time I

need to see someone about cash invest-
ments, I should ask my doctor."

Robert really laughed at this one, but
Eddie would not hold still. It was so fun to
tease him. So fun to see his eyes light with
passion for her. Their play might have gone
on indefinitely if Jackie hadn't come to the
door.

"Eddie?" she called innocently.

Eddie turned to her and Robert sprang.

"Gotcha!" he cried triumphantly.

"Oh!" Eddie let out a loud squeak as
Robert's arms came around her from the
back and pressed her to his chest.

"Robert Langley," Jackie demanded playfully. "What are you doing to my sister?"

"Well, I'll tell you, Jackie. She comes to
me and says she thinks she's pregnant but
won't let me near her. Now, isn't that rot-
ten?"

"Oh, Eddie." Jackie came forward, ignor-
ing Robert's question as her outstretched
hands searched for her sister. "Where are
you?"

"Right here."

Robert allowed Eddie to slip from his
grasp so she could hug her sister.

"Come to the sofa," Jackie pulled her. "I
want to feel the baby."

"It's too early," Eddie said with a laugh

but complied because Jackie wasn't listening. She sat still while the younger girl's hand came to rest gently on her stomach.

"You don't feel pregnant." Her brow was drawn in concentration.

"Not from the outside." There was a smile in Eddie's voice. "And I may not be, but if I am it's too soon to show."

Robert now came to his wife's other side. He sat down beside her, slipped an arm around her shoulders, and then pressed his lips to her temple and left them there.

"I want a girl," Jackie announced.

"I'll see what I can do." Eddie's voice was dry.

"What if I want a boy?" Robert teased.

"Well," Jackie cocked her head a little. "I guess you had better do what Robert tells you to, Eddie."

She was so serious that husband and wife shared an amused smile.

"Looking forward to Clayton returning tomorrow?" Robert asked. Jackie had made her decision on Tuesday, and this was now Thursday. Both husband and wife watched her blush.

"I think so," she told them, her face serious once again.

"Why do you look so uncertain?"

"Well, I just think he must have better

things to do. School starts a week from Monday."

"But he plans to come even after school begins," Eddie said reasonably. "You know, in the evening and such. That doesn't sound like someone who's too busy to come."

Jackie nodded but didn't answer. Her heart had made a complete turnaround in the last two days, but that didn't change the fact that she was in love with a man who would never be hers. In light of that, she'd been asking herself if seeing so much of him was a good idea.

But then she remembered the school year. Surely when classes began he wouldn't be able to come very often. The problem would be taken care of on its own. Jackie didn't want to think about why that made her want to cry.

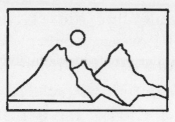

CHAPTER 36

Jackie was alone in the study working over the writing table when Clayton arrived on Friday, and because she was concentrating on moving her hands over the poetry book, she didn't hear him come in. The sound of his voice caused her to jump.

"Hello."

"Oh, Clay, it's you," she said on a gasp.

"Yes. You look like you're very busy."

"Well," she faltered, her hands fluttering in embarrassment. "You left the books here, and I thought it would be —"

"Don't apologize. I'm glad you're enjoying them."

"Um, well, I mean . . ." She was suddenly tongue-tied. "I know Robert talked to you and all, but if you don't have time to come, Clay, I'll understand." She finished rather lamely, wishing she hadn't brought the subject up at all.

He didn't reply right away. She listened as he brought a chair up to the other side of her writing table. He didn't touch her, but she could tell he was very close.

"I have plenty of time for this, Jackie," he said gently, when he'd settled across from her. "And if I didn't have time, I'd make some."

His voice was so warm that she blushed from the chin up. Clayton watched in amazement. She was like the Jackie from months ago, before the letters they had shared, the one who was so shy around him that she could barely form two sentences.

"Oh, well, all right. If you're certain."

"I am."

"Oh," Jackie said before Clayton could suggest they begin. "There's one other thing, Clay. I'm sorry about the hard time I've given you here, and well, about the letter from a long time ago. I'm . . . well . . . I'm sorry I lied. I made Lexa write it. I've asked Eddie to write to her and apologize for me."

Clayton's whole body vibrated with the pounding of his heart. Robert had told him about her decision, but to see it up close was an awesome thing. Very carefully, so as not to frighten her, Clayton placed his hand over the top of hers. In so doing, he watched Jackie take a huge breath, and in that instant also learned that she hadn't begun to understand the intensity of his feelings.

"Thank you, Jackie," he managed after a moment. "I assure you it's all behind us. All right?"

"Yes."

"Shall we start?"

She nodded, and he asked her to read to him. He hadn't translated the page she was on, but the poem flowed so beautifully that he knew she had read every word. From there they moved to her writing. She could not see how his suggestion would work, but Clayton had wanted her to give it a try.

"Okay," he said as he bent over her shoulder. "Feel the paper on the table. That's the one you write on. The other piece of paper is set over it."

Jackie sat quietly and felt with her hands.

"Now, just move slowly. Begin to write, using the top paper as your line, and when you get to the edge and want to begin a new line, move the top paper slightly downward."

"How will I know how far?"

"I'll tell you until you get the feel of it."

"What should I write?"

Clayton thought fast. "Wildflowers. Give me a paragraph on Colorado wildflowers."

"All right."

It was painful going, but Jackie did her best, the pencil feeling foreign in her hand after so long a time. None of her *i*'s were dotted in the right place, and the *t*'s were crossed in rather odd spots, but other than that it wasn't bad. Letters like *g* or *y* that went below the line of the other paper were cut off, but her attempt was still legible.

"Let me see." Clayton asked for the paper, and Jackie was very aware of the way he stood at her shoulder. "Good; very good. You'll have to dot your *i*'s and cross your *t*'s as you go, but it looks good. How did it feel?"

"A little strange. I wish I could feel the words."

"You'll be able to," Clayton told her. "After you get this down, I'm going to teach you to take notes. You'll dot out the words when someone speaks or you want to make a list and later be able to read it back to yourself. It won't mean anything to someone who can't read Braille, but it's handy for your own information.

"Now," Clayton said as he moved away from her. "I think you're doing well in all your subjects, so why don't you tell me what you'd like to work on today."

Jackie bit her lip. She knew what she wanted but was a little afraid to ask.

"No ideas?" Clayton prompted.

"Well," she began, but didn't go on.

"I'll make some suggestions, shall I? We could go over math facts or work on the writing some more. You could memorize a poem from the book and recite it to me. We haven't done much with geography, so I could get out a map. I could read to you or —"

"That one," Jackie cut in.

"Read to you?"

Jackie nodded, and Clayton noticed that she was almost tense.

"Did you have something in mind?"

Again she bit her lip, and this time Clayton waited. Silence.

"What is it, Jackie?"

"Clayton, could you read the Bible to me?"

Her voice was so hesitant, her look almost fearful. Clayton's heart broke.

"I'd love to," he told her truthfully. "Just let me borrow a copy from Eddie."

"You're going to, Clay?" she whispered before he could leave. "You're really going to read to me?"

"Sure."

The smile that lit Jackie's face was the first Clayton had seen from her in more than a year. It did funny things in the region of his chest. He moved toward the door, but ran into the doorpost because he was staring behind him, watching her. Eddie, who was headed that way, laughed when she witnessed it.

"Are you in a hurry?" Eddie asked, noticing that he looked a little dazed.

"She smiled," he said, his voice bemused. "I saw her smile."

Eddie's gaze became very tender. If Jackie could see him now, she'd know in an instant how much he still loved her.

"Are you taking a break?" she asked.

"No. She wants me to read to her. May I borrow a Bible?"

Eddie walked back into the study with him and showed him the one Robert kept in his desk. "He does his Bible study here," Eddie explained.

"Hi, Eddie."

"Hi, yourself. How are things going?"

"Good. I wrote a paper."

"You wrote a paper?" Eddie sounded uncertain.

"Well, just a paragraph really." Jackie's hand searched the desk and found the sheets. "It's one of these."

"Wow," Eddie managed. "You did great. You'll have to dot your *i*'s and cross your *t*'s as you go, but this is wonderful."

Jackie smiled at how closely she'd echoed Clayton.

"Well, I'll leave you to it."

"Are you going into town today, Eddie?" Jackie suddenly asked. In a flash Eddie realized how long it had been since she'd taken Jackie along.

"I was, but why don't I wait until tomorrow," Eddie suggested. "Then you could go with me."

"All right." Jackie didn't smile this time, but she was very pleased.

Eddie went out after that, and Clayton sat down to read. Jackie moved from the desk to the sofa and made herself comfortable. He began in the book of Luke, and Jackie listened to every word and detail. Things she had paid little heed to in the past now leapt out at her. She didn't ever remember hearing that Zacharias had been made mute until his son was born, but it was right there in the first chapter. Hearing it, Jackie burst out with a question in the middle of the verse.

"Why?"

"Why what?"

"Why was Zacharias made mute?"

"Because of his unbelief. Let me finish verse 20 for you, '. . . because thou believest not my words, which shall be fulfilled in their season.' "

"Oh," was all Jackie said, but Clayton could tell she was troubled.

"Is it clear to you now?"

"I understand what happened, but didn't you read to me that he and Elisabeth were upright, blameless people?"

"Yes," Clayton responded, thumbing back to verse six. " 'And they were both righteous before God, walking in all the commandments and ordinances of the Lord, blameless.' Is that the verse?"

"Yes." Jackie's voice sounded almost sad. "God takes unbelief very seriously, doesn't He?"

"Yes, He does," Clayton had to agree. He watched her face for a time and decided there must be huge regret involved in fighting God for as long as she had. He quietly prayed that Jackie would put the past behind her and begin serving God with her whole heart. Clayton told her what his prayer had been. Jackie smiled and thanked him, and they talked of the importance of this for a few minutes. After that he read on, finishing the 80 verses contained in the first chapter of Luke.

"What did the doctor say?" Jackie asked as soon as they walked from the office back onto the street.

"That we should put a nursery together sometime before next year."

"Oh, Eddie. Oh, Eddie!" Jackie nearly flapped with excitement. "I don't know if I can wait that long."

The expectant mother laughed.

"Are we going to see Robert?"

"No," Eddie told her immediately. "He's so excited about this that he's sure to make a scene right there in the bank."

"Oh, Eddie," her sister scolded. "He would not."

"You haven't seen him chase me around the house in the last few days, and we weren't even sure. All he wants to do is hold me."

"It must be torture for you."

This was Jackie's first attempt at humor since she'd come to live with them, and Eddie wanted to shout with laughter. It was too bad they weren't alone so she could give way to her mirth.

"What's on the list now?" Jackie asked, her eyes still shining over Eddie's soft chuckles.

"The general store. I want some yarn."

"Booties," Jackie proclaimed triumphantly. "You're going to make booties, isn't that right?"

"Hello," Eddie said congenially as someone passed. To Jackie, she said "Will you keep it down, Jackie? The whole street heard you."

Jackie laughed. "I'm not responsible for my actions," she declared. "I'm a delirious aunt-to-be."

Eddie told herself not to laugh because it would only encourage her, but Jackie could feel her shaking.

"Well now," a deep voice spoke as footsteps neared. "This certainly looks like a good time."

"Hello, Travis," Eddie spoke warmly, bringing her sister to a gentle halt.

"You look radiant, Mrs. Langley," he said kindly and tipped his hat. "As do you, Miss Fontaine."

"Hello, Travis," Jackie added, smiling. Eddie watched him blink at her. "We're going to the general store and then I think Eddie should take me to lunch, don't you agree?"

"Absolutely," Travis said, turning pleased eyes to Eddie, who was grinning at him.

"I think I should take you home," Eddie announced, "before you get us arrested."

"I've never spent any time in jail," Jackie said thoughtfully. Eddie shook her head.

"We'll see you later, Travis."

"All right. Goodbye."

"What has come over you, Jacqueline

Fontaine?" Eddie asked in amazement, but she was more amused than angry.

Jackie didn't answer. She was in great spirits right now but couldn't really tell Eddie why. It wasn't that she didn't know, but now was not the time or place. Only just last night she had been telling the Lord that she could live forever as she was. Eddie was probably expecting, so she would have a baby niece or nephew to play with, and Clayton was her friend again. She still desired to be his wife and have his children, but God had given her a deep contentment for the way things presently stood.

She now sighed to herself. Eddie didn't hear the sound, but saw that her sister's face looked very serene. They had come to the general store, and even the familiar smells and sounds were God's way of saying to Jackie that He was going to take care of her.

Has there ever been someone so blind? she asked the Lord. *Thank You, Father, for never giving up. Thank You for showing me the way.*

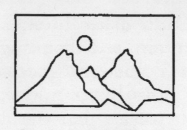

CHAPTER 37

Jackie had Eddie laughing again, this time from nearly tripping on the doorstep. She didn't fall, but her recovery and comments were so funny that Eddie didn't try to hold back.

"I've got to sit down," Eddie gasped as she moved into the living room. "I don't know when I've laughed so much."

"I'll get us something to drink," Jackie offered.

"Oh, that sounds wonderful. Lena was going to leave early today, but she usually makes lemonade."

"Okay. Don't go away now."

Eddie leaned her head back and sighed. It was as if her sister had been dead and had now returned to life. Eddie had struggled so many weeks trying to understand what she should do but finding no answers. She knew Jackie needed salvation, but in truth it had seemed so impossible.

Jackie was busy in the kitchen for a long

time, and Eddie made herself stay seated, wanting to think and pray. Suddenly, in the midst of Eddie's reflections, the front door opened. Eddie put her head up to see Robert come in. He was a few hours early, and she rose to greet him with a pleased smile on her face. Her welcoming smile changed to a look of astonishment when her parents came in behind him, followed by Lexa, Danny, and Sammy, all looking a little travel-worn but absolutely wonderful.

"Oh, Mother," Eddie said softly, noticing that they were all very quiet as she hugged each one in turn. Indeed, their silence was tense. Their eyes looked past her, taking in more than the house, and Eddie understood.

"Come this way," Eddie told them, her voice low. Less than a minute later they stood just inside the kitchen.

"Am I taking too long?" Jackie asked, having heard the movement.

"No," Eddie spoke with a teasing tone.

"Well, go back and sit down. I'll wait on you and not even get you wet."

"All right," Eddie told her, but she didn't move.

Addy had put a hand to her mouth to keep from gasping with delight, and now she waited until Jackie put her glass down.

"Hello, dear."

"Mother?" Jackie said immediately, turning from the counter, her excitement making her unsteady.

"Yes, honey, I'm here."

"Oh, Mother, Mother." Jackie's hands began to flutter in the air and continued until Addy came to hug her. The deed was enough to spark the whole family into action. They all began to talk at once. Jackie's mouth opened and closed, but no sound came out as she realized that everyone was there. They were together. For the first time in months they were all together in a good way. When Eddie and Robert had come to take her to Boulder, she had been impossible, and even refused to tell her family goodbye, but with the changes in her heart, this was like a dream come true.

"You can share my bed," Jackie found herself saying to Danny, and then Lexa was there. "Oh, Lexa, how long can you stay? You can share my bed, all right? Oh, no, this can't be Sammy. You're so tall. Share my bed, will you? Stay in my room so we can talk."

"Well, that's four in the bed now," Robert commented with a laugh. "Maybe Eddie should move in there too."

No one noticed the kitchen — no one noticed that they were standing and not comfortably seated in the living room. It was just too wonderful to talk and touch one another right where they stood. Jackie was filled with questions, and her father finally put an arm around her and answered them.

"We'll be here for five days, and then we're going to visit the Taggarts in Denver. From there we'll head home. We didn't write ahead of our coming because I wasn't certain when I could close the store."

"You actually shut the doors of the store?"

"Yes, I did. Doc Edwardson has a key in case there's an emergency, but I warned customers ahead of time that we would be gone when they usually shop for school. I've put a sign out that says we'll be back on September 5."

"We'll miss the first two days of school," Lexa added happily.

Jackie laughed. "You don't need to. Clayton is here, and he can give you lessons next week."

Lexa only groaned and said she didn't think she would be up to it.

Tours of the house were next. Addy wanted to see the bedrooms, so Eddie took her that direction while Robert led Morgan around the downstairs. For a few minutes, Danny found herself alone with Jackie.

"Tell me what's happened, Jackie," she said quietly. "You're not the same girl who left Georgetown on May 1. What's happened to you?"

Jackie smiled. "I'm so glad I'm not the same girl. I fought it, Danny; I fought it for so long, but I finally gave myself to Christ."

Danny hugged her older sister. They were very much the same height now, and Jackie clung to her. Upstairs the women were doing some hugging of their own.

"You have something to tell me, don't you, Edwina?"

Eddie smiled. "How did you know?"

"Because you're radiant."

They hugged, and Addy held her oldest daughter very close, her heart crying and rejoicing at the same time. They would be far from Boulder by the time this little one entered the world.

This is what my mother felt, Addy thought of the woman long dead. *This was what she experienced when I had my babies far from her reach. This is the separation she felt in not touching them or seeing them.*

"Mother," Eddie said gently. "You look about to cry."

Addy's smile wobbled dangerously. "For the first time ever I agree with your father about wanting you to move to Georgetown."

Eddie laughed and hugged her again. "I know," she suggested. "Let's have Robert pressure Father about moving here to Boulder."

"Oh, no," Addy said. "Just about the time we do that, one of you girls will meet someone from New York, and we'll be off across the country again."

"Mother, are you in here?"

"Here, Sammy."

"Oh. Is this your room, Eddie?"

"Yes. Isn't it pretty?"

"Um hmm," she agreed as she took in the green curtains and counterpane. It was not overly feminine but had enough masculine touches to make Eddie and Robert both comfortable. The greens ranged from a pastel to a deep forest, and the effect was very soothing.

"What have you been doing, Sammy?" Addy wished to know.

"Just wandering and wishing I could live here all the time."

The older women smiled. "We waited rather late to come this year," Addy said. "Maybe another year you can come and spend some time during the summer." She paused for the space of several heartbeats. "Especially if you can be a help with the baby."

Sammy's eyes shot to Eddie's, and Eddie's heart melted at the love she saw there. They embraced for many minutes, neither capable of words. Addy left them to find Morgan. He needed to see Eddie and learn firsthand of her news. Addy wanted to see the rest of the house.

"Did you know, Mother? I mean, could you tell?"

"Yes and no, Jackie," Addy confessed.

It was late in the evening now, and Addy had walked Jackie and Sammy up to Jackie's room. Sammy had gone to retrieve something from her mother's case, so Addy was given a few moments alone with Jackie.

"What do you mean, yes and no?"

Addy smoothed Jackie's brow as her daughter's head lay on the pillow.

"You made a confession as a child, and I thought it genuine as I talked to you that day, but then things didn't really change for you. They did for Danny, who accepted Christ at the same time, but not for you. I also must admit to you, Jackie, I *wanted* to believe you understood. I've had to confess that. It was very wrong of me. I told myself I couldn't judge you that way, and then God reminded me that I was still judging you: I was judging you saved. If that wasn't true, then that was the worst thing I could possibly do."

"So you think that if a person is saved it will be evident?"

"Yes. I didn't always. I mean, I tried to tell myself that if a person told me he had made that choice then I should believe him, but James puts it very well in James 2. He says I'll show you my faith by my works. If the conversion is real, my darling, then the whole world should be able to tell."

"Oh, Mother," Jackie took her hand. "It's never been like this. I want to pray all the time, and I love it when someone reads the Bible to me. I've always been so bored and restless with church, but I can't wait until tomorrow."

Addy leaned over and put her arms around Jackie, her heart so full that she couldn't even speak. They were still hugging when Sammy returned. Addy kissed her youngest daughter good-night and teased them both about giggling and talking in bed. As she then joined Morgan in their own room, she only hoped that Jackie would have a chance to tell him all that had happened. Since Jackie had left George-town, Morgan had been more attentive and at home as much as he was able, but Addy suspected that he was still trying to come to God his own way. Their marriage was more precious right now than she ever dreamed it could be, but Morgan's views on how to get to heaven still lay between them. As always, Addy continued to pray.

Clayton Taggart's face lit with surprised pleasure when he saw the Fontaine family. He hugged all the women and shook Morgan's hand. He was doubly pleased when Robert invited him to come for Sunday dinner so he could have a long visit. Such an invitation took all the pressure off him to talk to them at church. He was able to stand back while they met the church family, knowing his time with them would come.

However, his heart didn't completely step away. Whenever he was in the same room with Jackie, he was aware of her every move. The other girls had all grown so tall and were prettier than ever, but Clayton had eyes for only one, and she would never see him again. Amazingly, that didn't matter. Clayton's heart and attitude had not changed in the least, except that he wanted to cherish Jackie all the more. And he knew that he would.

Jackie, however, didn't know it. If there was one great advantage to her loss of vision, it was that he could look at her beloved face and still keep his feelings to himself. Someday she would know his voice well enough to know what he was thinking, but right now he'd kept a close watch on himself.

After he had told Jackie about his feelings concerning her spiritual state days before, Clayton had gone home to pray. In truth, he couldn't pray right away. His heart felt broken, and he wept off and on for two hours before falling into an exhausted sleep. When he awoke, he turned to his Bible. He read for the rest of the day and turned Jackie over to God. He knew an amazing peace, but he had no sense that something had happened. He simply knew for the first time since seeing her again that he could live without her. He told God he was going to pray for her salvation if it took the rest of his life, but he was also going to obey God's Word, and that meant no marriage to a nonbeliever.

When Robert had come the next day to tell him what had taken place, Clayton was so shocked he could hardly speak. He was not sorry for the way he'd talked to her, but it never occurred to him that God might use his words in such a powerful way.

It was on that day that Robert told him to come back on Friday to teach. He'd gone and found Jackie in the study. One look at her as she pored over that book, and he knew he was more in love than ever. When she asked him to read from the Bible, it was as if the Lord was saying, "She's yours now, Clayton. You can finally have her." Now, two days later, his feelings were just as strong. He even considered talking to Morgan but decided against it. The time to tell Jackie of his feelings might not come for months or even years. No matter to Clayton's mind. He could wait. Her friendship was beyond value to him, and the rest would come in God's time.

"I guess I'll see you next Sunday." Clayton's voice came low to Jackie's ears. The day was getting on, and Clayton thought it a good time to go. He found Jackie alone at the front, on the wide stone porch that swept halfway around the house. She was sitting on the stone bench, the skirt of her new green dress spread out around her. Clayton found her enchanting.

"Next Sunday?" Jackie looked uncertain

and shifted the glass she was holding to her other hand. "I didn't think your class started for another week."

"It doesn't, but I assumed you would want to have time with your family."

Jackie licked her lips. She did want time with her family but not without him. In addition, she began to doubt his excuse. Was that how he really felt, or did he need some time away from her?

"Well, I guess it's probably best." She tried without success to keep the disappointment from her voice. "You must want some time to yourself after all of this, and especially with school starting."

Her head had dropped forward, and although she couldn't see, it was as though she was avoiding Clayton's eyes. He couldn't stand it. He stepped to stand in front of her, and with a gentle hand he captured her jaw and raised her gaze. He bent from the waist and spoke directly into her upturned face.

"I don't need any time off," he told her. His thumb moved gently on her cheek, and her breathing became labored. "I was thinking only of you. I could come as usual or just for a few hours. Whatever you want."

"Oh, Clayton, I wish I could see you," she told him honestly. "I wish I could tell if you really mean it."

"I mean it," he said, the hand still in place. It was amazing that they'd managed to be alone as long as they had, but when Clayton heard footsteps behind him, he moved his hand and took a step back.

"What time shall I come?" he managed in a normal tone.

"Maybe I should ask Eddie, just in case they've made plans."

In truth, it had been Addy who was headed their way, but when she saw how close Clayton had been to Jackie, she stopped short, beaming with pleasure.

"Your mother is here," Clayton said loudly enough for that woman to hear. "Why don't we ask her?"

Addy came forward and Jackie did just that. Addy pleased her daughter to no end when she said, "Well, even if we do have plans, Clay can join us."

Jackie didn't comment on that, but her delight was more than obvious. Clayton knew some delight of his own, but his stemmed from the way Addy looked at him when he finally said his goodbyes. She was no fool, and his feelings for Jackie were more than clear. Her approval, given with kind, beautiful eyes, was crystal clear as well.

CHAPTER 38

The next four days with the Fontaines were so much fun for Clayton that for the first time in weeks he didn't miss the company of his own family. They all wrote to him, from Milly to his grandmother, and he answered every letter, but since moving from Denver he'd missed them with an intensity that surprised him. However, he recognized the strong cathartic his letters to them had become. In those missives he wrote his every thought and feeling.

Only Addy Fontaine had been in contact with his family since he moved to Boulder, so it was ironic that his mother received news of Jackie's blindness just days before Clayton wrote to her himself. His father had been the one to write back to Clayton, and the young school teacher had been surprised to hear what the other man had to say. He encouraged his son never to pity Jackie, even if she felt sorry for herself. Clayton knew this advice stemmed from the fact that his father was still not up and walking, and might never be, but his life at home, in the mill, and amid their church family was full and fruitful.

Now Clayton could see that Jackie was on the same track. She went everywhere with her family and asked dozens of questions about the places they visited. It was such a turnaround from the girl who left Georgetown. It was a wondrous thing to watch God take hold of a life. Morgan saw Jackie's changes as well but would not admit to himself that God was at the root.

Travis had made a point of inviting the family to visit his ranch before they left, and it was during this time that Jackie was able to have a few words with her father. They were outside the house, walking next to the closest corral.

"You're doing so well," he commented when they had a few moments alone. He stopped by the fence, and Jackie's hands came to rest on it.

"Yes," Jackie smiled. "It's amazing what a humble heart can hear."

"What do you mean?"

Jackie's head turned to him. She could feel his gaze. "My pride has been so big. I heard all the right things but didn't want to listen."

Had Jackie had her sight, she'd have seen Morgan's look become shuttered. He knew exactly what she was talking about, but since her accident, he'd become more certain than ever that he must take care of his family and himself on his own. The silence spoke volumes to Jackie.

"Please keep your heart open, Father," she whispered.

"All right," Morgan agreed, but only because he didn't want to hurt her. His head tipped back, and he looked into the bluest sky he had ever seen. It seemed to stretch for miles without a cloud in sight. He then looked at Jackie. She would never see the sky again. His heart cramped, and he wanted to ask how she could trust God at all after what had happened. At the same time he knew it would be the worst thing he could say. A moment later they were joined by the others.

The week passed way too swiftly for everyone, and it was a painful goodbye that was made on Thursday morning. It helped to have Clayton come and teach Jackie, but he could see that she was down.

"I think we need to get outside today."

"All right." Jackie stood and waited for further orders, but Clayton didn't say anything, so Jackie asked, "Front yard or back?"

"Hmm," he said thoughtfully. "Let's start in the front."

Jackie didn't know what he meant by "start," but she moved from the study to the front door, Clayton following in her wake.

Clayton knew she could navigate the steps on her own, but the new friendship that existed between them made him think he could offer his arm. He did so, and Jackie took it, holding on even when they'd reached the bottom. Clayton had planned to hand her leaves and wildflowers and ask her to identify them, but Jackie spoke as they walked through the grass.

"School begins Monday."

"Yes."

"Excited?"

Jackie felt his arm tighten, but he said only, "Yes."

She laughed softly. "I think you're more than excited; I think you're ecstatic."

Clayton laughed as well.

"Tell me about the schoolhouse," Jackie begged quietly.

Clayton came to an abrupt halt. "Why don't I show you?"

"The schoolhouse?"

"Yes. I'm sure Eddie would let us use the buggy; in fact, she might want to go with us."

Jackie was surprised at how swiftly events in the next few minutes transpired. Within 15 minutes Eddie had said she would love to go, and the three of them were in the buggy headed through the middle of town to the school.

It was a scorching-hot August 31, and even though everything was in darkness for her, Jackie kept the brim of her bonnet pulled low over her face. By the time they arrived, sweat had begun to trickle down her neck.

"Here we go." Clayton's voice came to her, and Jackie put her hand out. Making it seem quite natural, Clayton kept her hand in his own long after she was down from the wagon. Jackie loved it, but the action distracted her so much that she nearly tripped.

"Easy." Clayton's voice was close to her ear. "Here are the steps."

"How many?"

"Let's see. Eight."

Jackie began to count, but Clayton still held on. In fact, he never let go. He showed her the spacious schoolroom, the wall at the front that was all blackboard, the neat rows of desks, and the woodstove that would not be needed for many weeks yet. The whole room smelled faintly of chalk, and Jackie could tell by just moving in Clayton's grasp that it was larger than the one in Georgetown.

"What color is it?"

"Off-white, I guess."

"And the wood; is it oak?"

"My desk is, but the children's desks might be an ash."

"Come over here, Jackie," Eddie called to her. "Feel the size of these windows. They line both the side walls and give the most wonderful light."

Clayton led her over and dropped her hand to reach around her, putting her very nicely into his arms, in order to open the wood-framed glass. A hot wind instantly blew onto Jackie's front, but she hardly noticed. At the moment all she could feel were Clayton's arms around her, and he was no longer even there. Jackie put a hand to her heaving chest and tried to divert her attention. If she wasn't careful she was going to grab that man and kiss him.

"What was the verse you read to me last night, Eddie? Something about the fields being white unto harvest?"

"Yes. That was what Jesus said to the disciples after He'd spoken to the woman at the well. What made you think of that?"

It never occurred to her that Eddie would ask that. She gave a shaky laugh.

"Maybe Clayton will harvest his students."

As if she'd asked him to, he took her hand once again.

"Come stand at the front where I'll be teaching."

He helped her step up to the place and left her standing so he could take a seat at the back.

"I'm in a rear seat, Jackie. Eddie's at the front."

"Okay. How close am I to the edge of the dais?"

"About 18 inches," Eddie told her, and Jackie took a few steps to the left and then to the right.

"I'll have no talking in this class." Jackie tried for a stern tone but found herself far too amusing. "Do you hear me, children? I can be very nasty if you force me to be."

"You're nearing the edge now, Jackie," Clayton called to her.

"You're nearing the edge, *Miss Fontaine*," Jackie corrected him. Eddie laughed.

"I'm getting hot," the expectant mother complained. "Let's go back into town and see if the hotel has anything cool to drink."

"It's a little early, but I would treat for lunch if anyone is hungry."

"Why, thank you, Clayton," Eddie told him with a smile, watching as he went to get Jackie. Her eyes misted at the tender way he pulled her arm through his, and then at Jackie's sure step with Clayton leading her.

Please, Lord, she prayed as she had done so often of late. *Please help them to find a way. What does a man do with a blind wife? I honestly don't know, but, Lord, I want them to have each other, and I just know You can find a way.*

Clayton had already taken Jackie to the buggy and was now waiting to shut the door. Eddie's heart was still at prayer as she thanked him and climbed in beside her sister, but it wasn't until the middle of lunch that she realized she herself could be part of the answer.

"Thank you, Clayton," Jackie told him much later that day.

"For what?"

"For taking me to the school." She knew he would be heading for home soon and didn't want him to leave before she could express herself.

"You're more than welcome. I can hardly believe it's only two days away. Now that you've been there, you can picture me teaching and pray for me."

"I'll do that," she promised.

Clayton asked her to turn to a page in a new book he had found for her, but Jackie just sat still.

"We'll always be friends, won't we, Clayton?"

"Yes, we will," he told her without hesitation. "Why do you ask?"

"It's just so hard when you can't see a person's eyes." She tried to laugh, but couldn't quite pull it off. "I mean, you could be looking daggers through me, and I wouldn't even know it."

"Does it sound like I'm looking daggers through you?" he asked gently.

"No," she admitted. "But I do wonder what you look like now."

"Why don't you go ahead and see?"

Jackie tensed. Did he mean what she thought he meant?

"Here," he said. Her fears were confirmed. "Put your hands on my face and see."

Clayton picked up her soft hands and laid them on his cheeks. His beard was just beginning to feel prickly. Jackie held her breath. The temptation to forget who he was and who she was was overwhelming, so without allowing her hands to "see" him at all, she put them back in her lap.

"I can't do that, Clayton."

"Why not?" His voice was low, intimate.

"Because we're not married."

The silence that followed lasted only a moment.

"Well, maybe we should be."

Jackie couldn't breathe. Her mouth had gone to dust and she felt frozen to the sofa. She heard Clayton move.

"I guess I'd better be on my way, Jackie. I'll see you on Sunday."

With that, he kissed her cheek and walked from the study. The sound of his steps was long gone before Jackie realized she hadn't uttered a word.

"Keep an eye on her," Clayton said softly to Eddie as he moved for the front door.

"Why? Did something happen?"

"I hope so," was all he said before smiling contentedly and bidding her goodbye.

Eddie stared at the closed portal and then back toward the direction of the study. She bit her lip with excitement. She had been reporting the day's events and making plans with Lena since they returned from town. She now had more to add.

$\star\ \star\ \star$

Pastor Henley had finished his sermon, and the folks of the small congregation were rising to fellowship. The elderly pastor was working his way through the book of Genesis, and there was much discussion on the respective roles of husbands and wives. The sermon was positive and exciting to all but a few. Robert and Eddie were still seated and enthusiastically discussing it when Clayton approached. The room was too noisy for Jackie to tell that someone had neared.

"Jackie," Eddie said, not thinking of the noise. "Why don't you ask Tag to dinner at noon."

"Oh, well," Jackie replied uncertainly, not realizing she was being watched. "He probably has plans."

"No, I don't." Clayton had come up behind their pew and leaned over, his face near hers. Jackie started, but he only smiled. He waited, but she said nothing.

"Well?" He was closer than she realized. "Are you going to ask me?"

Jackie's hand fluttered nervously around her bare neck, and she wished that Eddie had not offered to put her hair up. She was silent for many seconds, her eyes searching the air. "I'm sure you have plans for today, don't you, Clay?"

"I'm not doing a thing."

Again her hand fluttered, this time around the ear he had spoken into. "Would you like to come for Sunday dinner?"

"I'd love to," he said, so low that Jackie melted.

Eddie and Robert watched with unabashed curiosity as Jackie's face went a bright pink. Eddie could only assume that Clayton was joining them for Sunday dinner as she couldn't hear a word he was saying. If Jackie's face was any indication, the news was good, but Eddie forced herself not to ask.

The church was swiftly clearing, and Jackie left with the Langleys. However, Clayton was near to help her into the buggy and to remind her that he would see her shortly. Eddie noticed that she blushed all the way home.

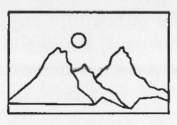

CHAPTER 39

Clayton looked out over the sea of faces in his classroom and felt an unbelievable sensation in his chest. They were here, and he loved them. He didn't know their names yet, but he had prayed for them every day, and in so doing, his love had grown. Not only that, he was the teacher. Mr. Taggart. The name was already written on the board in white chalk.

"As you can see, I've written my name on the board at the front of the room. I'm Mr. Taggart," he told them kindly. "Now I would like to know your names. We'll begin here at the front and work our way back. Please stand when you give your first and last name, and don't sit down until I've had a chance to check my list."

He took a seat at the desk up front, and they were off. There were half a dozen kids who obviously didn't want to be there at all, but for the most part the 32 students were eager to learn and participate. Clayton had more boys than girls and thought that might be unusual, but with the shy smiles he was receiving from a few of the girls who already looked smitten with him, he thought it might be best.

The day literally flew by. As tired as he knew he was going to be that night, he couldn't wait to tell Jackie all about it.

"How many of the girls fell in love with you?" she asked when she could get a word in. Eddie, who was with them, laughed uproariously.

"What's happening?" Jackie demanded.

"Oh, Jackie." Eddie was still overcome. "Clayton's face is lit up like a house afire. I think they all must have been enamored."

Jackie laughed as well, but then thought of herself. She had put absolutely no stock in Clayton's remark in the study, and so now her thoughts tormented her. At one time she had been one of the older girls in school. What if Clayton fell for one of his female students? *Stop it, Jackie,* she chastised herself. *You know he's going to be your friend, and you can't expect more than that. The day he meets someone and wants to marry, you'll just have to accept that. You could probably go back to Georgetown, and that would make things easier, but you're done with being selfish. Just because you can't have a normal life doesn't mean Clayton can't either. Help me, Father. Please help me to accept and believe this.*

Both Clayton and Eddie saw the odd look on Jackie's face, but no one questioned her. Clayton went on to share a little more about the day, and then he asked Jackie if she wanted her lesson now. He wasn't supposed to give it until evening, but as long as he was there, he thought she might want it then.

"Oh, sure," she said immediately, and then thought about how he might feel. "I mean, if you're not too tired."

"No, I'm fine. Why don't you get your books, and I'll meet you in the study."

"All right."

Clayton waited until she was gone before talking to Eddie.

"Has she been all right?"

"I think so. She didn't have much to do today, but all that's going to change tomorrow."

"How's that?"

Eddie shook her head. "I think I'll let her tell you if she wants to, but she won't know about it until morning."

Clayton thought that was more than fair and let the matter drop, but he was curious, especially because Jackie was a little quiet for their lesson. He left a few hours later and prayed all the way home.

When will I be in a position to ask her, Lord? When will I have the right to be what I want to be to that woman? I thought it was hard to wait for school, but this is torture. I want to hold her and calm her every fear. Clayton was halfway home when he finally heard himself.

I can't be those things I prayed about, Lord. Only You can do that. Please help me to remember.

"I can't remember how to do this," Jackie admitted, and Eddie looked at her in compassion.

"That's all right," Lena spoke up. "I will refresh your mind. You break the eggs, one at a time, over this bowl, the smaller bowl, and then you will have a chance to search for any shells that might have dropped before pouring the eggs into the larger bowl. Right here," Lena instructed, moving Jackie's hand, "is the wet towel to wipe the mess from your hands."

"All right." Jackie's voice was small, her face strained, and Eddie wanted to bawl. The younger girl was covered with flour and eggwhite, but she didn't complain. Eddie knew it would be a challenge for Jackie, but she never dreamed it would break her own heart to watch. She had waited until after breakfast that morning and begun by apologizing to Jackie.

"I need to confess something to you, Jackie," Eddie began. "I haven't treated you as I should."

"Eddie, what in the world could you be talking about?"

"I'm talking about getting you a schoolteacher but not helping you learn things you need to know around the house. You already serve your own food and drink. Why couldn't you learn to cook if Lena left all the ingredients in the same place all the time?"

Jackie's mouth felt like paper. She would burn the house down, she was certain of it, and said as much when she could find her voice.

"No, you won't." Eddie sounded so confident. "We're going to work up to this gradually. Beginning this morning and every weekday morning, you're going to work with Lena or me in the kitchen. What do you think?"

What do I think? What do I think? Jackie's mind nearly cried. *I think I'll fail at this like I thought I would fail at everything without my sight. I think this will get my hopes up, but I still won't be normal. Oh, Eddie, I love you so much and I'll do this to please you, but I think we're asking for disaster.*

"Jackie?"

"Sounds great," she replied, trying to convince Eddie as well as herself. "I'm just surprised and a little uncertain."

Eddie hugged her. "You won't be left on your own until you think you can do it."

Jackie nodded and prayed for strength, and then realized suddenly that she had much for which to be thankful. How many sisters would have sat her in a corner and told her to stay out of the way? But not Eddie, and not Robert either. She might be scared out of her wits, but they believed in her.

And it was a good thing they did, because Jackie was ready to throw in the towel by Friday. She worked every morning with Eddie and Lena, sewed, read, or wrote in the afternoons, and then worked with Clayton in the evening. She fell into bed every night, and Eddie had to call her each morning or she'd have slept until noon. Saturday never looked so good.

Eddie woke her at the regular time. Jackie didn't question her, but got dressed and made ready to leave her room. Not until that moment did she realize Clayton was downstairs. She heard his voice and then remembered that since they were getting time for school only in the evening, he said he would be coming on Saturday as well. Jackie knew she couldn't do it today. She stood in the upstairs hallway and fought the tears that threatened. She stood for quite some time until Robert came through on his way to the bank and spotted her.

"Jackie?"

Her back was to him, and she didn't answer. He circled to the front of her and saw the tears. With a gentle hand he led her back to her room and waited until she sat in the chair by the window.

"What is it, Jackie?"

She shook her head, and Robert read a certain hopelessness in her eyes.

"Jackie, Tag is here," Eddie called from the bottom of the stairs. Jackie rose wearily.

"She'll be a few minutes," Robert called down from the door. He then strode back into the room. "Sit down, Jackie."

She did as she was told, trying to remember the verse about doing all things in Christ because He gives the strength, not once realizing that she might be doing more than God was asking of her.

"Jackie, tell me what's upset you."

"I'm not really upset, Robert, just tired." A tear trickled down her face. "But I need to stay busy, and I think I'm being a baby."

Robert felt ashamed. She lived under his roof, but because things were busy at the bank, and Eddie was a concern with her pregnancy, not to mention Jackie's doing exceptionally well, he'd almost forgotten her personal needs.

"I need to go down now," she told him.

"Why don't you and Clayton just go for a walk today? I'm sure he would welcome the change."

"You don't pay Clayton to come here and walk with me, Robert," Jackie pointed out reasonably. Robert didn't tell her that Clayton had stopped accepting pay from him a long time ago.

Jackie went on. "If he's not going to teach me, I think he must have better things to do with his time. After all, he works all week long now and spends every evening here."

"And you work all morning, afternoon, and evening too," Robert added, but Jackie didn't comment.

"Stay here, Jackie. I'll be back."

She heard him leave and lay her head back. She felt ashamed for being tired and unwilling to work, but right now she didn't think she even had the strength to rise. She told herself not to go to sleep — she'd just awakened — but it was no use. Sleep was crowding in, and she didn't seem to have the will to fight it.

"Is Jackie coming down?" Eddie asked when her husband joined them in the living room.

"Not just yet." He looked at Clay. "I think she's pretty tired. I suggested that she go for a walk today instead of doing her lesson, but she said that's not what I pay you for."

Clayton's brows rose. "Well, that might have been true at one point, but surely she knows I come for more than her schooling."

"I think she does, but she's so tired right now that she's not thinking straight."

Clayton nodded. "She told me she's learning to cook all over again. I've noticed that anytime she learns something new, it exhausts her. She's doing great. I probably don't tell her often enough how well she's doing. Maybe Saturdays are not such a good idea."

Eddie looked shame-faced. "And I woke her as early as I always do."

"I think maybe we should back off a bit," Robert stated. "I've got to get into town now, but I think if you ask Jackie, she'll say she wants to rest today."

Eddie nodded, kissed her husband, and

started for the stairs. Clayton said he would stay and talk to Jackie awhile, but when Eddie returned, it was to report that Jackie had fallen sound asleep in her chair.

"I can feel the approach of winter," Jackie commented, fingering the leaf in her hand.

"Yes," Clayton agreed, but he didn't feel like talking more. Jackie looked utterly captivating in a dress of cream and navy blue, and all Clayton could do was stare. The beautiful Rocky Mountains rose majestically in the distance, but Clayton had eyes for Jackie alone.

Several weeks had passed since Jackie had been too tired to study, and from that point Clayton had spent every weekend with Jackie, but not to study or work. They had been some of the most wonderful weeks of his life. She grew more accustomed to his voice and inflections, and most of the time she was the wild, fun Jackie that he'd fallen in love with the summer before in Georgetown. Tonight they were supposed to be studying, but it was so nice that Clayton called for a nature walk and took her outside.

"Here's one for you." Clayton held a flower beneath her nose and watched her smile.

"Wild rose," Jackie breathed. "My favorite." She caressed the delicate blossom and smelled it again. She then realized how quiet Clayton had been that day.

"You haven't been very talkative today, Clayton Taggart."

"No," he smiled, "but I'm doing plenty of thinking."

"About?"

"About how lovely you look in that dress and how beautiful your hair is when the sun bounces off it."

Jackie's hand automatically went to a fat curl that lay on her shoulder. "I can't really remember what it looks like anymore."

"Shall I tell you?" Clayton asked and began before she could answer. "The color is richer than anything I've ever seen. Even without the red highlights, the sable brown is so full, dark, and soft to the eyes that you automatically want to touch it." Clayton's voice grew softer and deeper as he continued, and Jackie's heart began to pound. "It falls in ripples down your back and shoulders, and curls slightly at the ends. Even with the wind teasing it, it's smoothlooking and tempts my hand unbearably."

Clayton now looked at Jackie's eyes and saw understanding for the first time. "What did you just hear, Jackie? What does your heart tell you?"

"No, Clayton," she whispered. "It can't be. How can you love me after this? How can you possibly feel —"

She cut off when his arms came around her. He held her gently, but her hands clung to his shoulders.

"You don't understand, Jackie." Clayton had to bend his head only slightly to speak softly into her ear. "The blind Jackie who is indwelt by God is a thousand times more lovely than the sighted Jackie who didn't understand the things of the Spirit."

"But Clayton, how could I ever be anything to you; how could I ever really be —"

Her words were cut off again, this time with his mouth. He wasn't going to kiss her so ardently but every time he raised his head she had another objection. He ended up kissing her until his own heart was thundering and she was limp in his arms.

"I've never stopped loving you," he said when he could talk. "I begged God to save you, Jackie; not for myself, but for you. When it happened, I knew someday I'd make you mine."

Jackie's heart overflowed. She threw her arms around Clayton and held him with all her strength.

"I told myself that we would always be friends, and I would have to be happy with only that."

Clayton kissed her again, but then she pushed herself to arm's length and spoke with her hands on his chest.

"Clayton, we have to be serious now."

"All right."

"I almost set a towel on fire last week."

"Yes, you told me about it." He sounded calm.

"Clayton, you don't understand."

"Yes, I do. You're picturing yourself in Eddie's house and kitchen. We won't live there. We'll live at my house, and I work just steps out the front door. Not to mention, I'm always done in the schoolhouse by 3:30. Plenty of time to come home and help you start dinner."

"What about children? How could I ever take care of a baby?"

"When the time comes, we'll handle that."

He's thought this all out. He has an answer for everything because he's worked it all out.

Her heart was going to burst, and she had to be close. She moved her hands from his chest to his face, framing it carefully and tipping it down so he could see her.

"Clayton, do you know that I love you?"

"Oh, yes, Jackie," he replied tenderly.

"Can you see it, Clayton? Can you see it in my eyes?" She was only just holding her tears.

"Yes, Jackie, I can see it."

Jackie's hand smoothed his face for just an instant.

"Clayton." Her voice became very serious, her eyes searching the air. "Will you marry me?"

Clayton gathered her close, his lips brushing her forehead before bending to her ear.

"Absolutely."

"Right away, Clayton," she added. "No big wedding and no waiting for families to come. Right away, with just the family and close friends who are here."

Clayton looked down at her. "If that's what you want."

"Isn't that what you want?" She sounded uncertain of a sudden.

"Yes, it is." Clayton realized how true it was. He could have his family come later, but he and Jackie had been apart for so long; waiting seemed unnecessary. This way they could have a quiet beginning, and by the time family visited and they celebrated with them, his wife would feel confident as the lady of her own home.

"When?" he suddenly asked. "When will you marry me?"

"Right away," Jackie told him. "I don't need a fancy dress I can't see. I just want us to be together, Clayton. I think God's been preparing me for that for a very long time."

Clayton knew God had done some preparing in his own heart as well. He looked up just then to see Robert and Eddie coming their way.

"We're going to have company. Shall I tell them?"

"Yes, please," Jackie said with a smile that stretched off her face.

If the young couple had known any doubts about their decision, they dissolved in the face of Eddie's and Robert's joy. The four of them stood until the sun was sinking low in the sky and talked and planned. Robert himself suggested they marry right away, and Jackie couldn't even feel the ground beneath her as she walked back to the house.

She had never even dared to ask God for this, but He had given it to her. She had been content in Him, slipping only occasionally into dissatisfaction, and He had been faithful. So many plans swarmed into Jackie's head that she knew she would never sleep. She went out for the night, however, as soon as her head touched the pillow.

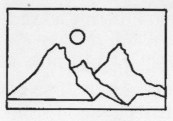

CHAPTER 40

The families had been wired the good news and were asked to visit later. Ten days after Jackie asked Clayton to marry her, just two days before Clayton's twenty-second birthday, Jackie stood in the Langley's living room wearing Eddie's wedding dress and preparing to become Mrs. Clayton Taggart. Much to everyone's astonishment, she was not nervous. Her eyes were shining with peace and happiness, and she stood very still, trying not to wrinkle, while Eddie and Lena ran all over the house.

Clayton could have used some of her calm. He and Travis were at his house, and Travis had offered to take him to the church. The young groom was beside himself.

"I can't stop shaking," he admitted.

"Second thoughts?"

"No." He smiled and laughed a little. "None of that, just, I don't know . . ."

Travis smiled compassionately and decided that now was not the time to tell him his hair was on end. Once they got to the church, he would hand him a comb.

"What if she's having second thoughts?" Clayton suddenly asked Travis.

"I don't think she is," he said calmly. "I think she was ready to marry you weeks ago."

This arrested Clayton's attention like nothing else could.

"Why do you say that?"

"It's just something I've observed, Tag. I'm no expert on women, but when a lady blushes every time she's in your presence, there's something going on."

"But she doesn't do that."

"Not now, but a few weeks back, before she really got comfortable with you, she was beside herself to say the right thing every time."

Clayton nodded. He of course had seen some of this, but never the way Travis would have observed. Things always looked different when your own heart was involved. Clayton wanted to ask his friend what else he had noticed, as Travis was a very observant man. The conversation would have helped Clayton's nerves, but instead he started to pace again. There was less than an hour to go, and it felt like eternity.

"I don't want to wrinkle," Jackie told Robert. Robert tried not to laugh. She looked so serious and solemn all of a sudden that he was reminded of Eddie on his own wedding day. Well, marriage wasn't something to be entered into lightly, so maybe serious wasn't so bad.

"Am I wrinkling?"

This time he had to laugh.

"What's so funny?"

"You. You're about to be married, but you're more concerned with your dress wrinkling."

Jackie grinned at herself. It did seem a little silly, and she told herself not to be vain.

"We'd better go or Eddie will look back from Ray and Lena's wagon and have heart failure."

"Has the dust settled?"

"Here we go again." Robert's sigh was long-suffering and comical. "First it was wrinkles and now dust. I'm going to wish I'd sent you with them."

Jackie tried not to smile, but she couldn't pull it off. In the next few minutes Robert tucked her neatly into the buggy and moved them through town. They didn't talk much, but he looked over at her several times.

Seeing Eddie's dress on her frame was a special treat for him. It looked better on Eddie — she'd filled it out more — and it was fun to remember how lovely she had been on that day.

"I hope Clayton is there."

"You're doubting?"

"Well, not that he'll show up at all, just that he'll get there first. Are you certain I look all right?"

"You look wonderful."

"I'll try to believe that."

It was quiet for a few minutes. Jackie listened to the sounds around her.

"It's an overwhelming thing at times, Robert," she told him softly. "I'll never see my husband's face or the faces of our children."

She had never talked about this before. Robert was surprised and didn't comment.

"But it could be so much worse," she went on. "I could have been blind from birth, and then Eddie's telling me the new dress fabric is blue wouldn't mean a thing. Do you see?"

"Yes. You've found things to be thankful for amid the difficulty."

"And it is difficult, Robert, but not impossible. I had to make the choice to live with this, and of course you and Eddie were a huge help in that, but I had choices to make so that God could make this bearable for me. My only worry is that I'll have a baby and someone will take her from me."

"No one is going to do that, Jackie. Why would they?"

"Because I can't take care of her without my sight."

"You don't know that. Look at the changes in you these last months. There isn't anything you can't do around the house."

"But she'll grow. What if she walks away from me and I can't find her?"

"We'll tie a bell onto her."

Robert's voice and matter-of-fact solution was so amusing that she began to giggle. When Robert said she was making her face all red, she laughed harder. They arrived at the church amid much silliness.

It was not a large wedding. The church family had been invited to a reception a week down the road, but today's gathering was small. The Langleys, Pastor Henley, his wife, Beryl, and Raymond and Lena, along with Travis, made the short guest list. Everyone was already inside when Robert stopped the wagon and Travis came out to lend a hand.

"Is Clayton here?" she wished to know.

"No," Travis teased her. "He jumped on

the stage and ran for it."

"Oh, Travis, you have to stop," she told him with more giggles. "Robert already said my face is red enough."

The rancher hustled her inside where Eddie and Lena were ready to make adjustments on her dress and to hand her over to Clayton. She had not wanted to walk up the aisle where she would have to grope about to find Clayton, so he was going to walk her up himself. When Eddie and Lena finally stepped back, Clayton, who had been watching all the proceedings with love-filled eyes, came to her.

"Hi," he said softly. Jackie beamed.

"I made it."

"Yes; you look beautiful."

She smiled and said, "How do you look?"

Clayton chuckled. "My hair was on end, but it's better now."

Jackie put her hand on his chest. He covered it with his own, and leaned to kiss her cheek.

"Ready to become my wife?"

"Yes," she said a little too loudly, and they both laughed.

Clayton turned her and started up the aisle. Jackie had not wanted music, and she'd asked everyone to stand for the ceremony. It was unlike anything any of them had ever done, but it was very special. The bride and groom stood opposite Pastor Henley while the rest of the party stood to the sides of them, forming a half circle around the clergyman.

It was not a long service, but serious and unique. Clayton and Jackie turned to each other and said the things that were on their minds. They wanted these special friends and family to witness these vows and hold them accountable.

"I love you, Clayton," Jackie began, her voice soft. "Before God and these dear friends, I promise to put your needs ahead of my own. I can't see your eyes, Clayton — not today or ever — but I put my trust in you that you will always tell me what's in your heart. I know God has prepared me for this day, and although I know there will be adjustments, I vow to you from this day forward that I will strive to be the wife you need."

"I love you, Jackie," Clayton began just after Jackie finished. "I vow before God and the ones gathered here that I will be the leader of our home the way God would have me to be. I promise to be there for you, Jackie, and also to tell what's in my heart every day of our lives. I praise God that He brought us to this place. I know He will show us how to serve Him better.

"It doesn't matter today that you can't see me and it's not going to matter tomorrow. I will always love you, Jackie, and cherish your love for me as a rare and precious gift."

Even before the pastor could pronounce them husband and wife, Clayton leaned forward and tenderly kissed the woman he loved.

Eddie bawled her way through the proceedings, and even Robert was overcome a few times. All in all, it didn't take very long, and there was much laughter and talking as they all filed from the church to head for the Langleys' for a special dinner.

Out at the wagons, Clayton helped his bride become comfortable. Robert was going to ride with Travis in order to give Jackie and Clayton some time alone. Eddie went ahead with Lena and Raymond. Pastor and Mrs. Henley were on their way as well.

The two men had just come to Travis' wagon when two girls, looking to be around 14, passed by. That they found the big rancher good-looking was more than obvious, and as the man climbed aboard the seat, they shared a smile.

"You get stared at by a lot of women, Travis," Robert suddenly commented.

"Do I?"

"Yes. I just never realized it before now. Maybe it's time you get married," Robert teased him.

Travis, who had raised the reins, went very still. He forced himself to turn and look at Robert, who looked right back.

"I'm already married, Robert. I'm sorry I never told you before."

The banker stared at him. "You're married?"

"Yes."

Robert was silent for a full 30 seconds. "Where is your wife?"

"I don't know," was the pained reply, and Robert only nodded. "Maybe someday I can tell you about it."

"Sure." Robert's voice was kind. "Whenever you want to or don't want to, Travis."

Travis thanked him and slapped the reins. Robert was a good friend, and Travis felt relief at having finally told him. Maybe someday it could all come out, but not now. Now he needed to go and help Clayton and Jackie celebrate and get off to a good start. His prayers were that their marriage would be far different than his own.

"Okay, do you remember where everything is?"

"I think so," Jackie told her husband, who

had just shown her around their bedroom.

"Would you like a few minutes alone?"

"Yes."

Clayton turned to leave, but Jackie's voice, a little uncertain, stopped him. "Are you going far?"

"No. I'll be right outside the door. When you call, I'll come back."

Jackie smiled. "All right. And my gown . . . it's here?"

"Yes. Right over the footboard."

Jackie smiled again and this time didn't call him back. She was married. She was married to Clayton. Her Clayton. It was just too wonderful to be true. With hands that shook just a little, she began to undress. She laid her clothing very carefully on the chair and slipped into her new white nightgown. It was lacy and soft, and Jackie checked the buttons twice to see if she'd matched them all up.

"Clayton," she said softly and stood very still by the edge of the bed.

"All set?" His head came back in the door.

Jackie moved her hands nervously down the front of her gown. "Eddie made me a new nightgown; is it pretty?"

"Oh, yes," Clayton breathed the words and came to her. He kissed her brow because it was one of their favorite things and held her close.

"Did you know, Clayton? Did you know it would be this special?"

"I don't think I could have imagined this," he admitted to her. "I love you, Jackie."

She raised her face for his kiss and moved her hands over his back. He was finally hers. She could "see" him all she wanted.

There was no wedding trip because Clayton had to be at the schoolhouse on Monday morning, but it didn't matter. They spent Sunday alone, talking, cooking, touching, and learning more than they had ever known before. It was the beginning of two lives joined at the heart and settled in for a lifetime of love.

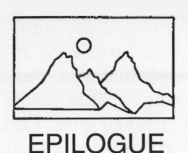

EPILOGUE

Spring 1877

Lena poked her head out the bedroom door. "Come in, Robert; you have a son."

The woman's voice was so calm. How could she be this calm? It had felt like years since Eddie's pains began. He'd been pacing the hallway for hours, and now he had a son. He walked into their bedroom as if in slow motion. Lena passed him on her way out, but he never saw her. Eddie's eyes were closed, and lying in the crook of her arm was a bundle of blankets. He stared at the unmoving bundle until he realized Eddie's eyes had opened and she was watching him. Robert smiled at her.

"Hi."

"Hi, yourself," she said with a weary smile of her own. "We have a son."

"Lena told me. How are you?"

"Sore."

Robert grinned. Their voices were both

very hushed. "Can I see him?"

"Yes, but I feel too tired to move."

Robert's long-fingered hand came out, and he shifted the blanket aside until a tiny, sleeping face peeked out. Eddie had been holding on very nicely, but when she saw her husband's tears, her own fell. They sat together, Robert close to her side and holding their son, drinking in his tiny features and limbs. He was a wonder to them, and all they could do was marvel.

"I need to see my sister," Eddie suddenly said. "I need Jackie."

"Okay."

Lena knocked at that moment, and Robert called for her to come in.

"Jackie and Clayton are downstairs. I did not tell them, but she said she needed to see you."

"Send her up," Robert said with a smile and opened the door wide. He took a seat across the room, between the two largest windows, and told himself not to make a sound.

"Eddie?" Jackie's voice finally called from the upstairs hall.

"In the bedroom, Jackie."

"Hi," she spoke when she came in the room. "I hope this isn't a bad time, but I need to show you something."

"Come on in."

On those words, Jackie knew something was different. She stopped a few feet inside the door, a scrap of lace hanging from her hand.

"Are you lying down, Eddie?"

"Yes."

Jackie stood frozen, then her hand flew to her throat. "The baby," she gasped. "The baby's coming. Are you in pain? We'll get Robert. Clayton — I've got to get Clayton!" Her hands were already reaching to find the door.

"Jackie." Eddie's voice checked her sister's flight. "He's here. I had a baby boy just a few minutes ago."

"Eddie; oh, Eddie." Jackie's hands were outstretched as she tried to find the bed. She started when Robert touched her, but forgot all about it when she sat by Eddie and a tiny bundle was placed in her arms.

"Oh, my darling," she spoke as she cuddled the infant under her chin for just a moment. "Oh, my little darling, you're here. You're finally here."

With slow movement and a gentle touch, Jackie laid the baby carefully in her lap. Robert and Eddie looked on as Jackie "saw" her nephew for the first time. Clayton came in the door while she was still unwrapping him, and Robert motioned him in. He grinned at the new mother and father before going to his wife's side and looking on in the same sort of wonder.

Jackie started with his head, her hands and fingers gently caressing the soft, downy hair and scalp. With featherlight movements she touched his facial features, the small nose and brows. Her hands moved down his arms to his tiny fingers and eventually down his legs to his toes. He didn't like his toes touched. A small fuss ensued, and then a louder cry came forth.

"It's all right," she coaxed him. "Aunt Jackie has you." With expert movements she rewrapped him and put him to her shoulder, kissing his silky temple. She bounced him gently and rubbed his back. Eddie and Robert exchanged a look that clearly said, *She was worried about having her own, but she's so relaxed and capable.*

Clayton finally spoke. "He's so tiny. I can't believe how small he is."

"Here, Clay," his wife offered, having known he'd arrived by the smell of his shaving soap. "Would you like to hold him?"

"I don't think so," he said, making everyone laugh.

Eddie was looking a bit uncomfortable, and Robert came forward to help her shift around in bed. Jackie stood, and with the baby still tucked close, she found the chair and sat down. Clayton came close once again, this time to stare at him over her shoulder.

"What did you name him?" Clayton asked.

"We haven't really had time to do that," Robert told him good-naturedly.

Clayton's brows rose. He bent over his wife and gently took the baby from her arms. "I think," he said with quiet conviction, "that we'll see how Lena's doing and check back with you in a little while."

Robert took the baby, thanking him with his eyes, and Jackie stood to leave with her husband. They were halfway down the stairs when she said, "I didn't even say congratulations."

"That's all right. I think they could tell you were delighted."

"He's perfect, isn't he, Clay?"

"Yes. So small and perfect."

"I want a baby, Clay."

"I know you do. It'll happen." He suddenly kissed her. "We'll just keep trying."

Jackie smiled with pleasure.

"I can't believe we were here to see him when he was so tiny and new," Clayton said as they moved past the living room.

"Isn't it fun? I just wanted to ask Eddie about that lace pattern."

Jackie was quiet for a few steps. "God has been doing that often these days."

"What's that?"

"Giving me little surprises and blessings. Your folks' visit was so special, and Milly's fiancé, Trevor, is wonderful."

"I wouldn't be too surprised if your parents come on the scene pretty soon. A first grandchild is a big draw."

"Wouldn't that be fun? I hope they come."

Husband and wife had wandered onto the porch and now took a seat on the stone bench. The evenings were still cool, and they snuggled together, Clayton's arm around his beloved.

"I think I like being married to you, Mrs. Taggart," he said as he laid his head against hers.

Jackie smiled. "I rather like it myself. How was school today?"

And with that they talked. It was Clayton's favorite part of the relationship. She was always ready to listen to him. The companionship they shared was more than he ever dreamed it could be, and they never ran out of things to say.

A deer bounded across the road in front

538

of them, and as had become the norm, he described it to her. The sun set while they sat on the porch, and he described that too. He never tired of telling her about their world or what was in his heart. They ended each day in bed with the lantern turned high and Clayton reading from the Bible or a good book that he had on his shelf. Their world was a wonderful place, but neither one felt content to remain as they were. They prayed every day for change, even if it meant testing, and the results were coming forth like the sunset, pure gold.

"I think we should wait until tomorrow to visit again, don't you? They need some time alone with their baby."

"Yes." As much as she would have liked to hold him again, Jackie agreed. "I'd like to go home now, Clayton."

"I'll be right back with you."

He went to tell Lena they were leaving and joined his wife in the small wagon they had purchased just that month. As Jackie's body lurched with the sudden movement of the horse, she clasped Clayton's arm tenderly against her and thought, as she often did, that the best was yet to come.

About the Author

LORI WICK is one of the most versatile Christian fiction writers on the market today. From pioneer fiction to a series set in Victorian England to contemporary writing, Lori's books (over 700,000 copies in print) are perennial favorites with readers. The Rocky Mountain Memories series brings to life the rugged strength and enduring faith of Colorado settlers in the last part of the nineteenth century.

Born and raised in Santa Rosa, California, Lori met her husband, Bob, while in Bible college. They and their three children, Timothy, Matthew, and Abigail, make their home in Wisconsin.